ENCHANTERS

K.F. BRADSHAW

Enchanters

By K.F. Bradshaw

Published By

Wishbox Press

Copyright © 2017 by K.F. Bradshaw

ISBN: 978-0-9987518-2-5

First Edition, 2017

Cover by TS95 Studios

Interior design by www.redravenbookdesign.com

www.enchantersnovels.com

ENCHANTERS

PROLOGUE

My dearest Ithmeera,

Forgive me for not writing sooner. No doubt you have heard the news, and I know you will understand why I must make this letter briefer than usual. What you heard is indeed true – King Caleb Taylor of Gurdinfield and his family have been murdered. To make matters worse, the assassination was carried out within the palace walls themselves! Several of the king's Guardians, his bodyguards, were slain as well. No one – not even Lord Moore or Lord Harrington, the king's advisors – are certain of who was behind this. Both seem eager to find answers, though I fear that their constant disagreement will cause Gurdinfield to become unstable as a nation. My presence here has maintained an uncomfortable peace between them, but I do not foresee it lasting after I depart. A civil war would be disastrous for the nation, but with no heir in the City of the Towers, the prospect appears more real with each passing day. War between the Moore and Harrington houses would no doubt be the beginning of a new, darker era in Damea, one from which the ramifications could be worse than that of The Starving.

As terrible as this predicament seems, you must not lose hope, my daughter. For there was, indeed, a time before The Starving. Before the Second Era, before Gurdinfield's Enchanters Academy closed its doors, before the famines and the wars – before magic was feared and looked upon as our end, it was our salvation. Our way of life. It was the inventions of enchanters – gifted people versed in the art of manipulating Damea's natural energies, of making common items precious and powerful – that powered our agriculture, weapons, and machines. They even healed our sick. Magic was a part of our land, our sky, and even ourselves. Our great founder, the explorer Dameas, encouraged us to share our knowledge of magic and use it to advance our farms, our technology, and our society. This was, of course, long before Damea evolved into a land of many nations.

Do you remember our time in Gurdinfield a few years ago? The great white spires in the City of Towers that allowed its defenders to see far beyond the Black Forest still stand today, but they are no longer the grand towers that I read about in the history books. Now they are just crumbling pillars that stand as a grim reminder of what used to be when the City of Towers and its Enchanters Academy were the pride of the eastern regions of Damea. It represented our knowledge, our potential, and ultimately our downfall. The cities of Gurdinfield and its capital are still there of course, but it is a very different place than our ancestors knew.

My dear, please do not believe for a moment that our great empire is to become a memory like Gurdinfield.

Our laws limiting the use of magic are strict, but they are necessary until we can discover why the magic left us, and how we can bring it back or find a new means of powering our empire and restoring the old ways of life to our people. For now, we must trust that our royal enchanters know how to conserve what little magic we do have.

I do not know why the magic left us or where it went. Most of the royal enchanters agree that its widespread manipulation might have had something to do with its loss. The magic was a part of this world, and we may have simply created so much imbalance that it is no longer in a form that is useful. To make matters worse, I have received more disturbing reports of non-enchanters going through the black market to acquire magical artifacts – for what purpose, I cannot say, though the Legionnaires I have spoken with suggest that these poor people have become addicted to the magic the artifacts contain. I have also lost several enchanters to the illness that now plagues even the most talented of magic users should they try to manipulate too much energy for their own use.

Over the course of my reign, I have sent alliance offers to the people of the Western Hills and even the merchants of the Gurith Coast so that we could join together and find a way to either conserve or restore the magic in Damea – if not for ourselves, then for our children. So far, my efforts have been in vain, but I will keep trying. King Caleb had agreed to hold talks regarding an alliance, but I cannot say what will happen now that he is gone. I hope when the time comes for you to rule that you will strive to maintain the alliances I have forged, for we cannot be alone in this and expect to survive long.

I will return home soon. Be kind to your brother and mind your uncle.

– Father

(A letter from Emperor Nardos Cadar to his daughter, Ithmeera Cadar, heiress to the throne of the Azgadaran Empire, 202 2nd Era)

Chapter 1

Andrea

Damea, 220 2ⁿᵈ Era
Ata, The Western Hills

"Andrea! Andrea, come inside when you're done!"

Eighteen-year-old Andrea looked up at her mother's calls and propped the rake she was using against the nearby wooden fence. She used her shirtsleeve to wipe the sweat off her brow. It had been a hot summer so far, and it would be a few more months before the cooler weather returned.

Her family's farm had been quite successful over the past decade, and most of the crops they harvested were sold to the rest of the town and were even sent as far as the Azgadaran Empire. While she was proud of what her family had built, Andrea would be even prouder if her parents would stop being so cheap and hire some extra hands so that she would not be the one working all day in the unforgiving summer heat of the Western Hills.

She wiped her hands on her black work pants and made her way back to the small wood and stone house that her family had built generations ago when they had first settled in Ata.

Her mother, Isabel, was waiting for her at the front door. Isabel had the same fair skin, dark, slightly wavy brown hair, and hazel eyes as her daughter, though her facial features were much more angular and defined than Andrea's softer, subtler features.

"I need you to take this delivery down to the inn. Can you do that and be back for dinner?" Isabel asked, frowning at her daughter's pants, which were caked with dirt. "After you change, of course."

Andrea sighed. She usually did not mind helping her parents with errands like this, but her mother's requests were seemingly *always* on the days she actually had plans. "Yes, Mother. I was going to see Master Jheran later, though. He agreed to continue with my lessons."

Her mother inhaled deeply and smiled faintly. "You really should be careful, Andrea. Your father doesn't like you spending so much time with that old soldier. To be honest, I'm a little uncomfortable with it as well."

Andrea was determined not to appear childish, but she had lost count of the number of times she had explained her arrangement with Master Jheran to her parents, and it was difficult not to be frustrated. "Mother, Master Jheran is the *only* enchanter in these parts. He's only helping me get better at controlling my power."

Isabel crossed her arms. "I do hope you plan on using this 'power' for useful things, not getting yourself locked up in some jail cell in Azgadar."

Andrea had to fight to keep from saying something she would regret later. She had begun to show potential for enchanting when she was only eight years old. Instead of sending her to a tutor, her parents had insisted she stay home and rarely allowed her to use magic. Having read and heard the stories of the great enchanters of Damea in the First Era, Andrea was convinced that with a little more training she could be of real use – maybe even help get the old machines that lay dormant on the farm working again – or even better, go to Azgadar and become one of the empire's royal enchanters, and make a *real* difference in Damea.

But right now she was stuck on a farm arguing with her mother over whether or not she was allowed to see the closest thing to a tutor she had. Master Jheran was a retired enchanter who lived alone in town. She had met him at Ata's only inn and tavern on one of her deliveries. Upon discovering that he was an enchanter, Andrea barraged him with questions ranging from where he had learned his trade to whether or not he could teach her.

After a few weeks of her begging, he grudgingly agreed to test her potential. Upon seeing that she indeed was gifted, he arranged to give her private lessons once a week. Her parents, particularly her father, were not happy about it, but after a few accidents where Andrea had burned nearly an entire field of crops, they reluctantly agreed to the arrangement.

Her mother was not entirely wrong – magic was dangerous to use these days, with the threat of sickness always present. But the laws restricting the use of magic in Azgadar had no power in the Western Hills, which consisted of a loose collection of farming villages and a few isolated manors owned by reclusive nobles who were perfectly happy being uninvolved in the day-to-day problems of Damea. Andrea doubted she would end up in a jail cell, and she was lacked the power or recklessness necessary to manipulate enough magic to cause sickness.

"I won't be gone long, Mother. I'll take the food and go to my lesson. I'll be back before sundown – I promise," she said.

Isabel observed her daughter for a moment, considering. Finally, she sighed and conceded. "Fine. Back by sundown, understood?" she said sternly.

Andrea couldn't hold back a grin. "Yes, Mother!" She ran into the house and into her room to change into something more suitable for traveling. As she was leaving the house, her mother called out after her.

"Please don't give all of the food to Kira!"

Away from her mother's gaze, Andrea rolled her eyes. Kira was the family's horse, and Andrea often rode her when she delivered food to the inn. She didn't see the issue with giving the horse a well-deserved carrot or two, but her mother clearly thought otherwise.

✳ ✳ ✳

"Now, try it again."

Andrea closed her eyes and tried to put all of her effort into focusing inward in order to channel the power she needed to complete the task Master Jheran had given her. In a few seconds, she began to feel the familiar vibrations of magic coursing through her.

"*Don't* close your eyes!" her teacher, a grizzled older man with long hair, barked at her, snapping her out of her concentration.

"Sorry...I'm sorry. I just...I was trying to concentrate," Andrea tried to explain. She wiped sweat from her brow. The heat was making it even more difficult to focus, and her tutor's yelling did not help much either.

"You can concentrate all you want. But if you can't see what or who you're shielding yourself from, you're not going to last very long," spoke Master Jheran. His face was wrinkled and leathery, most likely from spending years in the hot Azgadaran Empire as one of the empire's royal enchanters. He had dedicated years of his life to solving the magic problem in Damea, and Andrea deeply respected him.

Andrea sighed and sat on a tree stump in the field behind Jheran's small house. "Why are we practicing shields anyway? Shouldn't I be learning how to power things or something?"

Jheran chuckled. "Listen to me, girl. You've got a knack for this – I'll give you that. But before you can really learn, you have to master the basics. Shields are the best way to test your endurance and balance. Plus," he continued, "they come in handy sometimes. Especially when you're somewhere you don't want to be."

"Like where?" Andrea asked.

The old man grinned. "The slums of Azgadar, for example. But this is really all for practice anyhow. I don't see you ever ending up in a place like that, or at least I hope you wouldn't."

Andrea shook her head. "No. The most dangerous place I'll end up is probably in the fields of my parents' farm."

Jheran scoffed. "It's none of my business, but I would hope you've your own aspirations, girl."

Andrea shrugged. "As long as I have this...thing, I might

as well do something useful with it. My parents aren't exactly going to send me off to Azgadar to become an enchanter like you were."

"Now look here," Jheran said, staring intensely at his student. "We don't get to decide what we bring into this world with us. But you have a gift, Andrea, and you should consider using it for something useful."

"Helping the farm is useful," Andrea half-heartedly replied.

Her tutor didn't reply but instead extended his hand to Andrea, who accepted it and stood up.

"Now," he said, "try again. And don't close your eyes this time."

"Can't we try something different? Like powering something? *Please?*" Andrea begged. "I just want to see if I can do it."

Jheran raised an eyebrow. "Girl, you're not quite there. You're going to be disappointed."

Andrea sighed in frustration and looked up. She noticed that the sun was beginning to set. "Sorry, Master Jheran, I have to go. I told Mother I'd be back before sundown for dinner."

The old man gave a crooked smile. "Of course. You'll be back next week then?"

"Yes, assuming my mother doesn't have other plans for me. I'll see you later!" Andrea said as she mounted her horse and began to ride home.

* * *

Andrea arrived home shortly before the sun had completely set. Isabel did not say anything when her daughter walked through the front door, which Andrea was rather grateful for.

They ate soon after: a simple meal of stew with vegetables and hard bread. The meal was mostly consumed in silence, except for when Andrea's father, Garrett, inquired about his daughter's day.

"Your mother says you took the delivery to Bill's today. How did that go?" he asked. He was a tall, strong-looking man with short, dark curly hair and grey eyes. He was not very old, but years of working in the hot sun on the family farm had aged his appearance.

Andrea put her fork down. "It went fine," she said slowly, trying to decide if she should tell them about her time at Master Jheran's. "He said he needs some extra carrots if we can spare them."

Isabel nodded. "I think we can. Can you take them to him tomorrow, Andrea?"

Andrea tried not to sigh. Another errand, another day taken away from doing what she actually wanted to do. "Yes, Mother."

"Bill really should just start his own garden. He doesn't need so many carrots that we should have to send you every day to deliver them," Garrett said jokingly with a wink to his daughter.

"Garrett! Honestly, it's as though you'd rather we not have any customers at all," Isabel chided. "Andrea can take them to him."

"Andrea might have other plans, dear," Garrett said. "A girl her age shouldn't be spending her days making carrot deliveries. I'll take them."

"Father, it's fine," Andrea assured him.

But Garrett was insistent. "Take the day off tomorrow, Andrea. Go into town, see some of your friends."

Andrea looked at her father and then at her mother, who seemed a little disgruntled but had not objected further. "Uh... all right. Thank you, Father."

Garrett smiled gently and nodded. The rest of the meal conversation consisted mostly of small talk between Garrett and Isabel, with Andrea silently observing her parents.

After dinner, she stole away, making her way to the small field where the old machinery stood. The large, metal contraptions had been built by her family many generations earlier and were once powered by magic, allowing tasks such as planting and harvesting to be done many times faster than by hand. They had been laid to rest away from the rest of the farm when the magic famine had grown worse in the western regions of Damea.

Andrea wanted to change that.

It made no sense for her father and mother to work as hard as they did to keep the farm running when there were perfectly good machines specifically designed to alleviate their burden. But Andrea had a chance to make herself useful – to put the abilities that she had to good use for once.

She stood in front of the smaller of the machine. The light she had available to her was quickly fading as dusk fell, but she could see that the contraption was severely rusted from years of harsh weather and nonuse.

"All right," she whispered and held up her hands. "Let's see if we can get you to work, you piece of junk."

She concentrated and reached inward to find the power she was looking for. Even in the Western Hills there was not much magic left, but there was no one around to police her if she wanted to try to use it.

The magic hit her fast and hard, and the vibrations in her hand grew stronger and more uneven. She had not been prepared for a power influx of this magnitude, but she was going to try to make it work. She focused on wielding the newly manipulated power on the machine in front of her.

To Andrea's surprise, the machine immediately began to hum and whirl as it absorbed the power she was feeding it. She could feel her arms growing sore from the power transfer. But it was working...after generations of dormancy, the machine was powering up.

"Yes!" she exclaimed. "Come on, work!"

She felt a shift in the power transfer, indicating that the machine was running on its own new supply of power. She had done it. She could not wait to tell Master Jheran. Her parents would be thrilled that the machine was working and maybe, just maybe she would not have to keep her abilities so quiet around them. Maybe they might want to invest in her abilities more, and perhaps they would let her train with Master Jheran more often.

Her celebration was short-lived. She was suddenly knocked off-balance by an influx of power far too great for her to get under control before it could transfer to the machine. She tried to compensate for it, but it was too late – the magic had already transferred through her and to the newly running machine.

She screamed in alarm as another surge of power coursed through her before she could cut herself from the transfer. The machine groaned, emitted a flurry of bright orange spark with a loud bang, then finally let out a metallic cough and went silent.

"Oh, no...no, no, *no!*" Andrea cried. She knelt next to the machine and tried to see if there was any power left in it. But to her dismay, it was dead.

"That's…not good," she muttered, breaking the silence. She desperately hoped no one had heard the commotion. She stood up and glowered at the machine.

"You were working just fine. What happened?" she asked it, knowing her question was pointless as the machine was not going to answer her any time soon.

Feeling defeated and a little lightheaded from the power transfer, she began to make her way back to the house. Perhaps Master Jheran was right – perhaps she *wasn't* ready for powering objects yet.

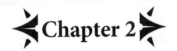

Chapter 2

The Enchanter

Ata, The Western Hills
One month later

By the time Andrea arrived at the old inn, the sun had begun to set. The temperatures were dropping, and she could take some comfort in the fact that it would not be such a miserably torrid ride home.

She had been finishing her afternoon chores that day when her mother asked her to make another delivery to the inn. Andrea did not mind, but this time her mother had insisted that she come straight home after making the delivery.

Upon arriving, she dismounted the horse and tied Kira to the dilapidated wood fence that surrounded the inn. The inn itself was not very big, but as Ata was quite far from the other villages, the establishment was almost always busy. The building itself was rundown – a wooden construction with many of its roof shingles missing or haphazardly patched. Most of its visitors were either regulars from Ata and the occasional merchant passing through.

She grabbed the canvas sack containing the food, swung

it over her shoulder, and walked into the inn. The scent of the trademark stew that Bill, the owner, usually had on hand permeated the inn along with the ever-present odor of whatever alcoholic drink was on tap.

Wrinkling her nose, Andrea tried to ignore the smell and walked up to the bar where Bill was serving drinks. He took notice of her and nodded in greeting.

"Here's this week's, Bill," Andrea said, setting the sack on the counter.

Bill, a balding middle-aged man with a bushy mustache, reached into his apron, pulled out a small bag of coins, and handed it to Andrea. "Thanks a lot. Tell your mother I'll be wanting two deliveries next week. Been getting more customers than usual lately. Lots of trading going on, maybe?"

"Hm. I don't know. But I'll tell her," Andrea said as she took the coins and offered a small wave goodbye. As she was leaving, a female voice spoke out.

"Delivering groceries is a little out of your domain, no?"

Andrea stopped and turned around. The voice belonged to a woman sitting alone at one of the tables near the door. She was dressed in brown pants tucked into riding boots, a dark green shirt, and a dark brown cloak, with a hood concealing most of her face. She gazed straight ahead, not at Andrea, at something Andrea could not see.

"Sorry?" Andrea asked.

The woman turned to look at Andrea. She looked young, perhaps in her late thirties. Most of her hair was concealed by the hood, but Andrea could tell that it was dark. Her grey eyes seemed small and faded, as though the fire that had once possessed them was long gone.

"Or perhaps you are just being kind and doing it as a favor to someone?" she asked. Her voice was light and airy, and Andrea found herself wanting to sit at the table with her.

Andrea shook her head in confusion. "I'm sorry, I don't know what you are talking about."

The woman beckoned Andrea over, and she slowly walked over to the table. "You are an enchanter, too, are you not? I just find it hard to believe that someone with your potential is delivering food to taverns."

Andrea did not know how to respond. Who was this woman, and how did she know about her abilities? "I…I'm not an enchanter," she stammered. "I live nearby. I was just making a delivery for my parents."

The woman laughed quietly. "Ah…I see." She gestured to the bench across from her. "Please, sit with me. What is your name, girl?"

Andrea hesitated for a moment before she slowly took a seat across from the strange woman. There was a small pot of stew on the table and a mug of which Andrea assumed was the inn's usual draught.

"Care for some stew?" the woman offered. Andrea shook her head. She fiddled with her hands in her lap, trying not to show she was nervous. What was she doing here, sitting with some strange woman? She knew she should excuse herself and leave. Her mother would be worried if she was not back before the sun set completely.

"Suit yourself," the woman said as she poured some from the pot into the wooden bowl in front of her. "Excuse me, you probably think I'm either rude or a lunatic. My name's Meredith." She extended her hand to Andrea, who tentatively shook it.

"Andrea," Andrea replied, feeling a bit more confident. "My parents own a farm nearby. I was just making a delivery here. I do every week." She raised an eyebrow. "How...how did you know I was–,"

"An enchanter? Gifted?" Meredith leaned in. "Because I know how to spot those with the talent to manipulate magic. I do it all the time when I'm not in my lab."

"Lab? You have a lab?" Andrea asked. She lowered her voice to a whisper. "You're an...enchanter?"

"Come now, dear, there's no need to be so secretive about it. We're not in Azgadar, after all," Meredith said with a smirk. She held out her hand and a small orb of blue light appeared over her palm. Andrea gasped when Meredith dispelled the light after a few seconds with a flick of her wrist.

The older woman calmly took a bite of her stew. "Yes, my lab – it's in the Black Forest. Quite a way from here but I enjoy traveling. Especially if I get a new assistant out of it."

Andrea thought she misheard the woman. "I'm sorry?"

Meredith laughed. "Don't be so shy! I knew you were perfect for the job the day I arrived in town. You gave off quite the projection last month."

"P-projection?"

Meredith sighed. "Goodness, they really don't teach the

young ones anything these days. Your energy projection. All those with magical abilities give one off, especially when they perform any kind of magical feat. I just happen to be very good at picking up the strong ones and tracking them."

Andrea thought back to a month ago. Sure, she was inexperienced and her attempt at starting up the old farming machine behind the barn was a complete failure, but for that to cause some sort of *projection* as Meredith referred to it was nothing that she and Master Jheran had ever discussed.

The fact that Meredith was tracking her based on that projection just made the whole situation seem impossible. *But it can't be so impossible if this woman is offering me a...job of some kind? Assistant? What does an enchanter's assistant do, exactly?*

"These projections, can you track all of them?" she asked.

Meredith shook her head and took a drink. "Oh, no," she said, putting the mug down. "Just the really strong ones. Usually they are produced by magic users who cannot fully control their abilities yet."

Andrea felt a little defensive, but relaxed when she realized that Meredith was complimenting her. "So," she said slowly, "what is it you want from me?"

Meredith grew serious. "I'm working on a project that has been a...long term investment. It's been very difficult working alone, and I've decided what I really need is a good assistant. Someone I can train as my apprentice."

Andrea was suddenly very attentive.

"Now," Meredith continued, "the key to this project

succeeding might also be the key to solving the energy problem in Damea. But one step at a time, right?"

Andrea's heart began to race. This woman, this *enchanter* had traveled across Damea to ask Andrea to be her apprentice! She would finally get the training she had been dreaming of for years!

"And," Andrea said slowly, trying not to show her excitement, "your lab, it's in the Black Forest?"

"Yes," Meredith said nodding. "It's quite a journey, so you might want to just pack the necessities, though I have everything else you might need. We would need to leave soon."

Andrea wanted to say yes with every fiber in her being. There was just one small problem she had overlooked.

"I don't think my parents would allow it," she admitted.

Meredith raised her eyebrows in surprise before returning to eating her stew. "I did not imagine it would be an easy decision to make. I will say that you will not get another opportunity like this though, Andrea."

Andrea was at a loss for words, but she tried to stay composed and not appear too upset. "It...it was nice meeting you, Meredith," she stammered. She stood up quickly, jostling the table and nearly spilling Meredith's bowl of stew. Muttering another frantic apology, Andrea backed away and practically sprinted out of the inn.

Meredith watched in amusement as Andrea left, then calmly returned to eating her stew. She noticed a small bag of coins on the table. Figuring it belonged to the girl, she decided she would pay her a visit in the morning. She waved the innkeeper over.

"Yes, miss?" Bill asked gruffly, holding a towel and the glass mug he was cleaning with it.

"That girl who was in here earlier, where does she live? She left this behind and I wish to return it to her," the enchanter gestured to the bag of coins on the table.

Bill finished cleaning the glass and said, "Girl lives with her parents right down the main road. First farm you'll see."

"Thank you," Meredith replied and pocketed the coin bag. She finished her stew and drink, then retired for the evening.

* * *

Andrea awoke with a start to sharp knocking on her bedroom door. Overnight, her normally wavy hair had become tangled to the point of resembling a bird's nest.

"Andrea? Are you awake?" her mother's voice sounded from outside her bedroom.

No. Bitter about being woken up before she was ready, she cleared what were probably unflattering clustered strands of hair from her eyes and mouth. "Yes," she replied in more of a grumble than normal speech.

"There is someone here to see you," Isabel said. "She's brought the money you left at the inn last night."

Her mother's last statement made Andrea sit up in bed. She recalled the awkward moment that had played out between her and her mother when she told her that she could not find the bag of coins Bill had given her. Her mother had scolded her and called her "irresponsible" before insisting that Andrea retrace her steps the next morning to try to find the coin bag.

Andrea quickly dressed and rushed out of her room and into the kitchen, where she was surprised to see her parents sitting at the table with none other than Meredith, the strange woman she had met at the inn the previous night.

"Um...good morning," she said nervously as she tried to control the frizzy mess that her hair currently was after a night of tossing and turning.

"Can I make you something to eat, Meredith?" Isabel asked.

"No, thank you," Meredith replied. "I just wanted to return this and again express my gratitude to your daughter for being kind enough to tell me about your wonderful village. No doubt I distracted her so much with all of my tiresome questions that she left the coin bag on the table." She gave Andrea a knowing smile.

Andrea, who was not really sure how to respond to Meredith's obvious lie, managed to croak out an answer. "Uh...of course! You're very welcome, Meredith."

"What is your interest in Ata, miss?" Garrett asked.

"Oh, I am actually only here for a few days before I head back to the Black Forest," Meredith explained.

"The Black Forest? My, that is far!" Isabel said.

"I didn't think anyone actually lived out there," Garrett quipped.

"Father!" Andrea protested.

But Meredith simply laughed. She had a certain grace about

her that Andrea could not quite place. Perhaps she was raised among nobility? What if she *was* nobility, but had given up that life to be an enchanter?

"It's true, there aren't many of us," Meredith said. "I have a lovely house there. It's a beautiful region – very peaceful. I'm originally from Darst, actually."

"Where is that?" Isabel asked.

"It's a village in Gurdinfield, just north of the capital city," Meredith explained. She glanced out the window. "Well, I should probably be going."

"Thank you for your assistance, Meredith," Garrett said, and Isabel nodded her agreement. "Let us know if there is anything we can do to return the favor."

"It's no trouble at all," Meredith replied. "Actually, there is one thing I could use some assistance with. I need to pick up some things in town today, but I'm not very familiar with the area. I was hoping it would not be too much to ask if I requested a guide."

"Of course. Andrea will go with you," Isabel offered.

Andrea looked at Meredith with wide eyes, but quickly tried to conceal her nervousness from her parents. "I...yes, of course I will. When would you like to go?" she asked.

Meredith's pleasant expression did not falter. "We could go now, if that is all right with you."

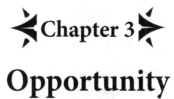

Chapter 3

Opportunity

"Such a charming town, don't you think?"

Andrea shrugged. "It hasn't changed very much over the years."

Meredith walked over to yet another merchant cart in the small marketplace in Ata, with Andrea dragging her feet behind her. As long as she had to show Meredith around, she wanted to learn more about the enchanter, not go shopping with her.

"What do you think of this, Andrea?" The older woman held up a midnight-blue cloak. It was imported from the City of Towers in Gurdinfield, and judging by the high-quality fabric and craftsmanship, Andrea could see that it was rather expensive.

"It's um…very nice," she told Meredith. To her surprise, Meredith gave the merchant some money and placed the cloak in the bag she was carrying.

"Now then," Meredith said as the two ambled along the dusty streets of Ata. "I assume you haven't spoken to your parents yet about joining me."

"I've already told you that I can't." "You haven't even asked them, have you?" Meredith accused.

"And *you* still haven't told me what you're working on in the Black Forest," Andrea countered.

"I've told you," Meredith began. "I'm working on finding a solution to our little magic problem."

"You mentioned a project," Andrea reminded her.

Meredith nodded. They found a small bench, and the enchanter motioned for Andrea to sit with her. "I am married, you see. My husband, Richard, is also an enchanter." She glanced down, and Andrea took note of the multicolored threaded bracelet Meredith wore around her right wrist. It was similar to the ones her parents wore – a tradition for most married Dameans. Most bracelets were created by weavers – specialized craftsmen and enchanters that often infused the threads with a bit of magic to bind the wearers of the bracelets. "Are you aware of the illness enchanters can get?"

"I only know that it happens when magic is cast without enough energy being available," Andrea replied.

"Exactly," Meredith said. "Richard and I were attacked in our home one night. He used a great deal of magic to save me at the cost of his own life. There was a tonic he had stored away that he instructed me to give him. It stabilized him, but it also put him in a deep sleep." She sighed. "It has been over twenty years. I cannot wake him."

Andrea suddenly felt sympathy for this stranger. Meredith just wanted to save her husband and Damea, and she needed help. Surely Andrea's parents could understand this.

"I'm sorry," she murmured.

"It's not your fault, but thank you anyway," Meredith said,

her tone not changing. "But back to why I am here. What were you doing that set off such a powerful projection a month ago?"

"I..." Andrea was sure that Meredith would think her incompetent or inexperienced if she knew that she could not power a simple farming machine. "I tried to power my family's old farming machine. It worked for a few seconds, but then there was too much magic. I didn't know what to do with it, and the machine broke."

She waited for Meredith to ridicule her, but Meredith actually nodded and gazed at Andrea with what appeared to be *admiration*. "I see," the enchanter said. "And it worked for a bit, you say?"

"Yes, only for a few seconds, though."

"That is remarkable, Andrea," Meredith beamed. "Few people of your age and experience could have accomplished that without formal training."

"I have a tutor that I see once a week. Master Jheran. He used to be a royal enchanter in Azgadar," Andrea explained.

"With all due respect to your tutor, I've seen students your age at the academy who have been trained by the greatest enchanters in Damea that couldn't light a streetlamp if they tried," Meredith said and laughed a little. "You have a gift, Andrea, and I do wish you would see that."

Andrea sighed. Everything she had been holding in for the past few months finally came out. "I don't know what you want me to do. My parents don't like magic. They don't trust it. They *hate* that I was born this way, as if I can help it! They'd rather I spend my life working with my hands on their farm than actually take what I have and use it for good." She buried her face in her hands. She knew she was whining and probably appeared immature and childish to the older woman.

"Then why don't you?" Meredith appeared unmoved by Andrea's plight.

Andrea glared at the enchanter. "Because I *can't*. They'd disown me if I left to become an...someone like you."

"Enchanter?" Meredith said quizzically. "You can say the word, Andrea. Look, I understand why you are troubled about this. I can wait a bit longer, but really, if you are serious about using your gift for good, then the question of what your parents will think of it should be irrelevant. Perhaps they will not understand now, but mark my words. When we restore magic to Damea and their farm is running on magic-powered machines, they will understand."

Andrea did not respond.

"Andrea, I learned one very important thing when I was very young: if you really care about doing something, you do it. You don't want to waste years of your life wondering if you should have or could have done it," Meredith continued. "I'll be town for a few days, so when you've decided, come tell me. I'll be staying at the inn." She stood up and turned to Andrea.

"Oh, and thank you for showing me around," she said with a quick nod before disappearing into the crowd.

* * *

Andrea and her parents ate in silence that evening. Her mother had asked how her day with Meredith had gone, to which Andrea had mumbled an "all right". Her father had given a polite greeting but had not spoken since they sat down to eat.

After what seemed like an eternity, the silence became unbearable. Andrea could not keep quiet anymore.

"Meredith offered me a job," she blurted out. There, it was out.

Her mother looked surprised, and her father appeared interested. "A job? What kind of job?" he asked.

Andrea put her fork down and took a deep breath. *Here goes nothing.*

"As an assistant," she explained, purposely leaving out the exact nature of the job. "Meredith is looking for someone to help her with her research in the Black Forest."

Garrett looked slightly uncomfortable. "The Black Forest is a bit far, no? Plus, you've got your responsibilities here. How are you going to keep up with those if you're out in the Black Forest?"

"That place is dangerous," Isabel warned. "I know Meredith said it was a peaceful place, but there's always talk of people winding up dead in those parts."

Andrea sighed. This was already not going well, and she hadn't even dropped the part about Meredith being an enchanter yet.

"What sort of research are we talking about here, Andrea?" her father asked sternly.

Andrea shifted in her seat. "Well," she began, "Meredith is an enchanter and–,"

"An enchanter? Certainly not!" Isabel exclaimed. "We've been over this many times, Andrea. I *knew* there was something strange about that woman."

"But it's a once in a lifetime opportunity, Mother!" Andrea protested. She did not care if she sounded like a small child throwing a tantrum. This was her future, and she wanted to have a say in it!

"You expect us to be okay with letting you roam the uncivilized parts of the land, risking your life, when you have a perfectly good life here?" Garrett demanded. "Damea is not a safe place for enchanters, Andrea. Is this something old man Jheran put in your head? Is risking the life of my daughter something that sounds like a 'once in a lifetime opportunity'?"

"No!" Andrea cried and stood up. "Master Jheran had nothing to do with this! Meredith asked *me*. I *want* to do this, Father. And it's not a risk! I would be safe–,"

"Safe?!" Garrett slammed his open palm on the table and stood up. "In case you've forgotten, enchanters are the reason for *every* problem in this land!"

"Garrett!" Isabel exclaimed. "Please, sit down. Both of you!"

"Enchanters didn't cause these problems, Father," Andrea snapped. "People did. People who were too blind and greedy and just cared about taking for themselves! That's all I am to you, isn't it? Just another tool to make your damn farm run." She knew it was unfair and untrue, but she was letting her anger speak for her now and there was no going back.

Garrett narrowed his eyes at her. "How *dare* you–,"

"Andrea!" Isabel cried. "That's enough!"

"*No!*" Andrea yelled. "I've had it. From now on, I'm doing what's right for *my* future, not yours!" she pointed at Garrett accusingly.

"If you feel so strongly about it, then leave!" Garrett shouted back.

The room went deathly silent as Andrea and Garrett glared at each other, with Isabel glancing worriedly at both of them. Finally, Andrea made the next move.

"I will," she muttered and walked briskly to her room to grab her old, worn-out cloak and throw a few personal items in her backpack. She walked to the front door and had barely grasped the door handle when she heard her mother's voice behind her.

"Just where do you think you're going?"

Andrea sighed. "I'm leaving. I'll have Bill bring Kira back." She opened the door and walked out, ignoring her mother's protests.

"You can't just let her leave, Garrett!"

"She'll come crawling back when she realizes how stupid she's acting," she heard her father say. She tried to fight back tears, but eventually ignored them and let herself cry as she prepared Kira for the short journey to the inn.

* * *

Meredith sat alone at her table listening to the soft, haunting voice of the minstrel playing the lute on the other side of the inn. Most of the patrons had gone home for the evening, but a few regulars and those staying the night at the inn remained.

"Another ale, my lady?" Bill asked.

She looked up at the man and shook her head with a faint smile. "No, thank you."

"As you wish," the innkeeper grunted and walked away.

The enchanter was just about to turn in for the night when the front door swung open. Some of the patrons turned to see who was there. When they saw Andrea, most just returned to their drinks and conversations. The minstrel continued her song.

Andrea removed her hood, walked over to Meredith and sat across from her. "Is that job still available?" she asked breathlessly.

Meredith looked surprised for a moment, then smiled and nodded. "It is."

Andrea extended her hand. "Then I accept," she said.

Meredith eyed her curiously. "And what of your parents? Are they no longer part of the equation?"

Andrea shook her head. "They're...irrelevant. Now, do we have a deal or not?"

Meredith gave a small laugh and shook her new apprentice's hand. "We do."

Andrea looked around nervously. "Can we leave tonight?"

Meredith nodded and stood up. She adjusted her cloak and turned to Andrea. "We can. But first…" She reached into her bag next to her and pulled out the fine blue cloak she had purchased in the marketplace earlier. "Here. You can throw your old one away."

Andrea tentatively accepted the cloak and looked at Meredith in awe. "How did you–,"

"I had a feeling you'd accept my offer. Now, put that on so you don't get cold while we travel tonight."

 Chapter 4

The Apprentice

The Black Forest

Three years later

"Andrea, dear, can you bring me that vial please? The one I just brewed."

Andrea glanced up from the dusty tome she was reading. "Of course," she replied and walked over to a metal shelf on the other side of the room. She scanned the numerous bottles on the shelves for the one she had remembered her mentor brewing less than an hour ago. She plucked it from the shelf and carried it over to Meredith, who was hovering over a complex-looking alchemy table.

"Thank you, dear," Meredith murmured as she added the vial to the mixture she was working on.

The room the two were working in was only one of the laboratories set up in Meredith's spacious mansion in the Black Forest. A thick, labyrinthine cluster of massive trees, the Black Forest was rarely traveled by merchants or soldiers. Too many had become lost on its paths and succumbed to starvation or animal attacks. Upon arriving at the abandoned house twenty years earlier, Meredith had used her power to create two mighty but mindless humanoid constructs that assisted her in repairing the old building.

The mansion consisted of three main laboratories on the main level, several bedrooms, a grand entry hall, and a large kitchen, among other rooms. Most of the drapery and rugs were torn and ruined when Meredith had arrived, but she had redecorated according to her own tastes over the years when she dared go into the cities. The mansion did have a large cellar, which contained the largest lab of all. It was here that she kept the preserved comatose body of her husband. She had created the conduits that would transfer the magical energy to restore him, once she had accumulated enough.

The enchanter had spent the first decade on her own traveling throughout Damea, attempting to collect enough artifacts to produce the magic needed to restore her lost love, but even with all the artifacts she procured and extracted energy from, it was not enough to bring Richard back. She had decided to attempt a different method. Alchemy was often practiced in tandem with enchanting at the academy, so she had spent the last decade trying to create a mixture that was powerful enough to work with the magical energy she had available. Her goal was to create a powerful reaction that would allow enough energy to be transferred to her husband to restore him. Alas, even with the help of Andrea, her apprentice of three years, success did not appear to be any closer than it was twenty years ago.

It was a small consolation that she had been able to acquire such a talented apprentice. Andrea was young and impatient, and at times her control over her abilities was less than predictable; but her potential was great – greater perhaps than Meredith's had been when she was that age. Had the academy existed today, surely they would have been eager to take Andrea as a student.

The girl had barely mentioned her home or her parents since they had left Ata that fateful night. Meredith was concerned at first, and tried to gently push Andrea to talk about it. But her apprentice would have none of it. The girl seemed to want to forget everything in her life up to when she and Meredith began working together. Meredith was fine with this; it certainly helped to have a focused apprentice. She herself had become more secluded over the last few years, speaking only to Andrea and never leaving the mansion. She feared any distraction would prevent her from focusing all her efforts on restoring Richard.

* * *

One morning, a loud, metallic crash woke Andrea with a start. The crash was immediately followed by what sounded like Meredith cursing loud enough for the entire forest to hear. Andrea blinked a few times before groggily sitting up. She did not jump to Meredith's side immediately – this had become a common occurrence over the last six months or so.

After a few moments, the young enchanter rubbed her eyes and climbed out of bed. The rain pounded heavily on the roof, and a flash of lightning lit up the room followed by rolling thunder. The quarters that her mentor had given her were vastly larger than any room she had lived in at her family's small house in Ata. Unfortunately, they were also within close proximity of the lab Meredith worked out of the most, so every few nights, when an experiment did not go as intended, Andrea would be awoken by the sounds of Meredith's tantrums. Not that she lacked sympathy for her mentor – quite the opposite, in fact. But after twenty years of trying and failure after failure, Andrea wondered when Meredith would cease her quest to restore her husband and focus more on finding a way to fix the land's magic problem. When she indirectly asked, as she often did, Meredith would dismiss her apprentice's concern as "impatience" and insist that the research to save her husband would eventually help all Dameans.

Andrea had been an excellent student in the last three years, however, and saw a potential flaw in Meredith's explanation. Over the years, the magic Meredith had used to experiment on her husband had most likely altered his condition. It was a known fact in the field of magical studies that too much exposure to magic decreased an individual's ability to tolerate it without experiencing unforeseen side effects. When Andrea pointed this out to Meredith, her mentor became agitated and insisted that those effects had never been proven and were "merely theory", at best. Andrea worried that even if Meredith found a way to restore Richard, that the solution would not help fix the magic problem in Damea. But she dared not object too loudly or often to Meredith's practices. She was relatively happy with her life as an enchanter's apprentice and wanted to keep things the way they were.

She changed into the long-sleeved shirt and pants that she normally worked in and navigated through the torch-lit corridor to find Meredith in her lab. When she got to the room, which was lit only by the eerie dim green glow produced by the magical equipment in the lab, she found her mentor on her knees, surrounded by shards of glass, her head buried in her hands. Various pieces of equipment had been knocked over and several vials of liquid, some of which had taken days to create, were shattered on the hard floor, their contents splattered everywhere.

Andrea sighed. "What happened, Meredith?" she said, and placing a tentative hand on the older woman's shoulder.

Meredith sniffed and stood up, wiping her eyes. Her hair was thin, greying, and stringy, and her eyes were bloodshot with dark, heavy bags underneath. "Oh, Andrea," she sobbed, "it's no use! Nothing works! I'll never bring him back." She threw her arms around her apprentice, who stood awkwardly and patted her mentor on the back.

"Don't say that, Meredith. It's one experiment that didn't work. We can try some more," Andrea said, attempting to sound calm and comforting but only managing tired and half-sincere at best.

The room was quiet save the thunder and rain outside and Meredith's soft sobs. Andrea looked out the large window in the lab just in time to see another flash of lightning. The thunder that followed it was much closer and shook the mansion. Suddenly, Meredith let go of Andrea and straightened up. Her grey eyes seemed more alive than they had been in some time. Andrea knew this look. She had seen it before, although not in quite a while.

"Meredith?" she asked.

Her mentor looked at her with wide eyes. "More."

Andrea tilted her head. "I'm sorry?"

"More. More magic. More energy. The storm, Andrea," Meredith whispered. "I've been an idiot. The storm!" She grinned and threw her arms around her bewildered apprentice again before bolting out of the room.

Andrea sighed and looked around at the mess her mentor had made. She would just have to clean it up later. Right now she had to follow Meredith to the lab in the cellar and find out what she was up to.

* * *

"Put this over there and get me that cable. And open the skylight. Hurry!"

Andrea rushed around the lab trying to follow Meredith's rapid orders. She was not exactly sure what was going on or what they were doing, but she could tell from Meredith's excitement that her mentor was onto something potentially groundbreaking.

The cellar was lit mostly by torches and the familiar green glow of the magical metal equipment that Meredith kept around. There were no windows, so the lightning was not visible; but Andrea could still hear and feel the vibrations of the thunder that rolled through the Black Forest as the storm grew stronger.

As she handed Meredith a long grey cable, she finally asked, "Meredith, what are we doing? What's going on?"

Meredith was hovering around the metal conduits near the

table where Richard lay, configuring the cables between them and connecting others to small glass tanks near the alchemy table. "Magic, my dear," she said cryptically as she worked. "Magic is everywhere. It lives in nature. That's where it comes from, you know." She wiped sweat off her brow and began pouring a variety of vials of liquid into the glass tanks.

"Yes, I know. But what does that have to do with the conduits?!" Andrea exclaimed. "And why are we opening the skylight? It's raining outside. Everything is going to get wet! The equipment–,"

"Weather is part of nature, Andrea!" Meredith interrupted. "Magic can affect and be affected by weather. The lightning," she whispered excitedly. "We can use it!"

Andrea looked at her mentor incredulously. "What? Then why have we never before?"

"When was the last time we had such a strong lightning storm? Besides, we need more than just the lightning. We need the equipment, the mixtures we've created, and every last bit of magic we have," Meredith explained. After a few more moments of configuring the conduits, she finally wiped her hands on her shirt and said, "There. They are ready. Hopefully the device on the roof will capture the energy from the lightning." She gestured for Andrea to stand near her. "Come, I'll need your help, Andrea."

Andrea went to stand by her mentor. "Are you sure this will work?" she found herself asking without thinking.

Meredith glanced at her apprentice for a moment and then looked longingly at her husband. "I…nothing is completely certain with magic, Andrea. Sometimes the right answer is a combination of several possible solutions. If this doesn't work, then I don't know what will," she admitted.

After a minute of silence, Andrea finally nodded and said, "Then let's do this and find out."

Meredith smiled at the young enchanter with pride. "Once lightning strikes the roof, the device I've placed there should relay the energy to the conduits. Once the conduits start to transfer the energy, we'll need to help contain that energy by manipulating the air around it. Can you do that for me, Andrea?"

Andrea's face was slightly paler than usual, and she was more nervous than she had been in years. She was unsure if her skills were developed enough to do this, but she nodded assent. This would be a true test and a chance for her to show Meredith she was ready to be a full enchanter.

"Yes, Meredith," she said shakily.

Meredith nodded. "Good. Wait for my command," she ordered. She briefly bent down to whisper something in her husband's ear before returning to Andrea's side.

They waited for what seemed like an eternity to Andrea but in reality was only a few minutes. The thunder seemed to grow stronger, and she suddenly heard and felt the humming of magic directly in front of her. She looked at the conduits. They had begun to vibrate. The vibrations became stronger until hot white sparks began to shoot off the top and bottom of the conduits.

"*Now, Andrea!*" Meredith shouted.

Andrea lifted her hands and concentrated all her focus on

the conduits in front of her. She immediately felt the energy in the air pushing against her–so strong, in fact, that she was nearly knocked over. But she had trained for this. She stood her ground, pushing back against the crackling magic that filled the cellar. The humming had become a roar. The room trembled, and the conduits shook violently.

"Keep it contained! Don't let any of it escape!" Meredith shouted, holding her own hands up as well, focusing all her willpower on containing the energy.

Andrea continued to stand her ground, but she could feel her body tiring. Beads of sweat rolled down her forehead and into her eyes, stinging them. Her head began to throb, and the strain of the energy pushing back at her made her arms ache painfully.

"*Yes!* It's working!" she heard her mentor yell.

Suddenly, a flash of light blinded her and she heard a loud bang, followed by a strong gust of hot wind as one of the conduits exploded, falling to the ground in several twisted metal pieces. Andrea was thrown to the ground as she heard Meredith's cries of horror. The explosion shattered the tanks designed to store the magical energy. The young enchanter covered her head and eyes to protect herself from the falling shards.

With so much energy lost, the device on the roof most likely destroyed, and most of the cables completely burnt, the other conduit ceased its shaking and the room suddenly became very quiet and still, save the harsh, shaky breathing of the two women in the cellar and the crackling of embers from the remains of the conduit. Andrea slowly removed her hands from her head, carefully picking tiny pieces of broken glass from her hair and back.

Richard lay on the table, his condition unchanged.

"NO!" Meredith screamed, kicking over the remaining conduit in rage. She turned toward the alchemy table and used all her strength to flip it over, sending everything on it crashing to the ground. Andrea scrambled to the corner of the room, fearful of what Meredith might do in her fury.

"*Why didn't it work?!*" Meredith yelled, tears streaming down her face. "Why?!"

Andrea was at a loss for words. There was nothing she could say that would make this remotely better. "I…" she stammered.

"Enough! Get out," Meredith snapped. "It's useless. *Useless!*"

"But Meredith–," Andrea tried, not sure what she was hoping to accomplish with those words.

"GET OUT!" the older woman screamed. "Leave me!"

Andrea did not need to be told again. She fled the room and ran back to her quarters as fast as she could. Once in her room, she locked the door, threw herself on the bed, and began to cry. She was worried for Meredith, disappointed in herself, and maybe a little terrified at what her mentor would do next. For the first time in three years, Andrea wanted to go back home to her family's small farm in the little, middle-of-nowhere village of Ata.

* * *

Meredith scanned the room and assessed the sight in front of her. The damage that had been done would take months – perhaps years – to recover from. She knew she had most likely made a mistake in losing her temper with Andrea, but she was too beyond grief to care enough to do anything about it.

She gazed at her husband.

Twenty years. Twenty years and I have failed to keep my promise.

"I'm sorry, love," she whispered.

There was a slight tug, then a stronger one. The tug became a pull. Meredith spun around, confused. There was no one else in the room, and the interval between thunder claps had become longer as the storm started to die down.

Then, above the pile of rubble where one of the conduits had stood, she saw it. Any untrained eye would have missed the slight ripple in the air, the distortion that was definitely not a natural occurrence.

She could feel it, though. The energy was tight, coiled, hyper-concentrated. It was powerful, more powerful than any artifact she had ever come across and even more powerful than the energy generated during their earlier, failed experiment. The distortion did not belong there – Meredith knew that much. But did she make it? Could she collect the magic from it?

She reached out, focusing on the anomaly and nothing else. The pull became stronger, harsher. At some point, the resistance was so strong it threatened to rip her arm out of its socket. Meredith's vision became blurry, and her thoughts clouded. But she knew she had to hold on. That magic had to be hers…

A flash of white light filled the room, followed by an earth-shaking boom that threw Meredith to the ground. She coughed and pulled herself up.

The anomaly was gone, but it appeared to have left something, or rather, *someone* in its place.

Chapter 5

Trapped

The unconscious girl who lay on the stone floor in front of Meredith appeared to be around Andrea's age. Her dirty blonde hair was pulled back and she had some charcoal streaks across her otherwise slightly tanned face, most likely residue from the magical reaction that had just occurred.

Meredith stared dumbfounded at the girl. Who was she and where did she come from? She turned her focus to where the distortion had been. The questions raced through her mind: Had the girl caused the distortion? Had the experiment? Was she dangerous? Did *she* cause the experiment to fail?

One thing was certain. Meredith detected a *very* strong magical presence from the girl. But the magic felt strange, alien. It was concentrated. In fact, it seemed less like a projection and more like a pulse. A very strong pulse. This girl was no enchanter. Meredith had no idea who or what this person was. Everything about the girl seemed foreign, including her clothing, which consisted of a strange, thick, black hooded shirt, and faded, rough blue pants tucked into short black boots. Her clothing was also streaked with a fine black powder. Meredith had visited most of the known regions of Damea, and had never seen clothing like this before.

She considered trying to revive the girl, but then thought twice and realized that there was a chance that the strange visitor could be dangerous, especially given the energy that radiated from her. She decided to summon one of her constructs.

The hulking, faceless creature, which was around the height of an average man but made of a grey crystalline substance, arrived less than a minute later and stood next to its master, awaiting orders.

"Take her to one of the unused bedrooms and lock the door. Keep watch outside and do not let her leave if she wakes," Meredith commanded. The construct grunted in acknowledgement, picked up the girl, who did not awaken, and carried her off. Meredith, now alone again, looked around at the wreckage in the lab. She sighed and summoned the other construct to begin cleaning the mess.

✶ ✶ ✶

When Cassie woke, her head was pounding and her entire body ached. She was surprised to find that the bed she now lay on was not her own. The room she was in was not her room, either.

"The hell?!" she breathed as she quickly sat up and scanned her surroundings. The room was large but the decor was like nothing she had ever seen before. It seemed older, like something that belonged in an exhibit. *Did I actually get drunk and wake up in a museum?* Sure, she had gone out with friends the night before but she had not drunk, and by all accounts she had returned home safely and had fallen asleep in her bedroom.

This was *definitely* not her bedroom.

Her clothes were the same as the ones she had worn to the bar. She remembered being exhausted and feeling too lazy to change into proper sleepwear, so she had just slept in her regular clothes. After working all day and spending a few hours at the bar listening to one of her friends complain for far too long about a bad date, not even the raging storm that had taken out power in half the city could stop her from passing out as soon as she got home.

But she was not home. Where *was* she? She swung her legs over the side of the high, large bed and jumped off, wincing in pain as she did so. The bedroom itself was dark and dusty, but she could see through the bright crevices of the outdated window drapes that it was daytime and no longer raining. The door was closed and she could not hear any sounds coming from outside the bedroom. She walked over to the door and tried to turn the knob to open it, but it was locked.

"Hello?" she called out. "Hey! I'm locked in!" No answer. She decided to try a different tack and began banging on the door.

"Hey! Unlock the damn door! Hello?!" she yelled. She waited a few moments and then attempted to kick the door down. But it was no use. Wherever she was, the builders of this house used very strong doors. She sighed and noticed an odd odor in the air. It smelled faintly of burned charcoal. She looked down and saw that her hands and clothing were streaked with a fine black powder.

"What the hell…" she repeated. She could feel her stomach tighten and she knew she was starting to panic. She tried to control her breathing. *Don't panic, Cass. Just figure out where you are first.*

There was an audible click, and she saw the doorknob turn. The door swung open, revealing a dark-haired, middle-aged woman wearing a long black skirt and a burgundy blouse. To add to Cassie's confusion, this woman did not seem surprised to see her.

"You're awake," the woman observed, her hands on her hips.

"Who are you?" Cassie demanded. "And where the hell am I?"

The woman raised an eyebrow at the girl. "I'm sorry?"

"You heard me," Cassie retorted, glaring at her. "Where. Am. I?"

"You are in my home, in the Black Forest. You were brought here last night, how exactly I do not know," the woman explained. "Would you like some breakfast?"

Cassie stared at her, confused. "Um…what? No…no, I don't want breakfast. Look, ma'am, I just want to get home. Why'd you lock me in here anyway?"

Her new hostess gave a knowing smile. "If a stranger suddenly appeared in your home, wouldn't you want to make sure they were properly contained if you were going to keep them overnight?"

Cassie took a step back. Was this woman crazy? Was she a kidnapper or serial killer? She didn't want to find out and considered trying to run.

The woman took a step toward Cassie. "I am Meredith. What is your name?"

"Uh…Cassie. Look, I'll just be going now if that's all right with you. I don't know how long it's going to take me to get home." Cassie was on the verge of panicking now, and Meredith could clearly see the fear and trepidation in the girl's bright blue eyes.

"I don't know where you are from, but I have a strong suspicion that your home is rather far from here, Cassie. You were brought here by magic – I am sure of that. Do you remember anything?" she asked.

Cassie shook her head. "Magic? Look lady, there's no such thing as magic. Now, I *really* have to be going–," she started to walk past Meredith, who quickly raised her hand. A force shook the room, and Cassie found herself blocked from moving any further.

"I'm sorry. You cannot leave yet. Not until I can figure out where you came from and why you are here," Meredith explained. Cassie reached out her hand and felt a slight push when she came in contact with the force field.

"What…what is this?" she gasped.

Meredith smirked. "Magic. Now, I'll be back for you later. I'll have food brought to you in a bit. There are facilities in the room should you need them." She gave a small nod and left, closing the door as she did so. Cassie heard the faint click of the lock sealing the door.

"Hey! Let me out!" Cassie yelled as she tried and failed to get past the barrier. She ran to the window and tore down the curtains. She covered her eyes momentarily as sunlight flooded the room. When her eyes adjusted, she gasped at the view before her.

The mansion was surrounded by towering trees that seemed to stretch on forever. The forest as well as the bright and clear blue sky gave away the troubling fact that she was indeed far from home. The bedroom window was not too high, so Cassie reached up to open the window to escape. She reeled back in shock when a small burst of energy painfully shot through her hands and up her arms. Whatever Meredith had done to keep her in the room was obviously affecting the window as well.

"Damn it!" she cried. Here she was, far from home, in the middle of some forest, locked in a room in a mansion that belonged to a woman who was completely insane and had some very...inexplicable abilities. She winced again as her headache worsened and stumbled back to the bed. She had barely made it onto the mattress when the world spun around her and darkness closed in on her once again.

* * *

Andrea spent most of the morning cleaning the lab closest to her room. Meredith's first outburst had resulted in the floor of the lab being littered with broken glass and other debris from the various ingredient shelves in the room. Andrea had not seen her mentor since the night before when the older enchanter had yelled at her to leave.

Andrea shook her head in dismay as she grabbed a broom and began sweeping up the broken glass. How many more outbursts would it take before Meredith realized that it was impossible to bring Richard back? How much more damage to their equipment, to their research, would there be before she understood this?

When she had retired to her room the night before, Andrea had blamed herself for the experiment's failure. But the more she thought about it, the less convinced she became that it was really her fault. And Meredith hadn't outright blamed her – in fact, she hadn't blamed her at all. Maybe she's finally coming around, Andrea hoped. Maybe she's realizing that we should focus on finding a solution to everyone's magic problem instead of just hers.

She was pulled from her thoughts by the stomping of a construct in the hallway. She turned to watch it walk by the room and noticed that it was carrying a limp body over its shoulder. Puzzled and curious, Andrea set the broom against the wall and followed the construct from a distance so that it would not detect her. Had they received a visitor during the night – worse, had someone been injured or killed during the storm?

Andrea was surprised to see the construct taking the body down into the cellar, the door shutting behind it. Clearly Meredith was down in the cellar doing *something* and did not want to be disturbed. Andrea had a nagging thought in the back of her mind that her mentor had grown so desperate that she had resorted to experimenting on other people, but she shook the thought from her head. While it was true that human bodies could be manipulated through magical means provided they were strong enough to survive the process, using people as energy sources was not only barbaric and unethical but it also required several very powerful enchanters to do, not to mention there had been no recorded incident of a successful energy extraction from a human since the First Era.

She did not believe Meredith was that desperate or foolish. However, there was still another person in the cellar, and Andrea wanted to find out who it was and why Meredith had brought another person into the mansion.

She knocked on the door. "Meredith?" No answer. She tried the handle, but the door was locked.

Andrea had a sinking feeling that something was *very* wrong. She did not want to make the situation with Meredith worse by trying to break the lock, but she did not want to sit idly by either. Either way, Meredith had a human being in that lab with her and she had locked the door to the lab. Andrea knew deep down that something was not right. Whatever Meredith was involved in now, it had nothing to do with helping Damea, and Andrea wanted no part in it.

She returned to her room and began to pack a small bag. She decided she would find this new visitor as soon as Meredith was finished and would quietly ask if her or she wanted to leave with her.

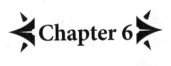

Chapter 6

The Test

Cassie opened her eyes and felt a chill run through her body. Her vision was blurry and her mouth was dry. She tried to remember what had happened after she had passed out on the bed in the strange room she had awoken in earlier. Or had that all been a dream?

She blinked several times until her vision was restored and looked around. The floor she lay on was cold and made of a dark, rough stone. Her heart sank when she realized that not only had that definitely not been a nightmare, but she was also still not home. The room was cold and lit only with a few torches on the walls. It appeared to be a cellar or basement. She could see fragments of glass and what appeared to be the smoldering remains of a machine of some kind. An old wooden table stood in the middle of the room. An unconscious, middle-aged man with short blonde hair and a trimmed beard lay on it. To the left of the table was a short, cylindrical metal box. There were thick cables running from the box to another table that was much smaller than the one the man was on. On it was a variety of bottles and vials as well as a medium-sized glass tank that emitted a faint green glow. There were broken glass tanks on the floor next to the table – no doubt the result of whatever fire or accident had occurred here some time earlier.

To make matters worse, her wrists had cold iron shackles clamped around them. The thick, heavy chains running from the shackles to the floor were long enough that she was able to stand up.

"Hello?" Cassie's voice was raspy from her dry mouth. Her head and body still ached and her stomach growled with hunger.

She heard only the crackling of the torches burning but was soon greeted by footsteps. Her captor emerged from the shadows.

"Good, you're awake. I thought you'd sleep through the night," she stated.

Cassie glared at the woman. "Look, you're obviously crazy. But if you let me go now I won't report you." She shook her wrists. "What's with the chains? Why are we in a dungeon?"

Meredith laughed quietly. "Dungeon? My dear, we are in my laboratory. And I'm not crazy, despite what you may think. As I said earlier, I cannot have you leaving before I know more about you. It's for all of our safety, not just mine."

Cassie struggled against the chains. "Right. So since I'm clearly *not* dangerous, can I go now? What about him?" She gestured to the man on the table. "Shouldn't you be finding out where *he* came from?"

Meredith narrowed her eyes. "That man is my husband. I'll forgive you for your insolence this time, but I will ask for some common courtesy from here on out."

"Common courtesy?" Cassie exclaimed. "Lady, you kidnapped me and locked me up in your dungeon...lab, whatever! Why would I show you any kind of courtesy?"

Meredith put her hand up to silence her visitor. "Enough!" she said. "The fact remains that I've discovered your secret and I'm willing to make a deal with you."

Cassie raised an eyebrow. "Secret? What secret?"

Meredith crossed her arms. "Oh come now, did you think you hid it that well? Any enchanter with an inkling of knowledge could detect it. My apprentice would have picked up on it immediately."

Cassie shook her head and continued to struggle. "I have no idea what you're talking about!"

"The magic!" Meredith exclaimed. "The magic that you have somehow stored in yourself." She pointed at Cassie. "Now, I don't know why you are here or what you want, but I have need of a great amount of energy. Provide that for me, and I will let you go. It's as simple as that."

Cassie rolled her eyes. "Again with the magic thing? I don't have any magic, lady."

"I beg to differ," Meredith said, taking a step closer to Cassie. She held her hand out and the immediate area around them began to hum with energy. "It's so strange. Most people have *some* energy in them, but it's impossible to extract. But you... it's as though the magic is surrounding you. How do you do that?" she said, her voice low but not quite a whisper.

"I...I don't know what you mean," Cassie stammered. "Please...let me go," she pleaded.

"I will, just as soon as you help me. I require magic to restore my husband. He has fallen ill, as you can see," Meredith explained and lowered her hand. The humming immediately stopped.

Cassie could not understand why this woman kept talking about magic. She figured Meredith was just a lonely woman who had gone senile over the years. That did not explain the dungeon-like setting, the man on the table, the shackles around her wrists, or that strange humming noise, but it was the only explanation Cassie had. She decided to try another method.

"All right then," she conceded, "how do I help you?"

Meredith looked surprised, but answered anyway. "You'll... need to stand still and not move. It's a simple enough process with inanimate items, but I admit, I've never performed an extraction on a living creature."

Cassie blinked. Meredith seemed to be legitimately convinced that there was going to be some kind of real result from whatever this "process" was. *What if she's not crazy?* She suddenly felt foolish. *That's insane – of course she's crazy! There's no such thing as magic.*

Meredith raised her hand and Cassie heard very heavy steps approaching them. When the construct arrived, Cassie suddenly felt very lightheaded.

"What...what is that?" she asked shakily.

Meredith shrugged. "One of my servants. It's here to make sure that you don't try anything, just in case." She positioned herself directly in front of Cassie and raised her hands tentatively. "Now hold still. I'm going to begin the process. Just a minor extraction at first, then we can go from there."

Cassie felt her heart racing and realized she was sweating, even though the room was cold. Something was definitely not right here. Magic was not real, and neither were giant autonomous crystal-creatures. "Wait!" she cried. "Don't. Please, I really don't understand anything about magic or whether I have it or any of that. I don't want to get hurt. I just want to go home."

Meredith lowered her hands halfway. "And you will. But you must first help me. Hold still, please."

She placed her hands on Cassie's shoulders. Nothing happened at first. But then a faint light enveloped her hands and grew brighter. The signature hum returned, and soon the air around them began vibrating. Cassie could only feel the vibrations from whatever it was that Meredith had triggered. Was this the magic she was talking about? How could this be possible?

The older woman's eyes were tightly shut, and Cassie could see beads of perspiration breaking out on Meredith's forehead. The woman's hands were trembling. Her fingers dug painfully into Cassie's shoulders. The construct motionless stood behind her.

Then there was a tug. Cassie felt it from within, as though something was trying to break free from within her. The tug grew stronger and more insistent, and suddenly Cassie found that it was becoming difficult to breathe. Out of the corner of her eye, she saw the glass tank on the table was glowing brighter than before.

Then the pain began.

The aura came first, almost letting her know that something significant was going to happen. Then it happened. A sudden rip that she felt everywhere began in her chest and tore through her body. Her head pounded and her vision faded. Whatever this was, it was unlike anything she had felt in her life, and she knew Meredith was causing it.

"Please...stop!" she whimpered.

Meredith did not audibly respond, but she did tense up as though she had been struck by something before finally ceasing her focus on Cassie and shakily removing her hands from the girl's shoulders. The humming and vibrations fell to a low rumble. Soon, Cassie could only hear the harsh rasping noise of her own breathing. Her body ached as though it was on fire. Her vision was still slightly blurry. Exhausted from whatever had just occurred, she fell to her knees.

Meredith was drenched in sweat and panting. She turned to look at the glass tank. It emitted a glimmering white light now. The energy transfer had been successful, and by the color and brightness of the light, she could see that the magic she had extracted from the girl was very potent.

"It worked," she whispered.

"Let...me...go...now," Cassie gasped as she weakly struggled against the chains.

Meredith's attention turned back to the weakened young woman. "I think that's enough for today. We will continue this tomorrow." She signaled for the construct to approach.

"Take her to her room, please," she told it and returned to hovering around her work table.

"What? You said…you'd let me go. You promised!" Cassie panted as the construct removed her shackles and hoisted her over its shoulder. She shrieked in pain but was too weak to struggle or fight back.

"And I will, once I've gotten all the magic I need," Meredith said curtly without even so much as a glance at Cassie, who had fallen unconscious again. As the construct left, Meredith marveled at the magic she now had stored. A few more sessions, and there could be enough for one more experiment on Richard.

This time, it would work.

Chapter 7

Cassie

Just after sunset, Andrea heard the heavy steps of the construct walking down the corridor near her room. She set down the book she had been reading and looked toward the open doorway. Moments later, the construct thundered on by. Sure enough, it had the same body hoisted over its shoulder. Andrea could see her vantage point that the person was definitely a young female, perhaps not much older than her. The fact that the girl was unconscious all but confirmed her earlier fears about Meredith.

She grabbed her packed bag and followed the construct from a distance. It stopped not far down the hall and entered one of the vacant bedrooms. After a few seconds, it exited the room alone and continued down the hallway.

Once it was gone, Andrea made her way to the room where it had dropped off the young woman, being sure to check that Meredith was not around. She found the door was magically locked but was not too worried. She briefly concentrated on the lock and was able to summon enough magic to disable it. She grasped the doorknob and cautiously opened the door.

The girl was sprawled out on her stomach on the bed. She

was unconscious but breathing steadily. Her dirty blonde hair was disheveled and her clothing and skin was covered with patches and streaks of magical residue. Her face was drenched in sweat and showed early signs of bruising. Andrea had never seen the fine powder on a person before, but after taking in the girl's state she realized in horror what had transpired.

She knew Meredith was desperate, but this? Experimenting on people? Perhaps this girl was not completely innocent – Andrea had never seen her before – but the thought of her mentor attempting to extract energy from a *human being* disgusted her.

She approached the girl and sat on the bed next to her. *Strange.* It had been well over a year since she had been out of the mansion and around other people. She had not interacted with someone her own age in at least three years – and even then, those had been just young shopkeepers or beggars in the city.

Observing the girl, Andrea noticed that her clothing was unlike anything she had seen before, even during her brief time in the cities. Everything about this new visitor was foreign, yet Andrea felt strangely drawn to the girl. There was something familiar about her, though the enchanter could not place what it was. It seemed to emanate from the girl's unconscious form, though, and Andrea could not help but reach out and place her hand on the girl's shoulder.

There was nothing, only emptiness. A cry sounded from far away. As she focused on it, Andrea realized it wasn't a cry, but a shrill noise that reverberated around her and into the ether in which she stood. There were voices, though…laughing? Conversations, though she could not understand what was being said. There was a ringing in her ears that only intensified the more she tried to ignore it.

She looked ahead. She saw the outlines of a familiar shape she had seen on countless maps. Damea. Andrea was not sure how, but she knew this was a massive magical projection of Damea. There were lights. They were tiny bright blue beacons that clumped together randomly, all scattered across the land. Larger clumps settled around the area that appeared to be the Black Forest. There was one larger, more noticeable beacon here. It flickered but still managed to burn brightly. She turned her attention to the entire map and noticed the more barren areas where she recalled magic being scarcer than in other regions.

Then, just north of Gurdinfield but deep within the Rhyad mountains, Andrea saw it. The largest beacon of all.

It must have been the size of a mountain, judging by how large it was. It pulsed and thrummed, and with every moment that passed, Andrea could see the smaller beacons gravitating toward it. Her chest suddenly felt tight and she found herself nauseated. The map began to contract and was violently sucked into the nothingness. A bright blue light burned her vision...

Andrea was torn from the experience as the girl's hands shot up and wrapped around her neck. The enchanter stared in shock into the bright blue eyes of the girl in front of her: the one who was now strangling her. Andrea clawed at the girl's hands frantically as she quickly ran out of air.

"Please..." she wheezed. "Stop..."

The girl did not loosen her grip. She pulled Andrea close and in a low voice said, "I don't care who you are. Get me the hell out of here, now!"

Andrea tried to reply, but she was already feeling lightheaded from lack of oxygen. Instead, she only managed a weak gasp.

"Are you going to get me out of here or not? Answer me, or I'll squeeze harder!" the girl threatened.

Andrea managed a weak nod, and the girl slowly released her grip on the enchanter's neck. Andrea coughed hard and inhaled as deeply as she could. When she had mostly recovered, she backed quickly away from the girl.

The girl stood up to face Andrea, her slight height advantage intimidating the enchanter. "What the hell–who are you?!"

"Please…I-I didn't mean any harm," Andrea stammered and threw her hands up in defense. The girl approached her again as though she was going to attack. Andrea cringed.

"Please! I yield! Don't hurt me!" she begged.

The girl looked amused and gave a harsh laugh. "Hah, hurt *you?* That's funny. You had your hands up like you were going to do that torture crap on me like the crazy bitch downstairs."

Andrea lowered her hands, puzzled. "What? Torture? No!" she exclaimed. "I thought…you're an enchanter and you seem really powerful and I just–,"

The girl threw up her hands in frustration. "What is it with you people and the magic thing? I'm not an 'enchanter', and I'm certainly not powerful. But if you don't get me out of here soon I'm going to start throwing punches."

"No! Please don't. Look, I'll get you out of here but you have to trust me, okay?" Andrea said.

The girl eyed her suspiciously. "How do I know you're not

just going to bring me back to your crazy friend…girlfriend – whatever she is?"

Andrea felt her face grow hot before she vigorously shook her head. "I-I promise I won't take you to her. And she's my mentor. I'm training…I *was* training to become an enchanter–,"

The girl stopped her. "Whatever. Are we going or not?"

Andrea tried to stay calm, but the entire situation – not to mention the girl's temper – was making it difficult. "Yes," she said slowly, looking around as she tried to decide how they would actually leave without Meredith knowing or interfering. Her gaze turned toward the window. The horses were stabled on the other side of the mansion. *We could just take mine.*

To where exactly, though? She had not thought that far ahead. She did know that what Meredith had done was unforgivable and violated the code of enchanting ethics. Leaving would surely terminate her apprenticeship and could quite possibly make her mentor even angrier and more unpredictable, but Andrea could not be a part of this anymore. She wanted to help the citizens of Damea, and right now she wanted to find a safe place where she could question this girl about the strange projection that she had seen.

"We can escape through the window," she said as she walked toward the floor-to-ceiling window, which consisted of two glass doors with worn handles. She sensed a magical lock was used here as well, and quickly dispelled it with a flick of her wrist.

The girl stared at her, astonished. "How'd you do that?"

Andrea flung the window doors open and inhaled the cool

night air. "Meredith has taught me quite a bit since I got here," she explained and she hoisted her bag over her shoulder. "Now, let's go. We should be able to make the jump down. Just run to the left and around the building to the horses. We can take mine."

The girl hesitated.

"Well? What are you waiting for?" Andrea said, exasperated.

"Before I go *riding off into the night* with you, I want a name," the girl demanded.

Andrea tried to hide a small smile. "Andrea. Of Ata," she added. "And you?"

"Cassie," the girl replied. She tilted her head. "What's 'Ata'?"

"The village I'm from," Andrea explained. She was growing impatient, worried that Meredith would see them. "Now, can we go?"

Cassie nodded. "Yep. Let's get out here."

Andrea jumped down from the window, and Cassie followed suit. She looked around to make sure the constructs were not patrolling the grounds around the mansion and quickly made her way to the small stables on the side of the building. She found her mount, a chestnut mare named Harriet, waiting for her there. The enchanter quickly saddled up the horse while Cassie kept watch outside the stables.

Once they were ready to go, Andrea mounted the horse and extended her hand to Cassie. "Ready?" she said quietly.

Cassie had so many questions she wanted to ask, but after a few seconds she quickly made a decision and nodded. She took Andrea's hand and allowed the enchanter to help her onto the horse. She settled behind Andrea, not really sure what to do, as she'd never ridden a horse before.

"Hold on to me or you'll fall off," Andrea said. Cassie obeyed and wrapped her arms around Andrea's waist.

"Sorry, I've never ridden a horse before," she admitted and looked down nervously. "Er…not really a fan to be honest."

Andrea guided the horse off the property and into the forest. "That's all right. I understand."

Cassie winced. "Can you try to, you know, not go too fast? Where are we going anyway?"

Andrea bit her lip. She honestly was not sure. She conjured a small light to hover in front of the horse and guide them in the dark. "I…don't know," she said. "Azgadar might be our best bet. It is just over a week's journey."

"Azgadar?" Cassie had never heard of the place but she was not paying much attention after she had seen Andrea somehow *create light* from nothing.

"I'd suggest Gurdinfield since it's closer but Azgadar is much stricter on magic usage. I don't think Meredith will think to look for us there," Andrea explained.

"It…it doesn't matter. You pick. I've never heard of either of those places," Cassie said.

Andrea shook her head in confusion. Where was this girl from that she wore such strange clothing and had never heard of the largest nations in Damea? *Perhaps she's from a really isolated village? Or another land entirely?* Somewhere far from Damea.

"Azgadar is fine," she decided. Her heart was still racing and she found herself thinking back to the projection she had seen.

She could hardly believe she had actually left Meredith and was admittedly terrified of what her mentor's reaction would be when she discovered both girls were gone.

"Why did you help me?" Cassie's question broke through Andrea's thoughts.

"Sorry?"

"You helped me escape, even after I tried to hurt you. That was your home, right? Why'd you drop everything and leave to help someone you just met?"

"Oh," Andrea said and rubbed the back of her neck nervously. "I guess it's because I do not approve of Meredith's methods. I want to use magic to help people."

"Yeah, seemed like all she cared about was helping that dead guy." Cassie still felt the painful reminders of her time with Meredith. Her head still hurt and her body still ached. Her face also felt oddly swollen in some parts and she wondered if she had bruises on it.

"Oh. Richard," Andrea said and nodded. "He's not dead. But Meredith's been trying to wake him up for the last twenty years. When I met her, she really did convince me that she cared about Damea and bringing back magic. I think…no, I *know* she's become more desperate in recent years." She sighed. "But to answer your question, what Meredith did to you was unethical and inexcusable. Also," she chose her next words carefully, "it seems to me that you're an innocent in all this."

"Heh, yeah you could say that," Cassie replied with a small laugh. "I went to sleep in my own bed last night and when I woke up, I was in that bedroom and Meredith was rambling on about magic and enchanters and some other nonsense. Then she had the nerve to hold me hostage and demand that I help her."

"She can detect the magic you have," Andrea explained. "I can, too. It's very concentrated. I've never encountered anyone who carried so much energy before and I suspect she hadn't either."

"See? Now you're doing it. I have no freaking clue what that means or what you're talking about!"

Andrea cringed. The last thing she wanted was to make Cassie angry again. "I'm sorry!" she rushed. "If you prefer, we can talk about all this once we reach Azgadar. I'll explain everything."

Cassie nodded. "That works for now."

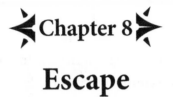

Chapter 8

Escape

Meredith had finally finished her work for the night and decided to retire for the evening. The energy she had collected from Cassie had been extremely potent and effective during the small tests she had run using her own magic and some of the alchemical mixtures she had. She decided to stop by Andrea's quarters to speak to her about their new guest and see if perhaps her apprentice was interested in assisting her with managing the girl.

"Andrea?" she called as she approached the young enchanter's bedroom. She poked her head in the open doorway. No one was there. "Andrea?" she tried again. She looked down the hallway. Perhaps Andrea had discovered that Cassie was staying in the mansion after all.

Humming softly to herself, she arrived to find Cassie's bedroom door ajar and the windows flung open. The magical locks had been disabled. Had Cassie done this? Was she lying when she claimed she had no enchanting abilities? No, Meredith would have been able to tell if she had abilities. Power, yes. But the ability to control it? She would have used it to get free hours ago. There was only one other person who could have disabled the locks.

Meredith realized she had been betrayed by her own apprentice.

She rushed out of the mansion and to the stables. *No, she couldn't have. She wouldn't.* But sure enough, Andrea's horse was missing, along with one of the saddles and some other equipment. Growing angrier by the minute, Meredith summoned the two constructs to her side.

"Find Andrea. She can't have gotten far." She concentrated and tried to detect Andrea's projection. If she had cast any magic recently, she would have left *something* for Meredith to pick up on.

There was something. It was small – probably just a light conjuration – but it was there. It began at the edge of the property and drifted out into the dark woods.

"Find her!" she commanded. "Follow that path!" She used her powers to light a temporary path that followed Andrea's magic. It would not last long, but her constructs were fast: much faster than she would be if she tried to follow on horseback.

The constructs grunted in acknowledgement and began running down the path of light, their objective clear.

* * *

Andrea and Cassie slowly but steadily made their way through the woods. Even with the light Andrea had created, she dared not move too fast and risk getting lost. It had been less than an hour since they left the manor and Cassie had not spoken much at all. The enchanter could tell that Cassie was still rather nervous about riding a horse, and she did not want to do or say anything to exacerbate that.

"It might be a while before we stop. I don't know how long it will be before Meredith discovers we're gone," she spoke, breaking the silence.

"I don't really have a lot of options, so whatever you'd like to do is fine," Cassie said half-heartedly. "What was this place called again?"

"We're in the Black Forest," Andrea explained. "It's the largest forest in Damea."

"Damea? What's that?"

"It's…" Andrea wasn't really sure how to explain Damea to another Damean. Unless Cassie *wasn't* a Damean. But that was impossible. Where else could she be from? Perhaps she had been injured – hit her head, and forgot where she was. But Cassie remembered her name and did not show signs of memory loss. One thing was certain. Cassie was not familiar with magic, a concept that was fundamental to Damea.

"Damea's our land," she tried. "You…you don't know this?"

"Never heard of it.""We're going to Azgadar. It's the capital city of the Azgadaran Empire – the largest nation in Damea, actually," Andrea continued. "They're very strict on magic usage. Anyone caught using magic without permission is put in jail, or worse."

"They sound smart," Cassie muttered. "I've had enough of this magic stuff already and I've only been here a day."

Andrea sighed. She wanted to protest, defend her trade,

but what was she defending exactly? Cassie was right – what Meredith had done was wrong and certainly did not help the case for bringing magic back for everyone. If that was her first and only experience with an enchanter, Cassie had every right to dislike magic.

"It wasn't always like this," Andrea said softly. "Magic was used to do a lot of good, too. My family's farm has these giant machines and back in the First Era they were powered by magic. We use it for keeping cities lit and even healing the sick."

"First…Era? How long ago was that?" Cassie asked.

"Over two hundred years."

"Two *hundred* years? You guys build things to last here, I guess," Cassie observed.

Andrea smiled faintly. "We try. Or rather, we tried."

She heard heavy thuds in the distance. They seemed to be coming from behind. She turned her head and exchanged puzzled glances with Cassie, whose eyes had gone wide with fear.

"What…what is that?" she asked.

Andrea tugged gently on the reins to stop the horse and concentrated on the noise. She peered into the dark, thick forest and saw two figures barreling at full speed toward them down the path they had traveled. The white light they emitted betrayed their identities.

"Harriet, hyah!" Andrea yelled at the horse and soon they were galloping through the forest, with Cassie holding onto the enchanter tightly as they tried to escape the constructs.

"It's those monsters that your crazy mentor made!" Cassie yelled.

"Meredith's constructs! She knows we're gone!" Andrea tried to focus on keeping distance between them and the creatures, but she knew from experience how quickly the constructs could move. There was only one way they could escape.

"Cassie, I need you to hold the reins and keep following the path!" she ordered and handed over the reins.

"What?! I can't drive a horse!" Cassie argued as she barely grasped the reins.

"Do it! We can't outrun them. I'm going to have to use magic to destroy them!" Now able to focus on the creatures, Andrea concentrated and raised her hands. She was able to conjure a small fireball.

"What the...is that *fire*?" Cassie cried.

"Yes! Watch where we're going! The fire's useless if we hit a tree!" Andrea yelled as she hurled the fire at the constructs, which were quickly closing the distance between themselves and the horse. The fire collided with one of the constructs and exploded on impact. The construct fell to the ground, but to Andrea's horror, it rolled and was quickly back on its feet and running after them again.

"It didn't work!" she wailed as the trees flew past. She glanced upward. "There's not enough magic here to create an attack that's powerful enough."

The constructs grew even closer.

"Magic can kill them?" Cassie asked.

"It should!" Andrea answered. She tensed when Cassie grabbed her wrist. She felt a surge of energy shoot through her arm and spread throughout her being. It was almost overwhelming, but once the enchanter had reestablished some control, she realized that she could easily take or ignore the new energy source if she wished.

"I have an idea. If the crazy bitch was right, if you're all not insane about this magic crap, I think I can help," Cassie offered.

"What? No! I won't do that to another pers-," Andrea immediately protested.

"You got a better idea or should we just keep throwing useless fireballs at them until they catch us?" Cassie countered.

Andrea glanced at her wrist where Cassie gripped her tightly and then back at the constructs. The horse was beginning to tire. They were out of time.

"If it starts to hurt, let go and we'll figure something out. Deal?" she warned.

"Yeah, whatever. Just *end them* so we can get the hell out of here!"

Andrea turned back to the constructs and raised her hand again, conjuring another fireball. This time, however, the fire was brighter, hotter, and Andrea knew something was definitely different. She'd never experienced magic like this before. The energy from Cassie flowed through her more strongly than any magic she had ever manipulated in nature – not even in the deepest part of the Black Forest. She could not deny that she enjoyed this newfound source of power.

She launched the fire at the constructs. It flew through the air, growing even brighter and larger as it sped toward the creatures. It exploded on impact with one of the constructs, but the flames spread quickly to the other one as well. In seconds, the constructs had mostly disintegrated, leaving behind only thin plumes of dark smoke and two small, glowing piles of ashes.

With the immediate threat gone, Andrea turned her attention to Cassie, who had slumped onto the enchanter during the energy transfer. Andrea quickly removed Cassie's hand from her wrist and snatched the reins while trying to push Cassie up. She slowed the horse down until they came to a stop.

"Are you all right?" she asked frantically. "I'm so sorry!"

Cassie blinked a few times as she struggled to hold herself up. "Yeah…yeah, I'm good. Don't worry about it – I'm fine. Did we get them?"

Andrea nodded. The familiar burned scent of magic still floated around them. "Yes, your idea worked. But," she looked at Cassie guiltily, "did it-are you in any pain?"

Cassie shook her head. "No, I'm good. I'm a little exhausted but I'm fine. It probably doesn't help that I've done this twice in one day." She let out a small laugh. "Weird. When the crazy bitch did it, it hurt like hell."

Andrea was unsure how to respond. Why had the transfer been excruciatingly painful for Cassie when Meredith had performed it but had only resulted in exhaustion when Andrea had done it? Maybe Meredith had taken more magic than was needed for a fireball?

"If you don't mind me asking, why did you do that?" she asked. "Offer me your power like that?"

Cassie tilted her head. "Um…because I didn't want to get caught by those things and it was the only idea I had? Honestly,

I didn't even know if it would work. I have no idea how any of *this*," she waved her hand back at the destroyed constructs, "works."

"They wouldn't have hurt you. Most likely they would have brought us back to Meredith," Andrea explained.

Cassie gave a small laugh. "Well, then I definitely did not want them catching us."

"Well, for what it's worth, thank you. You saved us," Andrea said gratefully.

Cassie shrugged. "I wasn't the one throwing fireballs at people. Also, if we could *avoid* going at top speed on this thing," she said with a grimace, gesturing at the horse, "that would be great. My stomach's not doing too great." She yawned. "So, on to this Azgadar place, right?"

Andrea nodded. "Yes. I'll try to go slowly, but we do want to gain some distance between us and Meredith." She spurred the horse to start moving forward. "There is one other matter I wanted to discuss with you before we get there, though."

"What's that?"

Andrea sighed. How was she going to explain to Cassie what she had seen in that...vision? She supposed it was a vision. A vision of all the projections. She was not sure how that was possible, but she had seen it and did not have any other explanation for it.

"The magic in Damea...it's run out. Mostly. It used to be everywhere – in the sky, the trees, the land, the water, and in every living creature here. Enchanters use the magic in nature and turn it into something else, like power or light or...fire," she explained. "We can even put the magic into objects and store it there and then extract it later should we need that energy again."

Cassie looked at the enchanter doubtfully, but said nothing and let her continue.

"At the end of the First Era, it seemed as though it had run out completely. Crops failed and there were wars over magic. A lot of people died. We call it The Starving." Andrea felt as though she were reciting from a history book.

"Why did it run out?" Cassie asked.

"Well, that's all theory actually. We don't know for sure that it ran out," Andrea said. "Some people think that it simply was manipulated so much that it's no longer in a form we can use anymore. Other people think it just somehow migrated elsewhere."

"Oh."

"After that, many nations in Damea enacted strict laws about when, where, and how they could use what little magic remained. That's when the Second Era began."

"Makes sense," Cassie said.

Andrea continued. "To make matters worse, enchanters everywhere were getting sick when they tried to perform too powerful a task and there was not enough magic around them to sustain it. That's what happened to Richard," she said. "Meredith is convinced that if she can gather enough magic then she can restore him."

"Seems a little selfish when people are desperate for the stuff," Cassie said bitterly.

Andrea nodded. "True, but when I first met Meredith, she told me that whatever the key is to finding enough magic to bring back Richard would surely be a step toward finding a permanent solution to Damea's magic problem." She sighed sadly. "I guess...she's not really thinking about the rest of Damea anymore. It was always a dream of mine though, to help people with my abilities. My parents weren't too happy when they found out."

"So, you ran off with Meredith because you thought she had the same goals as you? I get it, but that woman's a nutjob," Cassie said.

Andrea tried to stifle a laugh. "That's a funny word. Nut...job."

"Means she's crazy."

"I understood," Andrea said with a small smile. "So, now that I've told you a bit about magic here, I should tell you that when I...touched your shoulder earlier, I saw some kind of... vision. I know that probably sounds crazy."

"The last twenty-four hours have been nothing but crazy so at this point I'm not really sure what to believe anymore," Cassie said flatly.

"In the vision, I saw...well, I saw magic. The locations of magic throughout Damea," Andrea explained.

"Like a map?" Cassie asked.

"Yes! Exactly like a map," Andrea said excitedly. "But there was something even stranger about it. In Rhyad, which is in the far north, there was a massive concentration of magic, and all the magic in Damea seemed to be moving toward it. It was moving slowly, but it was definitely moving."

Cassie raised an eyebrow. "Sounds like your magic just got relocated. What's in Rhyad?"

"Mountains mostly. It's a cold region just north of Gurdinfield. Hardly anyone lives there," Andrea explained.

"Maybe all of your magic got stuck there? Is that possible?"

"Perhaps. It certainly provides some hope about Damea's future, though. If someone could go to Rhyad and investigate, maybe they could find a way to release the magic if it truly is trapped," Andrea said.

"*Someone*? Like you?" Cassie said, though Andrea could swear it sounded like she was teasing.

"Well, I…I would certainly be interested in an opportunity like that, yes," the enchanter said indignantly. "But," she continued sadly, "I only saw a general area. Rhyad is a vast region and I don't know exactly where the magic was."

"Let me guess – you need me for the map," Cassie said.

Andrea nodded. "Perhaps the closer we get to it the more specific the map will be? More importantly, I don't know if I could even release the magic if that's what is really there."

Cassie bit her lip and thought for a moment. "And what if you *can* release the magic? Will that fix the problem you guys have here?"

Andrea nodded. "I think there's a good chance that it will."

"This magic, could it be used for other things?" Cassie asked.

"Such as?"

"Getting me home. Look, I'll be honest – I still don't know if I believe all this stuff. I do know that wherever we are is nowhere close to where I'm from," Cassie admitted.

Andrea considered the question. She had no idea if magic had the capability to do that. She did not know where Cassie was from or even if she as an enchanter had the ability to send her back to where she came from. She did know she needed the girl to find out where the magic was, and that it could only help to have a portable magic source at her side. Not that she was planning to take advantage of her like Meredith had, but if they happened to run into trouble again and Cassie volunteered...

"If you don't mind helping me find this new source, when we get there and release it, I can probably send you home," she blurted out.

Cassie looked surprised. "Really? You'd do that?"

Andrea smiled nervously. What had she gotten herself into? Why had she said that? "If you help me help Damea then, yes, it's the least I can do. So...do we have a deal?"

Cassie nodded. "Deal. So, if Rhyad is in the north, why are we going to this...Azgadar-Azgadaran? I forget which."

"Azgadar. Well," Andrea said, "its official name is the Azgadaran Empire. Most people just call it Azgadar though – both the city and the nation."

"Right. Didn't you say Rhyad was north of that Gurdinfield place, though?"

"It is," Andrea explained, "but I think it would be best to find a safe place to rest and stock up on supplies first. No doubt Meredith will be looking for us." She felt a pang of guilt as she said this but tried to push it out of her mind. Meredith had betrayed everything about enchanting that Andrea held dear. *No need to feel guilty about walking away from that.*

"Oh, okay. Well, I hope we stop soon. I'm pretty tired," Cassie admitted.

Andrea nodded. "Of course. We'll rest soon."

She adjusted her grip on the reins and tried to stay alert as they continued to ride through the forest and toward Azgadar.

Chapter 9

The Empress of Azgadar

Azgadar, Azgadaran Empire

"Hold that sword steady, boy, unless you want it to fly out of your hands."

Kye sighed and adjusted his grip on the weapon he was forging – or trying to forge, anyway. This was only his second time helping his father in the family's forge, and he did not want to mess up this chance to impress the old man with something other than playing the lute. He knew his father, while appreciative of his love of music, was counting on him to become a good smith and take over the family business one day.

"Much better," his father, a burly man with thin, grey hair commented. His clothes were heavily covered in soot. "Keep that up and soon you'll be in here helping me every day."

Kye grinned as he continued working on the sword. His family had been responsible for forging weapons, armor, and riding supplies for the Azgadaran Legion for generations, and he could not wait for the day when he would take over the forge and make his father proud.

"If only you didn't have that damn curse," his father's harsh tone interrupted the young man's thoughts.

"Wh-what?" Kye stammered. "Curse? Father, I–,"

But his father had set down his hammer and was glaring at his son. "You honestly expect me to leave our family's legacy with you when you've done nothing but brought shame and ruin to us all?" He approached his son menacingly.

"Father, please! It's not my fault – I didn't know that–," Kye pleaded.

His father, now joined by his mother, younger brother, and several townspeople, continued to approach Kye. "You're a disgrace. You'll always be a disgrace. I wish you'd never been born, so that we wouldn't have to deal with the burden of having you for a son!" He pulled out a dagger with his ash-covered hand.

"Father, please!" Kye begged, backing away. He stumbled backwards over a broken wooden beam and fell hard. The old man raised the dagger.

"*No!*" Kye screamed.

✶ ✶ ✶

"No!"

Kye shot upright in the pile of hay that he had chosen for a bed the previous night. Breathing heavily and realizing that it was only a dream, he nervously ran his hand through his short blonde hair and rubbed the sleep out of his eyes. The same nightmare had been haunting the sixteen-year-old for months now. It did not occur every night, but often enough to keep him wary of how wanted he was in Azgadar.

None of this had been his fault, in his opinion. *But try explaining that to the Legion.*

He peered out the small window in the attic he had hidden in for the night. It was barely dawn, but still early enough that he should start moving to a new place before the guards searched in his current area. Only a few months on the run, and he felt like he had not had a proper meal to eat or bed to sleep in for years.

He grabbed the dirty white shirt beside him and pulled it over his head. After putting on his cloak and boots he scrambled out the tiny window and began sidling his way down the side of the house. Hopefully the guard assignments at the gates would be light.

* * *

The early morning breeze lightly shifted the fabric of Empress Ithmeera Cadar's long, red dress as she stood on the balcony of her bedroom, looking out over the hot, dry city of Azgadar and the sprawling grasslands beyond the city gates. Her palace stood imposingly above the hundreds of buildings that dotted the cityscape. Some had been built during the First Era, and had been constructed by enchanters during a time when magical energy was plentiful and the harsh restrictions on magic usage in Azgadar did not exist. These towering buildings came in a variety of shapes, were covered in gold and a spectrum of stones, and were beautiful through their uniqueness. Others had been built more recently and did not have the same intricate details crafted into them. Instead they were brown, squat buildings that did not stand from the collection of buildings that looked just like them.

The palace, however, had stood since the First Era, and was over five hundred years old. It had survived the renaissance of magical studies, the crushing blows that The Starving had delivered, the hundreds of skirmishes between the empire and other nations, and the dawn of the Second Era. The regal building, with its great domes and single spire, towered over all others in the. The blood red, gold-accented banners embroidered with the recognizable sword-and-shield emblem that were draped over its walls signified the might that was the empress and her mighty Legion.

Ithmeera had always loved watching the sun rise over the city. There was something about it that she could not express in words but the sight of the first light slowly revealing the great city one building at a time brought her a sense of pride. Her brother, Erik, probably would not understand – or worse, would tease her for being "a romantic", and her uncle, Alden, would most likely pester her again about when she was planning on meeting with her advisors to discuss the annexation of Gurdinfield. It had been over twenty years since her father's sudden and untimely death when she was only fourteen – a "rapid and incurable illness", the royal enchanters had reported later – and Ithmeera remembered her father and uncle speaking on the matter often, but it was put to rest shortly after the emperor had died.

Her uncle had brought up the topic again at dinner a few weeks earlier. It had been two decades since a ruler had sat on the throne in Gurdinfield, and the nation was still deeply divided. The houses of Harrington and Moore had battled for control of the region over the years. Ithmeera recalled receiving letters from Azgadaran messengers and spies reporting on the latest skirmish between the two houses, and more recently, the appearance of a new faction that had been ambushing the camps of both houses throughout Gurdinfield.

No doubt Alden would fill her in on what had been happening with the houses. But as far as Ithmeera knew, no one really knew anything about this new faction.

The empress looked out over the city again. Merchants were beginning to make their way to the marketplace where they would open shop for the day. Beggars took their places on the street corners, hoping to gather a few coins to afford bread or whatever addiction afflicted them. She could see the changing of the morning guard and the small groups of soldiers in the courtyard beginning their training for the day.

Her brother was nowhere to be seen, but Ithmeera knew he was probably handling the higher-level day-to-day duties and having his officers train the soldiers. Despite him being the empress's "little brother", Ithmeera was the first to admit that Erik Cadar had grown up to become the great general that their father had hoped he would be. Azgadar had not been at war in years, but the nation's crime rates had dropped dramatically since Erik had taken over command of the Azgadaran Legion. Bandit attacks on traveling merchants carrying enchanted artifacts still occurred, of course, but they were less frequent, as were city and town muggings and other crimes. The Legion itself had also grown over the years. Recruitment numbers were the highest they had ever been during peacetime, mostly due to Erik's popularity and the highly publicized stories of how he inspired his soldiers.

A knock on the door pulled Ithmeera from her thoughts. "Yes?" she asked.

Her lady-in-waiting, Petra, called from the other side of the double doors that opened into her spacious suite. "Your grace, Master Alden has asked for your company in the Great Hall."

Ithmeera sighed. No doubt her uncle wanted to talk about Gurdinfield again. Perhaps this time she could steer the conversation toward something interesting, like the Azgadaran Grand Ball to celebrate the bicentennial anniversary of the Cadar dynasty. There were arrangements to be made, food options to be chosen, musicians to be hired, and gowns to be ordered.

She could not help but smile. Yes, she would definitely bring the topic up.

"Tell him I'll be there shortly," she called back.

"Of course, your grace. Marco also asked for you. He is in his room," Petra replied.

"Thank you, Petra. I'll see to him after I've spoken with my uncle," the empress answered. She heard the servant's light footsteps on the marble floor as she walked away.

She was surprised her son was awake this early, but she knew that he was probably just excited about spending time with his uncle later. Erik had promised the boy that he would take him on a grand tour of the Legion once the general had finished with his duties for the day.

Marco was the product of a short marriage between herself and a merchant named Philip. She had met her late husband in the city during one of her visits to the marketplace and he had charmed her immediately. Their relationship was a scandal at first – the Empress of the Azgadaran Empire courting a commoner – but the people of Azgadar, enamored with their ruler, got over it quickly and just wanted to see the empress happy.

They were married within the year, and she gave birth to Marco the following year. The boy, now six years old, was the heir to the throne, but for now he was content with spending his days playing soldier and following his uncle around.

Ithmeera sighed sadly. Philip had been a loving husband and a doting father right up to that fateful day four years earlier when he had been killed by common bandits a few days' travel east of Azgadar while on one of his trading expeditions. He, like many other merchants, had made a decent living transporting the last of Damea's magically enchanted artifacts across the land. When they married, Ithmeera had offered him the chance to resign from his merchant job, but Philip had insisted that he still run his company and go on the occasional business trip.

Trying to push the gloomy thoughts from her mind, the empress finished making herself presentable before leaving her quarters to meet with her uncle.

* * *

Alden was in Great Hall, staring at the gold accents on the edges of the long wooden table where he sat waiting for his niece.

He had eaten breakfast already, a small meal of bread, eggs, and fruit. He glanced up as his niece walked briskly into the room. She wore her dark, curly hair down. The dark hair framed her olive skin and green eyes in such a way that she resembled her late mother, who had been lost to illness shortly after Erik's birth, more than ever.

"Good morning, Uncle," she greeted him cheerfully and took a seat next to him at the table.

"Hello, dear," the old man replied with a nod of his head. "I apologize for requesting to meet so early."

Ithmeera shook her head. "Uncle, it's fine. What did you want to speak about?"

Alden attempted a smile. "I wanted to inquire as to whether you had thought about the council's proposal from last week."

Ithmeera had to hold back from sighing in front of her uncle. He had been there for her and her brother after their father had died, but sometimes Ithmeera felt that her uncle overstepped his authority. She wanted to show the people of Azgadar and the council that she was a strong ruler, but it was becoming increasingly hard to do so with Alden always bringing up the topic of Gurdinfield when she would rather just put it to rest.

She paused for a moment before speaking. "I have already told you what I think of the Gurdinfield issue, Uncle. Why must you bring it up again?"

"Because there has been another attack on the Moores. One of their larger camps was ambushed less than a week ago. It seems this new faction has grown stronger and bolder."

"And you believe they will come for Azgadar next?" the empress asked.

Alden shook his head. "Most likely not; it's doubtful they have the resources for such a feat. However, Lord Moore has once again requested an alliance with you. He has even offered a share of Gurdinfield's magic should you assist him in winning his civil war." He shrugged. "It is clear he is not afraid to ask for help, but I am not sure I trust that man. He is a little too eager for my liking."

Ithmeera sighed, obviously this time. "You think he would seek a war with Azgadar after they've secured the country?" She rubbed her eyes. "I understand, Uncle, but why would the Moores want yet another war when they are trying to end a twenty-year-old one?"

"I believe that Moore's offer of an alliance is a mere trick, dear. I believe that once they secure Gurdinfield, they would seek to use their magical advantage to overtake our villages and eventually, the capital itself," Alden explained. He made a quick motion of his hand and a servant approached and took his plate and cutlery.

"They wouldn't dare attack Azgadar. Only a fool would be stupid enough to try that," Ithmeera said brashly. She knew her uncle did not always approve of her attempts to establish alliances with the other nations as opposed to trying to annex them, but she held firm in her conviction that her father had been right in his policies.

"Our energy sources are at the lowest they've been in years," Alden continued. "At this rate, we won't have enough to power our farms within a few years. The Legion will be much weaker without magic to power their weapons. You see what I am getting at, Ithmeera."

Ithmeera nodded. She believed her uncle this time – she knew the magic crisis was real and that it was affecting the lives of everyone in Azgadar. But she had taken measures to keep energy levels as high as she could.

"I could have Erik send his men on another search. Find artifacts that citizens have been keeping without going through inspections and regulation. Hoarding unauthorized magic is not acceptable," she said sternly.

"I'm afraid that will not get us very far," Alden explained. "With the Legion weakened and the Moores in power, there will only be war, and without magic, it will be a difficult one for Azgadar to win."

"You don't know that the Moores will start a war. Not for sure," she argued. "Helping Gurdinfield end its civil war and become a stable nation to trade with again might be worth the risk, Uncle."

"Perhaps, but do you really want to leave that up to chance? Think of your people...think of Marco, Ithmeera. The boy should not have to worry about a war with Gurdinfield when he is older."

Ithmeera sat back in her chair. This was not the conversation she had envisioned having with Alden. She had hoped to discuss the Ball, but it was clear what needed to happen.

"Very well, Uncle. Prepare a letter letting Moore know we will send him supplies and whatever else he might need in return for a share of Gurdinfield's magical lands. Once the civil war has ended, we can begin work on annexing them," she ordered.

"Surely Lord Moore will not be content with that."

"He will not know," Ithmeera explained. "We will hit Gurdinfield while it is still in recovery. Moore will have no choice but to surrender. We can offer him a position of governor or something of the sort."

"I...I see," Alden said with a slow nod. "Anything else I can do?"

"We need to begin preparations then. Have Erik start training the soldiers for combat."

"The entire Legion?" Alden asked incredulously.

"No," the empress said. "A small but focused force should do against Gurdinfield. Supply the Legion with whatever they need. We will take Gurdinfield before they take us," she finished, her eyes closed as she spoke.

"If you believe this is the best course of action, dear, then I am, of course, at your side," her uncle said.

Ithmeera nodded. "Thank you. Make the preparations then, Uncle, and inform me of any and all updates."

"As you wish. Can I do anything else for you, dear?" Alden asked, bowing his head.

"Yes," she said with a small smile. "We need to discuss the upcoming Grand Ball. There are still many preparations that need to be made for it."

Alden raised his eyebrows in obvious surprise. "Of...of course. Where shall we begin?"

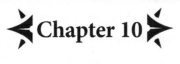

Chapter 10

Normal

Outskirts of the Azgadaran Empire, south of the capital

Andrea wrapped her cloak tightly around herself and moved closer to the campfire. The autumn days in the arid climate of Azgadar were mostly warm, but at night the air quickly cooled, making it necessary for any traveler to pack warm clothes for the evenings. Fortunately, Andrea had traveled quite a bit with Meredith over the last three years and was used to spending cold nights in front of a campfire.

Cassie, on the other hand, seemed to have little experience in traveling. She opted to sit next to the makeshift tent Andrea had set up with the remaining supplies they had picked up in a small town called Sadford, which was situated on the border between the Black Forest and Azgadar. While in town, Andrea had quickly gone into the general store while Cassie waited outside with the horse.

"You really should sit by the fire. It's much warmer here," Andrea suggested for the third time.

Cassie shook her head and crossed her arms over her chest. "I'm good," she said curtly.

Harriet, their horse, snorted loudly and shook her head. The horse was tied to a small tree next to the camp.

The enchanter sighed. After their discussion in the Black Forest, Andrea had hoped that Cassie was starting to trust her. But despite having traveled together for the last week, Cassie had gone from being openly hostile during their first meeting to acting coldly distant toward the enchanter.

"Are you hungry? You barely touched your dinner," Andrea tried again. She could still see the fading bruises on Cassie's face, no doubt inflicted from the forced magical transfer Meredith had performed on the girl combined with the incident with the constructs. Meredith had not followed them, but Andrea figured it was only a matter of time before she did.

"I'm fine. Look, you don't have to pretend to be my friend or anything," Cassie said bluntly. "I said I'd help you with your thing so you can send me home. You don't have to be all nice about it."

"I am not pretending to be anything," Andrea protested, although she was not exactly sure why she was arguing. Cassie had made it very clear several times during their journey to Azgadar that the only thing she was interested in was getting home, wherever that was. Andrea felt guilty again as she remembered her promise to Cassie. What would happen if they *did* find the long lost source of magic in Rhyad? Would she actually be able to send Cassie back? Andrea did not even know if that sort of magic was possible, let alone if she was skilled enough to perform a feat like that.

Then again, in the past week she had left everything she knew for the *second* time in her life to help a complete stranger who had been nothing but distant and unfriendly to her since their first meeting and who could also be the key to restoring magic to the entire land. She did not want to think about what was possible and what was not.

"Whatever. How much further is this city anyway?" Cassie asked, seeming uninterested in anything Andrea had to say.

Andrea took a deep breath to stop herself from saying something she would regret later. "I…we crossed into Azgadar two days ago. We should reach the capital in another two."

"And how long are we staying there?"

"Not long. But we'll need to sell Harriet when we get there to be able to afford transport to Gurdinfield," Andrea said.

Cassie glanced at the horse. "Why?"

"Harriet's not going to make it very far across Azgadar with both of us riding her. She's not made for those kind of distances. Also, I'm almost out of money since I didn't have much time to pack before we left, so we need something to trade," Andrea explained.

Cassie shifted uncomfortably. "Sorry."

Andrea tilted her head. "For what?"

Cassie shrugged. "I don't know…I guess for not giving you more time to pack. I still think your mentor is insane, but I get that it was your home that you left. Honestly, I'm surprised that you aren't as crazy as she is."

Andrea felt uneasy and was quiet for a moment as she looked at the campfire. "You don't know that I'm not," she finally said softly.

"What do you mean?"

The enchanter met Cassie's gaze. "Well, let's see, I left my family, my home, and all of my friends in a single night when I was eighteen and traveled to the Black Forest with a woman who I had just met a day before I left. I lived with her for three years doing every kind of experiment with magic there is, and just a week ago I left my second home one evening because I saw a map *in my mind*. And now I'm traveling with someone I barely know across the land because she *might* know the answer to the most difficult question in the history of Damea. So..." She shrugged. "I don't think I'd ever do what Meredith did, but I'm not exactly what most Dameans call 'normal' either."

Cassie looked thoughtful but remained silent. Finally, to Andrea's surprise, she stood up and walked over to where the enchanter was sitting and sat down next to her.

"Well, you haven't tried to kill me yet, so I guess that helps your case a little," she said. "'Normal' is overrated anyway." Andrea noticed Cassie's expression had softened for the first time since they had met.

Before the enchanter could say anything, Cassie spoke again. "I'm going to get some sleep," she stated and stood up again.

Andrea was not sure how to respond and stared at Cassie blankly before realizing she was expected to reply. "Uh...yes! You should. I mean, that's fine. See you in the morning?"

"Sure. You're not tired?"

"No," the enchanter admitted. "I think...I will stay up a bit longer. You should sleep though. We have another long day ahead of us."

Cassie nodded. "All right. See you." She walked back to the tent and opened the flap before ducking in.

* * *

Azgadar, Azgadaran Empire

It was high noon when Kye made his way through the marketplace in the city to get what food he could. He had been able to scrounge up enough coins from searching the streets at night to afford a few days' worth of food. His hood protected his identity for now, but the young man knew that it was only a matter of time before the Legion found him. He was already taking a risk by walking through the marketplace in broad daylight, but he had barely eaten in days. What other choice did he have?

He approached a general food merchant's cart and quickly purchased a few staples that would get him through the next few days. Hopefully he could acquire some more money by then – or with any luck, escape the city altogether. But he dared not hope too much. The Legion had placed double the guards near the city gates since Kye had been declared wanted.

Wanted. The word had reverberated in his mind many times over the last few days. It had never occurred to him that his boring, normal life would suddenly and violently be turned upside-down in a matter of minutes. But it had, and he was now living with the consequences of something he could not control.

Once he was back in the small attic that he temporarily called home, the young man quickly removed his hood. The thick dark cloak provided some protection from being spotted by guards but did nothing to counter the heat of an Azgadaran day. He set the food on the small hay bed in front of him and began to eat.

* * *

Meredith sat near the small campfire she had built for the night. After finishing a simple dinner, she spent the remainder of the evening pondering the events that had transpired. Where had she gone wrong? Why did Andrea leave? And what would this delay mean for Richard?

She knew she could not leave Richard alone, so she had used some of the powerful magic she had gathered from Cassie to create a new construct. It was a quick solution, for the other constructs had taken her years to create, but she no longer had time on her side. She did not know how long Richard had before his body would eventually succumb to weakness, but she knew that he could not last forever in his current state.

She did know at least partly why her apprentice had left. No doubt their visitor had told Andrea that Meredith had performed horrific experiments on her. Andrea had always been an idealist, an enchanter who hesitated when it came time to make the difficult decisions. She had hoped she would be able to train her apprentice out of that mindset, but it seemed that she had failed.

Their goal, *her* goal, had been and always would be to save Richard. Any magic powerful enough to bring him back would no doubt be viable for fixing the magic problem, if it was even repairable. Damea had taken enough from her. At this point, Meredith just wanted her husband back.

When her constructs had not returned, she left the new construct with Richard and set out to find the girl using her ability to read projections from the enchanter. Sure enough, she had come across the remains of her old constructs, blown to pieces by a fireball spell. While Andrea was powerful and had much potential, Meredith knew that her apprentice was not powerful enough to take down the two constructs on her own. It was not unreasonable to conclude that Andrea must have had assistance from Cassie in order to generate enough power to do a significant amount of damage.

She leaves me for my efforts in trying to succeed in our task, but then uses the girl's magic for her own purposes. Meredith clenched her fists in anger before trying to slowly calm down. *It will be fine.* She would find Andrea and convince her to stop this nonsense. The girl had no life without magic – no doubt, she would beg Meredith to take her back.

She focused inwardly to see if she could detect another projection from her apprentice. Closing her eyes, she harnessed a small amount of energy from the space around her. The fire flickered for a moment as the air shifted. The ability to detect magical projections was rare among enchanters, and it took a very precise level of control to determine where the projections were coming from. She reached for the familiarity that was her apprentice, for all enchanters had a unique marker in their projections. It took a few tries, but soon Meredith felt a faint tugging that indicated that she had been successful. The projection was coming from the north. *Azgadar. But why would they go there?* Azgadar was notorious for its little-to-no tolerance of enchanters, and the capital was by far the least hospitable place for a magic user to go.

In the end, the reason did not matter to Meredith. She would find both her apprentice and the girl, and she would bring them back to the Black Forest so that she could continue her work.

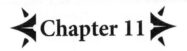

Chapter 11

The Azgadaran Empire

"Is that it?"

"Yes," Andrea replied. "That's the capital." She and Cassie stood next to each other on a high, grassy hill overlooking the great city below them. Their horse stood next to them, with Andrea holding the reins in one hand. The hot Azgadaran sun was high in the cloudless sky as noon approached. Andrea could see the great spire of the Azgadaran Palace from where they stood. She turned to her companion. "I should probably warn you – Azgadar has extremely strict laws on magic. It would probably be best if we didn't tell anyone that I'm an enchanter or anything about your...ability."

Cassie shrugged. "Yeah, sure."

They stood in silence for a while before Cassie spoke again. "So, after we sell Harriet, what's next?" She absentmindedly gave the horse a pat on the back and then proceeded to adjust her clothing, which, after over a week of traveling now sported a smattering of dirt and grass stains.

"Well," Andrea began, "we have to get more supplies, then take a carriage to Gurdinfield. From there, we head for Rhyad."

"And then we save the world and I go home, right?" Cassie said, her voice still laced with a tinge of sarcasm and impatience.

Andrea sighed for what must have been the hundredth time that day. She began to walk forward on the trail that would lead them down the hill and into the city. "Yes. I won't lie – it's a long and likely dangerous journey from Gurdinfield to Rhyad. I've only been to the City of Towers, and I don't know the countryside too well."

"Well, I mean, there are people we can ask for directions, right?" Cassie asked as she followed the enchanter down the trail.

"There are," Andrea said. "We just need to find them." Then, under her breath, "And hope they don't hate enchanters."

"What was that?" Cassie said.

Andrea shook her head. "Nothing. I just…" she didn't finish.

"No, you said something," Cassie objected and met the enchanter's gaze. "What was it?"

Andrea shrugged. "Nothing. Don't mind me."

Cassie looked as though she wanted to argue, to find out what Andrea had actually said. But she let the matter drop, and Andrea was not surprised she did. They were not there to be friends. They were there to get a job done. The enchanter could not even begin to think about how exactly she would hold up her end of the bargain with Cassie. It did not help that Cassie's mood was always changing either. *It doesn't matter – all that matters is getting to Rhyad and seeing if I was right, if the magic is actually there and–*

"You're doing it again."

Andrea snapped out of her thoughts. "Sorry?"

"Where you look like you're having this deep conversation with yourself," Cassie said. She kicked a small rock at her feet and it skipped down the path, landing several feet away from them. "Look, I'm not going to pretend this is fine, but as long as we're stuck with each other we might as well not stay silent the entire time."

The enchanter became somewhat flustered but continued walking. "I-I figured you wouldn't feel like talking so I thought keeping to myself might be better." It wasn't the most articulate excuse but it was all she could come up with in the moment.

Cassie shrugged. "I don't mind talking." She found the rock she had kicked moments earlier on the trail and gave it another kick. A small cloud of dirt rose from the ground where the rock had been before quickly settling again. "Crap, these boots are getting completely trashed," she said with a frown.

"I'm sorry. Are they new?" *Maybe she prefers to talk about the fashion of, well, wherever it is she's from.* Not that she was extremely well-versed on the latest trends coming out of Damea's cities, but it was worth a shot to connect with Cassie with it.

"No. They're just my everyday boots, so I would rather they last longer but I don't see that happening," Cassie answered and glanced at the rest of her clothing. "I don't even know if I'll be able to get these stains out anyway."

"I'm sure we could get some new clothes for you in the city," Andrea offered.

"It's fine," Cassie sighed. "Honestly, the faster we get this done the better. I'd rather not waste time shopping if we've got a job to do."

"You see this as a job?"

"Well, yeah," Cassie said. "I mean, isn't that what it is?"

Andrea gave a hopeful smile. "Losing all the magic is Damea's greatest threat. Perhaps there's a reason we were brought together to do this."

Cassie gave a brusque laugh. "Hah! Right. Destiny and crap like that. You seriously believe in that?" But when she saw the slightly hurt look on her companion's face, she felt somewhat guilty.

"Sorry, just...I don't really believe in that stuff," she said quietly.

But the enchanter smiled wryly. "A few weeks ago you didn't believe in magic, either," she said.

"I still don't know if I do."

Now it was Andrea's turn to laugh. "Really? We defeated magical constructs using fireballs and you still aren't sure if you believe in magic?"

"Hey, there is no 'we'," Cassie protested. "You're the one that did all the fireball throwing."

"There was a 'we' – it took the both of us to do that," Andrea reminded her.

"Whatever. I don't want to talk about this anymore," Cassie retorted. "Let's just get to this city so we can take care of what we need to take care of and go."

"What? Why? I don't understand why you're–," Andrea tried.

"I said I don't want to talk anymore. Can you understand that, or do I need to say it again?" Cassie snapped.

With the mood sullen, Andrea bit her lip and nodded before focusing her eyes on the city in front of them.

* * *

"Welcome to Azgadar. In accordance with city law, no visitor is to enter without being inspected for magical artifacts."

The Legionnaire at the massive iron gates of the capital spoke to Andrea and Cassie with the perfect lack of enthusiasm of someone who had said the words a thousand times before.

"Oh!" Andrea stammered, realizing what the guard meant. "Of course. We're not carrying anything."

The guard, a large, clean-shaven man, was clad in the traditional helmet and ornate red, black, and gold armor of the Legion. A large sword hung at his side. He looked them over with a weary expression. "And what is your business in the city today? How long will you be staying?"

"Just a day or so. We'll be needing to sell our horse," Andrea said carefully. Rationally, she knew there was no way the guard could tell if she was an enchanter or not, but that did not help ease her nerves. Cassie, on the other hand, seemed perfectly calm. But Andrea figured the girl was just very good at hiding her emotions when she needed to.

The guard eyed them for a moment. "Neither of you are practicing enchanters, are you?" he asked sternly.

Andrea was about to answer, to lie so that they could pass without trouble, but her nerves took over, and the words wouldn't come out, no matter how hard she struggled.

"No," Cassie spoke up, startling the enchanter. "We just spent a bit too much of our money in Sadford at the tavern there." She grinned. "You've probably heard this story a lot, but we need to sell our horse to make up our losses. Speaking of which, is there anywhere nearby where one could get something to drink?"

To Andrea's surprise, the guard's face broke into a knowing smile. "I hear you. Same thing happened to a friend of mine just last week. Lost his uniform in a bet gone wrong. Had to sell his father's sword to buy it back from the sod that beat him. Hopefully you ladies fared better."

Andrea was not sure whether to be offended or grateful toward Cassie for making them look like vagrant alcoholics.

"Not by much, but perhaps a tad better than your friend," Cassie said.

The guard laughed heartily. "Good to hear. The inn'll be down the main road and on the right – the Legionnaire's Rest. Best ales in the Market District. You can't miss it. Enjoy your stay in the city." He stepped aside and let them pass through the gates.

"Whoa," Andrea heard Cassie murmur. When she turned, she saw her companion was staring in awe at the city around her.

Azgadar was a bustling hub, and the smell and noise assaulted Andrea's senses. Crowds of people moved through the dusty streets – some alone, some with partners or friends, others with wooden carts drawn by animals. Children ran through the streets, ducking into alleys and screaming with excitement as they played tag with stray dogs. Buildings, mostly square brown ones, lined the streets, as did countless carts belonging to the street merchants who yelled out their sales at anyone who passed by.

"You okay? You look sick."

Andrea turned when she realized Cassie was talking to her. "Sorry?" she asked.

"You look really pale. Did you want to stop for a bit?"

"Oh," the enchanter replied. "I'm fine. I just…I'm not used to cities. I haven't been to one in a long time."

"You're from a small town, right?" Cassie asked as she led Harriet through the busy streets in the direction of the inn the guard had given them directions to.

"I'm from Ata. It's a village in the Western Hills. It's mostly farmland with a few shops and one inn," Andrea explained, grateful for the distraction from her surroundings.

"I see. Well, if it makes you feel any better, the cities where I'm from are nothing like this," Cassie shared as they arrived at the inn. A merchant surrounded by a few horses and a wooden cart full of hay across from the inn caught her eye. "That man looks like a guy who might sell horses. Maybe he buys them too?" She gestured in the merchant's direction without being too obvious.

Andrea looked in the direction Cassie was pointing and gave a small nod. "Perhaps. Wait here." She walked over to the merchant and began to speak with him while Cassie waited outside of the inn with Harriet.

"Sorry we only got to know each other for a short time," she said to the mare, which snorted and shook her head in response.

"Let's hope she can make a deal with that guy," Cassie replied.

A few minutes later, Andrea returned.

"Well?" Cassie asked.

The enchanter discreetly held out a small reddish-brown pouch. "He gave us a reasonable deal. We probably could have gotten more somewhere else, but I don't want to be here longer than we have to," she explained. "He said to leave Harriet outside the inn and he would take her. We might as well go inside and get a room."

"Can we eat?" Cassie pleaded. "I've been starving since we made it over that hill. Also, I think I really need a bath. I don't think I've ever been covered in this much dust before." She gestured to her partially torn and dust-coated clothing.

Andrea laughed a little. "That's a good idea. Er...the food part!" she suddenly stammered, realizing her odd choice of words. "Not that I'm implying you *need* to bathe. Unless you'd like to. I mean...I don't know what I mean anymore." She put her hand on her head. The day's events and their surroundings had given her a headache.

Cassie simply looked amused. "Let's go inside," she suggested, her face not showing any signs of anger or annoyance at the enchanter's rambling.

Andrea sighed, mostly with relief. "Yes, *please*," she said and followed Cassie inside the inn.

* * *

Later that evening, Andrea and Cassie sat in the corner of the inn's dimly lit tavern, waiting for their food to be delivered. The coins Andrea had acquired by selling her horse had given them enough to get dinner and a room for the night. Andrea had also gone to a nearby general store in the city and purchased Cassie some new clothes as well as some basic supplies for the journey to their next stop, Gurdinfield.

"I'm hungry," Cassie groaned. After the innkeeper had shown them to their room, she had bathed and changed into the new clothing that she now began to fidget with. The dark pants and boots were fine, but the midnight-blue shirt's lightweight material felt odd against her skin.

"Yes, you stated as much. A few times in fact," Andrea said tiredly as she rubbed her eyes. Between walking all day and dealing with the chaos of navigating the streets of Azgadar, she was close to falling asleep at the table. The low amount of light in the tavern contributed to her drowsiness, as did the comforting smell of food cooking, but the occasional boisterous laughter of a tavern patron would startle her awake when she dozed off.

"Sorry," Cassie mumbled. "I haven't had anything except the stuff we got at that store in that town. I need real food that doesn't taste like it's been sitting out in the sun for days."

Andrea raised an eyebrow. "You mean the town where we were supposedly wandering drunks who spent all their money at the tavern?"

Cassie flashed a rare genuine smile. "Hah. Yeah, that was hilarious. That guard totally fell for it, too. You should have seen your face. I thought you were going to pass out on me."

The other girl was unamused. "I'm sure. In any case, thank you for improvising when you did. I didn't really know what to say when he asked if we were enchanters."

"Um, you lie and say you're not."

"I know, I just…I suppose I froze up when I got nervous. I know they can't tell just by looking at us but being…" The enchanter lowered her voice as they were in a tavern in the heart of the most magic-restricted region in Damea. "Being in this city makes me nervous enough. When people ask me directly about what I am…well, can you see why I get nervous?"

Cassie shrugged. "I guess. Is Gurdinfield like that, too?"

A bored-looking young woman brought them their food and drinks. As the two of them began to eat, Andrea answered Cassie's question. "I've only been to the capital city, and that was a few years ago. But from what I remember, no, it's not like it is here. In fact, there used to be an academy dedicated to the study of magic."

Cassie took another bite of her dinner, while at the same time eyeing her plate suspiciously. "This is good, but I have no idea what's in it. I don't know if I want to know, though."

"Probably for the best if you didn't. These kinds of places aren't exactly the epitome of fine dining."

Cassie looked down at her food. Her shoulders shook slightly. At first, Andrea thought something was wrong with the food, but when she saw her companion's expression she realized the girl was laughing.

"What's so funny?"

Cassie took a moment to compose herself. "You. You made

a joke and it was funny. I didn't think you knew how to joke."

The enchanter was slightly offended but she tried not to show it. "I-I do joke! You...you simply don't understand my sense of humor!"

The other girl took a sip of her drink, a strong ale with a bitter aftertaste. She grimaced. "Your 'sense of humor' has so far ranged from 'we need to save the world' to 'I worry about everything'. Also, this tastes like crap." She gestured to the mug.

"Then why did you order it? Do you want some of mine?" Andrea offered her cider.

"I wanted to try it. The bartender said it was the best ale in the city," Cassie replied sheepishly. "And no, thanks."

They continued to eat in silence for a while before Cassie spoke again. "So, did you go to this academy?"

Andrea drank some of her cider, surprised that Cassie was so talkative tonight, but she did not want to ruin the conversation by dwelling on the fact that it was happening. She put her mug down before answering. "I did not. It closed down when I was very young. Meredith...oh. Sorry." She went quiet, ashamed of bringing up her former mentor in a conversation with the one person who had every reason to hate her.

But if she was uncomfortable, she did not show it, at least not to Andrea. Instead she gave a snarky smile and leaned in. "It's okay," she whispered teasingly. "You can say your girlfriend's name out loud. It doesn't bother me."

The enchanter immediately became flustered. "As I said before, we *weren't* involved that way. Meredith...attended the academy when she was younger. She was one of...one of the top students there," she continued haltingly. "She showed it to me the last time we were in Gurdinfield together. It's empty now, but twenty years ago it was the best place to go for magical studies in Damea. It was a place of research and learning and the people there really wanted to make a difference and solve the problems that the land has now because of what's happened to magic."

She realized as she spoke that her nervousness had turned into regret. Sure, she had studied under one of the best enchanters in Damea but it had been in secret and against her family's wishes. Would things have been different had the academy not closed?

"Sounds like you would have liked it there," Cassie observed. "Lots of people there that want to save the world like you."

The enchanter smiled shyly. "When I was younger, I dreamt of becoming a royal enchanter for the empress." She shook her head, shaking off the childish memory. "It's silly, I know. But their tutors are some of the best enchanters in Damea."

Cassie tilted her head in confusion. "You know, for a place where magic is supposedly running out, it seems to be doing pretty well. You sure this Rhyad place is important?"

Andrea frowned. How could she explain to Cassie in a few sentences what she had been brought up knowing over many years? "You may not see it in front of you," she said slowly, "but people are affected by it just the same. Many of our farms and businesses use machines that are powered by magic. Without power for those machines, crops fail, shops close, and people lose their way of life."

"Why don't you find another power source?" Cassie asked. It

seemed like such a simple question.

"You think we haven't tried?" Andrea said with a laugh that came out harsher than she intended. "After The Starving, most people just wanted a life that wasn't filled with war and famine. They want their life to be decent *today*. They don't want to waste resources trying to fix a future that isn't guaranteed."

"I still don't really understand why we can't tell anyone what we're doing," Cassie said. "I mean, wouldn't your governments want to know about this lost magic, if it's really in Rhyad?"

"I'd rather not risk it, honestly," Andrea explained. "Gurdinfield is currently in a civil war, and I doubt the empress here would just invite us into her palace for tea if we told the palace guards that we knew the location of the missing magic."

Cassie nodded and looked down at her food again. Andrea could not tell if the girl was uninterested or simply absorbing what she had said. She was too tired to find out, however.

"I think I'm done for tonight," she said and stood up. "You know how to find the room?"

"Yeah. I'll be there soon."

A thought crossed the enchanter's mind. "Um...you probably saw that the room wasn't that big so..."

Cassie rolled her eyes. "I don't mind sharing a bed. Just don't kill me in my sleep or start doing any weird magical experiments on me. I've gotten enough of *that* to last me a lifetime."

Andrea smiled faintly. "I won't. Good night."

"'Night."

Once Andrea had left, Cassie eyeballed the enchanter's

drink and tentatively tried a sip of it. She looked at the mug, disgusted, and set it back down on the table.

"Gross," she grumbled.

★ Chapter 12 ★

An Evening Stroll

Her dreams were filled with echoes of her parents and their resounding disapproval at her choice to leave. It wasn't her fault she had...abilities. She wanted to help people, wanted to help Damea. Why couldn't her parents just understand that?

The energy in front of her was massive, bigger than any she had encountered during her travels across Damea. She couldn't see it very clearly, for it had no form, but she knew it was there by the sheer power it gave off.

"Enchanters are responsible for every problem the land has today." Her father's harsh voice rose above the whispers that filled the great space she stood in.

"Why don't you just fix it?" Cassie's voice spoke. "Find another power source?"

That shouldn't be her job. This was too big for any one person to fix – too big for her to fix.

The energy, while formidable, seemed to offer a sort of peace as it remained stationary. The gentle humming was almost comforting and felt more familiar to her than anything had for the past few weeks. Suddenly, she felt it fading, the humming quieting. She called out to it in the hope that her pleas would make it stay but only a moment later, it was gone.

Andrea awoke with a shudder. Her brow and neck were covered in sweat though the air around her was chilly. She grasped at the bedsheets, which had bunched together at her waist. She turned her head slightly and did a double take when she saw that the space next to her on the bed was empty.

"Cassie?" she whispered. She remembered awaking sometime during the night when Cassie had gone to bed. But now her companion was nowhere in sight. *Perhaps she went back to the tavern.* She decided to get dressed and see if she could get Cassie to go back to bed. They had a long day of traveling ahead of them and she needed Cassie to be awake and alert for it.

After dressing and pulling her boots on, Andrea closed the door behind her and made her way downstairs to the tavern of the inn. It was quiet save for the quiet murmurings of conversations of late-night travelers. Her entrance garnered her a few mildly curious glances from the tavern patrons, but only for a moment before they returned to their food and drinks.

There was no sign of Cassie. She was not at the tables or at the bar. Trying to resist panicking, Andrea walked briskly to the innkeeper and asked if he had seen anyone with Cassie's description. When he told her he thought he saw a girl leave less than an hour earlier, the enchanter felt a lump in her throat as she muttered a "thank you" and rushed outside. She was immediately greeted with a strong, cool nighttime breeze that blew her dark hair into her face. Cursing herself for forgetting her cloak, she looked out at the mostly empty streets of Azgadar and chose a direction.

Why would Cassie just leave on her own? *It doesn't make any sense.* Andrea hastened her steps as she walked quickly down the dusty, dimly-lit streets. While nowhere near as crowded as they were earlier in the day, the streets still hosted a number of late-night business deals, gangs, and other unsavory activities that Andrea would rather not think about Cassie or herself getting involved in.

Where are you? Countless scenarios of where her companion might have gone or what could happen flashed into her mind. If something happened to Cassie, she could not get to the exact location of the magic in Rhyad. Returning to the Black Forest was no longer an option, so where would she go? She barely recalled her dream. She would definitely *not* go back to Ata, where she would no doubt be ridiculed and called a disappointment.

Seems like I'm making a habit of disappointing people lately.

She continued to walk down the street, hoping for a sign, any sign, of Cassie, or some clue as to where her companion might have gone.

* * *

Kye finished the last bit of his meal, a somewhat stale piece of bread, and brushed the crumbs from his stained white shirt. His food supply was getting low again and soon it would be time to search for more money or try to escape the city.

Unfortunately, such a feat was easier said than done. His

wanted poster was nailed to boards all over the city. Any guard who spotted Kye had the authority to kill him on sight.

He was not entirely hopeless, however. The small attic he had chosen for a hideout suited him for now. There were not many Legionnaires posted here, and it helped that the attic window offered a decent view of the streets below. From his vantage point, Kye could see every coin purse dropped, as well as where merchants kept extra stock behind their carts. He stared out the window, not focusing on anything in particular.

Wait. He took a closer look at the sight below. A young woman with light brown, maybe blonde hair walked the streets alone. Her mannerisms and facial expression betrayed the obvious – she was lost.

Four hooded figures silently crept after her, sticking to the shadows on the sides of buildings. *Not so alone after all.* Kye looked back at the girl. She seemed to have no idea she was being followed. He was certain the figures were going to attempt to mug her, though he had heard horror stories of gangs of thugs that would mug and murder their victims or kidnap them and demand a ransom from the victim's family.

He was indecisive. Part of him wanted to go down there and somehow help her. He knew that while he could not see any Legionnaires, there was always the chance of one walking by.

He shook his head, scolding himself. *Stop being a coward and* help *someone for once.*

He made his decision, hoping that he would not regret it, and grabbed his cloak before climbing out the window.

* * *

Cassie continued wandering down the street, hoping that the next turn might put her back on the more familiar main thoroughfare of the city. But when she reached the end of the dark road she was only greeted by a collection of small, dilapidated buildings and shady alleyways.

It did not seem that big of a deal to her – she could not sleep and wanted to take a walk to clear her head anyway. She had not *tried* to get lost. Yet here she was, wandering alone at night in a city she was unfamiliar with and in a *land* she was still trying to convince herself she was really in.

"Crap," she muttered. She crossed her arms over her chest in a vain attempt to keep warm. The streets were silent save the sound of her own breathing and what she assumed were the squeaks of rats scurrying in the gutters.

"You lost, dear?"

The voice startled Cassie, making her jump and spin around to face whoever had spoken to her. She found herself facing four people, three men and one woman, all wearing hoods and dark, tattered clothing.

"It's not safe for young ones like yourself to be wandering the streets at night, dear," the woman, who had spoken earlier, continued.

Cassie forced a straight face. "I'm fine," she said coldly. "Thanks for asking." She started to turn around with every intention of walking away.

The woman flashed a crooked smile that was visible even

with the hood blocking most of her face. Her companions began to spread out, flanking Cassie.

"My friends and I are just looking for a few coins to get us by for the next night. Surely you can help us with that." The woman pulled her cloak back enough to reveal the short sword that hung from her belt.

Trying not to panic but knowing a mugging when she saw one, Cassie put her hands up in defense. "Look lady, I don't have any money. You're better off wasting your time on someone else." She saw the men exchange wry glances with the woman, who gave a curt nod.

The man on Cassie's left lunged forward quickly and grabbed her arm hard, pulling her in close to him. "Hey! Get the hell off me, dirt bag!" she yelled as she struggled to break free of his iron grip.

"Hold her still," the woman ordered and began searching Cassie's pockets. Cassie responded by kicking the woman in the knee.

"Ahh!" the woman cried out as she staggered backwards. "You *stupid bitch!*" she yelled and hit Cassie in the face with the back of her hand. The impact made Cassie grunt in pain as her head jerked violently to the side. A red imprint began to form on the side of her face.

"Leave her alone!"

All focus turned in the direction of the new voice. Cassie thought he looked quite young, maybe sixteen or seventeen, though he was quite tall. His blonde, curly hair was short but uneven, as though he had attempted to cut it himself. His skin was slightly tanned, with a light dusting of freckles across his face and signs of sunburn on his nose and cheeks. She wasn't quite sure how he planned to help her as he was quite scrawny and looked as though he had not eaten well in a long time.

"You'd do well to leave us, boy, unless you wish to meet an unpleasant fate," the woman sneered while the man holding Cassie tightened his grip on her arm.

The young man's large brown eyes widened in fear, but he stood his ground. "I-I don't want to hurt you. Please leave her alone."

"He says 'please'!" the woman mocked as she drew her sword and held it to Cassie's throat, pressing the blade lightly against her skin. "I won't warn you again, boy. Leave us before this gets messy."

The young man stared at the woman for a moment before hesitantly raising his hands. At first it seemed like he was showing a gesture of surrender, but Cassie knew better. She had seen Andrea do the same thing with her hands a few times now. This boy was an enchanter.

She closed her eyes tightly, hoping that whatever magic he did would not accidentally kill her in the process. The air around her suddenly became almost unbearably hot, and the steady hum of magic started off faint but quickly grew louder. The grip on her arm was released.

Upon slowly opening her eyes, Cassie nearly jumped back at the ring of fire that now surrounded her and her assailants. The woman had withdrawn her blade and was staring at the fire, her eyes full of fear. Her cohorts were not faring much better – their glances darted back and forth between their leader and the fire.

In what seemed like less than a second later, the air rapidly cooled, almost too quickly. Smoke gave way to steam, and Cassie realized that the ring of fire had transformed into a ring of crumbling ice.

"You'll leave if you know what's good for you." Andrea stood a few feet away. A dim blue light emanated from her hands and she was breathing heavily. "Unless you want to deal with two enchanters."

The woman with the dagger muttered a curse under her breath and signaled for her men to follow her. They quickly left, retreating into the shadows and leaving Cassie alone in what was now a puddle of water.

Cassie let out a sigh of relief. "Thanks," she said, rubbing her throat gingerly. She turned to the young man who had intervened on her behalf. "And thank *you*. You didn't have to do that."

The young man gave a shy smile. "Ah…you are welcome, I think. I couldn't just sit by and let them rob you."

"*Maybe* if she had stayed at the inn like she was *supposed to* instead of wandering around the streets of Azgadar like an idiot you wouldn't have had to save her and we wouldn't all be standing here in the cold in the middle of the night!" Andrea exclaimed angrily as she strode over to Cassie, grabbing the other girl's arm. "Are you dense or just very stupid? You could have been killed!"

Cassie jerked her arm away. "I couldn't sleep," she said, glaring at the enchanter. "And who the hell are *you* to boss me around?"

Furious, Andrea began to retort when they were interrupted by the sound of shouts approaching.

"This way! I heard them over here! Pretty sure there was magic being done, too!" The voice was loud and authoritative and accompanied by strong, heavy footsteps and clanking armor.

The young man's eyes widened in fear. "Legionnaires!" he gasped.

Andrea felt the color drain from her face. "W-what?"

"We need to get out of here!" the young man hissed. "Follow me!" He made a move to run but stopped when he saw that the girls had not moved.

Cassie looked at Andrea for direction. The enchanter hesitated as she exchanged frightened glances with her companion.

The voices of the quickly approaching Legionnaires grew closer and louder.

"We don't have time to think about it! They're going to be here any moment!" he said.

Andrea finally found her voice. "R-right," she said hoarsely and turned to the young man. "Lead the way."

The three bolted down a nearby alley. Andrea and Cassie followed closely behind the young man, leaping over fallen crates, piles of garbage, and other debris that littered the street.

"This way! Follow me, *now!*" one of the Legionnaires shouted.

"Come on!" the young man exclaimed as he raced ahead of the girls.

"We *are!*" Andrea panted. *They're going to find us. We'll be thrown in prison.* She tried to force the thoughts from her mind and to focus on running as fast as her legs would carry her while making sure that Cassie was still close by.

"Crap!" the other girl cried out as the three came to an abrupt halt. "Now what?!"

The wall that blocked their way was too tall to jump, and Andrea could not see any obvious places around them to climb. There was little around them other than bits of trash and a small metal grate on the ground. Panic began to set in and she began to hyperventilate. "I-I–,"

"That's not helping!" Cassie snapped. She turned to the young man. "You got another place we can go?"

He shook his head nervously. "N-no. I-it's a dead end–,"

"I *know* it's a dead end – I'm standing right here looking at it!" Cassie exclaimed.

The screech of metal grinding against the cobblestone street startled all three of them. Andrea turned around and noticed that the sewer grate had been pushed aside and that someone had pulled themselves partially out of the tunnel below.

"You." The voice was low and female, but she had a hood on and the darkness made it difficult to discern her features. "Hurry up and get down here, now!" She quickly climbed out and gestured for them to approach her.

Without being told twice, Cassie grabbed Andrea's wrist and dragged her to the open sewer entrance. The young man followed.

Less than a minute later, all four were holding onto the long ladder that led from the streets to the sewer tunnels below. Their mysterious rescuer had replaced the sewer grate just before the Legionnaires started to arrive.

"They're not here," one of them said from above. He stepped right on the grate, knocking down a clod of mud.

"Didn't you see them go this way?" another asked.

"Thought I had but…there's no way they would have been able to get over this wall."

"Well, let's keep looking," a third suggested. "Perhaps you saw them go down another alley."

"I know what I saw. I heard magic being done as well!" the first soldier protested.

"Well, they aren't here and my patrol is about up. Let's head back and see if we can catch them on the way," the second said.

"On the way?"

"You still owe me a drink."

The first Legionnaire who had spoken laughed. "Thought you would have forgotten about that bet by now." Their conversation grew fainter until the group could only hear murmurs, then silence.

"All clear," their rescuer declared after quietly opening the grate and checking.

Andrea let out a sigh of relief as she loosened her grip on the metal bars of the ladder. She followed the others as the four began to climb back up to the street.

"T-that was too close," the young man breathed once their rescuer had closed the grate again.

"Yeah," Cassie panted. She turned to Andrea. "You done yelling at me now? Can we go back?"

The enchanter glared at her companion. "Don't you even care how close we were to ending up in a prison cell?"

"She's right. But this is probably not the best place to have this conversation." The lithe woman before them stood slightly taller than Andrea. She wore dark clothing layered with dyed black leather armor. Her hooded cloak covered all but a few strands of her copper hair. Two long daggers hung from her belt, one on each side.

"Whatever. They wouldn't have heard us if you hadn't started yelling at me," Cassie snapped at Andrea. She winced in pain as the side of her face where she'd been slapped began to throb.

The woman, whose age Andrea could not tell due to the poor lighting on the street, spoke again in a cold, even voice. "Follow me. We need to get off the streets. You, too." She pointed at the young man, who had been watching Andrea and Cassie's argument with fascination.

"Sorry, I don't make a habit of following strange people," Cassie said and crossed her arms across her chest.

Andrea ignored her companion's comment. She turned to the stranger. "We have a place to stay. If you'll excuse us–,"

"Those Legionnaires will probably be at the very inn you're referring to. You're not as subtle as you think you are. Follow me…or get caught and go to prison. It's up to you." The woman spoke with a calculated certainty that convinced Andrea that she was not lying.

The enchanter paused for a moment before turning to Cassie

and then back to the woman. "Fine. Lead the way. Come on, Cassie." She grabbed Cassie's arm again. This time, Cassie did not pull away. They followed the woman, who quickly led them back up the alley, around the corner and into an abandoned house. The young man stayed close behind them but said nothing.

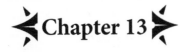

Chapter 13

The Legionnaire

"In here. Quietly, now." The woman opened the front door and gestured for them to enter. They stepped into the house, a small box of a building with a barely habitable living space and an even smaller kitchen.

"Thank you, Miss…" Andrea began but trailed off when she realized she did not know the woman's name.

"Elisa. Sit down, get comfortable. I'll put some tea on." The woman removed her cloak, revealing her fiery copper braids that stopped just past her chin and the pale green eyes they complemented. She looked to be several years older than Andrea and Cassie, perhaps in her thirties. She removed her belt and placed it on a small table near the tiny kitchen before hanging a kettle of water over the fire to boil.

"Thank you. I'm Andrea and this is Cassie," Andrea gestured to herself and her companion, who nodded in greeting. Both took seats at the small table.

"Right. An enchanter and the latest victim of Claudia and those idiot thugs she calls friends," Elisa observed, her voice still unwavering as she rummaged through the pantry. A minute later she returned to the table and set a plate of biscuits in front of the girls. Then she turned to the young man, who had stood by quietly the entire time. "And you're Kye. They've been looking for you for a while."

The young man appeared on the verge of panicking. "I-yes… I'm sorry. I can just go if you like–,"

"You wouldn't make it more than a few hours out there before they found you and put an arrow through your heart," Elisa said.

"Nice to meet you, Kye. Thanks again for saving my ass back there," Cassie offered.

"Yes, especially since it would have been *completely unnecessary* had you just stayed at the inn," Andrea muttered.

"Oh, stop it." Cassie waved her away. "You already lectured me once about it – I don't need another damn speech."

"I-erm…you're welcome," Kye said, rubbing the back of his neck. Seeing the dirty look Andrea shot Cassie, he decided not to say anything more. Instead he walked to the table and took a seat next to Cassie, who seemed to be the safest of the three women.

The water began to boil. Elisa finished preparing the tea and brought each of them a cup. Once she had her own, she took the last chair next to Andrea. "Now," she began, "we can talk."

"What were you doing down there anyway?" Cassie inquired. "It smelled horrible."

"The sewers usually do. But I know of no better way to move around the city undetected. You're fortunate I saw you when I did," Elisa explained.

"Not to sound ungrateful, but why *did* you help us?" Andrea wondered.

Elisa took a sip of tea and put her cup down before speaking. "You're an enchanter. You know very well what happens to enchanters in this city, at least the ones not working for the empress."

"I thought everyone here hated enchanters?" Cassie blurted out while looking at Andrea, who shot her another dirty look.

Elisa smirked. "The people with enough power to be allowed an opinion dislike you," she stated, looking at Andrea again. "And you," she said, turning to Kye. "You don't appear to be the serial murderer the wanted posters claim you are."

"Wanted posters? What are you, some kind of criminal?" Cassie looked at Kye suspiciously.

"N-no!" he exclaimed frantically. "I…it's a long story. I…I'd rather not speak of it."

Elisa regarded Kye for a moment but said nothing to him, turning her attention back to Andrea again. "I won't waste your time. I would not help you without expecting a favor in return. But perhaps we can come to an arrangement that can benefit all of us."

Cassie interjected. "Um…sorry, but we literally just met you and you want to start making deals? You don't know anything about us."

"Cassie, let me handle this," Andrea warned tiredly.

Elisa laughed quietly. "I know myself and everyone this side of the city could hear the two of you bickering in the middle of the street. But other than that, you are right. I don't know much about you and you know nothing of me. I would prefer it stay that way." She took a biscuit from the plate in front of them. "In any case, I don't need to know you well to know that you will consider my offer."

"Much?" Andrea raised an eyebrow.

Their new acquaintance nodded. "You enchanters think you're *so* discreet." She leaned in closer to Andrea. "Next time you visit Azgadar, try not to talk about magic so much. Anyone at the inn that wasn't drunk and had ears could hear you. Well, I could anyway."

Andrea sighed and buried her face in her hands while Cassie simply looked entertained as she plucked one of the biscuits from the plate.

"How much did you hear?" the enchanter groaned.

"I'm not here to blackmail you. You need to get to Rhyad though, yes?" Elisa asked.

"I-yes," Andrea admitted and flashed a worried glance at Cassie.

"I assume you don't want to hear this but you really should. Rhyad is completely blocked off to travelers. The Harringtons control the Northland Bridge and they aren't letting anyone in, least not as long as the civil war in Gurdinfield is still going on," Elisa explained.

The enchanter sighed again. "What do you mean 'blocked off'? Why would the Harringtons do that? Andrea was not extremely familiar with the details of the civil war that had raged in Gurdinfield for the last twenty or so years. She knew that King Taylor and his family had been massacred in their own palace and that the assassins had never been found. Since then, the ruling noble families of Gurdinfield, the Moores and the Harringtons, had pitted their private armies against each other, each house claiming that they were the next in line to take the throne.

"I do not know. Perhaps they want the advantage of the mountains to shield them from an attack should the Moores attempt a large-scale invasion in northern Gurdinfield," Elisa speculated. "The point is that if you want to get to Rhyad you're going to need my help. And if *you* want to get out of Azgadar without being killed in the process," she said, looking at Kye, "you will also want to listen to what I am about to offer."

When she saw the other three exchange glances and then look back to her, Elisa continued. "Very well. The empress is throwing a grand ball tomorrow night to celebrate the bicentennial of the Cadar dynasty." She did not hide the disgusted look that crossed her face. "There is a book, a journal, belonging to the empress that I need to acquire, and the ball will be the perfect time to get it." She paused and took another sip of tea.

"And you're going to get it for me."

Andrea immediately shook her head. "You're asking us, a couple of *enchanters*, to break into the Azgadaran Palace and steal a *book* from the empress of Azgadar? Are you mad?"

"What's so important about this book?" Cassie leaned forward curiously.

"Honestly? I'm not completely certain. I only know what my employer suspects based on intelligence they've gathered," Elisa admitted, "but I do know that there is a good chance that the information contained in it will have a significant impact on the civil war in Gurdinfield."

"What do they suspect?" Andrea asked.

"That the empress has allied with David Moore."

"Why would Azgadar care about Gurdinfield or its war?" The enchanter continued her line of inquisition.

"No idea. Regardless, I need this done."

"Wait. Why can't you do this yourself? You seem to know exactly what you're looking for. We don't even know what this book looks like or where to find it," Cassie pointed out before biting into another biscuit.

"Because," Elisa said slowly, "it cannot be me. I...have a history with the Legion and the guards will recognize me."

"You probably should have told your employer that before you took on this job," Andrea chided.

Elisa glared at the enchanter. "Perhaps I did tell them, and these are desperate times. But I don't expect you to understand that."

"Don't worry – she lectures me constantly," Cassie joked. Andrea narrowed her eyes at her companion but said nothing.

"You're a Legionnaire?" Kye finally spoke, surprising all three women.

"*Ex*-Legionnaire," Elisa corrected him. "And no, I won't tell you why. Now, do we have a deal or not?"

Silence descended upon them. Cassie looked to Andrea to answer for them and for some reason Kye also looked to the enchanter for guidance. Andrea looked around and rubbed her eyes. "Why are you all looking at me?"

"Well...you're kind of the boss," Cassie admitted.

"Oh, *now* you care what I have to say?" the enchanter retorted. She looked at Kye. "I barely know you. You're better off making this decision for yourself."

Kye shrugged. "I don't really have any other option."

"He's right – he doesn't," Elisa agreed, seemingly satisfied as she saw the young man cringe. She met Andrea's gaze. "If I can be blunt, neither do you. I know it is a lot to ask of you to trust me when we've only just met, but I can promise that I'll help you get to where you need to go if you do me this favor."

The enchanter switched her focus from Elisa to Cassie, then back to Elisa. The ex-Legionnaire was right – they didn't have a lot of options. Sure, they could get to Gurdinfield and then journey to Rhyad, but if the bridge was blocked then what was the point?

Finally, she nodded slowly. "What do you need us to do?"

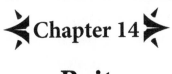Chapter 14

Bait

"It itches. Where did you get this?"

"None of your business. Stop fidgeting."

"I would be lying if I said I wasn't having second thoughts about this pla-ouch!" The enchanter gasped as their new acquaintance used the laces that fastened the back of the dark green gown she was wearing to jerk her hard to the side.

"Stop talking. You're making this more difficult than it needs to be," Elisa grumbled. She turned to Cassie and Kye, who were observing the entire process a few steps away in the room that Andrea and Cassie shared at the inn. "Does she always talk this much?" she asked.

Cassie shrugged, her arms folded across her chest, a smug expression forming quickly. "It's been pretty much nonstop, yeah."

At this, the enchanter turned her gaze quickly to Cassie and glared at the other girl. "Unless *you* want to be the bait, Cassie, I suggest you-ah!" she cried in pain as Elisa tightened the laces forcefully. "Was that really necessary?"

Elisa bit her lip and shot a disbelieving glance at the enchanter. "You're *still* talking. There." She stepped back to admire her handiwork. "Well, what do you think?" she asked the others. "Is she ready to attend a ball?"

The enchanter stood stiffly while she waited for her companions to make their judgement. The gown, a fitted dark green piece with long sleeves and trimmed with gold embroidery, nearly reached the floor but was not so long that she might step on it. Half of her dark hair was pulled back into a few small braids that cascaded over the rest of her hair. Elisa had even given her some simple but elegant bracelets and earrings to wear, as well as a silver necklace for which the ex-Legionnaire had threatened Andrea with death multiple times if it was lost or damaged.

"Well?" she asked impatiently. "It's ridiculous, isn't it? I told you this would never work and–," she stopped when she saw the expressions on Kye and Cassie's faces. For once, the other girl did not have a smart remark ready to go. Kye seemed to be internally debating between averting his eyes shyly as he had done most of the afternoon and saying something.

He opted to say something, though he appeared to struggle getting it out. "It…it suits you well, Andrea. You'll fit right in."

Andrea gave a small smile. "Thank you, Kye." She involuntarily looked to Cassie, wondering at the same time why she was even worried about what the other girl thought. They were doing this to get the book so that they could get to Rhyad, not so they could give each other fashion advice. Not to mention she was still somewhat annoyed at her companion for going into the city alone and putting both of them in danger.

Before Cassie could answer, however, Elisa broke in. "It's going to take more than a fancy dress and a pretty face to fit in at the Azgadaran Palace." She looked the enchanter up and down, her face contorted in deep thought.

"I'll have an invitation, will I not?" Andrea asked as she absentmindedly adjusted the sleeves on the dress.

Elisa nodded. "You will, but if we want anyone there to actually believe you're Andrea, noblewoman from the Western Hills, you've got to convince me that you can act the part, too."

The enchanter sighed. "Remind me why *I'm* the one doing this?"

Exasperated, Elisa explained for what must have been the third time that day: "Because *he's* a wanted criminal," she pointed to Kye, "and your friend there's got all the tact of a drunk Legionnaire."

"Wow, thanks. I can totally tell we're going be great friends," Cassie deadpanned.

Elisa ignored her. "Do you want to go over the plan again? We only have one shot at this so it *has* to be perfect."

When the others nodded, she began to recite the plan again. Andrea was to enter the Azgadaran Palace with the invitation Elisa had given her in hand, where she would be introduced as a wealthy landowner from the Western Hills. Cassie and Kye were to make their way to the back of the palace and wait outside the servants' entrance, making sure that no one saw them before Andrea could find an opportunity to get to the servants' wing and open the door for them.

Once Cassie and Kye were inside the palace, they would make their way to the empress's quarters while Andrea returned to the ball. Most of the palace guards would be in the Great

Hall and the palace gardens where the ball was taking place, and Elisa offered some very specific directions on how to get to the empress's room without passing through too many major corridors. There, in the top drawer of the empress's desk, they would find the book Elisa was after. After procuring it, they were to leave as quickly and quietly as possible.

"How will I know when to leave?" Andrea questioned.

The ex-Legionnaire donned her cloak. "I'll send a signal. There will be some kind of security alert, something minor, but you'll see the guards getting nervous and shuffling around."

"How do we know you're not going to just take the book and leave us?" Cassie demanded. Kye said nothing but his wide eyes gave away his interest in Elisa's answer.

"You don't," Elisa shot back, "but right now *I'm* your best chance at getting to where you need to be so you might as well get over any issues you have and just trust me. It will be easier going forward." When Cassie did not argue back, she turned back to Andrea. "I will warn you now," she said, her voice low and void of the sarcasm it held earlier. "When you are in that palace you *will* be in danger. The empress makes a point of socializing with all of her guests so she will most likely approach you at some point. Do not give her *any* reason to suspect that you are not who you say you are. Keep your answers simple but polite." She paused. "Do you understand?"

The enchanter took a deep breath and exhaled. "I…yes, I understand." Her throat was tight and she could feel her hands already trembling from nerves.

Noticing Andrea's nervousness but seeming satisfied with the enchanter's answer, Elisa nodded and clasped her hands together. "All right," she concluded. "Make any final preparations you need to. I will meet you outside the inn. Do not take too long."

"I'll go with you," Kye offered.

Once they had left, Andrea and Cassie let silence consume the room. Cassie sat down on the bed and folded her hands in her lap while Andrea stood, awkwardly, in the same spot she had been standing when Elisa was assisting her in getting ready.

Cassie broke the silence first. "You think you can do this? Thought you came from a farm or whatever. What do you know about being some nobleperson?"

While the other girl had put it harsher than the enchanter would have liked, Andrea knew Cassie had a point. "I don't know. I guess…I guess I'll just have to do what I can and hope that you two can get the book quickly," she said quietly. She gave a small laugh. "Besides, it's not as though I am a complete barbarian just because I was a farmer."

Cassie smiled wryly. "At least we won't have to worry about throwing fireballs at anyone this time."

"Yes," the enchanter agreed with a vigorous nod. "Let's *not* do that again anytime soon." She took comfort in the fact that Cassie was trying to establish more conversations with her. It didn't completely take her mind off this new sort of danger that they were about to venture into but it did ease her nerves a bit.

She adjusted her dress a final time. "We should probably meet Elisa and Kye. Are you ready?"

Cassie stood up and straightened her own clothing. "Yeah. Let's get this over with. And uh…Andrea?"

Andrea glanced up at the other girl in surprise. Cassie had never called her by name before. She waited anxiously while trying not to appear overly eager.

"For what it's worth, I think Elisa's all right. But...just be careful in there. This empress sounds like a piece of work if she runs a country that hates people like you," Cassie cautioned. "Oh and um...you look nice."

The enchanter smiled faintly and shook her head. "We'd better go. Elisa doesn't seem the type that likes to be kept waiting." She opened the door to leave the room.

Cassie shuffled after her, muttering, "She doesn't seem the type that likes *anything*."

* * *

"There it is," Elisa announced as she led her group down one of the many alleys that connected to many of the major streets in the city.

"It seems so much bigger when you're right in front of it," Kye breathed as he gazed up in awe at the massive structure that was the Azgadaran Palace.

They did not have to walk far from the inn. Only thirty minutes earlier they had left to make the short walk to the palace. Elisa had taken them through a series of side streets to avoid the guests arriving via the main road of the city. "Right, then," she said, stopping suddenly and turning to the group. "Is everyone ready?"

Andrea looked up and inhaled deeply, taking in the cool night air that had descended on Azgadar. From where they stood, she could hear the sounds of guests arriving and being greeted at the palace entrance. Hoping her steady breathing would calm her nerves, she spoke first.

"I think so. This dress really does itch, though," she complained halfheartedly and gestured to her gown.

"You can change once we're done here," Elisa told her. "What about you two?" She faced Cassie and Kye. "Do you have any questions before we do this?"

Cassie raised her hand as the others looked at her with raised eyebrows. "Yeah. Can there be food after we're done? I haven't eaten all day."

The ex-Legionnaire's stony expression remained unchanged as Kye chuckled and Andrea let out a longsuffering sigh, though she had to fight back a smile. "We ate a few hours ago," she reminded her companion. Part of her knew that Cassie was trying in her own strange way to lighten the mood despite the fact that they were going to be in very grave danger.

"All right. Andrea, you know what to do," Elisa announced. She handed the enchanter a rolled up piece of parchment. "Here is the invitation. I've altered it to have your name on it. Hand it to the guard at the front – they'll announce you."

"Okay," Andrea said as she grasped the invitation with both hands.

Elisa continued. "You two," she eyed Cassie and Kye. "You need to be ready to go when she opens the door for you. Got it?"

"Yep," Cassie answered as Kye gave a short nod.

"Good. Go, then," the ex-Legionnaire prompted and pushed Andrea toward the street. "Good luck."

The enchanter stumbled for a moment, regained her balance, and after a final glance at her companions, she began to make her way toward the Azgadaran Palace, hoping deep down inside that she would not mess this up in some horrible way.

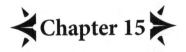

Chapter 15

Roses

"...the Lady Andrea of the Western Hills!"

Andrea hesitantly made her way through the grand foyer of the Azgadaran Palace as she was announced. The sheer size of the room was impressive, almost intimidating, as were the massive red and gold banners with the sword and shield symbol of the Legion that hung from the walls of the cathedral ceilings. She forced herself to focus directly in front of her, ignoring the curious gazes of some of the guests who had gathered near the palace entrance, no doubt to observe new arrivals like herself. The dull buzz of the conversations around her had grown to a roaring cacophony now that she was in the thick of the crowd. In the background, a small orchestra played a lilting waltz, though it was not a song Andrea had ever heard before. Taking a deep breath while trying at the same time not to be overwhelmed, the anxious enchanter pushed forward, gently nudging through the clusters of finely-dressed nobles around her.

She knew based on Elisa's information that the servants' entrance would be through a small door located in the rear of the Great Hall, but she could not go there just yet. First, she had to let herself be seen by some of the other guests. She also knew that there was a chance the empress herself might see her.

While Andrea had never seen Ithmeera before, she knew enough to know what to expect. Ithmeera had inherited the throne of Azgadar before she was even of age. She was a fair ruler, if strict, and the empire had flourished under her rule. Despite the additional restrictions on enchanters and magic that she had put in place, Ithmeera was very popular amongst her people, arguably more than her late father had been. Andrea knew the empress did not hate magic or distrust enchanters, but she was confident that Ithmeera would lose no sleep over throwing her in a jail cell if she was caught.

A tap on her shoulder startled her out of her thoughts. She spun around, nearly forgetting her place and character.

"Pardon me, miss! I did not intend to startle you." An older, balding man, perhaps in his fifties and dressed in a rather elaborate suit stood before the nervous enchanter. He looked at Andrea curiously before exchanging glances with his partner, a dark-haired and equally well-dressed woman that the enchanter took to be his wife.

"Oh, I-I'm sorry," Andrea stammered, struggling to maintain her composure. She took a deep breath and tried again. "What I meant to say, sir," she said slowly and deliberately, "is that *I'm* the one who should apologize for reacting as I did. My mind was elsewhere, you see."

The man smiled warmly before bowing slightly. "No need, miss. Lord William Moore. Pleased to make your acquaintance. This is my wife, Nia." He gestured to his wife, who gave a polite nod.

Andrea struggled at first to remember the proper greeting Elisa had insisted she use, but decided to go with what she was comfortable with. Better to appear natural than to draw suspicion with her nervousness. "Pleased to meet you. I'm Andrea…of the Western Hills." She flashed the most genuine smile she could manage and bowed.

Nia Moore's expression quickly changed from polite to pleasant. "The Western Hills? We were actually considering visiting on holiday there very soon. How is the weather this time of year?"

"We've heard it's nothing short of lovely," William added.

Andrea relaxed. If all these people wanted to talk about was the weather and her homeland, perhaps this would not be so difficult after all.

"It's actually very nice this time of year," she began. "The harvest season is particularly nice as many of the towns will be having festivals soon to celebrate."

"They have festivals? How quaint! We must go in time for them, William!" Nia exclaimed.

"Of course." Lord Moore looked around as though he were looking for someone in the crowd of guests before turning back to Andrea. "That is if those blasted Harringtons don't block the roads again. It's quite terrible."

Andrea forced a smile though she had no idea what to say in return.

"Honestly, William, must you bring that up *here*?" Nia chastised. "Surely we can enjoy one evening without bringing up this silly conflict!"

William took a sip of his wine and shook his head. "Those bastards have destroyed three of my caravans! I will not stand for it any longer!"

Nia placed her hand on her husband's shoulder and gave a sympathetic nod. "I'm sure David will sort it out."

"Most likely. My brother is resourceful like that. Ah, well. Forgive me, Lady Andrea," William said, calming down and turning back to the enchanter. "The troubles of Gurdinfield are surely of no interest to you."

Andrea froze up. She vaguely knew of the civil war that had been waged for the past twenty years, but beyond the generalities she knew very little. Would a noble from the Western Hills know more than she did?

"Ah…well, every region has its problems, yes?" she tried, cringing inwardly. But the Moores only stared at her a moment before Nia nodded enthusiastically.

"Oh, of course, dear. Even here, unfortunately," she said.

"That bloody enchanter?" William said, his face contorted with disgust. "I'm surprised the Legion hasn't caught him and thrown him in a jail cell yet!"

"Language, William!" Nia scolded. She turned to Andrea apologetically. "He gets so passionate about certain topics."

Andrea gave a slight nod. "I can understand that."

"Honestly, these enchanters, they're really more of a nuisance than anything," Nia said. "But every once in a while, you get those bad ones…the ones who hurt innocent people. It's such a shame, really. From what I understand, he's just a boy."

Andrea felt her chest tighten. *She's talking about Kye. What exactly did he do?* She barely knew the young enchanter, and while he had not been very forthcoming about why he was wanted, he *had* helped them so far.

"Erm...yes! A shame, really," she parroted back. Her mind wandered to Cassie. She was alone with Kye – what if he truly *was* a danger and was going to turn on her? *No, he didn't seem hostile...he was more scared than anything.*

"Oooh, I do believe they are serving dessert. William, dear, shall we browse Her Majesty's selection for tonight?" Nia suggested.

William nodded. "Of course!" He turned to the enchanter and bowed. "I thank you for your time, Lady Andrea. We will speak more later about your beautiful homeland. After dessert, perhaps?"

The enchanter nodded. "Of course. It was nice meeting you both," she replied and watched as the couple excused themselves and disappeared into the crowd. Once they had gone, she breathed a heavy sigh of relief. This was going to be a long night.

* * *

Cassie kicked in boredom at the gravel near the main path that led to the servants' entrance. She and Kye had been waiting for quite some time already, and the night cold had set in. She wrapped Andrea's dark blue cloak tightly around herself, thankful the enchanter had allowed her to borrow it.

While they were near the entrance to the palace, she and Kye had made sure to stay behind a cluster of trees and out of sight of any guards or other staff that happened to walk by, in the event that someone recognized Kye from the wanted posters scattered across the city.

"This is boring," she whined. "Andrea had better hurry the hell up."

"Not so loud – someone might hear us!" Kye hissed.

Cassie rolled her eyes. "Oh please, I didn't say it *that* loud. I just don't want to be standing out here all night."

"Do you think she's been spotted?"

"How should I know? In any case, I'm not really the one who has to worry about getting caught out here. That's *you*, remember? So what did you do? You supposed to be some kind of serial killer or something?"

"You know nothing about me," the young enchanter snapped. "I suggest we stick to the plan and not speak of anything except what that Elisa woman has asked us to do."

Cassie shrugged. "Fine by me. I'm going to ask you again and again until you tell me, though, so you might as well just tell me now."

Kye sighed. How could anyone be so insensitive? He suddenly preferred to be in the company of the other enchanter or even Elisa than to have to spend another minute being prodded and labeled a "serial killer".

"Oh stop making that face – I'm just messing around with you," Cassie said. She peered around the edge of the trees to see if the servants' entrance had been opened yet. Nothing.

"This really is going to take all night," she whined.

* * *

Andrea had spent much of her time at the ball walking around, giving polite nods to guests and engaging in the occasional conversation. More than once she had stumbled over her words, particularly when speaking about her homeland, once nearly giving away that she grew up a farmer, but she was able to recover in time before the guests showed any suspicion. She had also sampled the food in order to blend in better but admittedly was not fond of most of it. The meats had an odd aftertaste, and the desserts all had far too much alcohol in them.

She was waiting for the perfect time to leave the Great Hall and find the servants' entrance. *Now seems to be good.* No one's attention was on her, and her presence would not be missed. Elisa had given her general directions on where to find the servants' entrance, and so she began to make her way to the edge of the Great Hall.

"Everything's fine, everything's fine," she breathed aloud to no one. She slowly continued to the servants' entrance to let Cassie and Kye in.

* * *

"Cassie, the door!"

Cassie, who was sitting on the grass near the path behind the trees, leapt to her feet at the sound of Kye's alert.

The door to the servants' entrance was indeed opening. Cassie half-expected it to be a servant or a guard, but was actually surprised to see that it was Andrea who had opened the door. They quietly walked to the entrance, where the enchanter was waiting for them.

"Quickly!" Andrea whispered. "I don't know if anyone saw me leave, so I must get back soon." Once Cassie and Kye were inside, Andrea shut the door and locked it again. She turned to her companions. "Go get the book. Leave the way you came in when you're finished."

"What about you?" Cassie asked, quickly scanning their new surroundings.

"Elisa said she'll signal me," Andrea explained hurriedly. "Now *go!*"

Not needing to be told again, Cassie and Kye turned and quickly made their way down the hallway Elisa had said would lead them to their destination: the empress's private quarters.

* * *

It took a few minutes, but Andrea was able to return to the Great Hall without anyone noticing her absence. Hoping that Cassie and Kye would be able to retrieve the book without trouble, she distracted herself by sampling more of the strange-tasting food and trying to appear normal to the other guests. Aside from more curious looks from other guests wondering who the enchanter was, no one else spoke to her for some time – until she heard a voice behind her.

"Hold a moment. I don't believe we've been introduced." The voice that stopped Andrea was young and soft, but also convincing and commanding. Before she could even turn completely around, the enchanter knew who she'd be facing.

Though she had never seen Empress Ithmeera, the dark curls, bright green eyes, and regal stance gave the ruler's identity away. No one else in the room carried themselves the way Ithmeera did. She closed the few feet of distance between her and the enchanter, her yellow gown floating across the ballroom floor. It took a few moments for Andrea to spot the bodyguards who flanked the empress. They were mere shadows in the woman's presence.

"I am Ithmeera Cadar," the empress spoke. "I don't believe we've met yet this evening. And you are…?"

Andrea bowed, hoping with every inch of her being that Ithmeera would not see through her guise. "Andrea of the Western Hills, Your Majesty. This is a lovely ball that you've arranged."

Ithmeera examined the enchanter for a few seconds, though it felt like an eternity to Andrea. Suddenly, her serious expression was replaced by a radiant smile. "Isn't it? I hope everyone is enjoying it. It's been a very strange few weeks, and I admit I didn't have as much time to plan this as I would have liked."

Andrea blinked a few times, surprised at the empress's honesty. "I…well, it's amazing. This palace is beautiful!"

Ithmeera beamed at her. "Isn't it? I would give you a tour but alas, I have other guests who would object if they did not also get a tour." She delicately placed a hand on the enchanter's shoulder. "Forgive me for being so forward, Lady Andrea, but you are the first person here who I have not met three times already and who is not twice my age."

Andrea forced a smile as she screamed internally. Being cornered by Ithmeera like this was definitely *not* part of the plan. "Well, ah, I'm grateful for the invitation, Your Majesty."

"Of course!" the empress beamed. "I do hope you're enjoying the ball."

"I-yes, Your Majesty," the enchanter said with a bow.

Ithmeera smiled and looked around. The smile was quickly replaced by a mischievous grin. "Actually, I'm sure the other guests will be fine. Andrea, if it's not too much to ask, I'd like for you to accompany me for a short walk. I need to get away from the crowds for a bit for a breath of fresh air, I'm afraid."

Andrea's heart skipped a beat as she tried to stay calm. A private walk? Had the empress somehow identified her? No, she thought, rapidly rationalizing her thoughts. Ithmeera had never seen her before – there was no way she could tell who Andrea was or *what* she was. *Everything is fine.*

"Of course, Your Majesty. It would be my honor," she replied calmly, her confidence growing again.

"Excellent. Leave us, please," the empress said to her bodyguards, who gave an obedient nod and stepped aside.

"Follow me, then." Ithmeera took the enchanter's hand and practically dragged her away from the crowd and out of the Great Hall. They walked through a few short corridors and through a somewhat hidden small foyer that led out into the palace gardens. There, Andrea was presented with a sprawling array of well-manicured trees and bushes of all kinds lining various stone paths.

"Incredible," she breathed in awe.

"Isn't it? I love walking through here, especially when I need some peace and quiet away from the bickering of the bureaucrats and the other nobility," Ithmeera explained as they slowly walked down one of the paths. She pointed to a rather elaborate display of roses of different colors. "Those are my favorite. Roses have always been my favorite."

Andrea nodded, taking note of the lovely flowers and how perfectly the smell of them complemented the cool night air. If she ever had a place to call home again, she would try to obtain some for sure. "They are quite beautiful."

"Aren't they? They're my favorite for a good reason, too. Would you like to know why?" Ithmeera stopped walking and turned to face the enchanter.

* * *

"Have you found it?"

"Not yet – I'm looking! Stop asking me and keep an eye on things out there. You're a pretty crappy lookout."

Kye groaned in frustration and returned to his post at the doorway. It had taken them awhile to find the empress's bedroom, but Elisa had been accurate in her description – there were hardly any guards in the servants' passages and he and Cassie had been able to sneak past the few guards they did see. Now he stood watch while Cassie rummaged through the empress's private belongings in her desk, searching for the book Elisa had asked for.

"Ack! Where the hell is it? You'd think the empress would hide her extremely personal diary in plain sight," Cassie grumbled as she fished through several drawers.

Kye couldn't hold back a smile this time. "Yes, how thoughtless of Her Majesty," he deadpanned.

"Seriously! I hope there's some useful stuff in this book, otherwise this will all have been for –aha! got it!" Cassie held up the thick black tome victoriously. She opened the satchel Elisa had given her earlier and gently placed the book in it before closing the flap.

"Great! Now, let's get out of here before anyone sees us!" Kye pleaded.

"Yeah, yeah, quit whining. Let's go!" Cassie exclaimed and grabbed the young enchanter's arm before pulling him back down the hallway toward the palace exit.

* * *

"Of…of course," Andrea replied eagerly. She knew that this was not part of the plan – that she was to keep the empress busy only long enough to get bored with and move on from the enchanter. Then again, as long as Ithmeera was here, she was not in her quarters, and that meant Cassie and Kye would have more time to find the diary and make their exit.

Ithmeera gently touched one of the roses, a white one that was in a late stage of bloom. "They are so beautiful, perfect almost, but the flower is only the most visible part. Behind the flower are thorns…a reminder that sometimes things are not as they first appear to be." She released the flower and turned to the enchanter again.

"I don't believe you are who *you* appear to be, Lady Andrea."

Time seemed to stop as a deathly silence descended upon them, and Andrea could only hear her own shallow breathing. Out of the corner of her eye she could see palace guards making their way toward them.

"You have two options. You can make this simple and tell me who you really are and why Elisa sent you, or you can continue lying to me and I will have you killed right here, in the gardens. Your body, well," the empress mused, her voice cold and distant, "I'm afraid it will probably never be found. As for me…I've still a party to attend. So," she folded her arms across her chest, "what will it be?"

"I-b-but…how–," Andrea stammered, her face rapidly growing paler by the second.

The empress pointed at the enchanter's necklace. "*That* necklace," she said angrily, "does *not* belong to you." She lowered her arm. "Why did she send you? What does she want? To assassinate me? She knows none of this was my fault – *it was her own doing!*"

The guards had closed in on them now, and two stood on either side of Andrea as she trembled before the empress. "She…she needed something from you. I was only trying to help – honest. The name I gave you is my true name but…m-my reasons are my own!"

Ithmeera studied the girl for a moment before speaking again. "Your honesty is appreciated, whether you realize it or not."

Andrea held her breath. She knew this was it – she would die here, at the hands of these guards. No one would ever know what happened to her, and this would all have been for nothing.

"I do not wish to deal with this at my own ball. Lock her up." The empress waved her hand at the guards. "We will speak more later and you *will* tell me what Elisa sent you here for."

Feeling so faint she could barely stand anymore, Andrea released the breath she had been holding as the guards roughly grabbed her arms and dragged her away from the empress and out of the gardens.

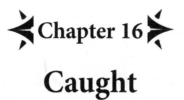

Chapter 16

Caught

Elisa waited silently, hiding in the shadows across the street from the Azgadaran Palace. She knew it was getting late and had been tempted more than once to abort the mission and rescue the others from whatever fate had befallen them, but she tried to remain optimistic. While Andrea had indeed seemed nervous, Elisa could tell that there was a streak of determination in the enchanter that gave the ex-Legionnaire some confidence that perhaps the operation might not fail after all.

Her eyes widened when she saw the familiar figures of Cassie and Kye making their way swiftly across the street and toward the cover of clustered buildings Elisa had made her rendezvous spot. She stepped out of the shadows slightly to make her presence known to them.

"Do you have it?" she asked once they had arrived.

Panting quietly, Cassie removed the satchel from over her shoulder and handed it to Elisa. Feeling the weight of the book, the ex-Legionnaire slung the satchel over her own shoulder before giving Cassie and Kye an appreciative nod. "Thank you. This will help more than you know."

"Sure. Where's Andrea?" Cassie asked as she slapped the dust kicked up by the gravel in the street from her pants.

"Wait here. I'll give her the signal," Elisa answered and briskly walked away, disappearing again into the shadows.

* * *

The ex-Legionnaire crept around the side of the palace, looking for the best spot to cause a disturbance so that the guards would be alerted. She stopped and hid in the bushes when she saw two guards approaching. One was walking quickly, the other following.

"Shift end early?" the one following behind asked.

"I wish. No, the captain needs me to cover another post. Seems the empress found herself a little spy or something."

Elisa gritted her teeth. *Fantastic.*

"A spy? At the ball? From who?"

"No idea, but I've got to get there now since he already left for the dungeon. I'll probably miss drinks tonight – tomorrow then?"

"Aye, tomorrow."

After the guards had left, Elisa emerged from the bushes and swiftly walked back to the building where she had instructed Cassie and Kye to wait. She was trying not to panic but was not yet sure yet what she was going to do about this. Though she had the book, leaving Andrea was not going to be an option, not after what she had promised them.

* * *

"Well? Is she coming?" Cassie demanded once Elisa had returned.

Elisa looked down and bit her lip. "I'm afraid it's a bit more complicated than that. Andrea's been caught and she's being held in the dungeons below the palace."

"What? How the hell did that happen? I thought the whole point of sending her in there was so we *wouldn't* get caught!" Cassie accused angrily. Kye said nothing, but the color in his face had quickly drained.

"Calm down and lower your voice, girl!" Elisa hissed. She took a deep breath and tried to keep her voice level. No, this was definitely *not* how things were supposed to go.

"How the hell am I supposed to stay calm when *you're* the one who got her locked up?!" Cassie snapped. "Who the hell knows what they'll do to her in there!"

The ex-Legionnaire grabbed Cassie's shoulders and slammed her against the side of the building. Cassie winced in pain and struggled a bit until Elisa held her still.

"I said *calm down*. Now." Her tone was even and low. "Andrea *knew* there was a risk going in and she still agreed. That was *her* decision, not yours. We can argue about that later. Right now, you need to *listen* to me and *trust* me, or she's as good as dead – after the empress has her tortured for information of course."

"T-tortured?" Kye stuttered from behind them.

Elisa looked back at the enchanter. "Yes. Don't let her looks fool you – Ithmeera is as ruthless as they come when it comes to extracting information from people who appear to be threats to her or her family."

Cassie finally pushed Elisa away from her. "Fine, we'll do it your way. What's the plan?"

"I know how to get into the dungeon from out here, but we need a distraction to keep as many guards off of us as possible," Elisa explained. The three of them stood in silence.

"I-I could distract them," Kye piped up. "They know who I am."

"No. That's stupid – we'll end up with two of us locked up instead of one!" Cassie protested.

But Elisa looked thoughtful. "Hm…actually that's not the worst idea I've heard tonight." She turned to Kye. "You'd be willing to do this at the risk of your own life?"

The young enchanter nodded. "Yes. I can run fast if I need to and I'm no stranger to climbing if I need to make a quick exit."

"They know your face just as well. Why don't *you* do it?" Cassie demanded of the ex-Legionnaire.

Elisa shook her head. "Without me you have no chance of getting into that dungeon." She nodded toward Kye. "*His* plan is better. I suggest we stop talking about it and do it."

Kye rolled his shoulders back, feigning confidence. "It's all right, Cassie. I've done this a few times already. Elisa's right – we need her to get into the dungeon."

Cassie looked at the enchanter and then back at Elisa before sighing. Going home sounded like a really great idea at this point. "Fine," she said wearily. "let's do this."

* * *

Andrea leaned back against the crumbling stone wall of her cell. Water dripped steadily from the ceiling, forming a puddle a few feet in front of her. The only light came from a poorly lit lantern. Based on the faint green hue of the light, Andrea concluded it must have been lit magically long ago. The stench of sewage, rotten food, and sweat assaulted the enchanter's nose and left her nauseous and disoriented.

She slammed her fists against the cold floor in frustration. Her once-radiant dress was stained from the filthy water and caked with mud. Her dark hair was a mess, tangled up in the hairpieces Elisa had placed in it hours earlier. Oddly enough, the empress had not taken the necklace from her.

The necklace. The enchanter gripped it in her hand. How could she have been so stupid? Of *course* the empress would have found out. The woman knew how to command the entire Legion before she was even of age – she was not going to miss a single, inexperienced spy at her own ball.

This made Andrea even more curious. Why had Elisa allowed her to wear a necklace that Ithmeera would recognize? Had the ex-Legionnaire set her up? *No.* The enchanter quickly stopped that line of thought. Elisa had nothing to gain from betraying them. Unless…

Unless her plan all along had been to get the book from Cassie and Kye and leave Andrea alone with Ithmeera to get caught and take the fall. *It doesn't matter anymore.* She had been caught, and no doubt the only reason the empress had kept her alive so far was so she could be interrogated and possibly tortured for information. There would be no getting to Gurdinfield or Rhyad, and definitely no restoring of magic.

Everything she had done so far had been for nothing.

I should have never left the Black Forest. I should have never left home!

A rather large rat scurried across the stone floor and observed Andrea for a moment before returning to the tiny hole in the wall from which it came. Feeling utterly hopeless, the enchanter buried her face in her hands. The tears she had been holding back since she and Cassie left the Black Forest flooded the room, her sobs echoing off the dungeon walls.

"Quiet, girl!" one of the two guards standing watch in the dreary dungeon barked at her. "No use crying. I'm sure Her Majesty will send for you after the ball's over."

"Aye, don't expect a friendly meeting, though," the other guard chimed in. "We don't tolerate spies in the empress's city, and especially not in her home!"

The enchanter sniffed and glared at the guards before burying her face in her hands. The tears did not stop and she continued to cry silently, trying not to dwell on what her fate would be.

* * *

"Wow, he *does* run fast."

"Let's hope he can keep it up without getting caught," Elisa said. She and Cassie had been able to sneak past the remaining guards that had not chased after Kye. They now stood above a metal grate outside the palace.

"This will take us through the sewers, which have a connecting door to the dungeon," Elisa explained.

Cassie wrinkled her nose. "That's disgusting."

Elisa raised an eyebrow and gestured for Cassie to help her lift the grate off the ground. "You want to save your friend or not?"

With a dramatic sigh, Cassie knelt down to assist Elisa. "Well, I mean," she began as they lifted the heavy grate and cast it to the side, "I don't know if she'd consider me her friend at this point. But I do know if we don't get her back then I'm pretty much screwed."

"That so?" Elisa questioned. She scanned their surroundings quickly to make sure no one was watching them. Fortunately, the lack of guards in the area, combined with the darkness that concealed them, allowed the two to descend into the sewers without being seen.

Elisa dropped down from the ladder to the sewer floor, her boots splashing in the water that came up to her ankles. "Careful, it's wet," she called up.

Cassie dropped down moments later. "Ugh!" she cried. "Gross. What the hell am I stepping into exactly?!"

"Trust me, you probably know, and it would do you no favors were I to share," Elisa replied, a slight smile forming on her freckled face. She began trudging through the water and mud with Cassie following closely behind. The sewer tunnels were pitch black, and Cassie could only tell where she was going by the sound of Elisa's boots splashing.

"This is disgusting."

"You've said that. A few times now," Elisa answered.

"Yeah, well, just want to make sure you know. This is the last place I thought I'd end up."

"Hold onto me and turn left here," Elisa instructed as she reached back with her arm, which Cassie grabbed. "So, how do you know Andrea anyway? Why do you need her?"

"Huh?"

"Well, you're clearly not friends, or so you've said. And she obviously needs you, otherwise she wouldn't have saved you from Claudia," Elisa pressed. "So...what is it, then?"

In the darkness, for a moment, Cassie considered telling Elisa everything. How she had woken up in a strange house and been tortured at the hands of Meredith, how Andrea had helped her escape – given up her home and life as an apprentice to get Cassie away from the Black Forest, and how the two of them had ended up on what was indeed a real but still ludicrous quest to save magic. She was not sure if Andrea would be comfortable with her sharing everything with someone they had met only a day earlier.

Cassie decided she would ask the enchanter after they had rescued her.

"Well?" Elisa asked.

Cassie shook her head, despite the darkness. "She helped me...and I owe her a favor. That's all."

Elisa nodded. "As you wish." She froze and held up her other hand to stop Cassie. "Shh! Quiet!" she whispered. She pulled Cassie around a corner.

"Get down and stay there!" she hissed. Cassie nodded as she

knelt down and held as still as possible while the ex-Legionnaire crept back around the corner to inspect whatever it was that she heard. The stillness seemed to magnify the foul smells to Cassie, and it took a great deal of willpower not to gag.

Finally, Elisa returned. "Just rats," she reported, taking Cassie's arm again. "We're almost there."

Cassie let out the pent-up breath she did not know she was holding in and stood up. "Gross, there are *rats?*"

"Of course, though they like to gather closer to the dungeon since the guards and some of the prisoners get food."

"Again, gross. I hate this," Cassie declared.

"You'd be surprised how many times I've had to take this route," Elisa said. "You never get used to it."

"Why would *you* need to take this way? And how do you know the empress anyway?" Cassie noted the walls were now dimly lit with a fading green light. She let go of Elisa's arm.

"It's a long and tedious tale that I'd rather not share in the confines of a sewer or dungeon. Perhaps another time," the ex-Legionnaire said. She stopped suddenly. "Here."

"What? I don't see anything."

Elisa pressed her hands against a small bit of stone that seemed less dense than the rest of the sewer walls. Cassie noticed a small opening in the center of the stone. The light originated from the opening.

"There. This is the way in." Elisa turned to face Cassie. "Here, take this." She reached toward her boot where she had equipped herself with a small dagger. Cassie stared at her hesitantly as the woman unsheathed the dagger and offered it to her.

"The hell's that for?"

In the dim light, Cassie could see Elisa roll her eyes. "There are *guards*, girl. Now," the older woman began, "usually there are only a couple posted in the dungeon – just enough to keep the prisoners quiet or subdue them if they need to."

Cassie stared at the ex-Legionnaire blankly. "I'm sorry, are you expecting me to *kill* one of these guys?"

Elisa sighed heavily. "Of course not. I gave you that so you could defend yourself if you need to. I can handle the guards. Assuming there are only two or three and they are the idiots that often get stuck down here, we should be fine."

Cassie raised an eyebrow. "So...*you're* going to kill them?"

"I'll do what we need to do to get out Andrea of there," Elisa said simply. After Cassie gave her a mildly horrified glance, she clarified. "Stop giving me that look. I'll *disable* them. I'll try not to kill them. Now, do you want to save her or not?"

Securing the dagger in her belt, Cassie answered, "Yeah. Let's get this over with."

"All right," Elisa said. "If I remember correctly, we just need to place our weight here and here." She pointed to the weaker parts of the wall.

Cassie did as she was instructed. "Like this?"

"Exactly. Now, just a small push...there!" Elisa grunted and pushed the stone in, causing the wall to break apart cleanly and revealing a narrow-barred door.

"Whoa! Secret passageway," Cassie exclaimed. "Why would they build this if prisoners could get out?"

"Because prisoners *don't* get out here. These tunnels were built long before The Starving. I assume the builders needed a way in and out of the dungeon while they were building the palace and this was their way of patching it up when they were done. It's also an escape route should the empress ever be in danger."

"Oh," was all Cassie could say to Elisa's explanation. She waited while Elisa fidgeted with the door, opening it a few minutes later.

"Let's go. Quickly," Elisa whispered. She crept silently through the doorway and into the palace dungeon, with Cassie following closely behind her.

* * *

"Three fives and two fours."

The second guard looked up from the dice he had just rolled. He took a swig of his ale and shook his head. "Sorry, friend. Now pay up. Come on, now!"

Andrea heard the distinct jingling of coins being exchanged as the first guard laughed. "Twice in a row – where's my luck tonight?"

"Clear across Damea if you're stuck down here instead of at the ball."

"Ah, let those fools have it," the first guard blustered. "At least no one's telling us we can't have drinks down here."

"Indeed – and it's far more entertaining taking your money anyway."

The enchanter sighed at the guards' conversation and tried to ignore it. No one had come to interrogate her yet, which was good news, but she still dreaded what was to come when someone inevitably did.

Dice were rolled again, clattering onto the rickety wood table a few steps away from her cell.

"Four sixes and one two!" the first guard declared. "Yes!" he yelled victoriously soon after.

"What?! You looked!" the second guard cried indignantly.

"Looked my arse! You owe me, friend!"

The grinding of stone in the distance startled Andrea from her dazed state. She stood up and looked around wildly, wondering with dread if her torturer had finally arrived.

Probably rats again. But then there were footsteps. Heavy footsteps.

The guards were still arguing.

"Hmph! I'll not play with a cheater!"

"Just hand over my mone-wait, you hear that?"

Andrea's chest tightened when she saw the faintest of shadows against the dimly lit walls approaching. The guards slowly stood up and drew their blades.

"Intruders! W-where'd they come from?!" the second guard bellowed.

"Who cares? Get them!"

The enchanter could not hold back a disbelieving gasp when she saw that the shadows belonged to none other than Elisa and Cassie. The ex-Legionnaire moved swiftly across the room, drew a long dagger, and deftly disarmed the first guard with it. His blade skidded across the stone floor. He swung his arm at her but she deftly dodged it and kicked him in the abdomen, knocking him breathless before she punished him with an uppercut to the chin. He crumpled to the ground, unconscious.

"*Intruders!*" the second guard yelled again, loud enough no doubt for those outside the dungeon to hear. Elisa turned on him and attempted to wrestle his weapon from his hands, but the guard was prepared. He moved to the side and sent a strong backhand blow to the ex-Legionnaire, catching her off-guard and sending her stumbling backward. Taking advantage of Elisa's dazed state, the guard advanced on her and drew his blade back, aiming for her chest before preparing to drive it through her.

"Elisa, *look out!*" Andrea screamed. She lifted her hand and was prepared to use magic, despite the dangerously low amount of energy in the room, when she heard another yell.

Cassie had surprised the guard by jumping onto his back and wrapped her hands tightly around his throat, choking him. The guard gasped for air and dropped his sword before clawing frantically at her hands while trying to throw her off.

"Feel free…to do something now!" Cassie shouted at Elisa as she struggled to keep her grip on the guard's neck.

Elisa recovered quickly and grabbed one of the metal tankards on the table. In a blur, she smashed it on the guard's head. The guard grunted and then with a groan, his eyes rolled back in his head and he collapsed. Cassie released her grip and jumped off of him before he hit the ground. Panting, Elisa bent down to find the key to the cell on the unconscious guards while Cassie rushed over to Andrea's cell.

"How…?" was all the enchanter could manage. She fell to her knees.

"Long story. We're getting you out of here," Cassie explained and knelt down so she could see Andrea face to face through the iron bars of the cell. "Are you okay?"

"Found the key!" Elisa announced, holding up the small silver key. She strode over to the cell door.

Andrea pinched the bridge of her nose and winced in pain and fatigue. "I…yes…I'm sorry. I made a mistake – somehow, she knew about this necklace, Elisa." She looked up at the ex-Legionnaire, who had begun to insert the key into the lock, and gestured to the necklace she wore. "She knew."

Elisa's expression rapidly shifted from surprise to guilt.

"My necklace," she gasped. "It…it was a gift from someone whose name I…I will not say. I didn't think Ithmeera would know it." She released the key and met the enchanter's bloodshot eyes. "Forgive me. I had no idea."

"Can we please just get that lock open so we can get the hell out of here?" Cassie snapped and stood up.

"I'm working on it!" Elisa shot back, her earlier softness vanishing. A moment later, there was an audible click and the door swung open.

"Hurry!" Elisa ordered. "We must leave the same way we came in." She turned and headed for the exit, motioning the other two to follow.

Andrea was able to grab the cell door bars to lift herself up, but stopped when she saw a hand extended in her direction.

"Ready to go?" Cassie stood next to her, offering her hand.

The enchanter nodded slowly and grabbed the other girl's hand. After being pulled to her feet and regaining her sense of balance, she turned to her companion. "Thank you. I-I'm sorr–,"

"Yeah, I know. We can talk about it later if you want, but right now I just want to get the hell out of this city," Cassie interrupted. With a slight nod from the enchanter, Cassie took Andrea's arm and began leading her out of the dungeon and back into the sewers, where Elisa met them near the hidden door.

Cassie offered the still-sheathed dagger to her. "Want this back?"

Elisa shook her head. "Keep it. Let's hope Kye was able to make it back to my house without getting himself killed," she said as she resealed the door.

"Kye's out there?" Andrea mumbled, letting herself be practically dragged by Cassie.

"Yeah. He's letting the city guard chase him for a bit while we get you out of here," Cassie explained as they trudged through the filthy sewer water once more. "Oh wow, I think the smell is actually worse now."

"You're just not used to it yet," Elisa said dryly. "It takes awh–,"

"Shh! Listen!" Cassie hissed, yanking Andrea back by her arm. The enchanter yelped in alarm but was quickly silenced when Cassie clamped her hand over her companion's mouth. Elisa stopped and focused her hearing on what was happening directly above them.

"That's right, sir, they were out cold. I could hear the shouts from my post, though," a muffled voice spoke just loud enough for the the ex-Legionnaire to just barely make out.

"And the spy?"

"Gone, sir. We're not yet sure on the why and how, however."

"Find her. Try not to cause alarm, though. The ball is still going on and I don't want Her Majesty to be disturbed with this nonsense," the superior officer ordered.

"Yes, sir. We'll search the entire dungeon and the palace. She couldn't have gotten far without someone seeing her."

"Very well. Keep me updated. I don't want this girl getting away. I doubt she's dangerous, but don't hesitate to kill her if you're left with no choice. I've got too many guards chasing down that bloody enchanter in the city streets, and I don't need another disaster on my hands tonight. Is that clear, soldier?"

"Yes, sir!" the guard replied quickly. The two parted ways, their heavy, armored footsteps growing farther and farther away.

After a minute or so, Elisa nodded. "Let's go." Cassie released Andrea, who let out a sigh of relief, and the three of them began to creep forward in the dark, dank tunnel.

They arrived at a junction where Elisa stopped and looked around. The others waited in silence until their guide had made a decision. "This way," she muttered and turned right.

"I-I didn't mean for anyone to have to risk themselves on my behalf," Andrea stated.

"Oh, stop. We all knew what we were getting into," Cassie said. "We have the damn book and we can get out of here now, right, Elisa?"

"Yes. I made arrangements to leave the city when I first arrived. We'll have to go through the sewers again, but we should be able to escape undetected. Assuming we find your friend, of course," Elisa explained.

"We'll find him," Cassie insisted. She pointed at the ladder several feet in front of them. A sliver of light peeked into the sewers, likely from the streetlamps on the streets above. "I see it."

"Let's get out of here and return to my house then," Elisa said. "Follow me." She pushed forward and gripped the ladder with both hands to make her way back up to the streets of Azgadar, the other two girls following close behind.

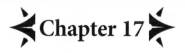

Chapter 17

Wanted

Ithmeera Cadar awoke with a headache the following morning to the sound of knocking on her bedroom door. Wondering what in the world she ate or drank too much of at the ball and who could be vying for her attention at this hour, she climbed out of her luxurious bed slower than usual.

The sun had barely crept over the horizon and the sky still had many traces of dark blue and violet hues in it. The empress could already tell it was going to be a *very* early start to her day.

"Yes?" she called out once she was decent for visitors.

"It is only me, sister," her brother Erik's deep voice resonated from the other side of the double doors. "I need to speak with you."

The empress padded to the doors and opened them both for her brother, General of the Azgadaran Legion. Like his older sister, he had the same dark curls which he kept cut short and tan skin, though his eyes were a pale blue like those of his late father's.

"Good morning," he said, though his voice lacked the confidence it usually had whenever he spoke to her. "I hear you had a visitor last night. Were you ever planning on sharing that with me?"

Ithmeera raised an eyebrow. "I do not have to inform you of everything that goes on in my life. Besides, I figured you would have found out sooner or later from your officers."

"A spy, Ithmeera? Really?" Erik asked, his voice laced with both sarcasm and concern. He stepped into the bedroom. "What did they want? Who sent them?"

The empress held up her hand. "Calm down, Erik. Our 'spy' is no more than a scared, meek little girl."

"You mean 'was'. She's gone."

"What?" Ithmeera shook her head in disbelief. "What do you mean she's *gone*? I had her locked up! Why didn't your men stop her?!"

The general shrugged. "The guards that were posted were knocked out. The rest of my men were busy either keeping watch at *your* party or chasing down the city's most wanted criminal. No one should have been able to escape the dungeon."

Ithmeera put her hands on her hips. "Well then, brother, do you want to tell me how *she* did?"

"Oh, *I don't know*, Ithmeera," Erik retorted. "Who else do we know that knows every inch of the city's sewer systems and can get past a lock in mere seconds?"

The realization slammed into Ithmeera and all she could do was clench her fists angrily. "Elisa…" she whispered. She turned to her brother. "Which criminal?"

"Kye. The blacksmith's son."

"If she really was here, then…" Ithmeera let her sentence trail off and rushed to her desk, where she hastily began rummaging through the drawers.

"What in the world are you doing?" Erik wondered.

"She would have known...she probably would have-but no...no, it can't be!" The empress stopped searching and instead slammed one of the drawers shut as hard as she could with a huff, making the desk shift a bit.

"She took it...that bitch *took it!*"

"Took what?!" Erik practically yelled.

"My diary. It has...I record everything in it, Erik." Ithmeera backed away from the desk and sat down on the bed with a heavy sigh. "She has it now, and she'll know everything about Gurdinfield. Everything."

Erik sat down next to his sister. "Do you really believe she's working for the other side now?"

"They're not the 'other side', Erik," Ithmeera corrected him. "They are our allies, and our arrangement with the Moores was supposed to make it easier to annex them. But now..."

"Fear not," the general said, placing a hand on his sister's arm. "My soldiers are nearly prepared to march on Gurdinfield. Even if she gets the information to whoever it is she's reporting to, it will not make a difference." He met Ithmeera's eyes. "Have faith in me, sister. We *will* take Gurdinfield, and we will do it whether *she* likes it or not."

Ithmeera looked at the floor sadly. "I just...I still wish things had not ended the way they did, Erik."

"She is a traitor, and had it not been for the *loyal* members of the Legion, you would have died," Erik said. He stood up. "I could not live with myself if I ever failed to protect you."

Ithmeera gave a half-smile and waved her brother away. "Oh,

stop it. You're being dramatic. Go…go prepare the Legion. We cannot delay any longer."

The general bowed theatrically. "As you wish, Your Majesty." He turned on his heel and swiftly walked out of the bedroom, leaving the empress alone with her thoughts.

＊ ＊ ＊

It was around mid-morning when Andrea was awoken by a particularly violent shake of the rickety wooden wagon that she, Cassie, and Kye rode in the back of. Elisa helmed the wagon and its horse as the group made their way away from the capital and toward the dry plains of Azgadar – their destination: Gurdinfield.

"Sorry…rocks!" Elisa called back.

The enchanter looked up at the cloudless bright blue skies of Azgadar feeling grateful that she had lived to see another cloudless day like today. Truthfully, she was still exhausted after that long night. They had arrived back at Elisa's house without being spotted by any guards. To their relief, Kye had met them there, having evaded the guards himself. Elisa had packed a few things before leading them back through the sewers and through several tunnels out of the city, where a man Elisa had paid awaited them with the horse and wagon. Now they traveled to Gurdinfield, to the town of Karrea, where they would meet with Elisa's employers who would hopefully help Andrea and Cassie get on the path to Rhyad.

Just thinking about all the things that still needed to happen for them to get to Rhyad made Andrea feel tired all over again.

She knew they were past the point of no return – Meredith was no doubt still looking for them, as was most likely the entire Azgadaran Legion. The enchanter had gone from being a mere apprentice to one of the most wanted criminals in Damea.

This is what I get for wanting to save magic and help people.

"Talking to yourself again?"

Andrea looked up when Cassie spoke. The other girl looked exhausted as well, though it seemed she had not lost her usual confident and sarcastic streak. "I was thinking."

"Careful, now. Look where that's gotten us," Cassie joked.

The enchanter narrowed her eyes at her companion. "Very funny. I was thinking about where we started and where we are now."

"Other than being hunted by your crazy girlfriend and an even crazier empress lady and on our way to meet some more people who – let's be honest – are probably also crazy, what else is going on?" Cassie said casually and leaned back against the canvas packs Elisa had made them carry from her house in Azgadar.

Andrea exhaled in frustration. "As I've said several times now, we were *not* involved that way. She was my mentor! If anything, she was more of an older sibling."

"Aw, you ruin everything. See, now it's gross," Cassie whined.

"I...I haven't implied we were anything other than platonic!" the enchanter protested. "Y-you're the one making it...weird."

"Sorry, say again? You were romantically involved with your former mentor?" Kye spoke up for the first time in hours, surprising them both.

Andrea threw up her hands. "*No!* And I'll ask you to stop bringing that up!" she snapped at Cassie, who laughed lightly.

"What's so funny?" the enchanter demanded.

Cassie put her hands up. "Was waiting to see when you'd finally wake the hell up. It was getting really dull with you moping and being all depressed ever since we got you out of that dungeon."

Andrea sighed heavily and rubbed her eyes. "I...I don't even know what to say to that."

"Well? Do you feel any better? Come on, you know you do," Cassie pressed. Kye laughed softly from the other side of the wagon.

Looking at both of her companions and then at the wagon floor, Andrea finally gave a slight nod. "Yes...I suppose I do feel a little better. But no more...*teasing* me about my relationship with Meredith!" she warned.

Cassie grinned. "See? There *was* a relationship!" she exclaimed and Kye laughed loudly.

Elisa said nothing but could not hold back a smile.

Andrea blinked. "I give up," she said and leaned back, hoping the conversation topic would change to something else...anything really.

✷ ✷ ✷

The usual silence enveloped her mind for a moment before she felt the walls blocking her from seeing her goal break down.

She waited. Hours seemed to pass, though it was probably only minutes until a single light stood out amongst the others. It was faint but it was there.

She focused on the orb, hoping that its location would be made apparent soon. The light flickered – perhaps she was getting tired? No, she needed to stay focused. There was no guarantee she would be able to find them again if she let herself lose track now.

Relaxing, she spotted a small cluster of lights not too far from where she had spotted her target. Having a good idea what – and more importantly, where – she was looking at, she began to gently pull her mind away from the tangle of lights.

Meredith opened her eyes and gently rubbed her aching temples. Tracking her apprentice's projection was growing more difficult by the day. The enchanter was not certain if the difficulties were due to Cassie being near Andrea or something else, but she did know that she needed to follow quickly if she was to have any hope of catching them.

Now Meredith sat outside her tent at a campsite not too far outside the walls of Azgadar. Andrea's projection could not tell her much, but she did know that her apprentice and their visitor had left the city and were heading east – toward her homeland of Gurdinfield.

But what was in Gurdinfield? Perhaps they had only stopped in the capital for supplies? It still made no sense that Andrea would stop in the most hostile place in Damea for enchanters. Unless...

Unless she knew that Meredith would not follow her into the city. Quite risky, the enchanter concluded, but also admirable if true. This still did not answer the question of why Andrea was going toward Gurdinfield, but it did give Meredith a new destination. *Something more accurate is needed.*

This was taking too long. Normally, Meredith would be cautious before attempting any magic outside of the Black Forest, especially of this magnitude, but these were not normal times. She reached into her bag and selected a vial that contained the last of the magic she had obtained from Cassie. She held the vial up to study it.

"Two weaker ones, perhaps," she muttered. Focusing inward, she channeled the bit of magic and began working on creating two final constructs. Once the crystal beasts were complete, she examined them. They stood slightly shorter than her original constructs and had a light grey tint to their build. While certainly weaker than her previous creations, they would still be faster than she would at reaching her apprentice.

The enchanter placed a hand on each of them to transfer her knowledge of Andrea's whereabouts to them. "Find her," she ordered. "Do something that would prompt a magical response from her. Now go!" The hulking creatures slowly turned and took off at a steadily increasing speed to the east, toward Gurdinfield.

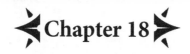

Chapter 18

The Guardians

Karrea, Gurdinfield

Six-year-old Amara laughed joyously as she ran from her friends, her tangled golden hair littered with crumbles of dead leaves and small twigs from the nearby woods. The other four children chased her at full speed, not caring that they had nearly knocked one of the village's fishermen into the water as they raced across the docks of the quiet town of Karrea. A few days' travel from the capital city, Karrea was primarily a fishing town that boasted a population of only a hundred people or so. Bordering the Rhyad River, Karrea also served as the first major trade hub to travelers coming from Azgadar to the Southlands of Gurdinfield, as the river represented the border between Gurdinfield and the empire.

The old fisherman yelped in surprise and barely managed to keep from tumbling into the water as the children ran past him, squealing and yelling at each other. He shook his head in faux dismay – the children did not bother him nearly as much as the adults usually did. He'd been fishing and selling his catches for decades and had encountered the best and worst of what Damea's tradesmen had to offer.

He noted the partly cloudy sky. It was just after midday, and many of the villagers had finished their lunches and were returning to work. It would most likely rain tonight if those clouds became something more over the next few hours.

He considered taking a break to get some food himself when he heard the distant but distinct galloping of horses. Removing his fishing pole from the water, he looked away from the river and toward the main path. If he squinted, he could just barely make out the black and yellow saddlecloths the mounts of the Moore militia wore on the horses that sped toward the village.

Knowing exactly why they had come, the fisherman began swiftly walking toward the town center, hoping to find the mayor and get as many of the villagers, especially the children, indoors as soon as possible.

* * *

"Good day, Mayor. I trust you and your people are well this fine afternoon?" The commanding officer of the militiamen was a tall, fair-skinned man with short dark hair that he hid beneath his leather helmet. Unlike the other soldiers in his company, he sported a short beard that allowed him to pass for older than he really was. He eyed the nervous mayor of Karrea, a hefty, balding man in his fifties and a carpenter by trade.

"Y-yes, sir," the mayor stammered. "I...I hope the journey here was not too rough."

The officer shrugged. "The plains of Gurdinfield are hardly 'rough', Mayor. *Boring* is what I'd call it." A few of the other soldiers chuckled.

"Of...of course." The mayor eyed the emblem of the Moore house branded into the hard leather armor the officer wore. The fierce bird of prey was recognized across Gurdinfield as the mark of the Moores. One of the two factions that had fought for control of Gurdinfield over the past twenty years, the Moore militia was known for being fierce, disciplined, and unmerciful. They had claimed stake over the southern half of the region while their enemy, the Harringtons, had claimed the north. Both demanded taxes of their subjects in the hope that they could build up their armies enough to defeat the other side once and for all and claim the City of Towers as their own.

"I trust this won't take long, Mayor. We've other destinations in our itinerary before we return to my superiors, so if you don't mind?" the officer pressed.

The mayor swallowed and nodded before summoning one of the villagers, who swiftly handed him a large sack of coins.

"Here you are, sir," the mayor said as he reached up and handed the officer the sack. Upon grabbing it, the officer weighed the sack in his hand momentarily before opening it. He studied its contents while a tense silence descended on the town.

"S-sir–," the mayor piped up.

"This is not what is due," the officer interrupted loudly. He looked down at the man practically trembling before him. "Where is the rest of the payment?"

The mayor shakily clasped his hands together. "Sir, that is all we could come up with this month. Trade's been rather slow what with the m-magic problems in Azgadar and–,"

"*Do not* blame the empire for what is *your* failure, Mayor," the officer spat. The frightened mayor stumbled backwards and some of the villagers who had been watching from their doorsteps began nudging their curious children into their homes.

"I-I'm sorry!" the mayor cried. "We can get you the rest of it next month!"

The officer held up his hand as he glared at the townspeople. "This is the third month in a row that you have not been able to make your obligation to Lord Moore. Unfortunately, without proper compensation, he cannot protect you from our enemies," he announced. "We move on, but understand that Karrea is no longer under the protection of Lord Moore and thus you will not be spared from the inevitable Harringtons attacks."

The village held its breath for what felt like an eternity to the poor mayor. The soldiers would move on and Karrea would be safe for the moment. They could always hire mercenaries and–

"Bloody bird scum!" a voice yelled out. A child started crying. A few of the villagers began murmuring in fear.

The officer narrowed his eyes at the town and then at the mayor. "I see your people cannot be civil even when I grant mercy, Mayor. Perhaps a lesson in common courtesy is required?"

"No!" the mayor cried. "Please, don–," but was cut off when the officer used the back of his armor-clad arm to knock the helpless man to the dirt.

"Idiot," the officer muttered while glaring at the whimpering man on the ground. He turned to his soldiers. "Lock them up and burn the town. They don't need their homes or their lives if they aren't willing to pay to protect them." A few of the soldiers looked surprised, but none questioned the officer's order. Within seconds, torches had been lit. Despite the screams and wails of the villagers, the soldiers began carrying out their commander's order.

* * *

Diana Telman held deathly still while kneeling in the cover of the thick forest brush as she waited for the perfect moment to release the arrow nocked in her bow, her slightly dirty but tanned face and dark eyes hidden under the shadow of her dark green hood. The deer was only several meters away and while it appeared distracted by the grass it nibbled on, Diana did not want to make any sudden movements that might startle the animal. After steadying her aim, she breathed deeply and prepared to release.

"*Diana?!*" Her name rang out amongst the trees, causing a flock of birds to flee the high branches. Diana exhaled heavily and cringed as the deer's head shot up from the grass it had been munching on before bolting off into the forest.

"Damn it," she muttered and gently released the tension in her bow. She stood up and returned the arrow to its quiver before slinging the bow over her shoulder.

"Diana!" the same voice rang out again. She sighed and removed her hood, allowing her long, dark hair to fall freely past her shoulders. *Alexander just couldn't wait for me to finish hunting. Typical.*

She began trudging back toward the site where Alexander and the others had set up camp. It was not too far from the closest major town, Karrea, but a few of their sentries had spotted Moore's soldiers riding in the area and had advised Alexander Telman, the group's leader and Diana's father, to stay in hiding for a few days until they could better assess the soldiers' route. Dubbed "The Guardians" after the late king's royal guards, Alexander and his militia had been operating across Gurdinfield for the past two decades, most of which had been spent ambushing both Moore and Harrington soldiers and stealing money and supplies from them before returning most of the money to towns and villages across the region and keeping the supplies to support their own operations.

As Diana strolled through the camp, which was littered with crates of supplies, horses, campfires, and several of Alexander's fighters either resting in their tents or preparing for their next mission, she could not help but feel a sense of pride at what they had accomplished so far. Though it had been several years since their operation in Gurdinfield had begun, Diana believed that if they kept the pressure on the Harringtons and the Moores, both sides would not be able to continue their civil war. A peace treaty could be signed and perhaps a new, stable government in Gurdinfield could be formed. "There you are!" Alexander exclaimed as his daughter approached his tent. A tall, stern man in his mid-forties with short, greying hair and light brown eyes, Alexander had years of fighting experience under his belt from both his time in the royal military back when the Taylors were still in power as well as the time spent training and leading his own fighters against the warring houses. He even served as a personal guard to King Caleb for several years before the royal family's untimely demise.

"Yes," Diana said tersely. She dropped her bow and quiver on the ground.

"We've been looking for you," Alexander stated.

"Could it have waited until *after* I was done with my hunt?" Diana replied haughtily. But Alexander's serious expression did not waver.

"The sentries just reported back. The Moores went through Karrea. We're not sure what happened yet but the town has been burned to the ground. We're heading out there now to see if there are any survivors," he explained.

All thoughts of her ruined hunt left Diana's mind as she registered the news. Karrea had been one of their routine stops as they knew the Moores passed through there often to collect tax money from the villagers. Diana had been there countless times over the years and knew many of the residents personally. She could not fathom an entire town being snuffed out or the Moores escalating to this level of brutality...until now.

"I-I," she stammered for a moment before regaining her composure. "What do you need me to do?"

"The sentries picked up the trail Moore's soldiers took when they left. I want you to take Jacob and two of the others with you. See if you can find out where they're headed next," Alexander instructed. A shadow crossed his features as he maintained eye contact with Diana. "Do *not* engage them. I don't know how many there are and there could be more on their way now. We don't need to risk lives unnecessarily until we know more."

"Yes, sir," she answered with a short nod. Although she was

Alexander's daughter, Diana had no issue with addressing him in the same manner that the rest of the fighters did. For the past several years she had trained and fought alongside the rest of the men and women who served under Alexander and in that time, their leader had never shown any signs of nepotism toward her, which Diana was grateful for. In fact, she was completely comfortable calling him by his first name as the others did, in order to maintain equality with the rest of the Guardians.

After being dismissed, she made her way to the other side of the camp to find Jacob, captain of the Guardians. Jacob had been with the Guardians for nearly fifteen years. Alexander had saved him from the brink of death when his family's trading caravan was ambushed by bandits taking advantage of the chaos in the war-torn region. Now in his early thirties, Jacob was an imposing figure standing taller than most of the other Guardians. His skills as a swordsman were unrivaled amongst his peers, and the other Guardians respected him as a leader and mentor. Diana had always been fond of him growing up, but for reasons unknown to her, Alexander rarely sent them on missions together. Figuring her skills were better used for reconnaissance than front-line fighting, she never considered this an issue. But the curiosity always lingered.

"Thought I might find you here," she announced as she approached one of the larger campfires in the site. Jacob sat on a crate next to the fire, inspecting and cleaning his battle gear for his next assignment. He looked up at Diana, though not by much due to her shorter stature and his great height. The sudden movement caused his shaggy blond hair to fall over his green eyes. "Afternoon, Diana. What is it?"

"Alexander sent me to find you. Karrea's been burned to the

ground," she explained.

Jacob's concern gave way to anger as he stood up quickly. "Burned? What-the Moores?"

Diana nodded.

"So they've moved from taking people's coin purses to taking their lives. Brilliant," he continued bitterly and began to equip his weapons, a long sword and two hunting knives. "Are we to head there then? It's not far."

"No," Diana corrected. "He wants us to scout out the path the Moores took and find out where they're headed next."

Jacob looked at her doubtfully and stroked his short beard. "Why? We should go to Karrea and see if we can help," he declared stubbornly.

"Alexander's orders. If the Moores have a new objective and if that objective is burning villages, then we need to stop them before they do it to another town," Diana pressed.

Jacob shook his head in dismay. "It makes no sense. Why would they burn towns? It's their source of income for their damn war!"

"That's what we're to find out, I think," Diana explained. "We're to take two of the others with us."

Jacob nodded. "As you say. I'll grab Roe and Victor and we can be on our way." He began to walk away but stopped when Diana called his attention again.

"Jacob, we're under specific orders not to engage them even if we do find them."

He sighed. "Well," he said slowly, "let's hope we don't end up in a position where we'd have to defend ourselves."

"You mean 'let's not be seen at all;'" Diana said sternly.

Jacob snorted. "Don't worry. I'll follow orders, but I won't cry over a few dead bird scum."

Diana gave a small chuckle. "I need to grab my weapons. Meet you at my tent. Bring the others and we will go." After they parted ways, she headed back to her tent to prepare for their mission, worried about what the Moores' next move would be. If they were not hesitant to burn an entire village to the ground, what sort of methods would they use to terrorize the people of Gurdinfield with next?

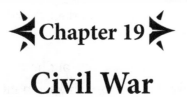Chapter 19

Civil War

"Diana, if you prefer, we can finish searching here if you want to report back to Alexander."

"I'm fine, Victor. We know they're nearby so hopefully we'll find them soon," Diana said as she and her companions crept quietly through the woods while attempting to avoid crushing the dead leaves and twigs that covered the forest floor.

Victor, a lean, long-haired man in his mid-twenties and the Guardian fighter who had spoken up, nodded. "Of course, Diana. Looking forward to teaching these bastards a lesson at some point."

"I am too," Diana agreed. "But Alexander ordered us to find out where they were going first. We'll just have to save the rest for another time."

Victor nodded again as an awkward silence passed over them. "Right," he finally spoke, his demeanor far less confident than it had been moments earlier. "Back to business, then?"

The other Guardian, a burly, bald man named Roe, nodded in agreement. "All right, then. You're the one stopping us for all this chit-chat so whenever you're ready we can go, yes?" he asked, giving the others a crooked smile, revealing a few gaps where teeth had been knocked out during past skirmishes.

Victor rolled his eyes. "Shut it. Was just stating what I thought. Shall we, then?" he muttered and trudged ahead. Roe followed, leaving Jacob and Diana staring at one another.

"They seem tense," Diana remarked. "Do they really need to go so far ahead?"

Jacob shrugged. "It's dangerous out here. Who knows what we'll encounter what with those bird scum murderers walking about?"

They began to walk, with Diana speaking up again. "We will be fine," she said with a smile. "You worry too much."

Jacob gave a short laugh, his serious demeanor vanishing. "Better to be cautious than dead I suppose. Not that–,"

"Wait." Diana held up her hand and was silent. Up ahead, Victor and Roe had also gone quiet. Faint laughter and voices could be heard in the distance. Diana exchanged alert glances with her fellow Guardians.

"Forward," she mouthed, leading them into a thicket of trees and brush so as to avoid being detected. The voices sounded closer and Diana was sure that they had found Moore's soldiers. A few steps forward revealed that the Guardians were positioned on a small hill that gave them a decent vantage point over the clearing that Moore's soldiers had set up camp in. A fallen, rotting log served as a good hiding spot for the Guardians, at least until Diana had figured out the next step. She inspected the site below them. The soldiers were seated around a small campfire, but Diana saw no sign of their commander anywhere.

One of the soldiers reached into his pack, but another stayed his hand. "We should wait for the captain before eating. You know how he gets."

The other soldier sighed before withdrawing his hand from the pack. "You're probably right. Considering how he's been lately, I wouldn't be surprised if he had us thrown in a dungeon for eating before he gets back."

"And how exactly have I been lately, soldier?" The Moore officer strode into the clearing, flanked by two more soldiers. A smug grin crossed his features before he narrowed his eyes at the soldier who had spoken ill of him.

The soldier scrambled to his feet, stammering, "I-I apologize, s-sir. I was only–,"

"Oh, save it," the officer dismissed his apology with a wave as the rest of the soldiers stood at attention. He looked around at them. "I tire of these woods and its dreary towns. We ride north in the morning. Be ready to go at sunrise. Understood?"

"Yes, sir!" the soldiers replied in unison.

"Did you already search the area?" the officer demanded.

"Y-yes, sir!" the officer who had spoken out of line earlier managed. "All clear."

"Then Harrington is having his sorry excuses for soldiers remain north as well, no doubt," the officer concluded.

"What of the rebel Guardians, sir?" another soldier asked.

The officer scoffed. "*Guardians.* The name in itself is an insult. Telman's arrogance is unsurpassed, it seems."

The soldiers exchanged nervous glances before the one who had asked spoke up again. "S-sir?"

"What?" the officer snapped. When he realized his subordinates were waiting for an answer, he threw up his hands in frustration. "If you say we are clear then we had better be clear! Set up a watch. I won't have anyone, Harrington or Guardian, sneaking up on us tonight."

"Yes, sir!" the soldier replied quickly.

Behind the log, Jacob turned to Diana. "I don't suppose you'd want to take care of them now, do you?" he whispered.

The leading Guardian shook her head. "We should report back to Alexander and–," she went silent when she heard a whimper, faint but still distinguishable from the other sounds of the forest around them.

"Over there," Roe mouthed, pointing at the thick brush near a tree behind him. Diana nodded at the man, who crept closer to the brush and slowly peeled back the low branches that concealed the source of the whimpering.

There, curled up and trembling in a pile of dead leaves, was a young girl. Her blonde hair was littered with twigs and her tear-stained face was caked with dirt. She looked up bleakly at Roe, who stepped back and turned to Diana for further instruction.

Diana hesitated. She looked at the girl and then back at the Moore soldiers below them.

"Diana!" Jacob hissed, his hand hovering over the hilt of the great sword strapped to his back. "We're out of time!"

Biting her lower lip, the commanding Guardian ran her hand nervously through her hair.

The Moore officer tilted his head slightly before looking up. "What was that?" His gaze shifted in the direction of the fallen log where the Guardians hid.

One of the soldiers looked at his commander curiously.

"What was what, sir?"

The officer rolled his eyes. "That sound." He closed his eyes for a moment and inhaled deeply before drawing his sword. "We are being watched."

Diana exhaled and turned to her companions. "Grab the girl. We're leaving," she whispered.

Jacob did not hesitate. He swiftly walked over to where Roe stood and scooped up the girl, who appeared to be in a state of shock and had been surprisingly quiet the entire time. After nodding to Diana, he began heading back in the direction of camp, the other Guardians following close behind.

Diana cautiously glanced back at the Moore soldiers before she too left her post behind the log and made her way back to camp.

* * *

"You are certain they did not see you?"

"Yes, sir," Diana said breathlessly, shadows cast by the campfires dancing across her face. She wrapped her cloak tighter around her to keep out the evening chill. "Though I think by the time we found the girl they might have been alerted to our presence."

Alexander frowned, looking older than he really was. "I see. And the girl? Who is she?"

Diana fiddled with her hands nervously. She knew Alexander was disappointed that she had allowed her group to be detected.

"She is sleeping now. I gave her a meal and clean clothes. She says her name is Amara, sir. Her parents have…had a home in Karrea. Her father is the village healer."

The leader of the Guardians was solemn as a grim expression replaced his frown. "You mean he *was*. Diana, we found no survivors in what was left of Karrea. Many of the villagers were forced into their own homes and the doors barred from the outside before the town was burned."

The younger Telman held back a gasp as she looked at her father in horror. Some of the other Guardians who sat around a nearby campfire looked over at the two. "That's…the poor girl! But…are you certain? You found no survivors?" she pressed.

"If there are any, they have not returned to the town and are probably on their way to the next closest village," Alexander explained. He placed a hand on his daughter's shoulder. "There's nothing we can do to help them now except to gather our strength and track down the people that committed this crime."

"North," Diana breathed. She swallowed and maintained her composure. "They're going north. Most likely to Fimen's Hope before they go back to their stronghold."

Alexander smiled faintly. "Well done. We'll leave at dawn."

"What of Amara, sir? The girl is terrified and keeps asking where her parents are."

"She may stay," the older man said, his smile remaining. "I'm sure we can find something to keep her busy until we reach the next village. After that…well, we will sort it out then. I need you ready to go at first light tomorrow."

"Yes, sir," Diana replied with a short nod. She watched for a few seconds as her father walked away before turning and leaving the camp to find Jacob. She already knew where he had gone.

* * *

The faint glow from the campfires barely lit the forest edge where Jacob walked. A cool autumn breeze picked up speed, rustling the drying leaves that barely clung to the branches of the trees around him. To Jacob, Gurdinfield had some of the most peaceful and beautiful forests in Damea. They were full of life and still ripe with magic unlike many of the forests across the land, except perhaps the Black Forest. Folks these days rarely ventured there, however, in fear that because there was very little in the way of paths or roads, they would be forever lost to the maze of twisted trees.

He breathed deeply, enjoying the night air and the whispers of the forest wildlife. Though he had grown up in a village not unlike Karrea, his years as a Guardian had warmed him up to a life in the woods. As dangerous as it could be, especially lately, there was no where he would rather be.

"You're here." Diana Telman's voice, though less confident than she had sounded mere hours earlier, pierced the forest sounds, silencing the area around them.

Jacob gave a low nod. "Yes, as are you." Even in the low light he could see his commanding officer side-eye him. Her expression quickly gave way to one of amusement, however.

"We're going to hold on to the girl for a while. Hopefully her family…hopefully they somehow made it out of Karrea," she said, her gaze fixed upon the ground.

Jacob stepped forward to close the distance between him and Diana. He gently took her hands in his. "Why don't we talk about something else for now?"

Slowly, Diana looked up at Jacob, who easily towered over her. He leaned down and kissed her softly. She returned the kiss eagerly and the two held each other for a moment before she slowly pulled away. "I apologize," she said quietly. "It's been a long day."

"True, but you are not the only one who should be carrying the burdens of today," he argued. "You have Alexander, you have me, you have our friends–,"

"*Do* I have you, Jacob? Is that really what you mean?" Diana asked.

Jacob met her eyes for a moment before pulling away and releasing her hands. "You know what I mean, Diana."

"And you know what I want."

Jacob sighed heavily. "You know he cannot find out about us."

"Why?" Diana demanded. "Because he's my father? Or because he's your leader?"

"I…Diana, it's not that simple–,"

Diana turned her back to him. "What was it you told me back in the Southland Woods?"

"Diana…"

She spun around to face him, her tone angrier this time. "What *was* it, Jacob?"

The Guardian captain sighed. "I *do* love you. But–,"

"'But what?" Diana snapped. "Jacob, you seemed so sure six months ago. You were practically ready to tell Alexander right then and there!"

"Our work together, though…if something were to happen–,"

"You think I would do that to you? Make you leave the Guardians if we had a falling out? Do you think I am so petty, Jacob?" she asked, her voice wavering slightly.

"Of course not!" Jacob exclaimed, throwing up his hands. "Diana, it's not as simple as you make it sound. We are in the middle of a civil war right now."

"We've been in a civil war for over twenty years, Jacob – that hasn't changed," Diana said sharply.

"It's not just that! It's…it's difficult to explain." He began pacing. "We are *so close* to ending Moore and that bastard's reign of terror in the Southlands. The last thing I want is for Alexander to be worrying about who you are courting during what is probably going to be the most critical point in our mission yet!"

Silence descended upon them for what felt like an eternity to Jacob before he heard Diana speak up again.

"I…understand. You're…you're probably right – damn you," she said with a harsh laugh.

Jacob looked at her apologetically and reached for her hand, but she pulled away. "I'm sorry," he said meekly.

"No, it's all right. As I said, I understand. We have a job to do, and we cannot let anything get in the way of it. Even...even this," Diana answered, her voice trailing off at the end. "I should get back." She sniffed and regained her composure quickly. "We leave at dawn and ride to Fimen's Hope. Alexander's orders." With that she started to head back to camp.

"Diana," Jacob called after her. When she stopped to face him, he continued. "I meant what I said. Back in the Southland Woods. Every word."

The younger Telman inhaled sharply before turning around and continuing toward the camp, leaving Jacob alone again, though he quietly admitted to himself that the forest was no longer as comforting as it had been with Diana beside him.

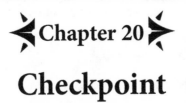

Chapter 20

Checkpoint

"...so we go south here, see? It will make more sense once we're actually moving again."

"Sure, if by 'sense' you mean that it makes absolutely *no* sense. It's another what, three months until we get to civilization?"

Andrea folded the map she was holding and closed her eyes while pinching the bridge of her nose. "It's just three *days*, Cassie. I've traveled this route before. Trust me, I think I know how to read a map of Damea."

Cassie leaned back against the large boulder behind her. "Ugh, I'm tired of traveling. I'm tired of walking...and riding. And anything else that involves me moving somehow," she pouted.

"What is it with you two? You're either talking incessantly or complaining about everything." Elisa returned to the small campsite and dumped a small pile of wood she had collected near the fire. Only a few steps away, Kye snickered in between bites of the dry food rations Elisa had packed nearly two weeks earlier when they left Azgadar. A cool, cloudy night had fallen, and the four of them were now situated around a small fire near two small tents. During their journey to Azgadar's neighboring region, the war-torn kingdom of Gurdinfield, Andrea and Cassie had shared one tent and Kye and Elisa had shared the other. They had not used the tents every night, but with heavy rainclouds hovering above them all day, Elisa had recommended they set up shelter just in case. A small tin teakettle hung above the fire.

Cassie shot Kye a dirty look. "Laugh it up, Convict Boy. Maybe it won't be so funny when I knock your tent over with you in it tonight."

"Cassie…" Andrea warned as the young man's dark eyes went wide with fear.

But Cassie simply shrugged as she began to eat her dinner as well. "What? Then he'll have something to complain about, too!"

"You still haven't told us anything about this employer of yours, Elisa," Andrea pointed out, ignoring Cassie.

Elisa began placing some of the newly acquired wood on the fire. "His name is Alexander Telman. He's a former Guardian of the King, and now he leads a group with the same name. We're to meet them near the town of Karrea."

"Wait, what's a Guardian?" Cassie asked.

"They are-they *were* the personal guards of King Caleb before he and the rest of the royal family were assassinated over twenty years ago," Andrea explained quickly as Elisa looked at Cassie oddly.

"And you work for him now?" Cassie continued, looking back at Elisa.

The ex-Legionnaire shrugged. "We have an agreement. I give them information and they pay me for it."

Kye raised his eyebrows in surprise. "Y-you're giving Gurdinfield information about the empire? Isn't...isn't that treason?"

"Is it?" Elisa challenged. "Treason would imply that I'm a citizen of the empire."

"Well, aren't you?" Cassie asked.

Elisa's green eyes flashed angrily. "No," she muttered. She stood up quickly, startling the other three. "I'm going to sleep. Try not to make a lot of noise."

After the ex-Legionnaire left, the remaining three exchanged awkward glances.

"Something I said?" Cassie suggested with a shrug.

"I think you might have offended her," Kye offered helpfully.

"It's obvious she doesn't like talking about her past, and it's none of our business, either," Andrea said.

"I did not ask her about her past!" Kye protested.

"Yeah, you were just the genius who brought up the whole 'treason' thing," Cassie pointed out. "And while we're on the subject, *you* haven't exactly been forthcoming about yours."

"Mine? What do you mean?"

"Your past. What's your deal, anyway?" she demanded.

"My...deal?" Kye stammered.

"Yeah," Cassie affirmed. "What did you do? You clearly can't be *that* terrible, or you wouldn't have saved me from those thugs in the city."

"Nor would you have risked your life to help rescue me," Andrea added quietly.

Kye glanced hesitantly at the enchanter and then at Cassie. "My family owned the smithy in the capital. I was to take over when I was old enough, but…there was…something happened. It wasn't my fault but I'm not…I'm not very good at controlling my powers." He sighed as his gaze turned to the fire. "Every time I try to help, things go wrong."

"How do you mean?" Andrea asked, leaning forward in interest. When Kye looked back at the enchanter apprehensively, she pushed again, her voice much softer this time. "Kye, when I was eight years old, I set a field of crops on my family's farm on fire. It was an accident, but I was terrified just the same."

"And your parents…what did they do?" the young man asked slowly.

The enchanter sat back again. "They were scared – understandably, of course. Enchanters aren't exactly common in Ata."

"Truthfully, I don't think I would have made a very good blacksmith, anyway," Kye replied with a shy smile and shrugged. "Was always better at music."

"You sing?" Cassie asked.

Kye nodded and turned to Cassie. "A bit, but the lute is what I really enjoy. I never asked, but are you an enchanter as well?"

Cassie smirked and shook her head. "No. Not even close."

"Then…why are you two traveling together?" he asked curiously.

The two girls exchanged glances. "Uh…" Cassie began carefully. "Well, I need to…to get to Rhyad. And um…Andrea knows the way, so she's helping me get there."

"Rhyad? There's nothing there, though!" Kye declared. A clap of thunder sounded in the distance.

Andrea clasped her hands together. "Right, well, what Cassie means is that she needs to get to a small village near the border of Rhyad and Gurdinfield. It's not really on the map, but I remember Mered-my mentor talking about it from when she visited it during her travels."

Kye nodded, though Andrea could not tell if he believed her. Still, he didn't press the topic further. "Well, it's late. I suppose I should also get some sleep."

Cassie looked up at the sky. "I think it's going to rain soon, anyway."

"We'll put out the fire," Andrea assured Kye. The two girls watched as the younger enchanter walked over to the tent he shared with Elisa before ducking into it.

"Nosy little guy, isn't he?" Cassie joked.

Andrea shrugged. "He seeks answers in a very confusing time – same as the rest of us."

Cassie grinned. "Is that your excuse for asking me a ton of questions all the time?"

The enchanter felt her face grow hot. "That's not-it's not the same thing."

"Isn't it, though?"

"No," Andrea retorted. A thought crossed her mind. "As long as we're here, Cassie, do you...you do mind if I inspect the uh...the map again? I just want to make sure we are on the right course." She expected Cassie to decline – or worse, to get upset and bring up the terrible things Meredith had done. But

Cassie simply nodded and held out her arm. "Go ahead," she said in a tone that sounded almost casual to the enchanter.

Andrea nodded. "Thank you," she said gratefully and gently wrapped her hand around Cassie's wrist. The same surge of power that Andrea had experienced during their escape in the Black Forest came at the enchanter in waves, but she tried to ignore it and pushed further into the magic that emanated from her companion.

Finally, she saw it. The same map that she had seen at Meredith's mansion only weeks earlier. The beacon of energy in Rhyad shone just as brightly as it had before, if not brighter. She saw a bright area in the very region they were in, and supposed it would not be an irrational theory that this particular bright spot was Cassie. Having seen all that she needed to see, Andrea began distancing herself slowly from Cassie's energy well. The map faded and disappeared, and within seconds she was back at the campsite and staring – rather awkwardly – straight into Cassie's blue eyes.

"Right so...we should probably get some sleep, too," Cassie said, rubbing the back of her neck. She stood up. "You got the fire?"

Andrea nodded. Cassie had taken no more than two steps when the enchanter called out to her again. "Actually," Andrea started, "there's something I wanted to ask you."

"Okay, what?" Cassie asked.

"What did you do? Where you're from, I mean," Andrea continued. Cassie had remained standing, her height advantage making the enchanter a bit nervous. She was not sure if it was even appropriate to ask about this sort of thing.

But the other girl simply raised an eyebrow and looked down at the enchanter suspiciously. "Why does it matter?" she demanded quietly.

Andrea felt a lump in her throat as she braced herself for another argument with her companion. True, Cassie had been… softer toward the enchanter since the incident in Azgadar, but that had not stopped her from making her usual offhand, crude, and often inappropriate remarks during their journey to Gurdinfield. The girl had a short temper, and was still not completely trustful of any of her traveling companions, or so it seemed to Andrea. "I-it doesn't matter. I was only curious. It seems you know a great deal about me and well, I don't really know anything about you," she pointed out.

Cassie appeared to be in deep thought for a moment before finally sighing and retaking her seat next to the enchanter. She removed the band she used to fasten her hair back, letting her blondish-brown hair fall to her shoulders. "Thing was giving me a headache," she explained. "Okay, so you have questions. Go ahead, then." She reached for the teakettle and refilled her tin cup before offering some to Andrea, who nodded and held out her own cup to be refilled.

"Really?" the enchanter asked incredulously.

Cassie rolled her eyes. "No, I'm lying. Yes, really."

Another clap of thunder sounded, this time much closer.

"That doesn't sound promising," Cassie commented as she glanced up at the dark, clouded sky.

But Andrea didn't seem too worried about the imminent rain. "Where are you from?"

"Not here," Cassie answered promptly before taking a cautious sip of her hot tea. "I live in a city. A big...city. It's different from anything I've seen here, that's for sure."

"How so?"

"Well, um..." Cassie didn't seem certain about how to describe it to the enchanter. "There are a lot of buildings – really tall buildings." She made sweeping motions with her hands to demonstrate. "They're um...made of metal. I live in one of them, actually. It's a little expensive, but the view is great." A small, genuine smile crept onto her face that she quickly but unsuccessfully tried to hide.

Andrea took this as a positive sign to push for more information. "So," she said, "what do you do? As a trade."

"Ah," Cassie said. "That's a long and complex story that I'm not sure we have time for right now."

"Oh," Andrea tried not to show her disappointment. "Really?"

"No, I'm kidding." Cassie grinned, earning her an eye roll from the enchanter. "I have a job. It's just boring. It pays the bills, and that's all that there is to say about that, honestly." She took another sip of her tea. "It's uh...not quite as exciting as say, being an *enchanter* and bringing people back from comas or throwing fireballs at magical walking rock monsters."

Andrea smiled. "I see you're coming around to the idea of magic."

Cassie side-eyed the enchanter. "None of that stuff exists where I'm from, so you'll understand if I'm a little skeptical."

Although Andrea nodded in understanding, she still had a

difficult time processing the idea that Cassie was actually from another land – no, *world* entirely. A world without magic. A flurry of questions sprang up in her mind. How old was this world? What was its name? Were there other worlds? How did people survive without magic without their nations going into crisis? Were there wars? Had Cassie ever seen war? What of her family? Her parents? Surely, they would have noticed she was missing by now. The enchanter was hit with a wave of guilt. She had, along with Meredith, taken this girl away from her home, her family, without permission and with no way to get her home. *And now you want her to help you when you have nothing to offer her in return.*

"Hey," Cassie's voice broke through Andrea's thoughts. "Let me guess – you have a million more questions." She placed a hand on Andrea's shoulder, surprising the enchanter and leaving her at a loss for words. "Come on," Cassie said. "How about instead of having another long, boring conversation with yourself, you get to ask me one last question?"

"I…all right." Andrea weighed her options carefully. Although a countless number of questions ran through her mind, she wanted to make sure that she did not waste this opportunity on a trivial one.

"Well?" Cassie broke the silence between them, her trademark impatience creeping back into her tone. Contrary to her tone, however, she still appeared to be waiting calmly for the enchanter's question.

Having decided on her question, Andrea finally took a deep breath and spoke up. "Do you miss them? Your family."

Cassie's brow furrowed as she appeared genuinely surprised

by the enchanter's question. "Um…" she mumbled. "I uh… that's a tough one. Can't say I have much of a family to miss, honestly."

"Oh! I'm…sorry," Andrea stammered apologetically.

"Ah, don't be. You had no idea," Cassie said with a shrug. "My uh…my mother died when I was fifteen. She was um…" She grew quiet for a moment and swallowed before continuing. "She'd been sick for a while."

Instinctively, Andrea reached out and placed her hand on Cassie's arm. "And your father?" she asked.

"Never knew him. My mother always said he had disappeared and was missing but…I don't know." Cassie shrugged again, though this time she appeared slightly uncomfortable.

"You don't know?"

"Well," Cassie clarified. "I think it's probably more likely he left. Us, I mean. Couldn't tell you why, though."

"I see." Andrea nodded as she understood. Another thought quickly surfaced in her mind. "There's…no one you miss, then?" A drop of water fell onto the top of her head, then another, and another. Within seconds, a light drizzle was raining down on them and growing heavier by the moment.

Cassie laughed quietly and gently pushed Andrea's hand away before climbing to her feet. "No," she said, pushing her quickly dampening hair out of her face. "We should put this fire out and get some sleep, especially if we have another, what, three months of traveling to do before we get to the nearest town?"

The enchanter stood up as well. "Three *days*," she corrected again.

"Whatever," Cassie said, waving her away. "Try not to step on me when you go to bed."

"For the last time, that was an accident!" Andrea protested as she put out the fire. Her tone softened. "Oh, and Cassie? Thank you...for talking with me. I...I admit – I haven't really had a lot of, well, friends since I left home." She stopped herself when she realized that she might have stepped out of line with that assumption. "Erm...sorry. I mean, not that I'm saying we *have* to be friends...unless you *want* to, of course–,"

Cassie sighed and shook her head. "Would you just *relax*? Yes, we're friends. Now, are you coming or you just going to stand out here like an idiot and get drenched?" she demanded while pointing up at the dark sky.

"Oh!" Andrea looked up, slightly embarrassed. "Yes, of course. Right behind you."

Chapter 21

The Path to Gurdinfield

The following morning, Andrea, Cassie, Kye, and Elisa continued on the road to Karrea. With the storm still delivering punishing amounts of rain, the ex-Legionnaire maneuvered their single horse and wagon down the bumpy, dirt road as mud splattered up against the sides of the wagon.

One of the wagon's wheels kicked up a large chunk of mud that flew up into the wagon and splashed onto Cassie's dark cloak as well as her face.

"Nice," she sighed, using her arm to wipe the mud off her cheek. She muttered a few profanities that were drowned out by Andrea and Kye's laughing. All four wore their cloaks tight with the hoods on in a mostly vain attempt to keep dry.

"What did I miss?" Elisa called back from the front of the wagon.

"Oh, nothing! Cassie was just telling us how much she *enjoys* the rain," Kye responded and grinned back at Cassie, who shot him a dirty look.

"You know," she said, her tone almost friendly, "I'm feeling very generous today, actually."

Kye's grin remained. "Lovely!" He turned to Andrea while

gesturing to Cassie. "See? This is why I like her. *She* can take a joke!"

Andrea glared at the younger enchanter and was about to retort when Cassie spoke up. "Yep. I also love to share!" she exclaimed before gathering some of the mud that had splashed onto the wagon and flinging it at the boy's face. The mud hit its target, causing Kye to reel back in shock. Cassie bent over with laughter and although Andrea covered her mouth, she was giggling silently.

Kye slowly wiped the mud from his eyes and mouth while letting out a small cough. "Well," he sputtered, "I suppose I deserved that. Just wait until we stop!"

"Is that a promise?" Cassie challenged.

"Hold on. If you two decide to engage in a mud-slinging battle, tell me beforehand so that I can be very, very far away when it happens," Andrea requested.

"Hah! No mercy for anyone, not even wimpy enchanters!" Cassie declared, shaking her fist in the air and making Kye laugh again.

Andrea wiped rainwater that had dripped from her hood to her face and narrowed her eyes at her companions. "'*Wimpy?* I'll have you know I've participated in my fair share of mud wars!"

"Right, and I'm the Empress of Azgadar," Cassie scoffed.

"You do realize I grew up on a farm, do you not? There's a lot of *dirt* on farms, you know. And on occasion, rain!" Andrea exclaimed sarcastically. "It's quite amazing, perhaps you'd like to–," She was cut off when a fresh splash of mud hit the side of her face, catching her in the eye, cheek, and mouth.

"Nice shot!" Kye exclaimed and clapped his hands slowly.

Once she had registered what had just transpired, Andrea slowly opened her eyes and stared at her companions. Kye appeared extremely amused while Cassie leaned back against the wagon across from her looking incredibly smug.

"You..." the enchanter fumed without bothering to wipe her face. "I'm...you're going to be very sorry!" She reached over to the edge of the wagon where more mud had gathered and flung it across at Cassie, hitting the other girl in the chest. Within seconds, a full-fledged mud battle had ensued, the three of them yelling various declarations and threats.

From the front of the wagon, Elisa raised her eyebrows in surprise and turned her head slightly to see what was going on. "Look, I don't care if you all kill each other," she announced, "but could you try not to get all of our supplies dirty in the process?"

"No mercy!" Kye cried, echoing Cassie's earlier words as he hurled another clod of mud. His target was Cassie, but his aim was slightly off and the mud flew past her and smacked into the back of Elisa's neck instead. The ex-Legionnaire froze in surprise before turning around to yell at the other three.

"All right, which one of you idiots threw..." she began to snap before suddenly falling quiet as she looked past her companions and out into the distance.

"What is it?" Kye spoke first. Andrea and Cassie looked to Elisa curiously.

"There. Something's behind us," Elisa said, her voice so low the others could barely hear her over the sound of the rain.

The others squinted into the distance. "Perhaps just a merchant? This is a major road, after all," Kye suggested.

Elisa shook her head. "Maybe. But it's moving rather quickly." She frowned. "Too quickly."

Andrea had been looking closely when a sudden, sickening realization hit her.

"Is that…?" Cassie whispered as a faint rumbling shook the ground below.

Andrea shot an alarmed glance at Elisa. "We have to go. Right now!" she cried. *"Go!"*

Elisa did not need to be told twice. She spurred the horse to run, and the wagon began hurtling down the muddy road. Glancing back for only a moment, she could now see the outlines of their pursuers, though she was not sure if she actually believed her eyes at first. "What are *those*?!" she yelled.

"Magical constructs!" Andrea yelled back, desperately clinging to the side of the wagon as it lurched and shook violently. "They belong to my mentor!"

"Your mentor?! Why would your mentor send them after *us*, though?" Elisa demanded.

"Let's just say we're not on very good terms with her mentor!" Cassie shouted.

"I'll explain everything later, but right now we've got to move!" Andrea promised. Panic welling up in her, she looked back at the two constructs barreling after them before she turned to Cassie, whose wide-eyed expression betrayed her own fear. The enchanter had an idea.

"Cassie," she said hurriedly. As though reading the enchanter's mind, Cassie quickly nodded and carefully crawled across the wagon to sit next to Andrea.

"Do it," she muttered and discreetly held out her arm. But before Andrea could grab it, Kye had already stood up halfway and was holding on to the side of the wagon.

"What are you doing? Get down!" Elisa yelled. "They're getting closer!"

"I'm going to try something!" Kye announced. He held out his hand and in less than a second, a bright, flaming sphere appeared in his hand.

"Kye, *no!*" Andrea shouted. She reached out to stop him, but was too late. He threw the blazing orb at the constructs, which had nearly caught up to them. She expected it to explode harmlessly off the construct, but was stunned when the orb began to slow down and wobble .

"Oh, no..." Kye muttered as he watched in horror as the orb shot high up into the sky before falling back down to the ground, slamming violently into the road and setting the fields around them ablaze. The constructs ran through the flames, unharmed.

"What the hell was *that*?!" Cassie yelled at the younger enchanter.

"I-I'm s-sorry...I thought...I thought-," Kye sputtered.

"Whatever you thought, you only made them angry!" Elisa informed them. "Any other ideas on how to get rid of them?"

"Just one!" Andrea answered. "My turn." She grabbed Cassie's arm and gasped as she felt the familiar surge of energy shoot through her.

"Well, hurry up! They're just about on us!" Elisa exclaimed.

Andrea turned to face the constructs and focused on creating a fireball with the same intensity and power as the one Cassie had helped her create that night in the Black Forest.

"Uh...Andrea?" Cassie warned.

"Not now – I'm concentrating!"

"They're...I think they're doing something!" Cassie pressed.

"Cassie, stop talking and let me focus!" the enchanter snapped as she was finally able to create a fireball in her hand. It was larger and brighter than the one Kye had conjured and caused the air around them to heat up.

"Wow!" Kye breathed in awe.

"Don't set *us* on fire, Andrea! Just get rid of them!" Elisa called back, momentarily getting the enchanter's attention.

"Andrea! *Look!*" Cassie yelled and pointed. Andrea looked back just in time to see one of the constructs throw a large boulder at the wagon. The other construct followed suit.

"No," she whispered, watching in horror as the massive rocks flew through the air toward them with terrifying speed. She had not realized how far her mentor would go, but never in a million years would she have thought Meredith was capable of *murdering* anyone.

"Andrea, kill them! *Now!*" Elisa shouted.

The enchanter looked up at the rocks and then at the wagon. *Not enough time.* She quickly made a decision and extinguished the fire in her hand before letting go of Cassie's arm, standing up halfway while leaning on the side of the wagon, and putting all of her focus into creating a barrier to shield them from the impact of the rocks.

"What are you doing?!" Cassie screamed. She stood up, hanging onto the side of the wagon to steady herself.

"Trying to save us!" Andrea cried as she created an energy barrier around the wagon. Her heart sank when the barrier began to flicker. She was either too weak to maintain a barrier of that size or there was not enough magic in the area.

"If you're going to do something then do it! *Now!*" Elisa roared. Kye held on tightly, his face having lost most of its color and his dark eyes wide with fear.

Cassie looked at Andrea, then the flickering barrier, and finally at the flying rocks hurtling toward them before leaping forward and throwing herself at the enchanter, immediately intensifying the strength of Andrea's barrier and causing it to glow brightly with a pulsing white light. The rocks slammed into the wagon, causing both the boulders and the barrier to explode and sending a volley of stone shards and wooden splinters everywhere as the wagon was flung onto its side. The axle snapped easily and the frightened horse squealed as it bolted away from the splintered wagon, which skidded harshly on its side over muddy grass and rocks until it finally screeched to a stop.

* * *

Andrea came to in a fit of coughing and gasping as she involuntarily inhaled some of the water and mud that had pooled around her head while she was unconscious. She opened her eyes to find she had to squint in order to see through the heavy rain that was still falling. Her head throbbed and a sharp pain shot through her side. A heavy weight held the enchanter down when she attempted to sit up to examine her surroundings.

"Cassie!" she gasped. Her companion was sprawled halfway on top of her, unconscious but still breathing. Blood trickled down the sides and front of Cassie's face from a gash on her forehead.

"Cassie…ah!" Andrea cried as she tried to push the other girl off of her, but the same sharp pain lanced through her again and she quickly lay her head back down on the dirt to take a breath.

"Cassie, we need to get away from here…wake up…*please!*" she pleaded, feebly trying to push Cassie off of her. Where were Elisa and Kye?

The ground suddenly rumbled beneath her. The hulking, crystal form of the constructs slowly came into view as they hovered over her and Cassie. The enchanter's breathing became ragged as she gazed at the creatures looming above her. She did not think Meredith would have the constructs kill them, but they would surely try to take Cassie and…

Cassie. She was not conscious, but perhaps her abilities might still work! *No…she's not awake; I can't just use her powers without permission.*

One of the creatures reached a massive hand down to grab Cassie. Fear spiked in Andrea as she inhaled sharply and made up her mind. "Sorry!" she muttered to her companion and focused on drawing power from Cassie. It was far more difficult to gather energy than when Cassie was conscious, but the enchanter soon had enough for one fireball, and she knew it would have to do. The pain in her head and her side was crippling now, and Andrea felt as though she might pass out.

Using the last of her remaining strength, she threw the fireball at the constructs. At such close range, it exploded almost immediately and Andrea used her arms to shield herself and Cassie from the blast. The constructs groaned loudly and staggered back a few heavy steps before crumbling into a fine black ash.

Letting out a heavy sigh of relief, Andrea lay her head back down on the mud. She was exhausted from manipulating so much energy in such a short amount of time, her clothes and hair were drenched and caked with mud, and Cassie's dead weight on her was not doing her injured side any favors. She laughed quietly at the desperation of the situation as rivulets of rainwater dripped down her face.

"Andrea!" The enchanter could hear Elisa calling her, though the ex-Legionnaire's voice was quickly fading as darkness began to close around her and finally took her.

Chapter 22

Intelligence Gathered

"Well, Diana seems to have a talent for picking up strays lately."

"Oh! I'm a *stray* now, am I Captain?" Elisa asked with a crooked smile. "You *do* realize this 'stray' is going to be providing you and your group with the information you need to win your war."

"She does have a point, Jacob," Diana chimed in as she exited the large tent that Jacob and the ex-Legionnaire stood in front of in the middle of the Guardian camp. It was late in the evening and the air was thick with the scent of rain from the storm that had passed through the southlands earlier and the smoke from the meat cooked over the Guardian campfires for dinner.

"How are they?" Elisa asked. "Alive, I presume?"

"The boy and the older girl...Cassie, was it? They're fine. Cassie had a few bad scrapes, but nothing serious. They'll be sore when they wake up, but they'll live," Diana reported. "The enchanter – what is her name?"

"Andrea."

"Right. She has a few bruised ribs and she was very weak when we found you – barely breathing, actually. What in the world was after you, Elisa?" The commanding Guardian looked very concerned now.

Elisa rubbed the back of her neck. "Ah, well, I'm still not sure, to be honest. They were created by an enchanter, that's for sure. Andrea mentioned that her mentor sent them after her. I have no idea why."

"And she destroyed them?" Jacob questioned.

"Yes. Kye, the boy, tried to take care of them with magic but ended up setting half the field on fire."

Diana looked curiously at Elisa. "He is also an enchanter?"

"Yes, though I do not believe he has complete control over his abilities," Elisa replied, shaking her head. "The way the grass caught on fire…it certainly was not intentional, but I fear that his uncontrolled magic could be dangerous."

"And this Andrea…she is trained?" Jacob asked.

"She mentioned a mentor, yes, and definitely seemed to have more control over her powers. She tried to get rid of them with fire as well at first, but then switched to a protective barrier once those…things started throwing rocks at us. Had it not been for her, we probably would have all been killed," Elisa explained solemnly.

"We saw her use a fireball on the creatures when we spotted you from down the road," Jacob said. "I assume fire is how one finishes these monsters off?"

"So it would seem," Elisa answered. "It is a good thing you arrived when you did. We were actually on our way to Karrea to meet you."

"We're heading for Fimen's Hope now. Karrea…Karrea is

gone," Diana said grimly. "Moore's men burned it to the ground and left no survivors."

"Well, almost no survivors. We found a child in the bordering woods," Jacob corrected.

"Ah," Elisa said with an understanding nod. "Thus the 'stray' comment you so cleverly came up with. Fortunately for you, I am very much worthy of your attention."

Diana turned to the ex-Legionnaire. "You've acquired the empress's book, then?"

Elisa gave a short nod before reaching into her pack and pulling out the thick tome that was the empress's personal diary. She handed it to Diana. "That is correct, though I cannot say exactly how helpful it will be. No doubt she knows it's missing by now, so there's a very good chance she might change her strategy."

"Which is?" Jacob asked.

Elisa bit her lip and turned back to Jacob. "Well, we know for certain now that Ithmeera has allied with David Moore."

"As we suspected," Diana said.

Elisa nodded. "What we did not know is that she means to invade Gurdinfield and add it to Azgadar's holdings."

Jacob frowned. "What? Invade? What does the empire have to gain from invading Gurdinfield?"

Elisa chuckled. "You're joking, right? Read the book."

Jacob rolled his eyes. "For goodness' sake, just tell us Elisa!"

Elisa turned to Diana and gestured toward the captain. "Impatient, this one," she joked. "The answer is actually rather simple. Magic." She folded her arms across her chest.

"Magic?" Diana asked incredulously. "What does magic have to do with anything?"

"It has to do with everything, unfortunately." Alexander Telman's calm but recognizable voice startled the ex-Legionnaire and the two Guardians. He gave a short bow to Elisa. "Good to see you are well, Lady Elisa. When I heard what had happened, I was a bit worried."

Elisa nodded. "I'm hard to kill, sir. Though I can't say I would have been so lucky had your best fighters here not found us when they did. And it's just 'Elisa', please."

Alexander smiled. "Of course."

"We were just performing a quick patrol of the area before returning to camp for the evening, sir," Jacob quickly explained.

"Well done, then. Now," Alexander continued as he turned to Diana. "Magic seems to be what the empress is after here, it seems."

"Ithmeera wants Gurdinfield's magic?" Diana repeated.

"So it would seem," Alexander replied. "We've known for some time that the supply of magic in Azgadar is abysmally low, so low that they barely have enough to maintain their farms or infrastructure."

"But why now? Why wait until now to attack Gurdinfield?" Diana asked.

"Perhaps that is where the alliance with the Moores comes in?" Jacob suggested.

Diana nodded in understanding as she flipped through the diary. "It appears Ithmeera plans to assist Moore in winning the civil war before invading, but she also intends to make him a governor of sorts once the Legion takes over."

"That snake," Jacob sneered in disgust. "All that bastard Moore cares about is sitting on the throne in the capital city. It's disgraceful!"

"Interesting that he's willing to give up Gurdinfield's sovereignty for an empty title," Elisa commented.

"Does Moore actually know about the invasion?" Alexander asked.

Diana looked up at her father and shook her head. "I don't believe so, according to this. It seems Moore actually believes he's forming the foundations of a long-term alliance with Ithmeera that includes sharing some of Gurdinfield's magic. But the empress just wants to take it all!"

Despite the new information, Alexander remained calm as he turned his attention back to Elisa. "Elisa," he said, "we are grateful for the information. Diana will give you your payment, but please feel free to stay with us for as long as you need to rest and recover."

Elisa bowed to the leader of the Guardians. "Thank you, sir. I'm sure my companions will appreciate that. Actually," she said as a thought crossed her mind, "two of my companions require passage to Rhyad. From what I understand, Harrington forces block the Northland Bridge."

"That is correct," Jacob confirmed. "No one is getting through. They seem to think hiding near the mountains gives them some kind of advantage in case the Moores decide to push further north."

"They are not wrong," Alexander stated. "But Jacob is right – there is no passage to Rhyad…for now at least."

Elisa took a deep breath. "I see. Unfortunately, I made a pact with these girls that I would get them to Rhyad if they helped me get that book, and as you can see, I must honor that pact."

Diana looked up at the ex-Legionnaire with interest. A curious smile crossed her features. "Commendable."

Elisa returned the smile, though she did not try to hide her dismay. "But impossible."

But Diana's smile never faltered. "Is it?" She closed the diary in her hands. "Elisa, you have already helped us get this far. We now have everything we need to do what was once thought impossible."

Jacob frowned. "We do?"

Alexander laughed quietly as he realized what his daughter was suggesting. "We do, Jacob. Elisa, I believe what Diana is asking is if you would do us the honor of remaining with the Guardians."

Elisa took a small step backward. "Remain? But…why? Surely there is more information I could acquire for you from the empire."

But Diana shook her head. "With this information, I believe we have everything we need to approach both the Harringtons and the Moores so that we can end this civil war before Gurdinfield loses its chance to remain a sovereign nation… forever."

The ex-Legionnaire stared blankly at the Telmans and Jacob before laughing loudly. "You…you're *joking* right?!"

"Well no, but–," Diana began.

Elisa interrupted her. "Your grand plan is to somehow get the Harringtons and the Moores – two families that have been at war for over *twenty years* – to somehow agree to end said war so that they can unite against the Legion?! Again, the *Azgadaran Legion*, the best-trained army in all of Damea?"

Diana smiled. "Yes, that is correct."

Elisa gaped at the Guardian commander disbelievingly. "Maybe you three should think about invading another country as well, because you are going to need *a lot* more magic than what you have here to make this insane plan work."

The four of them stood in silence for a few moments.

"Well," Jacob's deep voice broke the silence, "on the off-chance that Diana's 'insane plan' actually worked, it *would* mean we would have more negotiating power with the Harringtons to allow your companions to cross the Northland Bridge."

Elisa scowled at the Guardian captain. Although she knew he had a point, one real issue weighed on her mind. "The others – they're barely of age, especially the boy. They did not sign up for a civil war *and* an invasion."

"They seemed to hold their own well enough when being chased by magical creatures. And after all, you did say they helped you acquire the book, did you not?" Alexander pointed out.

The ex-Legionnaire sighed before reluctantly nodding.

"Talk to them, Elisa," Diana urged. "Perhaps if they hear it from you they will be willing to help."

"And we could certainly use two enchanters," Jacob added.

Elisa groaned in frustration. "Fine," she gave in. "But before I convince anyone to join in this war effort, I'm going to need a drink. Or three."

Alexander chuckled. "I believe we can help with that," he offered as the four of them began to make their way across the Guardian camp and toward the main campfire.

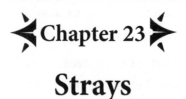

Chapter 23

Strays

The smoky scent of cooking food gently woke Andrea. She opened her eyes to discover that she was staring up at the ceiling of a tent and was greeted by a hot, sharp ache in her left side. She gasped and clutched her side with both hands.

"Careful," a low, commanding voice spoke from the other side of the large tent. Lifting her head up slightly, the enchanter saw a young, dark-haired woman in heavy traveling clothing and a dark cloak walking toward her. "Your ribs need time to heal. Try not to move too quickly," she said and knelt beside the enchanter.

"Oh…all right," Andrea answered weakly and winced as another stab of pain shot through her. She looked around, being careful not to move too much. The sunlight peeking in through the open flap of the tent and the absence of pattering on the roof told her that the rain had finally stopped. "Where am I?"

"At the moment? Somewhere between Karrea and Fimen's Hope," the woman answered. "If you don't mind, I would like to check your injuries once more before you try to move around."

Just the mention of her injury made Andrea's side throb with pain again. "Ah!" she cried out. "I-yes, that's fine."

"Try to hold still," the woman said. She gently lifted up Andrea's shirt, which to the enchanter's surprise had been changed into a clean white one, to examine the injury. Andrea inhaled quickly when the cool autumn air hit her skin. Still, she tried her best to remain patient and still.

Finally, the woman rolled Andrea's shirt down and stood up. "You should be fine, but try to move slowly. You could have been injured far worse."

Andrea nodded and slowly sat up, despite the pain. "Thank you," she said.

"Of course. I am Diana, by the way."

The enchanter nodded and offered as friendly a smile as she could muster in her current condition. "Andrea. How long was I asleep for?"

Diana looked thoughtful for a moment. "About a day, perhaps? You are an enchanter, yes?"

Andrea could not help but feel uncomfortable. How did this woman know what she was? Was she from the Legion? Where were Elisa and the others? "I-yes. Are you...with the Legion?" Had Ithmeera caught up to them? What about–

The constructs! The memory of the constructs looming over her as she frantically tried to destroy them with magic before they could take Cassie came back to Andrea in a rush. A wooziness took over for a moment and Diana had to help steady her.

"Careful," she warned. "Are you certain you don't want to lie back down?"

Andrea shook her head as she stabilized. "No...no, I'm fine. The others–,"

"They are all fine," Diana assured her. "A few scrapes and bruises, but nothing major. You actually had the worst of it, believe it or not."

The enchanter let out a sigh of relief. "I-good."

"To answer your question – no, I am not with the Legion, so please don't be alarmed. I am the commander of the Guardians. Elisa might have mentioned us, perhaps?" Diana tried calming the nervous enchanter. "Would you care for some breakfast? I believe our men brought in some fish from the river this morning."

The mere mention of food made Andrea's stomach rumble. "Y-yes, that would be wonderful, actually."

Diana smiled brightly. "Good. I can fetch some for you if you like."

But the enchanter held up a hand and shook her head. "No, no – I've got it. If you could help me up I think I can make the walk outside."

"Of course. Your friends are already by the main campfire if you want to meet with them," Diana suggested and offered her hand, which the enchanter took. After slowly standing, Andrea gestured to the tent's exit. "Lead the way, then?"

* * *

"Pass that fish over here please, Kye?" Elisa requested.

The younger enchanter nodded and reached out for the large pan that sat over the fire. He carefully handed it to Elisa, who used her fork to take another piece of the grilled fish that had been caught earlier in the morning.

Cassie took another bite of her fish. "This is actually really good," she said with a stuffed mouth. With the exception of a few bruises, scratches, and the small bandage she now sported on her forehead, Cassie had emerged from the incident on the main road to Karrea mostly unscathed.

"Yes, much better than what we've been eating lately," Kye agreed. He too had come out of the accident with a few bruises but was otherwise fine.

The ex-Legionnaire shot the young man a questioning glance.

Cassie noticed first and playfully nudged Kye. "You're in trouble now," she teased. The young man did not seem to understand at first until he saw Elisa staring at him and quickly realized how his words might have been construed.

"Oh!" he exclaimed, quickly becoming flustered. "I-I'm sorry, Elisa. I d-did not mean to appear ungrateful! I only m-meant that–,"

But Elisa simply waved her hand at Kye and cut him off. "Relax, boy. The fish is good – you're right."

Kye's shoulders slumped as he sighed with relief while Cassie just laughed quietly and Elisa shook her head. "Besides," the ex-Legionnaire continued nonchalantly as she took another bite of her food, "if I was going to kill you, I'd do it at night and in the woods where no one can see or hear you."

Cassie laughed again when she saw the color drain from the young man's face. She leaned in to take another bite of her food but stopped midway when she saw their newest acquaintance, Diana, approaching, with Andrea close behind her. The enchanter was walking slowly and haltingly with one of her hands hovering tentatively over her side. She met Cassie's gaze briefly before looking down at the others with a faint, tired smile. Cassie let out a dissatisfied huff, obvious enough for Andrea to hear.

"Good morning," Diana said warmly. "Good to see you all awake and well. I see you've tried the fish?"

"It's very good, thank you," Kye said, holding up a piece of the fish on his fork.

"Yeah, thanks," Cassie grumbled. Diana clasped her hands together. "Right, then. I shall return to check on you all. I need to speak with Alexander," she announced before leaving the enchanter standing on her own in front of her three companions.

Andrea bit her lip for a moment before speaking up, her voice barely audible. "I'm…glad to see that you're all okay."

"Sit down," Elisa commanded. "Eat." She looked at the others. "Move over and make some room," she ordered.

Cassie set her plate on the ground, the fork clattering loudly on the dish, and stood up. "It's fine, she can have my seat," she declared briskly before walking away from the group.

The others exchanged awkward glances. Elisa spoke first. "What's the matter with her?" she demanded.

Andrea sighed. "I'm not certain, but I believe she might be upset with me," she said as she slowly sat down.

"Why would she be upset with you, though?" Kye wondered. He cut a piece of fish for the older enchanter and served it to her.

"Thank you," Andrea replied gratefully as she took the plate and began to eat. "Cassie and I were staying with my mentor, Meredith, before we decided to leave. Meredith was…unhappy with that decision," she explained. "She sent her constructs after us. We disposed of them, but apparently Meredith had enough magic leftover to make more."

"So," Elisa pondered, "what you're saying is that my wagon being destroyed is *your* fault?"

"I-I didn't *know* that she was going to send more after us!" Andrea exclaimed, shifting in her seat. She winced and gingerly held her side again. "We-all enchanters have projections we give off. Meredith knows how to find them and track them."

Elisa studied the enchanter for a moment before asking, "Dare I ask why your mentor would be so displeased at you leaving?" Kye looked over curiously as well.

Andrea sighed and chose her words carefully. "We had been working on a project together. I disagreed with her methods and decided to leave. This…greatly delayed Meredith's progress. She wasn't too pleased with me."

"That's an understatement. She tried to kill you," Elisa pointed out.

"I still don't understand. Why is Cassie upset?" Kye asked as he put his finished plate down.

"You speak as though that girl is never upset. She is *always* upset," Elisa grumbled.

Andrea shook her head. "I don't know, to be honest."

Elisa climbed to her feet. "Well, it's immature, and we don't have time for it." She took a deep breath. "By the way, we've been offered an opportunity to remain with the Guardians."

"Remain? Are you serious?" Kye was stunned.

"What about the bridge and getting into Rhyad?" Andrea demanded. "That was part of our deal, remember?"

Elisa rolled her shoulders back and stretched her arms a bit. "Yes, well…about that. The Harringtons guard the Northland Bridge, and they are not interested in letting anyone cross as long as there is a war going on."

Andrea frowned. "What are you saying, Elisa? You are still going to help us like you said you would, right?"

"I will," Elisa said tersely, "but the only way I can possibly help you now is if we help the Guardians end this war. That book you helped me acquire? It has information in it that could help us convince the Harringtons and the Moores to unite under one banner."

"Unite? After twenty years of war?" Andrea said doubtfully.

"Yes. Apparently, Ithmeera is planning to invade and conquer Gurdinfield for its magic after she helps Lord Moore defeat the Harringtons," Elisa explained.

"That is why the book was so important!" Kye realized.

"Yes. What, you think I just wanted to browse through the empress's personal notes?" Elisa retorted, making both enchanters laugh.

Kye spoke in a snooty, high-pitched tone. "'Today I was rich and hosted a ball! Perhaps tomorrow will be better.'"

"'Maybe I'll lock up an enchanter or three if I get bored,'" Andrea added despite her own experience, mimicking Kye's impression and making the young man laugh harder.

The ex-Legionnaire stared at the two giggling enchanters with raised eyebrows. "So," she said slowly, "are you two all right with this arrangement, then?"

Andrea considered it. Elisa *had* promised her and Cassie that if they helped her acquire the book, then she would assist them in getting to Rhyad. But now that assistance came with yet another price. *Cassie is* not *going to be happy about this.* She did not want to be thrown in the middle of a civil war, especially *this* civil war.

Maybe I should talk to Cassie about this. The thought alone frustrated her. Why should she have to consult with Cassie about everything?

Perhaps because it's your *fault she's here with no way home?* Her side throbbed painfully as though responding to her troubled thoughts.

"Well?" Elisa asked impatiently.

The older enchanter nodded. "If you think this is the only way we can get to Rhyad, then I will help. I'm not certain what Cassie will say, however."

"Ah, leave that to me. I'll go knock some sense into the girl," Elisa replied. "Not literally, of course…"

"Erm…yes, please don't hurt her," Andrea pleaded, not completely convinced Elisa was joking.

"I will help," Kye offered. "It's bound to be better than anything I would be doing were I still in Azgadar."

"Considering your fate there was most likely to be hanged or beheaded, yes, I completely agree with you," Elisa said smartly. She turned to Andrea. "I am going to inform Diana of your decisions, then. Try to stick to the camp if you are going to wander. I don't want to have to go searching for you in the woods."

Andrea watched the ex-Legionnaire walk away before turning to Kye. "You're really all right with this? Fighting in a civil war?"

Kye shrugged. "It's either that or go back to Azgadar to whatever fate awaits me there."

"You could always leave and make your own path here. Maybe go to the City of Towers or one of the smaller villages?"

Kye gave a shy smile. "Oh, I don't know if I could do that. Make my own path? Like you?"

Andrea felt her face heat up. "I wish I could say that. No, I lived under the strict rules of my parents before living under the equally strict rules of Meredith."

"Well…then think of this as an adventure!" Kye encouraged her.

The older enchanter laughed. "An adventure, hmm? I think after all that's happened, I've had enough adventure to last me a good long while."

Kye placed a friendly hand on Andrea's shoulder. "What's the worst that could happen? We end a civil war, unite a country, and you and Cassie get to go to Rhyad?"

Andrea smiled and shook her head. "Yes, Kye – that's *definitely* the worst thing that could happen."

Chapter 24

Fire Lady

Cassie pushed some loose strands of her dirty blonde hair out of her blue eyes as a cool breeze blew across the grassy hills that bordered the forest where the Guardians had temporarily set up camp. The hill she sat on was among the tallest ones and provided an impressive view of the sprawling grasslands of the Southlands of Gurdinfield below her. Morning had gone and the sun's position high in the sky, although partially hidden behind clouds, told Cassie that midday was fast approaching. No one had followed her after breakfast and while she was happy for the privacy, part of her wished she had remained to sort things out with Andrea.

You could have at least asked if she was okay. But Cassie was tired. Her head still ached and parts of her body that she did not even know *could* be sore were sore. She was not upset that Andrea had used her still unexplained "abilities" without permission. She knew that in order to destroy the constructs the enchanter would have needed to draw on that power, but Cassie was still feeling fatigued from the entire ordeal.

But it was not just physical exhaustion that was weighing her down. Her life had been turned upside down since arriving in Damea, and she was waiting for things to start making sense any day now. Although she felt more comfortable with Andrea with each passing day, she was not sure if she completely trusted Elisa or Kye, though she could not deny that they had also played a crucial role in getting her and the enchanter this far. But this Rhyad place seemed so far away and it was clear that Meredith was still hunting for them – yet another thing to worry about.

Her thoughts were interrupted when she sensed someone sit down on the grass next to her. *Great.*

"I don't really feel like talking right now and-oh…Elisa," she stopped when she saw it was the ex-Legionnaire. "Sorry, I thought you were Andrea."

Elisa chuckled and looked out at the fields below them. "You would talk to me and not Andrea?" she wondered aloud.

Cassie shrugged uncomfortably. *Why does everyone here want to* talk *so damn much?* "I'm pretty sure that my life expectancy gets slashed by a week for every minute I'm around that girl. I feel like every time I catch my breath we have to run again because there's *something* trying to kill us or imprison us or whatever."

At this, Elisa gave a loud, harsh laugh. "You'd fit right in with the Legion, then."

"Yeah? Are they suicidal as well?"

"The training can be grueling – brutal, even," Elisa explained with a shrug. "Long hours, little sleep, and the most intense training a body can be put through. If you make it through without running home crying for your mother, then you're generally considered one of the best fighters in Damea."

"Hah. Sounds fun," Cassie joked.

"Not really, but you do what you have to in order to help your family."

Cassie glanced at the ex-Legionnaire curiously. "You have family back in Azgadar?"

Elisa shifted uncomfortably. "Not exactly, but my father lived there until his death."

"Oh. Sorry to hear that."

But Elisa waved her hand dismissively. "Don't be. My point was that I needed to support my family. I knew what my skills were, and I put them to good use."

Cassie sighed. "That's a nice story, but what has that got to do with me not talking to Andrea?"

"The two of you have both been tight-lipped about why exactly you are bound together, but like it or not, bound together you are, at least until you get to Rhyad to do whatever it is you need to do in that forsaken land," Elisa declared and met Cassie's gaze. "I don't completely believe either of your reasons, but one thing I *have* seen is that Andrea has taken great risks for you more than once." She looked back out at the hills.

Cassie snorted. "You mean she's taken risks for the *mission*."

Elisa quickly turned to glare at the younger woman. "You can toy with the words all you want, girl – the point is that I didn't see *you* serving as bait at that ball. I didn't see *you* locked up in that dungeon waiting to be tortured, and I didn't see *you* trying to protect the rest of us when those monsters were about a hair's breadth away from killing us all," she snapped. "Whether you like it or not, you're as invested in this 'mission' as she is."

"You don't know anything about me or what I've done, so why don't you just shove off and leave me alone?" Cassie growled and matched Elisa's glare. "Let me make something clear – all that girl cares about is getting to Rhyad."

"You say that, but you don't believe it yourself," Elisa replied. "While I was *trying* to sleep the other night and you two were chatting it up – rather loudly I might add – I happened to overhear quite a bit. And trust me, you're wrong."

"Whatever," Cassie retorted. "Why am I still talking to you? Ever since we met you bad things have happened."

"Hah! If I recall, *you* were the one who ventured off on your own into the slums of Azgadar. If Andrea, Kye, *and* myself had not intervened, you'd be dead," Elisa pointed out. "I don't know what village you're from where they taught you to make such terrible decisions, but you should consider going back because you're not going to last very long out here with that kind of attitude."

Cassie laughed quietly. "Yeah," she muttered, "that's…kind of the idea."

Elisa stood up and dusted the dirt and grass from her clothing. "Alright, I'm tired of lecturing you. Grow up, come back to camp, eat some lunch, and be nice to the enchanters."

Cassie sighed and shook her head as Elisa began walking away. "Whatever you say, Elisa. I'll be there in a minute."

After a few steps, the ex-Legionnaire stopped and called casually back to Cassie. "Oh, by the way – you're now a member of the Guardians. We've decided to help them stop the civil war so that you can get your bridge opened."

Cassie's eyes widened as she quickly turned back only to see that Elisa was already too far away to argue with. She turned back and buried her face in her hands before letting out a muffled cry of frustration. "You've *got* to be kidding me!"

✶ ✶ ✶

Southlands, Gurdinfield

A little more than five days north of Karrea, the Guardians found themselves traveling through the open green fields of the Southlands of Gurdinfield alongside the Rhyad River. They were just a day or so south of Fimen's Hope, the closest major town in the region, where Alexander Telman and his followers hoped to find the Moore soldiers responsible for the destruction of Karrea, or at the very least some clue as to where they might have gone next. He knew that Fimen's Hope also paid a tax to the Moores for their "protection", and he hoped that this town had not suffered the same fate as Karrea. Fimen's Hope served as the only major trade hub on the west side of Gurdinfield and sat on the border of the Northlands and the Southlands.

It was mid-afternoon, and Alexander could see the sun beginning the end of its journey across the sky as it neared the peaks of the taller hills in the distance. Glancing over at the men and women behind him, he noted that many were beginning to tire as those on horses began to slouch while those on foot began dragging their feet.

Amara, the child that Diana and her companions had found in the woods, began to express her disapproval – quite loudly, in fact – as she held onto Elisa's hand and walked behind one of the horse-drawn wagons carrying weapons and supplies. "I'm tired and my feet hurt," she whined and looked up at the ex-Legionnaire. "Lady Elisa, I don't want to walk anymore!"

Elisa looked down at the small girl and gave a long-suffering sigh when she heard Diana unsuccessfully restrain a laugh. "Diana, if you please," she said with a hint of desperation creeping into her voice, "would you remind me why I – a trained fighter and a considerably experienced spy – have become the Guardians' glorified babysitter?"

Diana laughed again from atop the horse she now slowly rode alongside her companions. "Come now, Elisa! You two have had a wonderful time traveling together haven't you, Amara?" she exclaimed, beaming at the blonde girl. Considering the girl had just lost her entire family and village, she had been in impressively good spirits, and Diana deeply hoped that Amara's family had somehow been able to make it out of Karrea alive, no matter how slim the possibility seemed.

"Yes!" Amara responded and tugged at Elisa's hand. "I'm tired. Can I ride on the wagon?"

"The wagon is full of very sharp knives and other things that a girl as young as you has no business sitting with," Elisa told her for what must have been the fifth time that day. She glanced up and looked around for one of her companions – anyone, really – to take the child off of her hands. She saw Cassie walking up ahead, looking down at the dirt more than straight ahead. Andrea walked a few paces behind her and Kye walked alongside Jacob who, like Diana, was also on horseback. Neither Cassie or Andrea had spoken very much to each other except when it was absolutely necessary. They were not unfriendly toward one another, but Elisa had noticed that Andrea had backed off from pressing Cassie with her usual barrage of questions and Cassie had eased off her usual teasing of the enchanter. The ex-Legionnaire had an idea.

"However, Amara, I believe Cassie would be more than happy to carry you," Elisa said just loud enough for Cassie to hear. As several of the other Guardians laughed, she smiled sweetly at the girl before slyly glancing at Diana, who it appeared could not decide if she disapproved.

Amara grinned and gleefully ran ahead and past Andrea. The enchanter watched with a blend of curiosity and amusement as Cassie continued walking with her head down while trying to pretend she had not heard Elisa's suggestion.

But the child was determined. "Cassie! Cassie!" she cried and tugged at the young woman's shirtsleeve. "Lady Elisa said that you would carry me."

Cassie stopped and looked back at Elisa long enough to give her an unimpressed look before turning back to Amara. "She did, did she?" she asked as Andrea watched the scene unfold with great interest. "It appears that the 'Lady Elisa' is very lazy," she stated solemnly. "But you probably already knew that, right?"

The young girl giggled and nodded.

"Good. Glad we're on the same page. Hop on," Cassie offered and hoisted an excited Amara up so that the girl sat on her shoulders. Andrea raised her eyebrows in surprise as she watched her companion start to walk again.

The sky slowly began to change from a clear blue to the familiar orange and purple hues that accompanied the sunset. Andrea watched with fascination as Amara proceeded to ask one question after another. Cassie patiently answered every single one of them.

"The sky looks like it's on fire!" the child commented.

"It does, doesn't it?" Cassie agreed.

"Is it like the fire that the Fire Lady made when the monsters came?" Amara asked.

Andrea could not hold back a smile when she realized the girl was talking about her. She sped up her walking pace slightly so that she was on Cassie's right instead of behind her.

"Uh…not really. Hey, how do you know about that?" Cassie asked, turning her head slightly to mouth, *"Fire Lady?"* questioningly at Andrea, who shrugged in response.

"Lady Elisa and Captain Jacob were talking about it," Amara explained. "The monsters were chasing you and the Fire Lady threw fire at them and *whoosh!*" The child flailed her arms to demonstrate Andrea's fire spell hitting Meredith's constructs. "The monsters were dead!"

Andrea giggled and covered her mouth as Cassie replied, "Yeah, I think that's pretty much how it went – 'whoosh' and all."

Amara gasped with barely contained excitement. "I would very much like to see the Fire Lady make *more* fire!"

Andrea saw Cassie catch her gaze again and could only respond with a nervous expression. Perhaps there was a time in Damea when magic could have been used for parlor tricks and amusing children, but that time was now long gone. She did not know these lands or how much magic they truly had, and she did not want to chance getting the illness that befell so many enchanters who were not careful. She briefly wondered if Cassie would push her to make a small demonstration just to placate the child.

"Well," Cassie said thoughtfully, "let me tell you something. The Fire Lady? Her name is Andrea, and she's an enchanter."

"Enchanter?"

"Yeah. She can do magic and stuff. Like the fire."

Amara nodded in understanding. "Oh. Can she do the fire now?"

"Well, here's the thing," Cassie explained. "I think she really wants to, but there's not enough magic to just make fire for the fun of it. She wants to save the magic for when we really need to use it."

Amara nodded thoughtfully. "For the monsters?"

"Yeah, exactly!" Cassie said brightly. "In case we run into more of those monsters."

As Cassie continued to answer Amara's seemingly infinite questions, Andrea breathed a sigh of relief and felt a swell of admiration and gratefulness toward her companion. *Well, at least she doesn't hate me for our situation.* She bit her lip and tensed up when she saw Cassie turn her head toward her, but was surprised when the other girl gave her a reassuring nod while Amara kept talking.

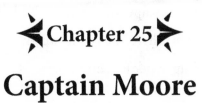

Chapter 25

Captain Moore

Fimen's Hope, Gurdinfield

The town of Fimen's Hope was a familiar sight to Andrea, who had been there with Meredith several times over the past three years during their travels together. Another river town, Fimen's Hope was slightly larger than Karrea and thrived mostly on its farmland as opposed to fishing. Tiny wooden huts made up the bulk of the structures in the village, which had a single main road that led to a small marketplace and a town center where its residents would often meet for important matters. A few old sheds could be seen in the distant fields, though Andrea knew from the occasional visit when she and Meredith had to sleep in one when the inns were full that most of those were well past their prime and had gaping holes in their roofs. With the day approaching late morning and having had breakfast hours ago, the enchanter's stomach rumbled in protest as she inhaled the various scents emanating from food out on display in the marketplace.

Kye's line of thought must have been similar. "We're here, are we not? Let's eat!" he declared.

Several of the townspeople took an active interest in the

Guardians as the fighters, along with their horses and wagons, made their way down the main road. Others kept their distance, glancing coldly and some even fearfully at Alexander and his militia. This did not escape the Guardian leader's notice.

"We're not the first here," he spoke quietly.

Diana looked up at her father as they kept a slow but steady pace toward the town center. "The Moores?"

"They are either here or have passed through," Alexander informed her. "I assume the town had the money for them since it has not been burned."

Overhearing the Guardians' conversation, Andrea looked around, half expecting to see a Moore soldier suddenly ambush them, before turning back to Cassie. Her companion was walking several steps behind her with Amara clutching her cloak, and did not appear to have overheard Alexander and Diana's conversation.

"Cassie," the enchanter whispered, trying to get the other girl's attention.

Cassie looked up briefly and was about to answer, but could not before a high-pitched scream rang out. A panic immediately spread amongst the townspeople, who instantly began scattering, running back to the safety of their homes or at the very least far away from whatever had caused the disturbance. Alexander began barking orders at the Guardians, who swiftly drew their weapons and began moving into a close-knit defensive formation. In a flash, Elisa drew her daggers. Kye stayed close to the ex-Legionnaire.

Andrea froze in place as she struggled to quell the panic that had welled up inside of her. She had instinctively lifted her hand up, ready to launch a fireball or put up a barrier if she absolutely needed to. She was not trained for combat – not really, anyway – but if her experiences over the past few weeks had taught her anything, it was to always be prepared to defend herself and those around her if necessary.

Amidst the escalating panic, Cassie grabbed Amara's arm and pulled her closer. The child's eyes were wide with fear and confusion and were not much different from Cassie's at that moment.

"What the hell is going on?!" Cassie demanded.

"Shut up and stay close to me," Elisa ordered. "I said *stay close!*" She gestured for Andrea and Cassie to move near her along with Amara, who had burst into tears. Cassie moved the young girl behind her and stepped in front of Kye and Andrea in order to shield the child better. Andrea could see Cassie's hand hovering over her sheathed knife, the very same one Elisa had given her when they rescued the enchanter from the Azgadaran dungeon.

A shout erupted from the town center and the remaining crowd retreated, leaving behind a single, motionless body in the dirt. Andrea could see immediately that it was an older man, perhaps a town leader. Judging by the deep head wound from which he was bleeding profusely, the enchanter knew the man was dead. A strong wave of nausea slammed into her. She noticed Kye cover Amara's eyes with his hands to block her view of the body. She could see Cassie tense up from her position behind her companion.

"*Silence!*" the voice that had shouted earlier commanded. The cries and screams died down, and an armored man sporting a short beard and carrying a long sword boasting a bloodied hilt stepped into view, flanked by several soldiers who were just as imposing. Andrea could see the man in charge was around Jacob's age, that he walked with arrogance, and that based on the bird of prey branded into his leather armor, he was indeed a high-ranking officer of Lord David Moore.

"Now then," he began calmly but without losing the authoritative edge in his voice, "it appears that there has been a gross misunderstanding in boundaries here." He glared at Alexander, who gripped his own drawn sword tightly.

"Fimen's Hope does not belong to the Moores," the Guardian leader spoke loudly but calmly. "What madness has afflicted Lord Moore that he would have his officers murder the citizens of Gurdinfield's towns?"

The officer's eyes flashed angrily as the tension between the Guardians and the Moore soldiers intensified. "I will thank you not to insult the rightful ruler of this kingdom, Alexander Telman," he said coldly. "Lord Moore has a message for you and your *Guardians.*"

Andrea was stunned when she saw the Guardian leader actually looked amused. "I see," Alexander said. "And to whom do I speak with that carries the burden of delivering such a message while completing the strenuous work of terrorizing the innocent?"

Several of the Guardians flanking Alexander chuckled quietly.

The officer glared. "You will address me as Captain Moore or not at all, fool. You'll find no admirers or support here, Alexander."

"*Captain* Moore, hmm?" Alexander exclaimed thoughtfully. "I would have thought the son of Lord Moore himself would have a grander title and role in this pointless war."

"You know less than you think!" Captain Moore sneered. His soldiers shuffled about a bit and several tightened their grips on their weapons.

"Indeed. I'm afraid we're going to have to ask you to leave, *Captain*. This town is not under Moore rule–nor are the rest of the Southlands. Feel free to deliver your message. However, if you offer a surrender, we will accept it so that we can move on to more pressing issues," Alexander said firmly.

The captain grinned and approached Alexander, taking very slow but purposeful steps. When he was nearly toe to toe with Alexander, Jacob moved forward threateningly.

"Not another step or I'll slice you open," the larger man growled. The other Guardians tensed and moved forward slightly, ready to attack on Alexander's order.

The captain rolled his eyes. "Tell your guard dog to back down, Telman. Lord Moore would like to assess the commitment of your fighters. He wishes to unite Gurdinfield under one banner and would accept your help, even offer you payment and… status," he spoke, giving Jacob a disgusted look before glancing curiously at Diana, "should you agree to take up arms with us."

Both sides went quiet save the faint jostling of armor.

"I believe," Alexander said slowly, "that my fighters are confident in remaining loyal to Gurdinfield. We too believe in a kingdom united. But mark my words, Captain, it will not be under the banner of Lord Moore."

"House Moore only employs those willing to die for the cause. What about your Guardians, Alexander?" The captain gestured to the fighters that flanked Alexander. "How far would any of *them* go to see this nation united? Would they die for it?"

Alexander leaned in dangerously close to the officer. "Of course," he said.

Andrea watched as Captain Moore's expression broke into an uncanny smile. The man gave a small chuckle before suddenly lunging forward and grabbing Diana, who cried out in alarm and dropped her sword as he pulled her roughly back against him and took a few steps back. Both Moores and Guardians broke into chaos as Jacob's eyes went wide with fear and Alexander held up his hand to command the Guardians. The enchanter quickly considered using her magic on the officer but as she looked at the situation before her she realized that any sudden movement or attack could jeopardize Diana's life.

The captain lifted his blade to the younger Telman's throat, a victorious grin spreading on his face as Diana immediately stopped struggling. "Ah, not so smug after all are we, Alexander?" he mocked.

Alexander sheathed his sword angrily. "That's enough, Moore! Let her go – she is nothing to you."

Captain Moore raised an eyebrow. "No?" he asked innocuously and pressed the sword tighter against Diana's throat, causing the young woman to whimper in fear. "Who is she to you, Alexander? Not that it matters – she is also willing to die a pointless, fool's death, is she not?"

Andrea looked on in horror as she tried to come up with something, anything really, that could possibly help Diana.

Almost as though her thoughts had been read, the enchanter staggered slightly as a surge of power rushed through her. She felt Cassie's hand gripping her wrist tightly and tried to remain discreet about it. Focusing inward, she attempted to harness energy from Cassie and possibly create a distraction of some sort. Perhaps it would buy Elisa or Jacob enough time to get Diana away from Moore.

But what?

A barrier would be useless – Andrea did not know if it was even possible to put one up around person without including herself. Fire would be too risky – she could not afford to throw anything at Moore and–*Throw the barrier.* She had done it only once before and it was on accident while under Meredith's tutelage. *When she had her stupid constructs throw whatever they could find on the manor grounds at me during one of our lessons.*

Under the pressure of time and Cassie's hurried gaze, the enchanter channeled the energy from her companion and rapidly formed a small barrier. Aiming it just past Moore, she threw it hard and hoped it would be enough to distract him without risking further injury to Diana.

The cluster of energy whistled as it flew through the air and slammed into the side of one of the small houses that ran alongside the main road, giving off a small shockwave and a distinct muffled sound. The remaining crowd of townspeople as well as both the Moores and Guardians immediately turned towards the disturbance, including Captain Moore himself, who lowered his blade slightly.

Diana immediately took advantage of the opportunity and elbowed her captor harshly in the chest, knocking the air out of him before she spun around and punched him hard in the throat, leaving the man gasping. The younger Telman freed herself of the officer's grasp completely and kicked the man in his ribs, sending him crumpling onto the dirt, his sword clattering on the ground next to him. She swiftly pulled a dagger from her belt and held it to the captain's throat as he pushed himself up.

"Do not move," she spoke, her voice low and commanding.

Realizing his precarious situation, Captain Moore glanced at his soldiers. "Stand down," he ordered, the urgency in his voice obvious. "I said *stand down!*"

With the Moore soldiers slowly backing away from the Guardians, Diana glared down at the captain. "Now," she said, her confidence quickly returning, "you will order your fighters to drop their weapons and move out."

"I will do no such thing!"

Diana pressed the blade harder against the captain's throat. Fresh beads of sweat broke out on his forehead as he grunted in pain. "You *will*," Diana threatened, "or your loyal soldiers can bring you back to your lord in pieces."

Captain Moore rolled his eyes. "Fine, fine!" he spat. Diana withdrew her blade but did not sheath it. The captain stood up slowly, rubbing his neck as he addressed his fighters. "Dis-dis-arm. We move out immediately. No point in wasting any more time in this filth they call a town." He leaned in closer to Diana, whose dagger hovered over the captain's chest. "Mark my words, this is not the last time we will meet."

Diana was unfazed. "I hope not," she answered plainly. "I

like to give cowards a head start before I put them down for good."

Moore stared hard at the Guardian commander, but said nothing before turning back to his bewildered fighters and harshly repeating his orders for them to leave their weapons on the ground and move out. The Guardians looked on as the Moore soldiers grudgingly dropped their blades and bows onto the dirt. They quickly assembled into a marching formation and left Fimen's Hope.

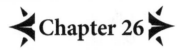

Chapter 26

The Saviors of Fimen's Hope

"You should have just left it alone! All of you!"

"Diana," Alexander pleaded as he followed his daughter, with Jacob trailing close behind him. The Guardians and their guests had set up camp just outside the town so as not to disturb its residents any further.

Diana spun around, fuming at Alexander as Elisa, Andrea, Cassie, Kye, and her fellow fighters discreetly watched the rather uncomfortable situation unfolding before them. "You said it yourself, Alexander – until this war is over we are *all* expendable. Showing Moore weakness like…like *that* is precisely what he wants!" she exclaimed. "Now he *knows* how to target us!"

"Diana, you don't understand–," Jacob tried.

Diana laughed harshly. "You of all people have no right to tell me what I do and do not understand." She turned to Alexander again. "The next time that happens you cannot hesitate!"

Alexander shook his head and spoke calmly. "I will do what I think is best, Diana. You cannot dissuade me from that, no matter how angry you are."

"Then we will lose this war! Is that what you want?" she challenged.

"We will press on as we always have. And I will *not* tolerate that kind of talk here," the Guardian leader said sharply. "You have a duty–,"

"My duty is to the Guardians and to stop Moore from burning another town," Diana spat.

"Your duty is to Gurdinfield!" Alexander yelled. "You *will* accept that or there will not *be* a Gurdinfield to save from Moore much longer!" Diana was swiftly silenced. Alexander rarely raised his voice at anyone, especially her. She looked around at her stone-faced companions. The campsite was dead quiet.

"Enough!" she finally cried, holding up her hand to stop Alexander from continuing. "I…I can't listen to this anymore. I need to be alone." With that, she stormed off, away from the camp and toward the town.

"Diana!" Jacob called after her. He began to follow her but was stopped by Alexander.

"No," the Guardian leader said calmly. "Let her go. She needs time to calm down before we can continue."

Andrea, who had remained quiet the entire time, spoke up timidly from the spot on the ground where she sat. "I'm sorry. I didn't mean to upset anyone. I was only trying to help."

"You did nothing wrong. Letting her die by that idiot's hand was not an option," Elisa said.

Jacob sighed. "Well then, what do we do in the meantime?"

"We need to seek an audience with Lord Harrington," Alexander replied. "It's time we stop hiding. Both houses need to know that Azgadar will invade."

"Sir, is Diana right? Will they try to come after her directly to get to you?" the captain asked.

"Perhaps. But the Harringtons are close to losing this civil war, and Edward will be desperate once he finds out that the Legion will be coming as well."

"Harrington will fall in line quickly, I believe," Elisa suddenly spoke up, surprising both the Guardian leader and the captain. "The Moores will be a problem, no doubt, but I think if we can take care of Lord Moore and his higher-ranking officers, we might be able to convince the rest to follow as well."

"How do you know this?" Jacob wondered.

Elisa smiled. "Let's just say I've been to enough parties back in Azgadar to know where our enemies' loyalties truly lie. Most of them are tired of the war. They want things back to the way they used to be, when they could be nice and lazy while someone else handled everything for them."

"What of the captain? We cannot just let him live after what he's done," Jacob declared. "We should go after him."

"No doubt he's returning to his father at Hathorn Hold," the Guardian leader stated.

"Hathorn Hold?" Kye finally spoke up. The young enchanter was sitting on a pile of burlap sacks containing supplies.

"The home of House Moore, at least for the last hundred years," Jacob explained. "It's a bit east of here, between Fimen's Hope and the City of Towers."

"If you know where he is, why don't you just take it? End the problem?" Cassie asked. She sat on the ground next to Andrea, and had also refrained from speaking for most of the afternoon while the Guardians had been conversing.

"That would be foolish," Elisa countered. "Hathorn Hold is well-guarded and has an army that could conquer Gurdinfield if it wasn't led by a complete imbecile. We are no match for them in a direct fight."

"Harrington's army might be!" Jacob said thoughtfully, his eyes brightening with an idea. He turned to Elisa. "You say Harrington would consider an allegiance if he knew the war would end quickly?"

Elisa gave a short nod. "No guarantee, but it is possible."

"Then Jacob, Diana, and I will take some fighters to the Northlands and gain an audience with Edward," Alexander decided. "Hopefully, he will see reason and will lend us the aid we need to bring Moore down."

Jacob shook his head in disagreement. "The Northlands? We'll be walking into a death trap, Alexander. What if he decides to simply kill us on sight?"

Alexander shrugged. "We are out of options, and there is no way we can face Moore in open combat – not with our current numbers." He looked to Elisa. "I am leaving you in charge, Elisa. You are to take everyone and meet me in the Gurdin Woods in six days."

"That's not far from Hathorn Hold," Elisa realized. "You are planning to bring help, I take it?"

"Yes," the Guardian leader confirmed.

"What of Captain Moore?" she asked. "Should we not track the coward down before he slinks back to his father?"

"No doubt he's sent a rider ahead of him to alert the rest of his house about what happened," Jacob muttered.

"No. I will not risk it," Alexander said sternly. He turned to the ex-Legionnaire again. "Prepare our fighters here for battle. Recruit anyone from town who is interested in joining our cause. When you are ready, come and meet me." He gestured to Andrea, Cassie, and Kye. "Take our new friends with you. It is time we see what our enchanters can do."

Cassie tentatively raised her hand. "Uh…I'm not actually an enchanter."

"You did well enough with that palace guard in the dungeon," Elisa cut in, actually nodding with approval at Cassie. "You can help us."

Andrea glanced worriedly at Elisa and then at Cassie. She knew that she had signed on to help the Guardians in return for their help in getting her and Cassie across the Northland Bridge to Rhyad. She did not expect them to actually have to fight, or worse, have Cassie – who did not have any combat experience that she knew of – participate in the fighting as well.

"Oh, um…all right, I guess," the enchanter heard Cassie say slowly. Andrea couldn't decide which was more surprising – that Cassie was going along with the plan without an argument or that Elisa was actually expressing her approval of something.

"Alexander clasped his hands together. "It is settled. I will alert those of you who are coming with me, and we shall make haste for the Northlands tonight."

"Ex-excuse me?" a quiet voice spoke up from behind them. Upon turning to face the visitor, the Guardians saw that it was a lanky, middle-aged man. He looked quite nervous.

"Sorry to interrupt," he continued. "I bring a message from

Fimen's Hope. We are…in the process of selecting a new mayor, however we are deeply grateful for your assistance in ridding us of those…"

"Bird scum?" Jacob offered helpfully.

The man chuckled nervously. "Ah. Yes, exactly. I was er… instructed to inform you that the town would like to host you and your companions for a celebration of our freedom tonight."

The Guardians responded with a chorus of interest, with most nodding or smiling in approval.

"Don't get too excited. They might come back, you know," Elisa deadpanned.

"Ignore her – she's never happy about anything," Jacob told the man as the ex-Legionnaire glared at him while several of the Guardians laughed.

The man wrung his hands together and gave a nervous smile. "Oh! Well then, we'll be awaiting your arrival at the inn after sundown. There will be food and drink for all."

At the mention of food, Cassie's eyes lit up.

"They might not have your *favorite* ale," Andrea quietly teased, taking the opportunity to test the waters of their recovering friendship.

Cassie shook her head and playfully shoved the enchanter. "You're getting better at this humor thing, but trust me – you desperately need more practice."

Andrea only shrugged and smiled back. It had been a long and terrible day, but at least a few things were looking up for her.

* * *

"Another one, miss?"

Diana Telman stared miserably at the empty glass in front of her from her seat at the rather rundown bar of Fimen Hope's only inn. She sighed heavily. It had only been an hour or so since she had left the Guardian camp. She had a headache and her throat stung where Captain Moore's blade had pressed against it earlier. "I shouldn't."

"Yeah, she will. And I'll have whatever she had." The Guardian commander was stunned to hear Cassie's voice as her newest companion walked up to the bar and took a seat in the chair next to her.

"Mind if I sit with you?" she asked.

Diana stared at the younger woman for a moment before shaking her head slowly. "Oh...no, not at all. Though I really shouldn't have anything else."

Cassie waved her hand dismissively. "You were almost killed. I think you deserve at least one more drink for all of this ridiculousness."

The Guardian commander could not hold back a small laugh as the innkeeper refilled her glass and placed a newly filled glass in front of Cassie. "Well," she said and lifted her glass up, "to you, I suppose."

Cassie raised an eyebrow but took a long sip of her drink anyway. She grimaced at the taste before regaining her composure. "I swear I will find a drink here that isn't disgusting," she muttered as she eyed her glass. She turned to Diana. "To me? What'd I do?"

Diana took a small sip before placing her glass back on the bar. "You did not ask to be here and yet you've been incredibly patient with us and our mission. You're a good sort, Cassie."

"Don't let Elisa hear you say that."

"Why not?"

"Nothing," Cassie dismissed. "She thinks I'm an entitled, spoiled brat despite the fact that since joining up with her I've nearly died. Twice."

The Guardian commander smiled. "Elisa told us everything and I do not believe she thinks you are any of those things. You, Andrea, and Kye have been nothing but cooperative. And..." She paused for a moment before adding, "Andrea *did* save my life. I feel like a terrible person for not thanking her yet."

Cassie rubbed the back of her neck nervously. "Yeah... about that...I don't think Andrea meant to screw up your strategy or whatever. She just wanted to make sure you didn't, you know, die."

Diana bit her lip guiltily. "I am sorry you had to be part of that...situation, Cassie. And I know that Andrea was only trying to help – I don't blame her in the slightest. My only concern now is that Moore will know our...weakness."

"You're not a weakness. You kicked that loser's ass in front of everyone!" Cassie exclaimed.

"Yes, but next time–,"

"Why does there have to be a next time? You beat him once; just do it again," Cassie said brazenly.

Diana laughed again. "If only it were that easy."

"You made it look pretty easy. I wouldn't mind knowing how to do that."

"Perhaps when all of this is over I can teach you a few things. Where are the others, by the way?"

"Oh," Cassie said and shrugged. "They're around. The town invited us to some kind of party tonight. I think Alexander was looking for you, though."

Diana sighed and pushed a loose strand of dark hair behind her ear. "No doubt. I take it he has a plan then?"

Cassie nodded. "Yeah. Something about someone named Harrington and ending your civil war."

"Of course. He probably thinks he can reason with Harrington now that we know Azgadar will invade," Diana sighed. "I should go meet with him."

"I think I saw him heading toward the center of town," Cassie informed the younger Telman as she reached into her pocket and pulled out some of the coins Andrea had given her back in Azgadar. "I'm still a little hazy on how this works, but this should be enough," she muttered as she counted the coins and set them on the counter.

"Thank you. You…this wasn't necessary," Diana said gratefully.

"Don't mention it. Seriously, don't," Cassie said, a crooked smile spreading across her face. She stood up and stretched a bit. "Well, then. I'm going to find out when and where the food will be. See you around?"

"Yes," Diana agreed and stood up as well. "Until next time." She took a moment to straighten out her clothing before walking with Cassie out of the inn, the two going their separate ways.

* * *

"To the Guardians!"

The large group of villagers, including its town council and small militia, echoed their praise for the Guardians as all lifted their glasses and mugs to toast the saviors of their home.

Jacob, along with the Guardians who had decided to attend the celebration at the town inn, raised his glass along with the rest before taking a long drink of Fimen Hope's finest ale that had been offered to them free of charge. He grinned as many of his companions clapped him on the back as they walked past him to enjoy the food and the festivities that had taken over the inn. A small but lively band of musicians played in one corner near the great fireplace where a variety of meats were roasting on a spit that rotated over the flames. Several of the villagers and Guardians had set down their food and drink to dance in the open space in front of the band.

Kye sat quietly at one of the tables, admiring the musicians as they played an upbeat song. He had heard it only a few times in Azgadar, but knew it was popular in Gurdinfield. He was perfectly content sitting and eating while listening to the lute player strum away the distinctive chords of the song when the table suddenly shifted as a plate clattered loudly on top of it.

"Let's see how well these barbarians cook their meat," Elisa muttered as she sat down across from the young enchanter.

Kye raised his eyebrows in surprise. "Barbarians?"

"Yes," the ex-Legionnaire grumbled as she began to cut into her steak. "What kind of tavern doesn't serve Azgadaran Red Ale?"

"Um…one that isn't in Azgadar?" Kye offered nervously.

Elisa took a bite of her steak and pointed her fork at Kye accusingly. "Enough of your logic, boy." When the enchanter snickered, she swallowed and spoke again. "So, I hear you play music. What sort?"

"Oh!" Kye immediately grew flustered. "I don't-that is…I used to play. The lute that is. And I…well, I suppose I sing a bit." He watched as the older woman attacked her food as though she had not eaten in days. "How did you know?"

"The three of you are terribly loud at night with all of your chattering," Elisa said with her mouth full of food. "So, you play. Are you trained or did your parents teach you?"

Kye smiled sadly. "No. I…I suppose you could say I taught myself. My father…" He suddenly felt very uncomfortable, but pushed himself to continue as the ex-Legionnaire watched him carefully. "My father bought me a lute a few years ago, and I guess I just started playing it on my own without anyone's assistance or training."

"But not anymore?"

The enchanter shook his head. "I'm afraid not. It was l-lost when…well, you know what happened, I'm sure."

Elisa took a sip of her drink and leaned forward. "Actually,

I don't. I know what you were accused of. Beyond that is all rumors and gossip."

Kye swallowed hard. He knew he could trust Elisa, but he was not sure if he should share everything that had happened. Then again, he knew that Elisa had her secrets, too. Perhaps if he shared his, then she might share a few of her own?

"Erm...well, by now you know that I cannot control my magic v-very well," he admitted. When Elisa merely nodded, he hesitated before continuing. "I only found out that I could even use magic a few months ago. I was helping my father in the forge – he was a blacksmith, you see."

"I know who he was. Everyone in the city knew who he was. He was a major weapons supplier to the Legion. So what happened?"

"Oh!" Kye felt his face grow hot as he struggled to find the courage to continue with his story.

"Go on, then," Elisa pressed and continued to eat. "You were helping him?"

Kye ran his hand through his short curls nervously. "Y-yes. While I was bringing him one of his tools...I can't describe it, but I remember fire just...engulfing my hand, the tool, and then the floor...and then the walls." He shuddered as the memory began to overwhelm him and blinked hard a few times to regain his composure.

Elisa stared at the young enchanter intensely. "And that was the first time you knew of your abilities?" she asked.

"I-yes," Kye answered softly. "M-my father was in shock and I can't really blame him. I couldn't move, and the flames swiftly

spread to the house where the rest of my family lived. They...
they couldn't get out in time."

Elisa's stony gaze did not falter. "How did you escape?"

The enchanter shifted uncomfortably. "Well, some
Legionnaires were nearby and they pulled me out before the
fire could...consume me. But when they saw my hands...that
I was creating the fire...that's when they knew, and...well, you
know the rest."

Elisa nodded. "Enchanters have no place in Azgadar."

"No," Kye agreed. "They do not. I spent the next few months
hiding in the attics of houses all over the city. The magic...it
would come and go, and I would try to control it as best as I
could. Then one night, I saw Cassie being cornered by Claudia
and her friends." He looked determined. "I couldn't just stand
by and let her get hurt."

Elisa took another sip of her drink. "Honestly, the way those
two are, I have a feeling that you and I are going to be spending
quite a bit of time making sure they don't get themselves killed
in some stupid manner."

The young man could not hide a smile. "You really believe
they would be so reckless? Andrea is a *real* apprentice to an
actual enchanter and–,"

"Andrea is a scared, emotional girl who keeps thinking with
her heart instead of her brain," Elisa retorted, "and when she's
not doing that she's bickering with Cassie about anything and
everything."

Kye raised his eyebrows. "I think they've been rather brave
in all this. Why do they argue so much?"

Elisa shrugged. "Who knows? But enough about them – you were telling me about when you had a lute of your own."

"Actually," Kye said and took a deep breath. "I was wondering if I could know a bit about you, Elisa."

Elisa took another bite of her food as she narrowed her eyes at Kye. "There's nothing to know about me."

"Of course there is. You used to be a Legionnaire, but you won't tell us why you're working for the Guardians. And I overheard some of the others calling you 'Lady Elisa,'" he argued. "I told you about me. It's only fair that I get to know about you."

Elisa put her fork down, showing no emotion, and for a moment Kye wondered if he had angered her. But she sat back in her chair and nodded. "All right. I suppose that's fair. But you're not to share what I tell you with anyone, you hear me?"

Kye nodded solemnly.

The ex-Legionnaire sighed. "What do you wish to know?"

The enchanter responded with barely-contained excitement. "Your title. Are you nobility?"

Elisa folded her arms across her chest. "Why am I not surprised you asked that first? No, not really. The title was given to me – I wasn't born with it."

"By the empress?"

"Yes," Elisa said casually. "It was mostly ceremonial at first. Being Ithmeera's sister-in-law can get you a lot in Azgadar."

Kye did a double take and stared blankly at the ex-Legionnaire across from him. "Hold on. You-your brother was the emperor consort?!"

"Philip, yes," Elisa said calmly with a short nod. She offered a crooked smile. "What, you couldn't see the family resemblance?" she asked while gesturing to her bright red hair.

"Well…no, but he didn't–,"

Elisa cut him off. "Didn't look like me, I know. I took after our grandmother."

Kye nodded, dumbfounded. "Did the empress give you the title after she married your brother?"

"No. I had already been a part of the Legion. Philip had a trading company that he had been growing when they met in the marketplace during one of her visits. When they began courting, my family was invited to the palace for dinner." She took another sip of her drink. "Turned out Ithmeera and I got along quite well. We became inseparable friends before she and my brother were even engaged."

Kye pointed to the silver chain that Elisa once again wore around her neck. "And your necklace – where did you get it? And how did Ithmeera know about it?"

The ex-Legionnaire unconsciously wrapped her hand around the pendant. "It was a gift. Philip gave it to me when Ithmeera named me her bodyguard. Ithmeera must have helped him choose it. That is probably why she recognized it when Andrea was wearing it that night at the ball."

"*You?*" Kye exclaimed doubtfully. "*You* were Ithmeera's bodyguard?"

"That I was," Elisa answered grimly. The young enchanter could see signs of hurt flash across the ex-Legionnaire's expression, but they quickly disappeared. "Look, I don't really care if you believe me or not. I don't even know why I am bothering to tell you all this. But if you so much as *whisper* anything–,"

"I wouldn't–I won't!" Kye protested before offering a shy smile. "For what it's worth, I am glad you came to our aid when you did."

Elisa narrowed her eyes at the young enchanter. "As I said, if you so much as utter a word of any of this I will kill you."

Kye's smile did not falter. "I won't tell."

An older man walked by to take the empty plates and cups off the table. The festivities were still going on strong and Kye could see that many of the patrons, Guardians and villagers both, were already quite intoxicated. He looked around for the rest of their friends. Andrea was not in sight, but he spotted Cassie sitting at the bar with Jacob, Victor, Roe, and a few other Guardians. From the volume of their shouting and laughter Kye concluded they were all very drunk.

"Looks like it's going to be a long night," Elisa grumbled. "And I refuse to nurse any of these idiots come morning when they are all sick from the rancid drink they serve here." She pushed her chair back and stood up. "Now, I am going back to camp so I can go to bed. We've a long day ahead of us tomorrow and I already have a headache from all of this talking."

"Good night," Kye said.

"Try not to be so noisy when you three return to camp tonight," Elisa muttered as she walked away, leaving the young man alone to resume watching the musicians play.

Chapter 27

Fimen's Fire

Even from the Guardian campsite, Alexander could hear the music coming from the inn as he watched the festivities begin moving outside and into the town square. He stood next to the main campfire looking out at Fimen's Hope, arms crossed over his chest as the night cold began to set in. He shivered and glanced up at the clear, starry sky. Autumn was ending and winter would soon be upon them. He considered for a moment. The frigid winter of Gurdinfield would certainly give them an advantage over the Legion, which trained primarily in southern Azgadar where it was much warmer and drier throughout the year. They could technically wait a bit longer before going to Harrington so that the Legion had no choice but to invade sooner before Gurdinfield regained its strength. But with winter came supply shortages and with this civil war…

No. He would not risk it. They needed to end this now and prepare for the inevitable invasion. *Twenty years is long enough.*

"Thinking about winter?"

The Guardian leader blinked in surprise and looked to his left where his daughter now approached him. He chuckled despite their heated conversation only hours earlier. "How did you know?"

Diana smiled wryly. The bright, orange flames of the campfire cast dark shadows across her face. "Because every year you get that pensive look on your face and keep gazing up at the sky as though you expect it to start snowing any minute."

"You know me well," Alexander commented with a smile.

"I know my father," she said simply. An awkward silence descended on them, the only sound coming from the crackling fire.

"Diana," Alexander began hesitantly.

She cut him off, her tone void of emotion. "So, we are to meet with Harrington? Hoping to gain an alliance?"

The Guardian leader inhaled sharply but forced himself to answer anyway. He cleared his throat. "I-yes. With Moore becoming more aggressive, Edward knows he needs to make a major move soon. He is old and tired of this war, Diana."

"And you think he will just *accept* our information about the empress? No questions asked?" Diana seemed doubtful.

Alexander shrugged. "Perhaps. That is my hope at least."

"Your 'hope'? That is what all of this hinges on?"

"If I recall," Alexander said, "reuniting Gurdinfield was *your* idea."

Diana sighed. "Fair enough. I just hope you're right about Harrington and that he doesn't have us killed for showing our faces in his home."

The Guardian leader smiled again. "I've known Edward a long time. We'll be granted some protections, though of course nothing is guaranteed."

"I don't even know what I would say to him," Diana grumbled.

"Leave that to me," Alexander assured her.

The younger Telman rubbed her eyes, visibly exhausted after the day's events. "Well, I should start packing then. I'll be by my tent if you need me," she announced before abruptly walking away, leaving Alexander to his thoughts once more.

* * *

Cassie failed to choke back a cough as the latest draught of her new favorite drink burned its way down her throat. She slammed her glass down on the bar counter.

"Good, isn't it?!" Victor laughed and slapped the girl on her back, forcing her to cough again. She nodded meekly as she fought back tears from both the drink and her attempts to breathe normally.

"Nice, Vic. Maybe you can help *all* of our new allies *choke to death* before we meet the Moores on the field," Roe barked at the smaller man.

"Nonsense, she's fine! Aren't ya, Cass?" Victor exclaimed, turning back to Cassie, who nodded again before speaking in what sounded more like a slurred squeak than her normal voice. "Fine!" she replied. She cleared her throat, the burning almost completely gone. "Just...fine."

"See?" Victor pointed out as Roe rolled his eyes. He turned and waved down the bartender, who was serving up drinks as quickly as he could to the crowds of patrons in the inn. The festivities were still going strong and both villagers and

Guardians showed no signs of fatigue. "Another one for our friend here, sir!"

Jacob, who had been calmly observing the amusing sight before him, chuckled at his comrades. "I apologize for Victor, Cassie. Alas, intelligence has never come naturally to him."

Cassie grinned at her newest friends. "No worries. You three have done the impossible. Everything else I've tried so far has tasted like something died in it." She gestured at the glass in front of her. "This is actually not that bad."

"'Fimen's Fire'. Oh, other towns claim to have invented the recipe and have given it different names, but as far as I'm concerned," Jacob declared as he watched the bartender refill Cassie's glass before setting it back down on the counter, "*this* is the true source!"

"Right you are, friend," Roe boomed. He lifted his own mug. "To Fimen's Hope."

Echoing his toast, the four of them drank from their cups again. This time, Cassie was able to keep herself from coughing as she set her half-empty glass back down. As she used her shirtsleeve to wipe a bit of spilt liquor from her mouth she noticed Andrea walking into the inn and going to sit at one of the few empty tables. She continued to observe Andrea as the enchanter ordered a drink from a passing waitress and took in the scene before glancing over at the bar, her expression shifting from boredom to curiosity upon spotting Cassie.

Cassie decided she had gone long enough without bothering Andrea over the past few days. "I'll…catch up with you guys in a bit," she said to the three Guardians. But as she made her way toward Andrea's table she quickly realized she was far more intoxicated than she had initially thought. She stumbled slightly – enough that she had to hold on to a nearby chair to steady herself before being able to continue. She finally came to a stop, practically collapsing in the chair across from Andrea.

Amused, the enchanter raised an eyebrow. "Having a good time, I see."

"Yep," Cassie replied brightly. "What did you order?"

The harsh stench of Fimen's Fire slammed into Andrea, causing her to reel back and shake her head a few times to rid her senses of the scent. "Oh my...what in the *world* have you been drinking?!" She covered her nose and mouth with her hand to further demonstrate her disgust as Cassie simply laughed at her.

"Want some? Victor had me try it. It's my new...it's my favorite. My favorite drink. 'Fimen' something. You guys have weird names for things," she slurred.

"Ugh...no, thank you," Andrea answered and coughed. "It smells horrible." She frowned and then looked at the other girl incredulously. "Wait, 'Fimen's Fire'? *That's* the drink you chose as your favorite?"

"Hey, don't knock it 'til you've tried it!" Cassie protested and slammed her fist down on the table. "Just because I don't like... whatever you like doesn't means it's bad."

The enchanter laughed quietly as the waitress returned and set a full mug down in front of her before leaving. "I think I'll stick to wine and cider, thank you. I'm...glad you found a drink you like, Cassie."

Cassie smirked. "Whatever. More for me." She began tracing

the wood grains on the table with her finger. "So where were you, huh? Haven't seen you all evening."

Andrea shrugged. "One of the villagers knew Amara's family. They offered to take her in, so I was helping with that."

Cassie nodded, though the enchanter was unsure if the other girl was actually listening based on how intensely she was staring at the table. "Out of curiosity, just how many of your new 'favorite drink' have you had?"

"Oh...a few, I guess. And then there was that other one I had with Diana earlier, which was gross. You sure you don't want any?" Cassie offered again.

The enchanter smiled and shook her head. "I will pass. Perhaps I might see if there is a spare tent, however."

Cassie looked up with a roguish grin. "What's wrong? The uptight enchanter doesn't want to sleep in the same tent as me after I've had a few drinks, hmm? Nervous?"

Andrea blinked in disbelief a few times as she felt her face quickly flush with heat. "I-no!" she snapped. "I just don't want to be around you when you decide you can't keep that foul liquid down anymore."

"If you say so," Cassie teased.

The enchanter closed her eyes and inhaled deeply. She wanted to confront Cassie about the other girl's behavior over the past few days, but was not sure how to go about it without upsetting her. *Might as well do it now. No doubt we'll argue again about something else soon enough the way things have been going.*

"Cassie...can we talk about what happened a few days ago?" she asked hopefully.

Cassie raised an eyebrow in mild surprise and appeared in thought for a moment before leaning in closer to the enchanter. "Maybe. You have to try some of my favorite drink, though."

"What? No, I've already told you – Fimen's Fire is disgusting."

"Have you even *had* it?" Cassie challenged.

"As a matter of fact, yes!" Andrea countered indignantly. "Cassie, I really do think we should talk about this–,"

"Why do you always want to *talk* so much?" Cassie threw her hands up in frustration, all traces of humor in her voice gone. "Yeah, I was pissed, okay? Every time we barely escape with our lives from something or someone we have to run again because something *else* is after us. First, it was your crazy mentor. Then it was the crazy empress. Then it was your crazy mentor *again*...or her monsters or whatever! Now it's some other batch of crazy," she fired off. "Oh, and don't even get me started on the fact that we've been thrown into the middle of a damn civil war! But hey, as long as we save the world and bring back magic, that's what counts, right?"

Everything I've done so far has put us in danger. Of course she'd be upset. Andrea wanted to respond defensively at first, but quickly realized that Cassie had a point when she spotted the fading cut on her friend's head. Ever since they had left the Black Forest, they had been in danger. She wanted to point out that this was what Cassie had agreed to, but quickly dismissed the thought when she reminded herself that Cassie had volunteered out of necessity, not by choice.

Rather than immediately argue, the enchanter decided to try something different. "I...you're right to be upset. It's my fault that we're here."

Cassie looked as though she was about to reflexively protest, but stopped short and stared at Andrea in surprise instead. "What?"

The enchanter suddenly felt very self-conscious but pushed herself to continue anyway. "Erm...well, let's be honest – we wouldn't be in this mess if it wasn't for me."

Cassie shrugged. "Eh. You...you didn't know what would happen," she admitted slowly, the alcohol having a more apparent effect on her speech than before. "I get it. You just-you just wanted to help. You always want to help. You're just one of those people, I guess."

Andrea nodded apologetically. "I really am trying to do the right thing here. I had no idea Meredith would be so... so desperate." She looked down at the table uncomfortably. "I truly am sorry that you got hurt."

But Cassie waved her away. "Ah...I got a scratch – it's not a big deal." She laughed loudly, startling the enchanter. "You know what you need?"

"You're not going to try to make me try your foul drink again are you?"

"No, though you should because it's good," Cassie declared. "You...need to seriously *relax*. Stop worrying all the time. I get that you want to save the world, but last time I checked we are not in a freaking apocalypse and even if we were, I'd rather focus on other stuff so that when we *do* all die horribly I'm not extremely depressed about it."

"We're not going to all die horribly," Andrea corrected with a faint smile.

"Good. See, you're getting better already!" Cassie praised, earning a short laugh from the enchanter. "It *is* possible to save the world and not be a total bore about it, even if we're talking about *you*."

"I am *not* a bore!"

Cassie snorted. "Of course you're not."

Andrea folded her hands together. "If I recall correctly, *I've* been the one throwing fireballs at Meredith's constructs *and* I played the bait at the ball in Azgadar. I think that hardly qualifies as 'boring.'"

Shaking her head, Cassie said, "Sure. But let's not forget that it was your brilliant, talented, witty sidekick helping you make those fireballs. I can't take credit for you getting caught by Ithmeera, however, I *did* help in the…" She grabbed Andrea's mug and raised it victoriously, "*grand* plan of breaking you out of that dungeon!" She ended her speech by taking a long sip of Andrea's cider before slamming the mug back on the table. "Ew! This crap again? How the hell do you drink this?!"

The enchanter rolled her eyes and took the mug back. "As anyone else would…and why are you shouting?" She briefly glanced around her and lowered her voice to a hushed and worried tone before she leaned in toward Cassie. "You-you haven't told anyone about your abilities, have you?"

Cassie winked. "What if I did? I bet they'd be impressed."

"Cassie!"

"Oh, stop. No, I haven't said a word. What did I just say about worrying so much?" Cassie exclaimed.

"Fine," Andrea grumbled. She sat back in her chair and drank some of her cider.

"So, when all this is over, what are you going to do? Go back home to your little town and show your parents what a big hero you are?" Cassie asked.

The enchanter set her mug down. "I...no. No, I don't imagine I'll see my parents again, to be honest."

"Why not?"

Andrea took a deep breath. "Because we didn't exactly part on good terms. No doubt they are still furious at me and coming home bragging about magic won't exactly reconcile things between us."

"I thought saving magic would help everybody here. Wouldn't they be happy to know that you were the one who saved it?" Cassie wondered.

The enchanter bit her lip in frustration. "I doubt it."

The other girl appeared more interested now as she leaned in again. "All right," she prompted. "What, being an enchanter wasn't the future your parents had in mind for you?"

Andrea shook her head. "Being a farmer is what they had in mind for me. My mother never approved of my abilities, but she would allow me to see a mentor every once in a while, so that I would learn *some* measure of control of magic. My father...my father was not so accepting." She tried to hide the hurt and disappointment that seeped into her voice every time she thought of the last conversation she had had with her father, but Cassie picked up on it even in her intoxicated state.

"Ah...they probably just didn't want you to end up in the exact situation you're in now," she suggested flippantly.

"Easy for you to say. One of the last things my father said to me was that enchanters are behind *every* problem in Damea," Andrea muttered, not bothering to hide the bitterness in her voice as she tried to quash the emotion from the memory and ignore the tightening in her throat.

"He probably wasn't talking about *you*. Just…enchanters in general. Like Meredith," Cassie offered.

Andrea narrowed her eyes at her friend. "You weren't there. How could you possibly know?"

"You can't blame him, Andrea. Shoot, look at where we are now," Cassie exclaimed, gesturing around them. She pointed to the cut on her head. "Look at this! We barely survived that whole ordeal with the wagon. I don't know your father, but I am pretty sure he didn't picture a future for his kid where she was being thrown into a dungeon by some empress or nearly getting killed because her ex-girlfriend wasn't okay with breaking up."

Shifting from frustration to anger, Andrea rubbed her temples and closed her eyes momentarily. "I can't tell if you're really bringing that up again because you're frankly, quite drunk, or because you just really want to upset me!" she snapped. "My reasons for leaving Ata were my own and if you can't agree with them then that's a problem you'll have to deal with on your own! You didn't know my parents and I'm starting to believe that despite my efforts, you don't really know me."

"Oh, great. More whining?" Cassie shot back. "Look, I may be a bit drunk." She laughed a bit despite herself. "Well, maybe a lot drunk. But here's the thing. You've been whining and bugging me for weeks about how you want to get to know me and asking me question after question. So there you go – we're friends." She leaned in again. "You know what friends do, Andrea?"

Andrea tried not to cough as she smelled the Fimen's Fire on Cassie's breath. "They don't smell like the worst drink in Damea, that's for sure," she muttered and folded her arms across her chest.

"Shut up and let me finish. They're *honest* with each other. And right now, I'm telling you that I think you probably acted like a spoiled brat when your parents were just trying to keep you safe," Cassie retorted. "I can't say I wouldn't have done the same thing as you, but I think you owe them a bit more credit than what you're giving them now."

Andrea was shocked by Cassie's outburst but she refused to back down so easily. "You weren't there, Cas–,"

"I don't need to have been there to tell you what I think. And I think that in all of this…this crap, that you've forgotten why the hell you're even doing this to begin with. What are you trying to prove?" Cassie challenged, her blue eyes bright with anger.

"I'm…I'm not trying to prove anything!" Andrea answered haughtily. "I'm *trying* to help Damea!"

"Bull," Cassie cut in. "You could have helped Damea a long time ago if you wanted."

"I didn't know where to look! Not until *you* came along."

"Oh *please*, like there wasn't any other way you would have figured it out?" Cassie asked coldly.

The enchanter finally slammed her fists on the table. "Fine," she whispered harshly. "Maybe I was *tired* of being nothing but my parent's farmhand. I was *tired* of living in that boring town and delivering vegetables to the inn instead of practicing powering on the farm's machines. I was *tired* of seeing Meredith weeping over Richard's body when *every* experiment, *every* trial failed miserably, and I was *tired* of cleaning up her messes after she would have her...episodes."

She felt tears of anger quickly welling up, but made no move to wipe them away. "Maybe I just wanted to *do something* with my life that didn't involve taking orders from someone else or letting them control how I live! Parents be damned – *I'll* decide what kind of life I want for myself, regardless of how risky or... or dangerous it is. *You* don't have to help me if you don't want to – none of you do!" She stood up furiously, causing the table to tip slightly and Cassie to move back in silent surprise. A few of the Guardians and other patrons looked over curiously at the two, though most returned to their conversations after a brief stare.

"Here. You can have my drink," the enchanter sneered. She made to turn and leave but lingered for a moment. "And don't bother waiting up for me. I'll get my own bloody tent!" With that she stormed away and walked briskly out of the inn, slamming the door shut behind her.

Cassie sat alone at the table, dumbfounded. She had not completely processed what had just happened when Jacob, Victor, and Roe joined her.

"The enchanter bothering you, Cass?" Victor queried, setting his glass on the table. "I've been sayin' they're trouble from the start!"

"Shut it – you just finished telling us what a nice lad that boy, Kye, is!" Roe observed. He sat down next to Victor, his immense size making the small chair creak ominously.

"Ah, but that's different! The boy doesn't lash out at our

friends and leave like that," Victor reasoned. "You want us to talk to her, Cass?"

Cassie looked up blankly at the three men for a few seconds before shaking her head a few times. "What? No...no, it's fine."

"Everything all right?" Jacob asked, his tone more concerned, albeit less aggressive than Victor's.

"Yeah, it's fine," Cassie said with a casual shrug. "We just had a little disagreement is all. Nothing new."

The Guardian captain patted Cassie on the shoulder. "I'm certain it will blow over by morning, Cassie. Andrea probably just had a long day."

"Didn't we all?" Victor sighed. "Those bird bastards give me a headache every time we deal with them."

"Indeed," Roe deadpanned. "Sure you don't want us to talk to her, Cassie?"

Cassie smiled gratefully. "It's all right, guys. I should probably get to bed anyway." She stood up and pushed her chair in. "Thanks for the drinks tonight."

"Anytime, Cassie," Jacob replied before turning back to the other Guardians as their newest companion made her way toward the inn's exit.

* * *

"Almost ready, Alexander!" one of the Guardians selected for the journey to the Northlands announced as he finished preparing a few of the horses.

"Aye, same!" another one reported.

Alexander nodded. "Very good. Be ready to leave shortly. I will fetch Jacob in a bit." He double-checked that all his weapons were packed and ready before inspecting his own horse. He had barely finished when he heard Elisa's voice from behind.

"Take care. No doubt Moore will be waiting for us to move," she cautioned as she approached.

Alexander chuckled. "Well then we had better hope we are not spotted." He tilted his head. "Done celebrating already?"

The ex-Legionnaire shrugged. "Was never very fun at parties," she admitted.

"You? Not fun at parties? I don't believe it!" Diana emerged from her tent, a heavy sack slung over her shoulder.

Elisa exchanged amused glances with Alexander. "You are sure you don't want me to accompany you?"

Alexander shook his head. "The Guardians need you here, Elisa. Prepare the others. They will need your help should the worst occur."

Elisa nodded and watched as Diana fastened the last of the supplies to her horse. "As you wish. If there is nothing else, I am going to retire for the evening."

"Of course. We shall see you soon," the Guardian leader replied.

"Yes, good night, Elisa," Diana added.

Elisa gave a final nod before walking across the Guardian campsite toward her tent. As she approached, she heard a faint sniffling and was surprised to see Andrea sitting on the dirt right outside of the tent. The enchanter had her arms around her knees, which were tucked up against herself. She looked up at the ex-Legionnaire. Even in the faint glow of the fire, Elisa could see that the enchanter's eyes were bloodshot and that she had been crying.

"Oh, what in the world…what is it *now*?" she demanded.

Andrea scrambled to her feet. "I-I'm…sorry," she stammered, brushing the dirt from her pants. "I was just…just–,"

Elisa was beyond caring. "I don't really care anymore. The two of you need to figure things out or one of you needs to leave. I certainly don't have time for it." She tried to move past Andrea, but the enchanter grabbed her arm, stunning her momentarily.

"Let go," she growled.

"You promised you'd help us. What are we doing here?" Andrea pressed as she tightened her grip on the older woman's arm.

Elisa sighed. "We are doing what you agreed to do. Once we've united the houses you will be free to go to Rhyad, though why you would want to be anywhere *near* there is a mystery to me." She shook her arm. "Now. Let go."

The enchanter appeared as though she was about to protest, but she finally let go of Elisa's arm. Annoyed, the ex-Legionnaire put her hands on her hips. "Look, girl. I don't know what happened between the two of you and to be honest, I don't care. You are free to leave whenever you want, but if you wish for my help then you're going to have to toughen up a bit and deal with the situation we are in." She gestured around them. "This is not your farm or your mentor's home or some posh classroom at the academy. *This* is what the world is like and if you wish to stay alive, you are going to have to come to terms with what I am asking you to do. Understand?"

Andrea bit her lip, but said nothing.

Elisa stared hard at the enchanter before finally nodding. "All right. I am going to bed. Good night." She attempted to move past Andrea again.

"Wait!" the enchanter cried. "I…do you really think we are that pathetic?"

The ex-Legionnaire sighed. She *really* just wanted to go to bed. "No," she admitted. "You've actually all been quite useful, even brave. I need you to continue to act like that."

Andrea nodded as she rubbed one of her eyes. "Right. O-okay, then. My apologies – I shouldn't have disturbed you, Elisa."

The older woman grudgingly shook her head. "It's fine. What were you doing here anyway?"

The enchanter sniffed. "It's stupid."

"I am certain it is, but I am interested now."

Andrea shrugged. "I was going to ask if there was a spare tent I could use. Cassie…Cassie and I got into an argument about…it doesn't matter anymore."

Elisa eyed the enchanter curiously for a moment and nodded. "You two are in this together. It is important to not forget that, no matter how obnoxious both of you are to each other," she said with a straight face. She glanced around them.

"I don't know where one would find an extra tent. You're better off asking Alexander."

Andrea shook her head and smiled faintly. "It's fine. I think…I think I'll be all right for tonight. Thank you…for listening."

"May I get some sleep now?" Elisa demanded. The enchanter nodded silently and walked away.

Finally alone, the ex-Legionnaire ducked into her tent and prepared her bed. As soon as her head hit the makeshift pillow, she was asleep.

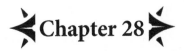

Chapter 28

Nothing According to Plan

Northlands, Gurdinfield

On the second night after leaving Fimen's Hope, Alexander, Jacob, and Diana sat around the small fire in the campsite they and the Guardians who accompanied them had set up shortly after crossing into the Northlands. The northern region of Gurdinfield was noticeably colder than the Guardians were used to, though the breathtaking view of the formidable Rhyad mountains in the distance made bearing the chilly air worth it. Their campsite was located on the top of a grassy hill and overlooked the impressive stone tower that was Northland Keep, stronghold of the Harringtons.

After finishing her dinner, Diana turned to Alexander. "Should we discuss what exactly we are going to say to Lord Harrington tomorrow?"

Alexander glanced up from his food, his expression one of momentary surprise. "I believe I told you I would handle it," he said, his voice calm.

"Of course, but I think we should still discuss what to do should things go wrong," Diana pressed. She noticed Jacob lean in with interest but the Guardian captain remained silent, as he had for most of their journey.

The older Telman put his plate down on the ground. He glanced across the fire at Jacob. "Jacob, I believe we need some additional firewood for tonight. Go with a few of the others to collect it. Take weapons – we cannot be too careful here."

Jacob gave a solemn nod. "Of course, sir. I shall return shortly." He stood up, securing his sword to his belt, and walked deeper into the camp, leaving Alexander and Diana alone.

The Guardian commander raised an eyebrow. "You sent him away for a reason," she noted quietly.

Alexander smiled. "We do need more firewood. But yes, there is something I wish to speak to you about before we get to Northland Keep tomorrow, Diana."

Diana bit her lip. "If…if this is about my conduct in Fimen's Hope, I apologize. Accusing us – our cause – of weakness was not acceptable." She hung her head. "I know that."

Alexander's smile did not falter. "Of course you do. And I'm aware of how deeply you care for our cause, make no mistake." Clearing his throat, he reached into his pocket and pulled out a small cloth pouch. "Here," he said. "This belongs to you. I've had it for quite a while, and I think it is time that it was returned to you."

Diana glanced at the Guardian leader curiously before tentatively taking the pouch. She opened it and gently dumped its contents into her hand, revealing a thin, gold chain. A heavy pendant hung from the chain. While it was slightly worn, its shape was obvious at first glance.

"It's a lion," she said blankly.

"The Great Lion, yes. There used to be an inscription on the back of it, if I recall correctly," Alexander mused.

The Guardian commander turned the pendant over. "It's still there," she confirmed and read slowly. "'One land. One legacy.'"

"The Taylors united Gurdinfield in the First Era," Alexander explained. "Unity without tyranny was King Caleb's way. He had hoped to pass that way down to his children."

Diana studied the necklace for a moment before looking up at the Guardian leader again. "That is interesting but...why are you telling *me* this?"

Alexander sighed sadly. "I...have not been completely honest with you, Diana." He looked down. "I've kept secrets from you, not just for your own good but also for the good and security of Gurdinfield."

Diana tilted her head. "What secret? What sort of secret would be so great that it would affect myself and all of Gurdinfield?"

The Guardian leader locked his gaze with hers. "The one your father, your true father, would have wanted me to keep."

Diana tilted her head. "My-my father? What are you talking about? You are my father."

Alexander shook his head. "No, my dear. I have had the honor of raising you, but I cannot call myself your father through blood. That title belongs to another man. A man I served for many years and...one who I failed to protect at the very end."

The color drained from Diana's face. "You're...you're joking, right?" she exclaimed. "I-*you're* my father, Alexander, not–,"

"Caleb Taylor was your father," Alexander interrupted, his expression remaining serious. "Your mother was Helen. You are the last surviving member of the Taylor line."

Diana simply stared at him. "But-I…that's impossible. My mother died after she had me. That's what you told me."

Alexander nodded guiltily. "I did. No, your family was murdered, Diana. You were almost part of that terrible loss, but I was able to find you in time and bring you to safety. I am sorry for lying to you – truly I am. But I did not want to risk you knowing too soon. Knowing all of this would have made our situation even more complicated. You were not ready."

Diana gaped at him in shock. "B-but you think I am now? You think it was okay to…to lie to me?!"

A few of the Guardians looked over at the two curiously as the atmosphere grew tense. Diana glanced back at them before the realization hit her.

"Did-who else knows? Jacob…did he–," she stammered, remembering her encounter with Jacob in the woods near Karrea.

"Yes," Alexander admitted. "I told Jacob that he needed to make a choice. Any other option would have been selfish and not in your best interest. Every Guardian knew and was sworn to secrecy," he explained. "I had to make certain they would fight for our cause and be loyal to the crown. To you, Diana."

Diana buried her face in her hands as tears sprung to her eyes. "How…how could you keep this from me, Alexander? You–,"

"I am sorry," the Guardian leader repeated. "I was not being fair to you by hiding this, just as it was not fair that you did not get to grow up with your mother, father, and brothers."

Diana looked up at him. "My brothers? I have-had brothers?"

She sniffed and shook her head. "I mean, I know the royal family had more than one child but–,"

"Two brothers. Abner and John." Alexander smiled at the memory. "Abner was quite a bit older than you, but he was so ready to be king. Your parents were so proud of him – of all of you."

Diana held up the necklace. "And this? Where is it from?"

"It is yours," Alexander replied with a nod. "You each had one."

"I...I see," Diana murmured, clutching the jewelry in her hand. "Were you-were you there? When it happened, I mean."

The Guardian leader nodded solemnly. "I was. I was about to retire for the evening. There was..." He sighed. "There was commotion from the great hall. By the time I got there it was too late. Your parents had already been slain...by magical means. The Guardians who had been with your mother and father were also killed. The remaining ones, including myself, began frantically searching the palace, looking for the enchanters who had done this."

Diana stood up and went to sit down next to him. "How did I survive?" she asked quietly as she cradled the necklace with both hands.

"Well," Alexander continued, "I split off from the other Guardians, hoping that I could get to you and your brothers before the assassins could. Your brothers...they..."

Diana nodded. "But not me?"

"No. You had...you had been unable to sleep that night and had gone to your parents' bedroom. The assassins did not think to look there, for they had already murdered the king and queen." He swallowed, the memory still as clear as it had been twenty years earlier. "I found you. You were still fast asleep. Your parents must have left you there during the night before they went to the great hall."

"What of the other Guardians? Did they find these enchanters?"

"Yes," Alexander said with a grimace. "I only heard the sounds of battle, but they did encounter the assassins. They... killed them all. I knew I had to get you away from there, so I grabbed you as quietly as I could and ran out as fast as I could. I knew the palace corridors well, and the enchanters never saw me." He looked at Diana sadly. "I am sorry, Diana. Truly, I am."

Diana looked down at the necklace for a long time. When she looked up at Alexander, her dark eyes were filled with tears. "You saved my life. It's...I won't lie – this is a lot to take in. It doesn't even seem real." She took a deep breath. "Did...do you know who–,"

"No. I only know they were enchanters and that they did not know their target very well. Perhaps they had been looking for you when they ran into my fellow Guardians."

Diana frowned. "Do you believe they were sent by Moore or Harrington?"

Alexander shrugged. "It is possible. Both Moore and Harrington repeatedly denied it afterward. The capital city was in chaos less than a day later. Moore took his army to Hathorn Hold to plan his takeover, and Harrington came here to do the same. You know the rest."

Diana glanced at the inscription on the necklace again. "I can't believe I really don't remember any of this. How am I supposed to convince armies to follow us when I don't even know where I come from, Alexander?" She scoffed. "Is Diana even my real name?"

Alexander laughed. "Indeed it is – well, your middle name anyway. You are Lydia Diana Taylor. As for the armies, well, you've never had a problem improvising, Diana. You've led the Guardians and you've gained the loyalty of the villages. Think of this as just a...formality."

Diana snorted. "'A formality'. I think it's a bit more complicated than that, Alexander."

"It is, but I believe you are more than ready for the task, Diana," he said, the pride in his voice obvious.

Diana studied the Guardian leader for a moment before glancing back at the necklace. She exhaled heavily before she finally put it on, the cold pendant suddenly feeling much heavier against her chest. She looked up at Alexander again.

"What must I do?"

* * *

Azgadar, Azgadaran Empire

"Ithmeera, dear. We've received news from Gurdinfield."

Ithmeera Cadar looked up from her desk in the palace study, where she had been reviewing the tax law proposals from her council of advisors. Now her Uncle Alden stood in the doorway, a piece of parchment in his hand. Since the Grand Ball, she had not seen her uncle much. He had traveled to the coastal region of Gurith during the yearly harvest festival that took place across Damea in autumn, and had only recently returned.

The empress of Azgadar sighed and put down her quill. Tax laws would just have to wait. She forced a smile. "Welcome back, Uncle. Did you have a good trip?"

The aging Cadar gave a short bow. "Forgive me for my abruptness. Yes, it was quite nice. Though I'll never understand why Gurith tends to have their festival so late in the season," he whined.

Ithmeera shrugged and gazed out the large window behind her. The mostly sunny afternoon was drawing to a close, and the sun would be setting soon. "We have our way and they have theirs, Uncle." She turned back to Alden and leaned back in her chair before gesturing to the seat in front of her desk. "Now, what is this news from Gurdinfield?"

Alden strode across the room and took the offered seat. He placed the parchment on the empress's desk. "We received this from an informant who was at Northland Keep. Edward Harrington has allied with Alexander Telman, Ithmeera."

Raising her eyebrows in surprise, Ithmeera leaned forward and folded her hands on the desk as she glanced over the letter. "Telman? The name sounds familiar…" she asked, not quite having read the note in its entirety.

Alden shook his head. "He is a former Guardian of the King. Well," he mused, "I suppose 'former' does not really accurately describe his position any longer."

Puzzled, Ithmeera shook her head and glanced back at her uncle. "What do you mean?"

"There was a young woman with Telman at the keep, Ithmeera. Lydia Taylor somehow survived the assassinations all those years ago."

The empress's eyes widened as she stared bewilderedly at Alden. "Lydia-you are joking, yes?"

Alden's gaze remained grim. "I am not, dear. And with this information comes a greater threat, I'm afraid."

Ithmeera could not help but smile. "Alden! Don't you realize what this means? With a Taylor back in power, we could send out ambassadors. If the civil war ends, we can form an actual alliance with Gurdinfield!"

But Alden's somber expression still did not change. "I'm afraid it is not as simple as that, my dear. The new queen knows of our planned invasion. I am not sure how, but–,"

The empress suddenly felt very ill. "I…" she hesitated, the smile vanishing. "At the ball," she admitted, "I encountered a spy. Elisa had sent her to distract me while she…stole my diary." She sighed heavily. "Oh, Alden, it had *everything* in it! Our plans with Lord Moore, sending out the Legion, everything!"

Alden nodded slowly. "And now Lydia Taylor has that, no doubt. And the spy?"

"Escaped," Ithmeera muttered. "Erik was right…of *course* he was right. Elisa has been working for Gurdinfield this entire time!" She clenched her fists angrily. "Possibly even before… before she left. I was a fool not to see it!" she cried and buried her face in her hands.

"Now, now, dear," Alden comforted his niece. "There is no use dwelling on past mistakes. Your father would not have any of it. I believe continuing with our original plan would be the best course of action. If she successfully recruits the Moores, this new queen will have a force that could rival the Legion. Even if they do not have the numbers, Gurdinfield still has far more magic than the empire. If she knows of our plan, Ithmeera, she could be coming for us to assert her claim to the throne."

Ithmeera raised her eyes to meet Alden's. "I don't even know this woman. Do you really believe she would do that? After all the years of war the country has endured?"

"She fought under Telman for decades, Ithmeera. Telman's spent years trying to put a Taylor back on the throne. I would not put it past him to persuade this new queen to attack the empire," Alden explained.

The empress glanced down at the letter again and ran her hand through her long curls nervously. "This...this should not have been so complicated," she said.

"The Legion is ready, Ithmeera. Your brother awaits your orders," Alden said firmly.

Ithmeera stood up and turned to stare out the window again, her arms folded across her chest. "And what if we fail, Uncle? They are nearly united now. Things are not what they once were."

Alden stood and walked over to his niece. He placed his hand on her shoulder. "You must trust in your brother and your Legion, dear. Our empire has overcome far worse. This *must* be done now, before it is too late."

The empress nodded thoughtfully as she turned to her uncle. She spoke, her voice quiet and determined. "Tell Erik to move the Legion out tonight."

✳ ✳ ✳

Gurdin Woods, Gurdinfield

"Again, now."

"Put your sword up. No one will fight you because they'll be laughing too hard at your terrible posture, boy."

Victor slowly lowered his sword before turning to Elisa, who sat on a fallen log in the clearing where the Guardians had made camp hours earlier. "It's not helping," he complained.

Elisa gestured dramatically at Kye, who had actually listened and now stood with the perfect posture that the Guardian captain had been trying to drill into him for the last hour. "Of course it is! He is now doing exactly what you've been telling him to do the entire time."

Kye cringed. "I'm sorry! Should-should I be doing something else?"

With a heavy sigh, Victor shook his head and raised his sword again. "You're doing fine, lad. Elisa…is right, I suppose. Now, *again*."

Kye adjusted his grip on the weapon before attacking Victor once more. The older man parried and pushed the enchanter backward with his sword. Kye nearly staggered, as he had done several times before, but held his balance this time.

"Better!" Victor exclaimed with approval. "Now do that a hundred more times and you'll be on your way to fending off dirty Legionnaires in no time."

"*'Dirty Legionnaires'?* This is coming from a man who's spent the last few years prancing about in the woods," Elisa fired back.

"Insulting me, now? I should have my newest recruit challenge you in my stead," Victor announced as he proudly held his sword up and pointed it at Kye.

Elisa stood up and straightened her clothing. "Well, I suppose if you wish to duel I shall have no choice but to accept," she said solemnly and approached the young enchanter.

"I-I think perhaps we should take a break? Yes? Erm... please?" Kye stammered hopefully.

"Nonsense, you'll do fine!" Victor laughed and clapped Kye on the back. "Just keep your sword up and do exactly as I showed you." He lowered his voice just loud enough for Elisa to hear. "Oh, and uh...don't go *too* easy on her."

The ex-Legionnaire rolled her eyes and drew her daggers, silently amused at Kye's twitching and the fact that the boy was clearly very nervous. "Fix your stance or you'll be eating dirt for lunch. Or your opponent's blade, were this a real fight."

The enchanter listened as best as he could to his new teacher's instructions as they carried on with a mock duel. It had been six days since Elisa and the Guardians along with Andrea, Cassie, Kye, and even a few new recruits from Fimen's Hope set out from the village to the Gurdin Woods, the last stretch of forest between the river villages in the west and the City of Towers in the east. They had arrived at the clearing early that morning and were now waiting for Alexander, Jacob, and Diana to return with the remainder of the Guardians and hopefully a new ally. The Harringtons had been their enemy for two decades, but the possibility of an alliance made the reunification of Gurdinfield seem feasible for the first time in twenty years.

The cool, sunny day helped brighten the moods of the Guardians as well. Cassie quickly found that she preferred this climate to the hotter, drier weather of Azgadar as she carried the pile of branches and sticks she had found in the camp's immediate surrounding woods back to be used for the fire later. As she stepped back into the clearing, her boot caught a half-buried rock and she tripped, falling forward. She managed to keep her balance, but gasped as some of the wood began to leave her grip.

"I've got it!" The falling branches were deftly caught by another before Cassie lost them. She looked up and raised her eyebrows when she saw Andrea standing in front of her.

"Oh…thanks," she blurted after staring at the enchanter for a moment. Andrea nodded and offered a polite smile before taking some of the firewood off Cassie's hands and walking back to the camp's center without a word.

Cassie sighed as she followed closely behind Andrea. The enchanter had barely said more than a few words to her after that night at the inn in Fimen's Hope. She had gone to bed shortly after their argument only to find that Andrea, who had angrily declared she would find her own tent that night, was fast asleep in the tent they had been sharing. Not wanting to cause another argument, and quite possibly too drunk to, Cassie had lain down in her bed next to the enchanter as she had done every night for the past few weeks. Neither one of them had brought up that night since, though Cassie knew that it was only a matter of time before Andrea would bring up Rhyad again.

As she deposited the firewood on the ground near where the campfire would be later, she grudgingly admitted to herself that she actually missed talking with the enchanter, even if it was mostly Andrea talking and even if that just meant the enchanter asking her a bunch of questions.

Maybe you shouldn't make her do all the work. Cassie shook her head. They could not keep going like this. She did not know when they would be able to get to Rhyad or when they would find the magic, if it even existed. Elisa was perpetually grouchy and Kye was nice enough to talk to, but Cassie still felt that she did not know enough about him or what he had done to trust him completely. Not to mention the entire situation they were in was ridiculous, especially if they truly were about to go into battle against some noble house she had never heard of.

"The uh…the forest here is really nice. I think I saw a deer back there," she finally tried.

Andrea set down the wood she had been carrying and dusted off the dirt and splinters that had gathered on her clothing. She looked blankly at Cassie and hesitated as though choosing her words carefully. "Yes, there are…a lot of deer here," she stated slowly.

Cassie actually laughed. "Been sitting on that secret for a while now?" As soon as the words were out she instantly regretted saying them. *Annnd you just can't help yourself, can you? She's probably still upset and doesn't want to hear any of your stupid jokes right now.*

The enchanter paused for a moment, but to Cassie's relief she laughed softly and shook her head. "Sorry," she said. "I think my mind was elsewhere." She gestured toward the cluster of trees. "These woods are one of the few places in this region where there is still a great deal of magic."

They walked together to the fallen log where Elisa had been sitting. "So…what you're saying is that while we're here you don't need me to help with your fireballs or shields or whatever?" Cassie guessed as she sat down.

Andrea took a seat next to her. "That's not true," she told her. "Of course I need you." She immediately tensed and stumbled over her words. "Wait – that's not…I-I mean…you *know* what I meant!"

Cassie elbowed the enchanter lightly. "*Right.*" She considered continuing to tease her friend over her choice of words, but at this point she knew that the enchanter had a habit of doing this and Cassie truly did want to make amends after their fight. "No, really – you can't get that sickness thing you were telling me about while we're here, can you?"

Andrea sighed, seemingly with relief, and nodded. "I shouldn't get sick as long as I'm careful. That's honestly the best approach no matter where we go."

"That must suck though! Always having to be careful like that and not being able to actually do any magic!"

"It's not as bad as it sounds," Andrea said with a shrug. "Like I said, as long as I don't try to do anything that could use more magic than what's available, I'm fine."

Cassie nodded. "Like what happened to your craz-to Meredith's husband?"

"Oh, Richard," the enchanter clarified sadly. "Meredith didn't like to talk about it. They used to live in the capital city and were having dinner when some men tried to rob them."

Cassie frowned. "That sounds pretty terrible."

"It was," Andrea agreed. She shook her head. "Richard used lightning magic on the men. He killed them, but…well, the capital city doesn't have as much magic as it used to." She shifted uncomfortably. "It takes a *great* deal of energy to…to take a life." Her voice grew quieter as the end of her sentence trailed off.

Cassie did not know what to say. She could tell the enchanter was clearly uncomfortable with the fact that Richard had killed people, but she knew that without being in that situation she honestly did not know what she would have done, either. She remembered when Claudia had attacked her in the street of Azgadar and Kye and Andrea had come to her rescue. Would they really have used their magic to kill if Claudia had not backed down?

A thought occurred to her. "Meredith didn't even need magic. She just used those monsters she sent after us," she pointed out.

To her surprise, Andrea did not argue. "I'll be honest, Cassie – I don't know why Meredith would allow her constructs to try to…to–,"

"Kill us?" Cassie finished for her. "Because that's what she did, Andrea. I was there. And we'd probably be dead if that shield of yours hadn't worked."

"I'm not–I'm not defending her, Cassie," Andrea insisted. "It's just not...Meredith's *never* talked about doing anything like that in all the time I've known her. Even after all the times we failed to wake Richard and...but she's changed, Meredith has. Releasing the magic will change the balance of magic in the land and will probably ruin all her work on Richard. And...I think she knew this." She bit her lip. "I'm sorry. I–,"

Cassie stopped her. "It's okay," she said calmly and held up her hand. "I mean – it's weird that she'd want to kill us because I thought she wanted to use me for my...abilities or whatever. But it's not *your* fault."

"I never thanked you for that, by the way."

Cassie looked puzzled. "Huh?"

"Saving me...us. On the wagon. My shield *was* going to fail. If you hadn't...and then with Diana–,"

"Don't worry about it," Cassie broke in quickly. "Really, I don't mind. Whatever gets us to Rhyad so that we can get this magic thing taken care of and you can send me home. No big deal. Okay?" She tilted her head when she saw the enchanter cringe slightly. "What? Did I say something wrong again?" she asked worriedly.

Andrea folded her hands together and took a deep breath. "Cassie, about the magi–,"

An arrow flew through the air, whizzing past them and barely missing the enchanter's leg before embedding itself in the log they were sitting on.

"What the hell?!" Cassie cried and jumped off the log. Her throat quickly tightened as she looked around wildly for whoever had fired the arrow.

"*Cassie!*" Andrea grabbed Cassie by her shirt and pulled her back roughly. Another arrow flew by, missing Cassie but striking one of the Guardians behind them. The Guardian went down gasping in pain as he clutched his wounded shoulder.

"We're under attack! To arms! *To arms!*" Elisa bellowed. The Guardians all scrambled to grab their weapons.

The next minute was a blur for Cassie as she watched helplessly while Elisa barked orders at the Guardians and their attackers began moving into the clearing. They were fighters armed with swords and bows and clad in black and yellow, with birds of prey branded or stitched onto their armor and uniforms. She had seen these soldiers only days earlier and knew all too well what they were capable of.

"Stay close to me," Andrea ordered, her voice uncharacteristically low and calm. But Cassie could see the intense fear in the enchanter's hazel eyes and knew that Andrea was anything but calm. She watched as her friend moved her hands in the familiar gestures of magic usage as Cassie had seen her do several times before. Andrea's hands were trembling severely and Cassie was worried that they'd be struck with another arrow if Andrea didn't do something *now*. She had little in the way of weapons save the dagger Elisa had given her back in the sewers of Azgadar. Shaking, she slowly drew it, desperately hoping that she would not have to use it.

"*Do* something!" she hissed.

"I'm *trying*!" Andrea snapped. She closed her eyes and Cassie held her breath as she waited for the enchanter to do something, *anything* that would help them as the Moores closed in.

A cold metal blade pressed against her throat, making her

blood freeze and her breathing stop. She dropped the dagger. "Drop your weapons or she dies," the blade's owner announced loudly. The voice seemed familiar to Cassie. "Drop them, *now*. I will not hesitate this time!"

Next to Cassie, another Moore soldier grabbed the enchanter. Andrea's voice broke out in a small, ragged squeak. "Elisa…?" she pleaded fearfully while holding as still as possible.

The ex-Legionnaire met Cassie's eyes before nodding angrily and tossing her daggers to the ground. "Do it," she muttered.

Cassie heard the dull thud of metal upon dirt echo around her as the Guardians dropped their weapons. She shuddered as the blade was pressed harder against her throat. Andrea's shaky, uneven breathing next to her was audible but still sounded so far away, and Cassie could not decide if it was the fear, the adrenaline, or the sheer reality of the situation sinking in, but she found herself suddenly feeling very weak.

"Thank you. Now, let's do this quickly so that Lord Moore does not have to wait too long." The blade was withdrawn and Cassie remembered how to breathe again. The blade's owner grabbed her arm and Cassie could finally see that it was Captain Moore, the man who had threatened Diana's life only days earlier.

"Back to Hathorn Hold," he barked at his soldiers. "Kill any that struggle."

As the Guardians were rounded up by the Moore fighters, one of the higher-ranking soldiers approached the captain. "Sir, I believe that girl is the enchanter you spoke of," he informed him, pointing at Cassie. "The one who disrupted us in Fimen's Hope!"

Captain Moore glanced down at Cassie curiously. "Is that so? Well, we do not wish for any *rogue* casting on the way back home now, do we?" he sneered, squeezing her arm tightly.

Cassie did not have time to react as Andrea's protests were drowned out by Jacob and Elisa's shouting. A sharp pain in the back of her head was immediately followed by the enchanter screaming...and then darkness.

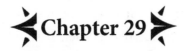

Chapter 29

Hathorn Hold

"The rules are quite simple here," Captain Moore stood in the outer courtyard of Hathorn Hold with a few of his soldiers alongside him and the Guardians on their knees, their hands bound before him. "I will ask a question and you will give me an answer. If you choose to cooperate, I will move on and you will be treated as any other prisoner. If you decide to lie, disrespect me, or be clever..." He stared pointedly at Elisa. "I don't think I need to elaborate on what will happen."

It had been less than an hour since the Moores had ambushed the Guardian campsite. The Moore soldiers had taken the Guardians back to Hathorn Hold, including the injured, where the captain now held them for interrogation. A small fortress built in the First Era atop one of the rolling hills, Hathorn Hold stood near the edge of the Gurdin Woods.

Andrea stopped struggling with her binds to look over at Cassie, who was also on her knees but had been fading in and out of consciousness since they arrived at the hold. Judging by her dazed state and the trail of blood that had dripped from her head wound to the back of her neck, it appeared that Captain Moore had hit the girl quite hard with the hilt of his sword, and the enchanter was concerned that Cassie's head injury would only grow worse if she did not get healing soon. Andrea had some knowledge of healing, but not enough practice to know if she could actually help her friend or not.

She scolded herself for not being fast enough – not being ready when her friends needed her. It should have been her, not Cassie, that Moore's subordinate had accused. No doubt the man had seen their faces back in Fimen's Hope and made his assumption without proof. *You could have put a shield around her sooner. What good is saving magic if you're not* doing *anything with it?* She had tried to protest, tried to tell Moore that she was the enchanter, not Cassie. But the captain had made up his mind and the enchanter knew why – he needed someone to blame for his failure at Fimen's Hope.

"Where is Alexander?" the captain demanded.

"Where is Lord Moore?" Elisa asked coldly. "We need to speak to him."

The captain glared at the ex-Legionnaire and walked slowly toward her. "You seem familiar," he observed before the realization hit him and he snapped his fingers. "Ah, yes! I remember you! Elisa of Sadford. You were the empress's bodyguard, weren't you?" He chuckled. "My, has it really been so long since I've been to one of Ithmeera's parties? I was shocked when I found out she fired you, what with you being her little lapdog and all, though I do remember you being rather rude at the last one I attended."

The enchanter looked over at the ex-Legionnaire in surprise. Elisa knew Ithmeera personally? And had been her *bodyguard*? Andrea noticed that Kye, who was kneeling next to Cassie, did not seem surprised by this. Had Elisa told him?

Elisa's stony gaze did not falter. "If you behaved then the way you do now then I am not surprised. Now, we need to speak to your father. It is imperative that he know about–,"

A backhand blow to the face silenced her. She hissed in pain as blood trickled from her lower lip.

"That was a warning. You will think twice before speaking to me that way!" Captain Moore declared furiously, his right hand shaking with rage.

"You'd be a fool not to hear us out, Moore," Elisa insisted. "Gurdinfield depends on–,"

The captain drew his sword and pointed it at her. "I am well aware of the needs of my own land without some Azgadaran trash telling me what they are."

Elisa leaned forward despite the blade that stayed precariously near her throat. "This Azgadaran trash is trying to save this kingdom," she growled through clenched teeth.

A deafening crash reverberated throughout the courtyard, startling all. Moore rolled his eyes and looked to his bewildered second in command. "Go see what that was. *Now!*" he yelled. The subordinate along with a few soldiers slinked away quickly as the captain turned his gaze back to the Guardians.

"Now, then," he began again. "Where were we?"

"You were just about to go fetch your father so that the adults can speak," Elisa answered with a smirk.

Moore redirected his weapon so that it was pressed against the ex-Legionnaire's neck. "You're really set on testing me, aren't you, Azgadaran bitch?"

"Leave her alone!" The other Guardians stared in shock at

Kye. The young man glared defiantly at the captain as Elisa shoved him slightly. "Not here, boy," she muttered.

Captain Moore laughed. "Having the young ones defend your honor for you, Elisa?" He withdrew his sword. "That's quite a change from your usual preference. Or is this whelp a Legionnaire as well?"

Elisa spat blood at the man. "You don't know what you speak of."

The captain was unmoved. "No? I accompanied my father to meet with General Cadar not too long ago. He told me everything about your unfortunate...betrayal. How you even managed to manipulate his second in command I'll never know. Really, it was a complete scandal and a black mark on the Legion, I am sure."

"Enough! What do you want, Moore?" the ex-Legionnaire demanded wearily.

"Simple. Alexander's location as well as the location of the woman with him that caused me a lot of trouble." He held his sword to Elisa again. "Who is she? His protégé? His daughter? Hmm...though I don't recall him having one."

"She is a Guardian who will make your life miserable if you don't let us go," Elisa declared.

Captain Moore simply smiled. "Your cowardly threats mean nothing here. You think I'm afraid of–,"

He froze, his eyes widening as he began gasping for air. Dropping his sword, the captain fell to his knees, the arrow impaled in his neck visible to all. A silence descended on them as Moore coughed up blood before collapsing face-first into the dirt.

Diana stood several paces in front of the bound Guardians, her bow slightly lowered after taking her shot. Alexander and Jacob stood to her right, and an older man with shoulder-length white hair dressed in chainmail over a dark green and white robe stood on her left. The great bear, the house insignia of the Harringtons, was embroidered in several places on his robe. A vast army of fighters stood behind them, many standing on the remains of the destroyed gates of Hathorn Hold.

Chaos erupted.

"To the gate! Attack at the gate!" Moore's remaining soldiers drew their weapons and began assembling in attack formation to drive out the invading army.

"*Push forward!*" Edward Harrington roared, his fighters spreading out around him and moving into the hold alongside Alexander's Guardians.

Diana and Jacob ran over to their companions and began cutting their binds. "You're alive!" Diana breathed with relief as she used her knife to cut Elisa's binds first. "We saw from the hills as they took you here and feared the worst."

"You're a hard one to kill," Jacob chuckled, earning a dirty look from Elisa.

"Where are the others?" Diana asked hurriedly. She moved from Elisa and continued to cut the binds of the other Guardians.

"Most are here. Some were locked away. You'll need to talk to Lord Moore about that, no doubt," Elisa explained after she was freed. She stretched her arms and wiped the blood from her mouth and chin.

"Where is he?"

Elisa began freeing the remaining Guardians as the area around them became more chaotic with fighting. "I don't know. Probably hiding until he knows he has to show his face." She nodded toward Captain Moore's body. "I'm sure he won't be pleased to see that."

"He decimated a village. He deserved worse," Jacob said as he finished freeing Andrea. "There."

"*Archers!*" Kye screamed.

In what seemed like less than a second, Andrea's hands shot up and a translucent, dome-shaped barrier was rapidly raised around the group. The arrows fired by Moore's archers bounced harmlessly off the edges of the shield, which crackled loudly with magical energy.

The others stared at the enchanter in awe as Harrington's fighters swiftly eliminated the archers. Andrea was not quite sure how she had reacted so quickly, but she was grateful that she had or they would all most likely be dead. She lowered her hands and the barrier dissipated.

"Nice reaction time," Elisa commented with a nod. She turned to Diana. "We need to go."

Jacob turned to the other Guardians, including Victor and Roe. "Find a weapon and find our companions. Leave the Moore-killing to the Harringtons. They're good at that."

"Aye, as you say, Captain!" Victor replied excitedly. Roe and the other Guardians echoed his acknowledgement.

"Andrea, you should take Cassie and Kye and find a place to hide," Elisa spoke as she pulled a barely conscious Cassie to her feet. "Come on, girl. Up you go."

Cassie winced as Elisa steadied her before holding her head with her hand. "Don't…feel great," she groaned. "Would rather…have a nap."

"Take her," Elisa repeated sharply to the enchanter. Andrea walked over and put her arm around Cassie, allowing the other girl to lean on her.

"I will fight," Kye announced.

"No," the ex-Legionnaire immediately answered. "You need to help get them to safety."

The younger enchanter shook his head. "I'm tired of standing by. I'm helping, and you cannot make me do otherwise," he insisted stubbornly.

Elisa looked at Jacob and Diana for help, but they did not object.

"I've got Cassie," Andrea said hurriedly, already struggling under Cassie's weight. "Find us when it's safe." She began dragging Cassie away, leaving Elisa facing a determined Kye. "Fine!" she exclaimed. She looked around and grabbed the sword from Captain Moore's body. "This is not a game. Those men will try to kill you. If you die, *I* will kill you," she threatened the young man.

"That doesn't make much sense!" Victor pointed out.

"Shut up, man. Let's go find the others!" Roe said before the ex-Legionnaire could say anything. They left, leaving Jacob, Diana, Elisa, and Kye alone amongst the fighting. Moore and Harrington clashed all around them, with the Harrington fighters having the upper hand from catching the Moores by surprise. The fighting had spread from the outer courtyard to just outside the hold's walls.

"We need to get to Alexander," Diana urged. "He can–,"

"*Down!*" Elisa yelled out and lunged at Diana's attacker with the slain captain's sword. Diana swiftly ducked as Elisa blocked the assailant's weapon with a harsh clang. The ex-Legionnaire slammed into the Moore fighter's stomach with her boot, causing him to stagger backwards. With a heavy downward swing of his sword, Jacob finished the fighter off.

"T-thank you," Diana panted as she tried to catch her breath.

Elisa used her boot to roll the Moore fighter onto his back to ensure he was dead. "Would be a shame if you died now," she said with a shrug. "Let's get to Alexander. I saw him head outside the hold walls."

Jacob frowned as he saw the horde of Moore soldiers blocking the exit. "How are we supposed to get through there?"

Elisa thought for a moment before turning to Kye. "Can you make a path for us, Kye?"

Kye tensed.

"You asked to be here and now you must do what I ask of you. Now...can you make a path for us?" Elisa asked again.

"I...yes...yes I can. Stand behind me!" he cried.

"Behind you? Why? Will you kill us too?" Jacob said worriedly.

"Maybe!" Kye focused on drawing energy from the area around him until a dark, purple sphere formed in his right hand. "This might do it! Ready?"

"Do it," Diana ordered.

The young enchanter threw the sphere at the cluster of

Moore fighters that stood between them and the hold's exit. It hit with impressive force, sending several fighters falling to the ground and opening a path to the exit.

"Excellent work, boy!" Jacob praised. "Now, let's–," Before he could finish, a sharp crack sounded and within seconds the Moore soldiers on the ground were screaming as flames engulfed them and part of the structure of the hold's exit.

"W-what's happening? What did you do?!" Diana demanded as Kye stared wordlessly at the scene before them in horror.

"Less talking, more running!" Elisa urged and led them through the inferno the enchanter had created, avoiding the fire as best they could until they finally escaped the hold walls. The magic-based fire quickly extinguished on its own, its purpose complete and its energy run out.

Jacob took a moment to catch his breath. "Did you know – did you know that would happen?!" he gasped at Kye.

"I-I don't know! Sometimes…I don't have very good control over my magic and–," the young man stammered.

"Diana! Jacob! There you are!" Alexander called as he ran toward them, flanked by several of Harrington's fighters.

"How are we doing, sir?" Jacob asked.

The Guardian leader nodded. "Well. We've demanded Moore's surrender, but he has not come out yet." He glanced at the smoldering remains of the burned section of the hold and the bodies scattered on the dirt. "What in the world was that?"

"Our newest enchanter, sir," Diana informed him.

Alexander shook his head. "It almost killed our own fighters. We *must* be more cautious," he said sternly.

Kye wrung his hands together. "I-I'm sorry, sir, I was only-,"

"Victor and Roe are freeing the others. We should gather our forces and finish this, sir," Jacob cut in, glancing at Kye momentarily before focusing on Alexander again.

A horn sounded deeply, followed by a cacophony of shouts and cheers from both the Harrington and Guardian fighters.

Alexander observed the situation surrounding them before taking a deep breath. "He's called a surrender. It is time. Gather the others and let's go meet Lord Moore," he commanded.

Chapter 30

The Heir

Amidst the chaos, Andrea used her remaining strength to practically carry Cassie over to the side of the hold's central building, a shaded area where they would be mostly hidden. Once they were out of range from the fighting, Andrea helped Cassie sit down on the grass and lean up against the stone wall.

"Ugh…what's going on? What are we doing?" Cassie mumbled, her eyes still mostly closed.

"I need to look at your injury," Andrea answered. "Tilt your head down a bit."

"No, I'm tired."

"Please, Cassie. It could be serious," the enchanter pleaded. A loud cry from the fighting startled her, and she struggled not to panic. She suspected they would be safe where they were, but the combat was still too close for comfort.

Cassie groaned and tilted her head slightly forward. "Can you really…do anything…about it? Where is Diana? She… knows stuff, doesn't she?"

Andrea began inspecting the back of her companion's head. The girl's dirty blonde hair was matted with dirt, tiny twigs, and dried blood, but had somehow managed to remain tied back.

The enchanter removed the hairband and winced when she found what she was looking for – a small, swollen area on the back of Cassie's skull where Moore's sword hilt had struck it. There was some dried blood in the hair and skin surrounding the wound, much of which had already scabbed over, but there was still a steady trickle of blood in one spot.

"I know how to heal a bit. Meredith taught me in case…it's very basic but it might help for now," she admitted. *What if it's not enough? She could die right here and it will all have been for nothing. You could have said something else to Moore; could have stopped him. This will be* your *fault.*

"No." Cassie opened her eyes just enough to glare at the enchanter. "I don't…mind helping you, but I don't want…I don't want any of that magic crap done to me. Not after–,"

"Cassie, it's not the same thing as what Meredith did – I promise," Andrea rushed in a shaky voice. "Please, you're…it's bleeding quite a bit still. I just want to help. I *promise.*"

Cassie closed her eyes tightly and groaned in pain. "Damn it!" she grunted. "*Fine.* Hurry up."

Trying not to let the chaos around them break her concentration, Andrea bit her lip as she tentatively extended her hand toward the back of Cassie's head. "Hold still. This might hurt for a moment."

"Right. Because the bleeding cut and the giant bump on the back of my head feel just *great* right now. Just…do what you have to do," Cassie muttered through gritted teeth.

For a moment, Andrea could only hear the sound of her own ragged breathing as she cupped the back of Cassie's skull with her palm. Immediately, she felt the surge of power that always occurred when she made physical contact with her friend. This time, however, she ignored it and focused on drawing power from the air around her, concentrating on stopping the bleeding and restoring the skin to its normal state. Drawing power from Cassie to heal her probably would have worked, but Andrea knew from experience that the transfer left her friend exhausted. She did not want to risk that in this situation.

"Ow...I think...I think it might be working," Cassie grumbled, sounding more like herself than she had in the last hour.

"It is," the enchanter confirmed with a heavy exhale, not even bothering to try to hide the relief in her voice. "I've...I've never had to do something like this before." When she felt the wound completely close she slowly withdrew her hand.

Cassie shifted against the wall and laughed softly. "What? Get kidnapped and fight an army or do that healing magic thing you just did to me?"

Andrea smiled. "Both. Your wound is closed. I think your head should be fine now."

"On the outside at least."

The enchanter sighed and shook her head, but her smile remained. A loud horn blasted from the top of the building. Both girls looked up toward the sound's origin.

"The Moores...they've surrendered," Andrea breathed.

"Great, can we go now?" Cassie asked.

Andrea looked around. Most of the soldiers had stopped fighting and were beginning to gather toward the center of the hold. She spotted Alexander and Diana in the distance. "Yes, let's rejoin the others."

* * *

"Alexander Telman. How long has it been?" Lord David Moore, an older man with short, greying hair stood on the worn, stone steps below the hold's inner entrance. He was dressed in black and yellow robes and clad in a single metal-plated chest piece. The trademark bird of prey shone in gold on the armor. A long sword hung at his side.

"Over twenty years, Lord Moore. I trust you've been well?" Alexander spoke, his voice steady and calm. Diana, Jacob, and Lord Harrington stood behind him with Elisa and Kye further behind along with the rest of the Guardians and Harringtons. Moore's soldiers had gathered behind him.

Moore narrowed his eyes at the Guardian leader angrily. "You slay my son, you threaten my lands, invade my home, and bring this…this *traitor* to my doorstep and expect a conversation? You are deceitful, Telman!"

"Your reign of terror over the Southlands is over, Moore. It is time that we put aside our differences for the sake of Gurdinfield's future," Alexander declared, the strength of his tone unfaltering.

"Gurdinfield's future lies with its rightful ruler. The Moores had claim to these lands long before the Taylors did and certainly more than you and your rabble ever have or will!" Moore sneered.

"House Moore surrendered its claim to the throne in the First Era, David," Lord Harrington called out, surprising both the surrounding fighters and Lord Moore.

"He is right," Alexander said with a nod to Harrington before turning back to Moore. "The Taylors united Gurdinfield when we were simply warring houses. They protected us from the empire, and they have earned the right to rule."

Lord Moore shook his head. "Telman, you cannot hold us responsible for the death of a line simply because its family could not properly defend itself. The Taylors are gone. That line has ended. It is time to set aside this nonsense and unite under one banner! Mine."

"You seek a banner to unite under, but why not unite under the banner of the Great Lion itself?" Diana's voice was clear as it reverberated throughout the hold's walls. All eyes turned to her.

Moore chuckled and took a step forward. "Dear girl, were there a member of the Lion's line left we would not have been at *war* for the last two decades." He shook his head, a condescending smile spreading on his face. "Perhaps the outskirts village you were born in did not teach you this?"

Diana was unfazed by his insult. "I was born in the City of Towers, so you'll forgive me if my education isn't up-to-date with your house's teachings, Lord Moore." She approached him. "Unfortunately, my parents were not around to choose my teachers for me. Had they been, I'm sure I would have learned the most interesting things about *your* house."

Moore glared at her. "Alexander, I was not aware you were so liberal with allowing your subordinates to speak out of turn," he said, not turning his gaze from Diana.

Alexander smiled knowingly. "I think, given the order of rank here, that I do well to allow her to speak, Lord Moore."

Moore laughed harshly. "Hah! This woman leads your Guardians now, Telman? She is barely of age! Is the burden of leadership truly too much for you?" he asked mockingly.

Alexander crossed his arms over his chest. "I am more than happy to lead, Lord Moore, however I am also relieved to finally reclaim my former position." He held Moore's angry gaze. "You *do* remember my former duties, yes?"

Lord Moore's jaw dropped as he stared speechlessly at Alexander before slowly turning back to Diana. "You…who are you?" he demanded. His hand hovered over his sword.

Diana took one more step forward. "My name is Lydia Diana Taylor," she announced to the crowd, which answered with a wave of gasps and murmuring. "Daughter of King Caleb and Queen Helen. Sister to Abner and John." She turned to face Moore again. "Gurdinfield is in grave danger, Lord Moore. I ask that you and Lord Harrington put aside this war so that we are prepared when the Azgadaran Legion invades!"

More gasps sounded from the crowds as well as shouting and some cheering. Lord Moore grew red in the face as he lashed out at Diana. "You think you can just walk into my hold and declare yourself the sovereign of Gurdinfield?! You think I am blind? I have protected this land for decades, and I will *die* before I see it back in the hands of those who would weaken it!"

"That can be arranged!" Diana shot back as she held Moore's furious gaze with a defiant one of her own.

"Edward, are you hearing this?" Moore yelled. "You would

give up your stake in Gurdinfield's future simply because this...this *imposter* told you a lie?!" He stepped forward. "Lydia Taylor is *dead*, girl, along with the rest of the royal family. Do not waste my time with this."

Diana reached for her necklace and unfastened the clasp. "You require proof? Here it is!" she retorted and shoved the necklace at Moore. The golden lion pendant dangled from her closed fist.

Lord Moore's angry stare shifted to one of disbelief as Diana put her necklace back on.

"It is her, David," Harrington said calmly. "Surely you recognize her face."

Moore vehemently shook his head. "Regardless of who you *claim* to be, the fact of the matter is that the Taylors abandoned their role as ruling house when they *did not return* to the City of Towers. *I* am the leader of this house and as leader, I have declared Gurdinfield under the protection of House Moore. That includes protecting it from those who would otherwise threaten it." He glared pointedly at Diana and Harrington. "You've killed my son. I demand that you leave. *Now!*"

"Your son was a murderer who killed innocents in cold blood. He deserved far worse," Diana spat.

"My son may have decided his fate, but *you* and your kind have threatened the stability of this nation. For that, you should be tried for treason and executed!" Moore yelled back.

Diana folded her arms across her chest and narrowed her eyes at the man. "Very well, then. I challenge you to a duel, Lord Moore. To the death, in fact."

The hold became deathly silent until only the sound of the grass rustling gently in the light breeze could be heard.

"I do not have time for *games*, girl," Moore sneered.

Diana shook her head. "This is not a game. I challenge you to a duel, and the winner will take this hold and the armies inside it."

The crowd of fighters broke into murmurs once more as Harrington side-eyed Alexander, a worried glance crossing his aged features.

Moore quickly assessed the Guardians and Harrington's fighters. "All of the armies?" he asked.

"All of them," Diana confirmed.

Moore stared intensely at the Guardian commander for several seconds. He drew his longsword. "Very well. To the death, then."

Alexander stepped forward. "As a Guardian, I offer myself as her champion," he announced.

Lord Moore frowned. "She cannot fight for herself? Hmph, I don't like it, but it is your right."

Diana quickly turned to face Alexander. "What are you doing? He's responsible for the murders of countless people! He *needs* to pay," she whispered. "I can do this, Alexander."

But Alexander simply nodded and placed his hand on her shoulder. "I have no doubt that you can, Diana. But you've many battles ahead of you. Allow me to finish what I should have done twenty years ago. Let me protect my charge."

"But that wasn't your fault!" Diana protested.

"I'm waiting!" Lord Moore taunted.

Alexander gave a wry smile. "I am a Guardian. Please, allow me to do my duty."

Diana glanced back at Moore worriedly and then at Alexander again. "This could be a trap," she tried.

"This needs to end *now*, Diana," the Guardian leader replied sternly.

"I do not have all day to wait, girl!"

"Fine," Diana breathed, exasperated. "I...please be careful."

Alexander gave a short bow. "Of course." He turned to face Lord Moore. "Shall we commence, Lord Moore?"

Moore waved his hand dismissively. "Yes, yes. Let's get this over with." He drew his sword and Alexander did the same. Diana and the others stepped back to give the men space.

They assumed dueling stances and began circling each other. Alexander knew he had more recent combat experience, but he knew Moore, despite his age, was still a very capable swordsman with decades of training.

"You can still stop this, Moore," Alexander called out. "The empress is misleading you in this false alliance."

Moore adjusted his grip on his weapon. "You know not of what you speak, Telman. Ithmeera and I have an agreement, one that benefits *all* of Damea." He struck the first blow, a heavy downward swing that Alexander quickly blocked before they pushed back on each other.

"The empress...seeks Gurdinfield's magic. What happens to you afterward is inconsequential to Ithmeera. She wants...to annex Gurdinfield for the empire," Alexander panted. He lunged at Moore with a hard swing from the left. Moore attempted a dodge, but the blade tore into his shoulder. He grunted in pain as a crimson red began to spread onto his clothing.

"You think this will be easy?!" he gasped. "Gurdinfield was *lost* without my house! *I* made it great again, so great that the empire wishes to share in our wealth! You…you and your selfish band of traitors seek to throw that away because of a pathetic remnant of a dead line? I will not allow it!" He suddenly thrust his sword with a cry of rage, catching the Guardian leader off-guard and causing Alexander to drop his sword. Moore's blade easily sliced across his arm, cutting into it and sending a small splatter of blood flying. Alexander yelled out in pain and fell to his knees, scrambling for his sword.

"Alexander!" Diana screamed and covered her mouth with her hands. The crowd of fighters had begun to grow restless and were shouting at both combatants.

Lord Moore strode over to Alexander and placed his blade at the Guardian leader's neck. "A pity. I was hoping for a real duel before taking you down. Perhaps you are not the fighter I thought you were. Perhaps that is why the Taylors died."

Alexander held still, breathing steadily as the cold blade pressed into his skin.

"The great Alexander Telman is speechless for once!" Moore crowed as he stood over his opponent. "A good run, but I'm afraid I have business to attend to, now." He withdrew his blade and pulled it behind him before putting all of his strength into the final execution blow.

Alexander swiftly rolled, barely dodging the blade, and

grabbed his sword. In a single, fluid movement, he thrust his sword upward and into Lord Moore's side, one of the few areas that the older man's armor did not protect. Moore cried out and immediately dropped his weapon, He fell to his knees as Alexander pulled the sword out and climbed to his feet. He used his boot to push Moore onto his back, where the older man gasped at the blue skies for several seconds before finally lying still.

Bruised, bleeding, and covered in dirt, Alexander tossed his sword onto the ground and turned to a stunned Diana. "It is done," he panted and wiped his brow with his shirtsleeve.

Diana chose to forego words and ran to her adopted father. Throwing her arms around him, she whispered fiercely, "Don't *ever* do that again!"

"Are you all right, sir?" Jacob asked. Elisa stood next to him, along with Andrea, Cassie, and Kye.

Alexander nodded as he patted Diana on the back. "I am fine." He pulled away from her. "I believe you have some unfinished business."

Diana sniffed and offered a small smile. "Yes...yes I do," she said before turning to the crowd of people looking on.

"Lord Moore is dead. We are victorious," she announced, her voice calm and steady. "I ask now that you join with us. The empress of Azgadar is preparing to invade. She believes us to be fractured and weak. We will not be."

Some of the fighters nodded in agreement while others exchanged tentative glances with each other.

"It is time for this civil war to end," Diana continued. She turned to Edward Harrington. "Lord Harrington. Will you and your men join us? Help us end this war so that we can keep Gurdinfield free."

Harrington took a deep breath. "Strange times are upon us indeed if I'm once again swearing allegiance to a Taylor monarch. Though, had things played out differently, I would have served your father to the very end." He looked at his men and gave a short nod before dropping to one knee. His next declaration was quiet, but every person in Hathorn Hold knew the immense weight that it held.

"Long may you reign, Queen Lydia."

Diana slowly looked around as one by one, every fighter – Moore, Harrington, and Guardian – dropped to one knee in an overwhelming act of fealty. When she had finally turned around completely, Diana met Alexander's gaze.

"The capital city awaits us, Your Majesty." The Guardian leader spoke with an informative tone, but the edge in his voice made it obvious that he was beginning to suffer from his injury sustained in the duel.

Overwhelmed by the events that were unfolding before her and concerned for Alexander's health, Diana bit her lip worriedly and nodded. "Let's not waste any more time, then," she decided. "We make haste to the City of Towers."

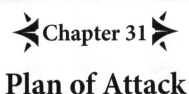

Chapter 31

Plan of Attack

Gurdin Woods, Gurdinfield

After yet another long day of walking, Elisa was more than happy when Alexander's order to set up camp in the forest sounded early in the evening. The Gurdin Woods were vast. Nowhere near as large as the Black Forest, but certainly the largest stretch of woods in Gurdinfield and the only thing separating the recently united Gurdinfield army and the nation's capital, the City of Towers.

The ex-Legionnaire exhaled heavily as she lowered her heavy traveling pack to the ground. The woods had many evergreens, but were also home to a variety of other trees whose leaves had long turned to the reds and browns of autumn and were littering the forest floor. Elisa breathed deeply as she felt at ease for the first time in weeks since she had departed Azgadar.

"Finally!" she heard Cassie exclaim several paces behind her. "I'm starving. Also, I'm pretty sure I walked into a spider web back there. My face keeps itching."

"Better to walk into a spider web than to fall on your face like an idiot," Victor advised as he began to set up camp with the others. The Guardian's face was streaked with more dirt than was typical for a trek through the woods.

"Perhaps had you watched the roots on the ground you might not have tripped so often," Roe reasoned with a grin.

The camp was quite large as it encompassed not only the Guardians, but also the Harrington and remaining Moore forces. At Alexander's recommendation, Diana had used her new authority to pardon all the Moore soldiers who had joined them. A table had been set up near Alexander's tent to plan the army's next move, which was to settle in quickly in the City of Towers and prepare for the imminent Legion invasion. After dinner, Alexander, Diana, Lord Harrington, and Jacob stood around the table, maps and diagrams laid out before them, trying to determine the next course of action.

"The palace is still standing. With it lying in the outer area of the city, neither side really went near it out of respect for the Taylors," Harrington explained, glancing at Diana, who nodded gratefully.

"Then we can convene there and have the forces set up camp along the palace walls," she decided. "I don't want to impose on the inns or the residents in the city unless we have no other options."

"Do they know we are coming?" Jacob asked.

"I have sent word ahead. The city has a governor, but I use the term loosely," Alexander said. He turned to Harrington. "Edward, it will be important that we acknowledge Dia-I mean, Lydia as queen to the public there. I'd rather they see your support for her as opposed to us requiring a show of force to convince them."

Harrington nodded deeply. "Agreed," he spoke.

"We've also received word from our scouts in Azgadar," Alexander continued. "The empress knows of our reunification and has released the Legion. They are on their way to the capital city as we speak."

Diana bit her lip. "Then we must get there before they do." The others nodded in agreement.

Once they had set up a tentative course of action, they went their separate ways – Harrington with his army and Alexander with the Guardians. Diana pulled Jacob to a small area on the outskirts of camp where they were provided with some isolation.

"You wish to speak with me, Your Majesty?" Jacob asked with a smile as he stoked the campfire where they sat across from each other.

Diana frowned. "Don't call me that – it's unsettling."

The Guardian captain shrugged. "What else am I supposed to call you, then? I don't know if I can get used to 'Lydia.'"

Diana sighed. "Just…call me what you've always called me, Jacob. No need to make this complicated."

Jacob chuckled. "Ah, I'm afraid that time has come and gone, love." He stopped himself too late as the word slipped out and glanced at the new queen nervously. But Diana merely smiled and shook her head.

"I cannot simply erase my feelings for you, Jacob," she admitted quietly. "Not even if they made me Empress of Azgadar tomorrow."

"Can that be arranged? I would prefer we *not* have to fight the Legion if it can be helped." After a brief laugh between the two of them, he paused and stared at the ground. "I cannot deny what I feel, either," he mumbled. "I am sorry for keeping the truth from you."

Diana raised an eyebrow questioningly. "Did Alexander really know about us this entire time?"

To her surprise, Jacob laughed loudly. "Hah! Yes, yes he did. He didn't want to make things even more complicated for you. Gallivanting around with a common soldier is probably not very seemly for the Queen of Gurdinfield to be doing."

Diana shook her head and stood up. "It is not for Alexander to decide who I 'gallivant' with!" she declared furiously.

The Guardian captain stood up as well and walked over to her. "Too true," he said solemnly and tentatively took her hands in his. "You cannot blame him when he was only doing what he thought was best for you."

"Perhaps he should have asked."

"Yet here we are."

Diana sighed as she calmed down. "Yes." She looked up at Jacob, her dark eyes sad yet hopeful. "I...I don't wish for this to be something we continue to discuss, Jacob. Either you want to be with me or you do not. I would...I would prefer to know now so that we can continue with our mission." She focused her eyes on the ground.

Jacob let go of her hands before gently cupping her face in his hand and forcing her to meet his eyes. "So business-like. Must be the queen in you talking," he teased. When she said nothing, he continued. "I was a fool to let you go at all, Diana. Alexander be damned. This royalty nonsense be damned." He inhaled deeply. "I want to be with you."

She held his gaze. "And why should I believe you after what you said to me earlier? If being together during a civil war isn't a good time, then what makes you think an invasion is any better?"

Jacob released her and let his arms drop to his sides. "I... Diana, please–,"

But she continued angrily. "What's to stop you from deciding that I'm not worth it anymore, hmm? When Alexander says this is no longer acceptable? What of the people of Gurdinfield? What of our friends? I refuse to hide this from them."

"I was *wrong*, Diana!" the captain exclaimed helplessly. "Is that what you want to hear? That I was wrong? *You're* right – I should have told you the truth from the start. I should have told Alexander that I would not be a part of keeping secrets for him. Even if that meant putting *you* at risk. Is that what you want to hear?!"

"No," Diana said quietly, her calm tone surprising Jacob as the tension between them began to dissipate. "I...I do care for you. I really do. And while I still disagree with what Alexander did in keeping, well, my *life* a secret from me, I understand why he did it." She reached up and touched his cheek. "I understand why *you* did it."

Jacob leaned into her touch before taking her hands again. "Then say you forgive me so that we can put this mess behind us."

Diana hesitated still.

"*Please*, Diana. Don't make me beg. I shall have to make a big scene and honestly, I don't think I could survive the humiliation of it," he grinned.

She snorted. "Afraid Victor and Roe won't let you live it down?"

"More like *Elisa* wouldn't let me live it down," he corrected. "She probably has at least a dozen different ways she could kill me if I did anything to hurt you anyway."

Diana squeezed his hands and nodded. "As entertaining as that might sound, I prefer you alive…and with me."

"Truly?" he asked, beaming at her.

She breathed deeply and nodded. "Yes. I…I love you, Jacob. I think…I think I have for a long time. No war, no invasion could change that."

"I love you," he returned before leaning in and capturing her lips in a soft kiss. They stood by the campfire holding each other until Diana finally felt the great weight she had been under for what seemed like an eternity lift from her. Regardless of what the future held, she had Jacob, and that was enough.

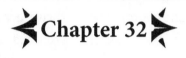

Respite

After devouring a quick dinner, Elisa walked toward her tent to take stock of the weapons that the group had fortunately recovered from the Moores. The ex-Legionnaire had grown rather fond of her daggers and found using them much more freeing than a single longsword.

She passed by Kye and stopped. The young enchanter was sitting by himself on a crate, staring out at seemingly nothing. Elisa sighed. The boy had been quiet for days and a haunted gaze had been his default expression ever since he had single-handedly taken down that group of Moore fighters at Hathorn Hold. She recalled the magic he had summoned and the fire that had broken out afterward, burning those soldiers to ashes. She had a sinking feeling that the power he wielded was both powerful and terrifying, and wondered what would happen should he ever lose control of that power...or if someone with malicious intent were to gain control of him. *He would never hurt innocents intentionally. Perhaps Andrea could train him.* She knew that was not a long-term solution as the older enchanter was barely of age herself and had probably been training for a few years at most.

She had an idea. After quickly stopping by the supply wagons, she returned to where Kye sat and approached the enchanter.

"You," she called. The boy barely glanced up and appeared generally uninterested the ex-Legionnaire.

"You've been moping long enough. It is time that you made yourself useful," she continued. She thrust her arm out at him. His eyes widened. The object she extended toward him was worn and the wood was scratched in several places. "It should still be playable," she said.

Kye looked at the lute in shock and then at Elisa before switching his gaze back to the instrument. "H-how did you get this?"

"Before we left Hathorn Hold we took any supplies we thought we might need. I found this in the main hall of the hold. I'm sure Lord Moore had some idiot playing it for him. I thought it might be more useful in your hands," she explained. "Now, take it."

The young man raised an eyebrow. "You are certain? I... don't know if I am any good anymore. It's been a while since I–,"

The ex-Legionnaire narrowed her eyes at him. "If you don't take the lute, boy, I swear I will smash it over your dense skull."

But Kye simply chuckled and reached for the instrument, gingerly handling it so as not to damage it further. "It needs some tuning," he muttered after a single strum, "but I think it will play nicely." He looked up at her, his dark eyes shining gratefully. "Thank you. This–I appreciate you getting this for me."

Elisa nodded and sat down on a neighboring crate. "You may not understand now, but you helped us a great deal back at

the hold. It can be difficult to do what is necessary to survive…
and win."

Kye shrugged and shook his head sadly. "I killed those
men, Elisa. They didn't even have a chance to get help or save
themselves." He sighed heavily. "I know what I am capable of. I
do not have very good control of it and I know this worries you
and Jacob and the others."

"I warned you that this was not a game. It's going to get worse,
especially when the Legion invades. You will need to learn to
control your powers before someone else tries to control them
for you," she said bluntly.

He nodded. "Yes. I've heard that the City of Towers once
had an academy for…enchanters. Do you think if we win that
perhaps–?"

"That is something that Diana would be responsible for
deciding, not I," she interrupted before standing up. "Enjoy
your new toy. Please do not set it on fire."

"Thank you," he said, grinning at the instrument as he held
it in his arms. "This means a lot to me."

Elisa cleared her throat. "Yes, well, hopefully you're as good
with it as I hope you are or the others will have my head for
giving you that." She left him and headed back to her tent. Her
daggers needed a good sharpening and she wanted to get to
bed early in case the young enchanter actually *was* a terrible
musician, though deep down she suspected he was not.

* * *

"Diana?" Andrea called out as she approached the campfire she thought she had seen the Guardian commander go to earlier. After passing by a few clusters of trees on the outskirts of the camp, she found the new queen and Jacob sitting around the fire. They appeared deep in conversation, but both looked up as they watched her approach.

"Oh! My apologies," she said awkwardly. "Erm...that is, I had something I wanted to ask you, Di-Your Majesty." The enchanter was not used to addressing royalty save her encounter with the empress, but she wanted to give Diana the respect the new monarch deserved.

"Ah, Andrea...there is no need for that," Diana said with a wave of her hand. "We are all friends here – there is no need for formalities."

Jacob chuckled. "You say that as though you honestly believe people will listen to you, Diana," he joked.

Ignoring the Guardian captain, the queen turned to the enchanter. "What can we do for you?"

Andrea swallowed nervously. "Well, it's about the Northland Bridge. You see, Cassie and I–,"

"Have to get to Rhyad, yes, Elisa told me," Diana finished for her. She sighed. "I'm afraid it's not as simple as just opening the bridge for you, Andrea."

The enchanter's throat tightened. They had come so far and had done what Elisa had asked of them. Now, after everything, Diana would not open the bridge for them? "It's...it's not? Why?"

Diana stood up. "With the Legion on their way we have to

consider the possibility that we will lose the City of Towers. If that happens we will need Harrington's forces to remain in the Northlands to block off all routes should the Legion try to invade there."

"Cassie and I are only two people, not the Legion. Can they not just let us through on your order?" Andrea demanded.

Diana took a step forward. "And what if the Legion finds you and captures you? Elisa told me what happened in Azgadar. You are wanted by the empress herself, I believe. No, I cannot allow you to risk yourself like that."

Flustered, Andrea protested again. "I…that was an accident and one that was not my fault," she insisted. "And we would not get caught. I've–,"

But Diana interrupted her again. "I will not risk the lives of my friends on this. Not until I can be sure that Ithmeera and her Legion are no longer a threat. Were they to find you and capture you, she might force you to use your abilities to serve *her* for all we know. I don't need that additional complication on my hands."

"But–,"

The queen gently placed her hand on the enchanter's shoulder. "I am sorry, my friend, but I must ask that you and Cassie remain with us for the time being." She smiled faintly. "You've already helped us get this far. Come with us to the City of Towers and fight with us!"

"We could certainly use your skills," Jacob added, standing up as well.

Andrea looked at the two of them before nodding slowly,

trying to hold back her frustration in front of Diana. "As you wish, Your Majesty," she said quietly, her shoulders slumping in disappointment.

Diana withdrew her hand, her smile remaining. "Thank you," she said, her gratitude not lost on Andrea despite her frustration.

"Of-of course," she mumbled with a short bow. She shuffled away, trying to navigate through the dimly-lit camp and suppressing the emotion that threatened to creep up in the form of tears. This was not what she had signed up for. *It's certainly not what Cassie signed up for, either.* They were supposed to get to Rhyad, find the magic, if it even existed, and then...

Then what? You'll send her home with the power you don't *have?* She had tried to tell Cassie the truth back when they had first entered the Gurdin Woods before Moore had captured them. *She'll despise you for lying to her. She already hates being here. She was nearly killed* again. *Maybe you should just go back to Meredith, tell her what happened. Maybe she can find a way to send Cassie home–* No. Andrea shook her head and struggled to push back the tears. They had come so far. She would tell Cassie, of course, and she would deal with that when...when the time came. Going back to Meredith was not an option and it never would be. *After what she did to Cassie, she doesn't deserve to go near her and–* Andrea blinked in confusion as she approached the area of camp that she, Cassie, Elisa, and Kye shared. *Deserve?* When had she suddenly become the authority on who could be around her companion and who could not? Since when did she care?

She sighed at her own internal fumbling. She was tired and

needed sleep. She knew Cassie was probably sitting by their tent waiting for the enchanter to bring word from Diana that they were free to cross the Northland Bridge. This was not going to be a pleasant talk.

Yes, sleep will definitely help.

She finally returned to their tent only to find Cassie gone. Elisa was sitting next to the fire polishing her daggers. Kye, who had been away earlier, was in his tent strumming on a lute, the notes not forming any particular melody that Andrea recognized. Funny, she hadn't remembered him owning a lute, only talking about how he enjoyed playing. Perhaps he had gotten it back in Fimen's Hope?

"Where's Cassie?" she asked.

"She left," Elisa muttered without looking away from her task.

Andrea folded her arms across her chest and stared at the ex-Legionnaire with an annoyed look on her face. "Yes, I got that much. Where did she go?"

"How should I know? *You're* her keeper, not me."

"I'm not her keeper," Andrea said wearily but didn't continue the argument. By this point she knew how Elisa could be. "You really haven't seen her?"

"Think she might have gone out towards that part of the forest," Kye spoke up from inside his tent, pointing in a direction. "Perhaps for a walk?"

Andrea nodded. "Thank you, Kye. That was very *helpful*," she said and narrowed her eyes at Elisa, who laughed quietly.

"Do you want help looking for her?" Kye asked eagerly as he

poked his head out of the small opening in the tent where the flap was pulled back.

"Thanks, but I'll be fine," Andrea replied. "I'll be back soon." She left them and began making her way into the dark gathering of trees ahead. The night sky was clear and well-lit by the moon and stars, but even so Andrea conjured a small orb of blue light to make it easier to see in front of her as she ventured deeper into the woods.

Chapter 33

Floating Lights

As she walked, Andrea heard the faint rustling of various nocturnal animals moving and going about their nightly activities. She worried for a moment about wolves or some other dangerous beast and briefly wondered if she should have armed herself before leaving camp. She dismissed her fear, though – if something wanted to attack her, she was still close enough to the camp to signal for help and was fairly confident she could use her magic to defend herself until her friends arrived.

As she traveled through the clusters of trees, she knew immediately that these woods had not been traveled often, if at all, for the magical energy that flowed throughout them was running past her and embracing her in strong pulses. The orb of light she conjured glowed brighter, taking it from a faded blue to an almost brilliant white.

The silence of the forest made Andrea uneasy. "Cassie?" she called out. No answer.

She was about to try again when she noticed a clearing up ahead, and a figure standing in the middle of it. The pale moonlight that was somehow able to penetrate the top layer of the forest revealed that the figure was indeed Cassie. She stood alone, hands in her pockets, staring at the trees around her.

"There you are," the enchanter exclaimed as she approached Cassie, the orb illuminating the clearing around them. "Why did you leave? We were worried." A half-truth, she admitted to herself, but *she* was worried and that was all that mattered.

Cassie would not face the enchanter. "I…don't know what I'm doing here anymore," she admitted quietly.

Andrea slowly approached her friend. "What do you mean? You left the camp and wandered out here."

"No," Cassie said and finally turned to face Andrea. She looked tired and wan. For the first time since they had met, Andrea could see the toll their mission had taken on Cassie. "I mean *here*. Damea."

Andrea was not sure how to answer. She tried anyway. "Well, we have to get to Rhyad. The magic–,"

"*Enough*, okay?! I *know* about the stupid magic thing!" Cassie suddenly yelled, startling the enchanter. "What I *don't* understand is *why* I'm still doing this. I told you before – I just want to go home. My life wasn't supposed to be like this. I was supposed to wake up in my own bed, in my own home, so that I could go to the same crappy job I go to every day, but *no*. Instead, I'm stuck in some weird land where everyone seems to hate each other and way too many people keep trying to either use me or kill me or both. Honestly, I don't know why you even want to save it, Andrea. This magic crap seems to have caused more problems than it's solved and it makes normal people act horribly. I just want to go back to living my *normal*, boring life!"

Silence descended upon them as a cool breeze blew through the forest clearing, making them both shiver.

Andrea wanted to try to convince Cassie again of the importance of their mission but she stopped herself upon realizing that Cassie might be right. Everywhere they had gone, Cassie had seen the worst of what Damea had to offer. Magic did cause wars, tragedy, death, and much more. Why exactly *were* they trying to save it?

She remembered her parents and the farm she grew up on. The machine that she tried so hard to power on. How broken Meredith had seemed when each experiment to bring Richard back failed. The empress of Azgadar invading Gurdinfield and putting countless lives in danger for what? Magic? Power?

Magic did not cause all of these problems – the enchanter knew this – and bringing it back would not fix them all either. But if it could help fix a few, Andrea knew it was worth trying to save.

And magic wasn't all bad. Surely even Cassie could understand how it could help. Andrea had an idea.

"Someone once told me that being normal is overrated," the enchanter said with a smile.

Cassie rolled her eyes but could not conceal the smile on her face. "What idiot told you that?"

The enchanter laughed softly. "Here, let me show you something." She raised her hands.

Cassie backed away immediately. "What are you doing?" she asked worriedly.

"Just watch. I'm not going to do anything dangerous. This forest has a lot of power in it still," Andrea explained. She focused on drawing power from the air around her and soon felt energy coursing through her. The orb of light she had conjured earlier was extinguished and darkness once again enveloped the forest.

But the enchanter continued to focus her abilities and within a few seconds, a new, smaller orb of white light appeared near the ground where they stood, hovering just over the forest floor. Then another orb, this one a faint purple, appeared near Cassie's shoulder. A third orb appeared above them, then a fourth, and before long they were surrounded by what appeared to be hundreds of tiny balls of light in various hues of blue, white, purple, and green.

Cassie looked around in awe. "What...what is this?"

"Magic," Andrea said simply.

"Yeah, I know, but...what is it doing? I mean it's pretty and all but..."

A rush of air blew past them again, this one caused by magic as Andrea sent the cluster of lights in all directions. Each of the orbs embedded itself in a tree, a branch, the foliage, and everything around them. The forest around them lit up brightly in a dazzling display of colorful lights that pulsed slowly. The trees themselves glowed blue and purple, the leaves a brilliant green.

"Whoa..." Cassie breathed as she slowly spun around.

Andrea, pleased with herself, put her hands on her hips and admired her work. "Magic is just a tool, Cassie. It was used for good for hundreds of years and it can be used for good again."

Cassie snorted in response. "Yeah, I know. I don't need the lecture again. Nice work, by the way. It's very pretty."

The light began to fade.

"What's wrong with it?" she asked.

Andrea looked around, unalarmed. "Oh, it only lasts for a bit before it fades. Keeping it lit up would require a lot of focus and power that I don't have right now."

"Seriously? You are the *laziest* enchanter I've ever met!" Cassie retorted. She quickly closed the distance between them and grabbed Andrea's hands. The enchanter gasped as a rush of power surged through her.

The forest around them exploded with light, the trees glowed much brighter than they had earlier, and the light spread to other trees beyond the clearing. Small white particles began to fall around them like glowing snowflakes. The quiet sounds of the forest were instantly overpowered by the low hum of magic.

"I...why?" Andrea whispered, feeling slightly dizzy after the sudden intake of power. The combination of the energy from both the forest and Cassie made it difficult for her to focus. She could see the map of Damea that Cassie had projected, the bright blue beacon of magic that was still present in Rhyad, and the strands of light that shot out across the land and intertwined with one another. Andrea had never experienced anything quite like this before.

"Because making fireballs for you gets boring after a while," Cassie quipped. When she saw the confused look on Andrea's face, her expression softened. "I don't know...I thought it was nice and I wanted to watch it some more."

"But the magic...it will drain you and–,"

"Hey, hey...we talked about this, remember?" Cassie interrupted. "Relax?" she asked hopefully.

Andrea said nothing, but was thankful the light had cast enough shadows that Cassie could not see the blush that spread across the enchanter's face.

They stood in the clearing staring at the spectacle around them for what seemed like hours but was in fact only a few minutes when Cassie began to feel fatigue setting in. She waited for Andrea to pull away, but the enchanter made no attempt to move. The expression of awe and serenity on the usually stressed and anxious enchanter's face as she looked around was enough to convince Cassie to not let go, even if she was growing weaker with each passing moment.

Fortunately, Andrea snapped out of her trance and noticed Cassie was looking weaker than usual. She quickly cut off the flow of magic but did not release Cassie's hands.

"Sorry," she said quietly. "I could tell you were getting tired."

Cassie shrugged but still did not let go. "It's all right. At least we got to see the show for a bit."

The forest around them began to darken, the lights fading from the trees and leaves. The trees glowed faintly for a bit longer, but soon the only light remaining came from the moon and stars. The humming had ceased, but now the forest seemed quieter than ever.

"It...it was nice," Andrea mumbled. She still felt slightly woozy and there was something else, a tightening in her throat as she suddenly found herself feeling very nervous. She could not explain why, however. She focused intensely on the ground, even though there was nothing of interest to be found there.

"Maybe magic isn't entirely horrible," Cassie tried to joke, but was quiet when she noticed the enchanter was avoiding eye contact.

The two stood there, each one waiting for the other to speak. But neither did.

"We...we should probably head back. The others might be worried," Andrea said quickly. She suddenly pulled her hands back and tucked them underneath her cloak.

"Right. I mean, Elisa probably doesn't give a crap, but yeah we should head back," Cassie agreed. "Lead the way."

Before they got more than a few steps away from the clearing, Cassie stopped and said, "Andrea?"

"Yes?"

"Thanks for coming to find me and...talking and stuff. I guess...I think it helped a little."

"Oh," Andrea replied. She was...disappointed? *That's...odd.* "Of course. Anytime." She hoped Cassie would not notice and to her relief, Cassie simply nodded as she continued following Andrea back to the camp.

As the enchanter summoned another orb of light to guide them back, she heard Cassie's voice pierce the silence again. "You talk to Diana already?"

Andrea tried not to cringe. "Yes," she said slowly. "She ah... she said that–,"

"They're not going to let us go, are they?"

The enchanter stopped and turned to face her friend again. "I'm sorry, Cassie. Diana won't ask Harrington to reopen the bridge until the Legion is dealt with."

To Andrea's surprise, Cassie did not seem angered by the news. The enchanter did not know if this was because Cassie was too fatigued from the magic transfer or if perhaps she had been worrying too much all along. *Cassie did say you needed to relax.*

"She say why?" Cassie asked.

Andrea nodded. "Should the City of Towers fall, she wants to ensure that we-that *I* don't get captured and taken back to the empress."

Cassie snapped her fingers in realization. "Oh yeah, because you're a wanted criminal and all!" She began to walk again and Andrea followed her.

"I guess that makes sense," Cassie continued as they stepped carefully through the trees. "So, what's the plan then?"

"Diana asked if we would help defend the capital city once the Legion invades," the enchanter explained. "After that…well, I suppose we'll see."

Cassie sighed. "Seeing as how the last time we tried to 'help' resulted in us getting captured, I'm not sure what Diana has in mind."

"Me neither," Andrea admitted as they approached the camp. "Whatever it is, I hope it results in us winning.

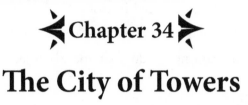

Chapter 34

The City of Towers

City of Towers, Gurdinfield

"There it is. The City of Towers."

"Yeah, I know – it's right in front of us."

Kye laughed when he saw Andrea's face turn a slight pink after Cassie muttered her response to the enchanter's announcement. It was difficult not to be impressed, however. The three pillars that stood imposingly on the corners of the great city and behind the massive metal gates loomed above them, the sun reflecting brightly off the white stone, and the young enchanter could not help but feel excited and the slightest bit jittery over the prospect of actually getting to see the capital of Gurdinfield. The city was situated on a hill, its roads gradually winding up the grassy slopes until finally ending at the palace itself.

"I am so done with walking," Cassie whined. "Is it bedtime yet?"

"It's not even midday," Andrea answered with a longsuffering sigh. The newly formed Gurdinfield army had finally departed the Gurdin Woods a few days earlier and was looking forward to setting up camp for a short respite before the Legion inevitably arrived.

"Fine. Lunch? Ow!" Cassie reeled back as she was hit in the back of the head with something hard that fell on the grass at her feet. She picked it up to examine what had struck her – a chunk of hard bread covered in cloth. Looking back, she saw Elisa. A sly smile appeared on the older woman's face.

"I've been wanting to do that for a while," she said in pleased tone.

"You and me both," Andrea muttered, to which Cassie responded with a faux-shocked look.

"You've graduated from bad jokes to just flat out insulting me!" she said. She pretended to wipe a tear from her eye. "I'm just so proud!" she added dramatically.

The enchanter shook her head. "My jokes are just fine, thank you. You, on the other hand, have been complaining about eating since we left camp this morning."

Meanwhile, Diana walked alongside Alexander, Harrington, and Jacob at the front of the group. She was worried about the challenge that lie before regarding the Legion as well as whether or not the citizens of the capital city would accept her as their leader. The golden lion pendant that hung from her neck felt heavier than it had in days as she was reminded that her actions over the next several hours would determine the fate of Gurdinfield. It was a massive responsibility, and other than being entitled to it by blood, Diana was not confident that she was ready for it.

"You seem troubled, love," Jacob's voice broke through her thoughts.

She looked up, a bit startled. "Oh," she said, "just thinking about, well, *this*." She gestured to the city ahead.

Jacob looked out in the distance and nodded. "We'll be fine. We've got all of Gurdinfield behind us now and soon the City of Towers. The Legion won't have a chance."

"Don't be so certain, young man," Harrington spoke sharply, surprising them both. "The Legion is the greatest army in Damea for a reason."

"Have confidence in your soldiers, Lord Harrington," Alexander joined in. "The city walls offer an excellent defense against anything the Legion can throw at us. Holding them off from the walls until they tire enough that we can take them in the field might be the best approach."

"I wouldn't be so sure of that, sir." Elisa had quickened her pace to catch up with the four of them.

Diana tilted her head. "You know something, Elisa?"

The ex-Legionnaire nodded solemnly. "Perhaps. I can only share what I remember back when I trained under General Cadar. But there are...factors that we have not considered yet that I believe may be key to this battle."

"Such as?" Alexander asked.

But Elisa shook her head. "Not here. I can explain more once we set up in the palace." She looked at Diana. "If that is all right with you, Your Majesty."

"Of course. And really, Elisa, just 'Diana' is fine," the queen said with a mildly annoyed look. Alexander and Jacob exchanged amused glances as Harrington focused on the path once more.

Thunder rumbled in the distance. From where they stood, the group could see dark clouds clustered to the north, nearly blocking their view of the formidable Rhyad mountains in the distance.

"That storm will be here in a few hours," Alexander informed them, any trace of amusement gone from his tone. "No doubt that will make things difficult."

Diana frowned at the storm worriedly. "We will figure this out," she said.

"Or we'll just get very muddy," Jacob deadpanned as they approached the city gates.

* * *

A flash of lightning closely followed by thunder lit up the long, dark, dismal corridor of the palace that Alexander, followed by Diana, Jacob, Lord Harrington, Andrea, Cassie, Elisa, and Kye as well as some of the higher-ranking officers in the Gurdinfield forces walked through. Although it had been decades since these halls had been walked, the palace was in surprisingly decent condition. The once-polished wood floors were dusty and littered with debris, and most of the furnishings and walls were coated in cobwebs. The only light save the occasional flashes of lightning was from the torches the group carried.

Shortly after arriving in the city, Diana, Alexander, and Harrington had met with the governor, who had been chosen years earlier by the nobility of the City of Towers to keep order and handle the day-to-day issues. He confirmed that he had indeed received the letter sent by Alexander and graciously resigned his post to Diana upon meeting her. He even offered the use of the inns to the Guardians for as long as they required.

At Alexander's suggestion, the group had decided to go to the royal palace to plan the defense of the city, for it had been decades since anyone had set foot in it and the Guardian leader suspected that there might be some information in the palace library that the Gurdinfield army could take advantage of.

"The library is up ahead. We can set up there," Alexander said as he briskly led them down the corridor.

Diana struggled to keep up as she repeatedly stopped to look around at their surroundings. This place...had it really been her home so long ago? She had *lived* here? With the royal family – *her* family?

"Your Majesty? Diana?"

Diana snapped back to reality and saw the concerned expression on Alexander's face. "Oh," she muttered, shaking her head. "I'm sorry, did you say something?"

The Guardian leader flashed a tired smile. "Just making sure you were all right." He looked around. "Do you...remember this at all?"

"No," she admitted and shook her head again. "I'm trying to, Alexander, but...I'm afraid I have no memory of this place." They continued walking.

"How long do we have until the Legion gets here?" Kye wondered, saying aloud what everyone else in the room was thinking.

"If we're lucky, the storm should delay them a few hours," Jacob answered. The usually jovial man now showed obvious signs of agitation. "We should plan our attack and be ready within the hour if we want to have any chance of standing against them."

"An *hour*? There's no way you'll be able to mount a proper defense against the Legion in an *hour*," Elisa argued as Alexander opened a set of double doors at the end of the corridor and led them into a large round room. There were a few small tables in the room as well as several rows of massive bookshelves. Tomes on nearly every subject save anything that had happened over the past twenty years filled the overflowing shelves. A thick layer of dust covered just about every object and surface in the room.

"We can push the tables together," Kye suggested and began moving the tables toward the center of the room to form one larger surface for them to plan on. A few of the Gurdinfield soldiers assisted him with the task.

"You mentioned earlier that you had some information about the Legion that you wanted to share with us, Elisa," Diana said. "Anything you can tell us about how they might attack, what their defenses will be like…anything really – would be most helpful."

The ex-Legionnaire nodded solemnly. "Of course, Your Majesty."

Jacob revealed a faded and partially torn map of the city and laid it flat on the table. "According to the information gathered from Ithmeera's journal, it will be a fraction of the Legion's full force. We can have archers posted on the wall while the rest of our forces move out and–,"

"That's not going to work," Elisa declared. She reached out and pointed to the scribbled depiction of the city gates on the map. "You need to have as many people as you can holding that gate. Keep the archers if you must, but don't try and take the Legion in the field."

"You must be joking," Jacob said. "We have the numbers now; we can take them."

"I don't think Elisa ever jokes, to be honest," Cassie quipped from the back of the room.

"Cassie…" Andrea warned.

"Why do we need so many to hold the gate, Elisa?" Diana asked, ignoring Cassie.

"Back when I was still training with the Legion, the royal enchanters had devised these containers filled with magic that were designed to explode upon impact. If such a thing were to be repurposed for combat use, I imagine Erik – General Cadar would not hesitate to use it," Elisa explained.

"Explosives? How are we supposed to stop *that*?" Cassie asked incredulously.

The room grew quiet save the rumbling of thunder outside.

"How are they able to get so much magic contained like that?" Andrea wondered aloud.

Elisa shrugged. "I'm not sure. I do know that the royal enchanters had spent a great deal of time working on them."

"Hold on a moment," Jacob said, holding his hand up to silence the room. "We don't even know if Cadar will be with the Legion. The empress is only sending a small force, after all."

"Trust me, he'll be there," Elisa said forcefully. Her expression hardened. "He wouldn't miss the fall of the capital city."

"We are *not* going to fall–," Diana began protesting.

Elisa glared at the queen. "The Legion is the best army in Damea. We are a barely united militia, with extra weight on top of it all." She gestured at Andrea, Cassie, and Kye. "The best thing we can do is to protect the city for as long as we can."

"For how long, though?" Alexander finally spoke up. "I respect your experience, Elisa, but we still have the people of this city to protect. We cannot protect them if we don't keep the Legion out for good."

"Even if we hold them off for the night, Cadar is a patient man," Lord Harrington spoke up. "They will siege the city until we run out of resources."

"There *must* be some way we can launch an offensive while maintaining a strong protection around the city," Diana declared.

"If the Legion has their device, then they will use it on the gates. Any barrier we form will be broken. They'll overrun the city before the night is over," Elisa stated, though Andrea could swear she heard regret in the fighter's voice.

Barrier. Andrea had an idea.

"There might be a way!" she exclaimed. She saw Cassie look at her oddly. The others stared at her, their attention wavering between her and Elisa.

"Well?" Jacob said impatiently. "What is it?"

"I…" Was this even a realistic idea? Or would it hasten their defeat because she might not be able to perform even the most basic of magical tasks? Andrea knew she had to try at the very least.

"If I can create and hold a magical shield in front of the gates, it might give you the time you need to launch your offensive," she rushed.

To her surprise, no one said anything at first. Diana was even nodding slowly. Lord Harrington remained silent but gave a single nod of approval. Andrea felt an odd combination of pride and fear as the reality of exactly what she had volunteered for set in.

"No," Cassie blurted.

"What? Why are you saying 'no'?" the enchanter asked.

"Because it's a stupid idea."

Elisa folded her arms across her chest. "How exactly is Andrea giving us more time to attack a stupid idea?"

"Because it's a suicide mission," Cassie retorted.

"It's a mission that will buy us time," Jacob pointed out.

"Sure, but if Andrea gets blown up by some *magical exploding device* then *our* mission is pretty much dead," Cassie said angrily.

"I can do it," Andrea firmly stated. Then, more quietly, "This is my choice, Cassie. If we don't win this, we don't get to Rhyad."

Cassie looked as though she was about to protest but bit her lip and remained silent, only glaring at the enchanter as the room shook from another clap of thunder.

"It is settled then. Jacob and I will lead the charge on the field while Andrea maintains a shield for us," Alexander said. "Diana will stay within the city walls in the event that the gate is broken through."

"Why can't I be on the field with you and Jacob?" Diana protested.

"It probably wouldn't do for the Queen of Gurdinfield to die so soon into her reign," Elisa said. She looked at Alexander. "I'll be on the walls with the archers. I assume at least one of them knows how to use a bow properly?"

"They'll await your orders," Jacob said with a sigh as he tried to ignore the ex-Legionnaire's biting comment. He turned to Cassie and Kye. "You two will stay in the inn until I give the order that the city is safe."

Cassie and Kye immediately protested.

"That's a load of–," Cassie began angrily.

"I can fight. You've seen me! Let me join you!" Kye cried, his pleas drowning out Cassie's profanities.

But Jacob stood his ground. He gestured at Cassie. "I can't spare any men to guard you, and you don't have the training to stand out there on your own. As for you..." He looked at Kye. "Your magic is unstable and unpredictable. I don't need you accidentally setting half the field on fire." Andrea noticed the captain exchange a tentative glance with Elisa.

"It's for your own safety," Alexander added.

Cassie continued muttering expletives under her breath and Kye slumped his shoulders in defeat.

"Right then," Jacob concluded. "I suggest we prepare for battle then."

"Agreed," Alexander said. "Dismissed."

As Elisa, Alexander, and the others walked away to prepare

for the upcoming battle, Diana grabbed Jacob's arm and looked up at him accusingly. "I should be out there with the rest of the soldiers. With *you*."

Jacob smiled faintly as he took the queen's hands. "We *need* you, Diana. The people of Gurdinfield need you now, more than ever. We'll have a greater chance of winning that offensive if I'm not worrying about you the entire time."

Diana raised an eyebrow. "I can fight well enough, you know."

"Of course I know. But you're not just a Guardian anymore. You're our queen…you're *my* queen. And as your captain, I am sworn to protect you. Surely you understand that," Jacob said and gave her hands a squeeze.

"I do…Jacob, I do. But," Diana lowered her voice, "am I…I mean, I'm more than just your queen, right? You know that, yes?"

Jacob gently placed his hand on the queen's cheek. "Of course I do."

Diana grinned and didn't bother to conceal her blush this time. "I…all right. Be careful," she said softly.

"I always am," the captain said before leaning in and placing a kiss on her lips. Diana barely had time to react properly and before she knew it, Jacob had pulled away and left, leaving her alone in the room.

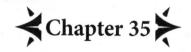

Chapter 35

Desperate Times

Most of the group and several Guardians retired to the city's largest inn, The Lion's Den, shortly after the battle's strategy had been decided upon. The inn was the newest out of the three that existed in the capital city, built near the top of the hill during King Caleb's reign. With a sweeping view of the city and the surrounding land, a full tavern, and seemingly endless entertainment courtesy of visiting musicians, the inn was by far the most popular of the three.

Andrea was on her way to the room that she and Cassie shared when Elisa pulled her aside in the main tavern hall. Cassie had refused to speak to the enchanter after their meeting in the palace, and had stormed out of the room ahead of her. While she understood why Cassie might be concerned about the mission, Andrea did not think that Cassie giving her the silent treatment was warranted and hoped to talk some sense into her friend once she met up with her. But first, she had to deal with Elisa.

"In my room, please," the ex-Legionnaire requested. The enchanter reluctantly followed.

"What is it, Elisa? I should probably get ready so that Diana and Alexander are not kept waiting," she insisted as Elisa closed the door behind them.

"Yes, because I fully intend to waste your time with idle chatter and ask you things such as what adorable little shop you acquired your cloak from," Elisa said dryly as she knelt next to the bed, from which she pulled out a large burlap sack.

"In Ata, actually. Meredith bought it for me before I left with her." Andrea could not stifle a laugh.

"Ah, your vengeful mentor," Elisa replied and tossed the sack onto the bed.

The enchanter immediately grew uncomfortable. "She's not- she's not 'vengeful.'"

"Of course. She was just testing you to see if you could survive having giant boulders thrown at your face." The ex-Legionnaire shot the enchanter a knowing glance before gesturing at the sack. "Here. I picked this up in the old barracks on my way back here. It's not custom, but it should fit well enough."

Andrea approached the bed and slowly peered into the sack. She raised her eyebrows before glancing back up at Elisa. "I don't know about this."

"I am not giving you a choice, girl. *You're* the one who volunteered for this stupid task. Your friend is right – it will most likely be a suicide mission," Elisa answered flatly.

"I'll be fine."

"Perhaps, though from experience I can tell you that your odds are quite poor." She bit her lip and Andrea could once again hear the regret in the older woman's voice. "Look, what you are doing is admirable, and it might even be the key to us not getting destroyed by the Legion. But I would not be doing my job if I did not warn you of the probability of you never making it to Rhyad."

The enchanter smiled warmly. "I appreciate you caring, Elisa."

"I've expressed no such sentiment. You are being foolish and stupid, as I've come to expect from you."

Andrea nodded and picked up the sack, struggling with it for a moment before regaining her balance.

"Andrea."

The enchanter turned.

"What's in Rhyad?" the older woman asked, her tone more curious than demanding.

Andrea considered for a moment before setting the sack down on the wood floor. "I'm not certain I should say, to be honest."

Elisa snorted. "Considering everything I have done to assist you and Cassie in getting this far, I think you owe me an explanation."

"You've never pressed the issue," the enchanter said with a puzzled look.

"Well, now I am. Obviously, there is something extremely important there for you to be risking your life like this," Elisa pushed.

Andrea looked around the room, only to realize she was being slightly paranoid as no one could hear them through the walls. "You cannot tell *anyone*."

"I have no desire to."

After taking a deep breath, Andrea finally let free the secret she had been keeping from the group for weeks. "You're aware of the shortage of magic?" Elisa nodded.

"Cassie and I believe we know the location of the magic that's been missing from Damea all this time," Andrea continued.

"You believe it's in Rhyad?" Elisa asked. The enchanter thought the ex-Legionnaire appeared interested, but only mildly. *Which is...significant I suppose?*

"Yes," she replied steadily. "That's why we need to get to Rhyad." She intentionally left out the part about Cassie's abilities, as she did not completely understand them herself and was still not sure if she could trust anyone else with that knowledge.

"And Cassie? She is no enchanter. What part does she play in this...mission of yours?"

"She...knows where it is," Andrea answered cautiously.

Elisa studied the enchanter for a moment before shrugging. Andrea was certain the older woman suspected she was holding back information, but she made no effort to volunteer more. "I see. Well, best you get that armor on and go meet the queen. We've a battle to win if you two want to get to Rhyad before the year's end."

Andrea nodded politely. "I will. And thank you, Elisa. I will see you soon," she said. She opened the door before picking up the sack again and slowly began making her way back toward her own room.

＊ ＊ ＊

"You're not doing this."

"It's been decided already," Andrea said firmly as she walked into her room, sack in hand. Cassie sat on the bed, looking anything but happy about the situation. She had jumped up when Andrea entered the room and walked over to shut the door behind the enchanter.

"You could have said something to Jacob. You know I can help. I could make sure we win that fight. At least let me go out there with you and–," Cassie leaned back on the door.

Andrea spun around quickly. "*No*," she snapped, dropping the sack. "We already agreed – we don't tell anyone about your abilities."

"But I can help! I can actually make a freaking difference in that battle!" Cassie argued. Andrea swore she heard sadness in Cassie's voice but stood her ground.

"*I don't care*. I'm not risking it. Now, I'm going to put up a shield in front of that gate tonight. You can't stop me."

"Have you ever actually fought in a battle before? You *know* that the second you go out there it's only a matter of time before the Legion blows that gate to bits! They aren't going to hesitate if you're in the way," Cassie pointed out.

Andrea reached into the sack and began pulling out its contents – a set of hard, leather armor – and setting the pieces on the bed. Not completely sure how to proceed, she finally grabbed the leather chest piece and pulled it over her head. While attempting to fasten it, she tried to reason with Cassie. "The whole point of the shield is to give Jacob and the others some time *before* the Legion uses their weapon, if they even have it."

"They'll have it. I can't imagine any army with that kind of weapon would just leave it at home," Cassie said bitterly.

Andrea exhaled in frustration as she struggled with the

straps of the armor. "I'm…trying to do…the right thing," she said between futile bouts of battling with the armor. She sighed. "Can you give me a hand?"

"And encourage this ridiculous idea that you have? I don't think so," Cassie replied smugly.

"*You're* the one being ridiculous."

"No, I'm trying to keep you alive. A little gratitude wouldn't kill you. This crazy idea, however, will."

"I don't know why you're so upset about it. It's the only chance we have to win this," Andrea explained. "If we don't win, Gurdinfield can't help us get to Rhyad. If we don't get to Rhyad, we can't find the magic and you…you can't go home." The enchanter could not help but cringe inwardly at her last comment.

Cassie slammed her fist into the door behind her, making Andrea jump. "*For once in your life* can you stop thinking about the freaking magic and think about yourself?! If you die, all of this – the magic, Rhyad, walking halfway across Damea, and… everything – will all have been for nothing!" she shouted.

The enchanter was puzzled by Cassie's outburst but made an attempt to understand anyway. "Cassie, even if something were to happen to me, you…you know the way to Rhyad," she said quietly, the weight of the situation and its possibilities growing heavier by the moment.

"Elisa or Diana…they could make sure you got there. There must be some other enchanters out there that could…you don't need me to do this necessarily." She turned around and made a weak attempt to try to fasten the straps of the armor again, unsurprised when she failed.

She was startled when Cassie came up from behind and grabbed one of the straps. "Here," Cassie said, exasperated, and began to fasten the straps tightly. "As long as you're going to be an idiot we might as well make sure you're not completely doomed from the start."

Andrea attempted a small laugh. "The odds have never really been in our favor since this all began."

"I don't know about that," Cassie mused as she finished fastening the last strap. She began to help Andrea slip on the wrist guards that had come with the armor set. "We did escape your crazy mentor girlfriend, break into the Azgadaran Palace, steal a book, become fugitives, *and* do the whole 'fix our civil war' thing for Gurdinfield without getting killed in the process. I'd say we've done pretty well for ourselves."

Andrea smiled. "Perhaps you're right," she said. Then Cassie's words registered more clearly. She looked mortified and pushed her friend lightly. "And for the last time, Meredith was just my mentor! I've never...our relationship was purely that of a teacher and an apprentice."

Cassie put her hands up in defense. "Relax, I was just joking. The look on your face just now was pretty funny, though."

The enchanter rolled her eyes. "Very mature. Now help me get the rest of this armor on so we can get this over with."

Cassie complied and assisted Andrea with putting on the remaining pieces. When they were done, Andrea put her hands out, twirled and asked, "Well? How do I look?" She had meant it as a jest to lighten the mood, but when she saw the worry on Cassie's face, she pushed herself to continue. "Thank you for helping me. I should go see the others. It's probably almost time."

Cassie shifted her weight from one foot to the other. "Uh...
yeah, probably. So, I guess I'll...stay here then."

The enchanter nodded. "Right. That's what Jacob said," she
said forcefully as she walked to the door. She felt foolish for
not saying something more comforting, something to instill
confidence in both of them, but what could she say that would
convince both herself and Cassie that everything would be all
right? "You'll...be all right here." It was a question more than a
statement.

"Yeah," Cassie muttered from behind, though the sadness in
her voice was unmistakable this time. "Try not to get killed."

"I...I will," Andrea mumbled, feeling slightly ill suddenly.
She wrapped her hand around the door handle and made a
move to turn it but then stopped. She barely had time to process
her own actions as she turned and grabbed Cassie's shoulders,
pulling her in for a rushed kiss.

Cassie nearly reeled back in shock, but was able to overcome
the initial surprise enough to respond by grasping the
enchanter's arms. Startled, Andrea quickly pulled back and
pushed Cassie away.

Cassie stared at the enchanter with wide blue eyes, unable
to find words.

Horrified at what she had just done, Andrea felt the color
drain from her face. She quickly turned and flung the door
open before rushing out of the inn.

Cassie, now alone in the room, simply stared blankly ahead
as she tried to register what had just happened. "Um...right,
so...that was new," she said to no one.

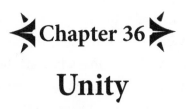

Chapter 36

Unity

"Andrea! There you are!" Gurdinfield's queen jogged toward the enchanter just as she exited the inn. The rain was coming down steadily and Andrea could see that the queen's hair and clothes were already soaking wet. She wore her dark, thick hair back and a leather helmet over it. A longsword hung from her belt and her bow was slung over one shoulder. Her armor glistened as rivulets of water ran down the hard leather pieces that protected her chest, legs, and arms. Andrea could see a small crest, the Great Lion of Gurdinfield, branded into the chest piece.

"Sorry I took so long. I'm a bit inexperienced when it comes to putting on armor," the enchanter admitted. She was still shaken up from earlier and her thoughts kept wandering to her encounter with Cassie. *Why did I kiss her?* What was she thinking? What was Cassie thinking? She knew she would have to face her friend again at some point, assuming they both survived the battle.

Clearly you were not thinking that far ahead.

"You all right, Andrea? You ready?" Diana asked, concern crossing her features.

"What?" Andrea asked and shook her head as she tried to clear her mind of what had happened at the inn. "I'm sorry. Yes. How are we doing?"

Diana began to walk toward the city gates, where the Gurdinfield army stood ready to defend the capital. She gestured for Andrea to follow. "Alexander's had all the officers gather their groups and meet at the gates. Jacob has been rehearsing the strategy with them – and inspiring everyone, no doubt." She laughed quietly, but the enchanter could hear the pride in the queen's voice.

They walked down the wet cobblestone roads of the city, passing scores of people. Some of them nodded or bowed in to greet and show respect to the queen and the enchanter, while others looked on in interest or fear. A few cheered loudly as others began moving their families into their homes in the hope that the army would be able to hold the gates. Andrea smiled faintly at the crowd as she walked along the street, wondering if they knew an enchanter would be playing a large role in what stood between them and the Legion. Despite all the wrongdoings her mentor had done, Andrea grinned inwardly, knowing that Meredith would be proud of her for what she was about to do.

"I have to admit – I am not used to this," Diana said quietly as they neared the gates. "Of all the things that had crossed my mind of things I would do in my lifetime, being queen was never one of them."

Andrea laughed. "You'll have plenty of time to get used to it, I'm sure."

Diana tilted her head. "You think so? You really think we'll win?"

Andrea nodded. "Gurdinfield deserves to be reunited. You've worked too hard not to win."

The queen raised an eyebrow. "And what about you? You've asked for nothing except passage to Rhyad. Surely there's something else you desire once this is all over."

The enchanter shook her head. "Passage to Rhyad is all that Cassie and I require. I wouldn't say no to some supplies and horses, though."

"Of course. Dare I ask what your purpose in Rhyad is?"

"I...it's something that I'm not quite sure about myself, honestly," Andrea admitted. She didn't want to lie to Diana, but she was not entirely sure how to explain much more without divulging the true purpose of their quest.

Much to Andrea's relief, they were quickly approached by Alexander and Jacob, both clad in full battle attire, as soon as they arrived at the city gates. A clap of thunder shook the ground beneath them.

"Lovely," Jacob grumbled. "Let's hope we don't all slip in the mud and let the Legion just walk over us."

"Then we'd better exercise caution," Alexander suggested. "Are your men ready, Jacob?"

"They are, sir," Jacob answered. "Roe's on the other side of the gates with Harrington and his fighters."

"And Elisa?"

"Up on the battlements, ready for orders. Victor's with her as well. She had some choice words for me when I asked if she was sure she could manage the archers. They tend to backtalk a lot," Jacob said with a lopsided grin.

Diana could not hold back a smile, but Alexander simply nodded and turned to Andrea. "Are you prepared?"

"Yes," the enchanter said, hoping her voice did not sound as shaky as she felt. "What do you need me to do?"

"Once it is time, I will give the order to attack. Elisa and the archers will go first, followed by our trebuchets from the towers. She will then give a signal to Jacob, who will charge with his men once he is ready," Alexander explained.

"Ideally, we won't need to use your shield at all. But if we do, Elisa will light the signal fire on the battlements," Jacob said and pointed up at the stone walls that surrounded the city.

"Hold that barrier for as long as you can," Alexander pressed. "Don't let anything or anyone past it. We will have some soldiers guarding you and the gate, but we cannot spare too many or we'll not have enough resources for our offensive."

Andrea nodded solemnly. "Understood."

"Are Cassie and Kye at the inn?" Jacob asked.

"Yes," the enchanter answered. She wondered what Cassie was doing. Was she scared? *She seemed...sad or was it angry? Was it at me? Or was it because I was leaving her at the inn?* Would she and Kye actually be safe there? What if the barrier failed and the Legion deployed their device? She knew Cassie could defend herself to a point and that Kye's magic, while unpredictable, was powerful. But against trained Legionnaires, the odds were not good for either of them. Whatever happened, Andrea knew she *had* to hold that barrier.

"Good. Diana, you'll stay inside the gates and watch for anything the Legion might try to hurl over the wall," Jacob ordered.

The queen nodded. "Be careful. All of you," she said, though Andrea could see Diana's eyes meeting Jacob's.

"You, too," Jacob said with a nod. "We'll be–,"

The low blast of Gurdinfield's battle horn sounded, silencing all and alerting them to look across the great field beyond the city. In the distance, only just visible on the horizon, was the seemingly endless wall of Legionnaires that made up the force Azgadar had sent to conquer the city. Some carried flags with Azgadar's crest on them, the sword and shield adorned with the blood red and gold motif that represented the empire.

"They are here," Alexander breathed. No one responded for a moment until Diana spoke up.

"This ends now," she said forcefully. She mounted her horse and rode through the city's entrance to where Gurdinfield's massive army stood. Jacob and Alexander followed suit, with Andrea riding on the back of Jacob's horse.

Diana rode out to the front of the army, making sure to position herself so that all could hear her. Then, in a voice that started out small but quickly rose in volume and confidence, she spoke to them.

"My-my friends!" she called out, her voice hesitant and shaky. "Today…today we have achieved what was once thought impossible! For twenty years, we were divided and broken. Today we are united – a new and stronger nation." She pointed at the massive army approaching behind her. "The Azgadaran Legion wishes to destroy that unity. They seek to take the very thing that makes us a sovereign nation. We *cannot* allow that!"

The soldiers of Gurdinfield yelled out in unison, an agreement that thundered within the city walls.

Diana took a deep breath and drew her sword. "We are a united, independent Gurdinfield, and that is something that no one – not an empress, not even an empire, can take from us again. That will not stop them from trying, however." She raised her sword. "I ask you this – will you deny them?!"

Another roar of agreement. The rumbling of the army seemed to shake the very ground, easily overpowering the thunder from the storm.

Once Andrea had dismounted outside the gate, Jacob rode up to Diana and positioned his horse next to hers. The queen nodded to him.

"You all know your duty!" he yelled, drawing his sword as well. "I stand for my queen, just as I stand for Gurdinfield. Will you fight beside me for her, the future of this great land?"

The final roar of agreement reverberated across the field and the city. The soldiers drew their swords and raised them up as their captain had done. In the city walls, citizens of Gurdinfield stood outside their homes and cheered in response.

Jacob lowered his sword and turned to Diana. "The city is yours, Your Majesty," he said. "That was an inspiring speech by the way."

Diana smiled. "Thanks. It was my first."

"The first of many. Now, behind the gates with you," the captain ordered.

The queen nodded. "Be careful, Jacob," she pleaded.

Jacob met her concerned gaze and nodded. "I will."

The queen paused for a moment. "I…Jacob, if by some miracle we do win, I want–,"

But Jacob would not let her finish the sentence. "After," he said kindly. "I dare not make that promise to you until I know I can keep it. But I will fight to make it, this I swear."

Diana bit her lip but quickly regained her composure and nodded. She gave the Guardian captain one last glance before riding past the army, through the gates and back into the city.

"Close the gates!" Roe shouted once he saw that Diana had entered the city safely. With a metallic groan, the chains that held the massive gates began to move, lowering the gate, leaving Alexander, Jacob, and Andrea on the field with Gurdinfield's army.

* * *

Elisa focused on the horizon at the quickly approaching Azgadaran Legion. It was still daytime, but the clouded sky made the field much darker than she was comfortable with. Luckily, the torches carried by the Legion's soldiers lit up the grassy field, making it easy for her to spot areas of opportunity for her and the archers. She could not spot General Cadar, but she knew he was there somewhere.

She waited.

* * *

Jacob and Alexander waited on the field with the army, waiting for the signal from Elisa. The closing distance between them and the massive army across the field was making the captain nervous.

"She hasn't signaled yet. Something must be wrong," he stated worriedly.

"She will signal when it is time," Alexander said calmly.

They waited a bit longer, looking up at the battlements on the wall for a signal from Elisa. For what seemed like an eternity, there was no word. Finally, Jacob heard the loud and distinct blare that was Elisa's horn, a confirmation to let him know that Elisa and the archers were in position and that it was time to strike.

Alexander did not hesitate. "Archers!"

＊ ＊ ＊

Elisa watched the field intensely and raised her arm, commanding her archers to ready their bows. The army was in clear focus now and the time to fire was quickly approaching. She waited until the Legion was within range. Turning her head, she saw that her men had prepped their arrows with fire on the tips of them.

"Get ready!" she shouted, holding her hand up. Closer and closer the Legion marched, until their commander, no doubt one of Erik's top officers, shouted an order. The march broke into the beginnings of a charge.

"FIRE!" she screamed. Streaks of fire flew over and past her head as the arrows rained down on the charging Legionnaires below. She watched as one by one, Azgadaran soldiers fell, many crying out after being struck in the chest, shoulder, or neck.

"Trebuchets!" Elisa yelled. "Ready!" She waited for another opportunity on the field to present itself before issuing her next command. "*Fire!*"

Massive blocks of stone and burning projectiles were launched from the great white towers of the city. They flew across the field and hurtled downward, smashing into the ground and leaving crushed Legionnaires in their wake. Large chunks of debris and dirt scattered outside the impact radius.

Her confidence high, Elisa raised her arm again and prepared to order the next hail of arrows.

* * *

Jacob watched in awe and pride as his archers took down Legionnaires. He raised his sword.

"Prepare to charge!" he yelled. He waited until the Legion was close enough before looking to Alexander, who simply nodded. The captain's sword came down.

With a great roar, the army of Gurdinfield began charging the Azgadaran Legion, becoming a blur of red, blue, green, and black, while the rain beat down on both armies. The initial clash left scores of soldiers on the ground, injured or dead. Jacob yelled out as he swung his sword into the nearest Legionnaire, who was quickly cut down by the captain.

Chapter 37

Shattered

Nausea nearly overwhelmed Andrea as she watched in horror as the battle unfolded in front of her. The screams of the Legion's soldiers after the fire arrows had hailed down on them had terrified her, and she knew that if she survived this she would never be able to forget them.

Still, she had a job to do and she was going to get it done, no matter what. She looked up at the battlements, waiting for the signal fire that would be lit once Elisa deemed it time for the barrier to go up. She looked around. She was mostly surrounded by soldiers who were there to protect her if Elisa failed to give the signal in time. They had their swords drawn and were waiting, fear showing through most of their hardened expressions.

Then it happened. The enchanter heard a shout and looked up. The fire had been lit. It was time.

With all the energy she could gather, Andrea concentrated inward on manipulating that energy into something that would surround not only herself, but the area around her. Forcing herself to remember everything Master Jheran and Meredith had taught her, she took a deep breath and pushed the newly shaped magic outward using a strong gesture of her arms.

There was a flash of bluish-white light and the barrier was up, a mostly transparent field of magic. The edges of the barrier glowed with a dazzling white light.

I did it. She relished in the intense energy that pulsated throughout her being.

"It's up!" she yelled. *"The barrier is up!"*

* * *

Jacob roared as he dodged a Legionnaire's sword and charged into the soldier with his shoulder. The soldier staggered and tried to recover but not before Jacob ran him through with his blade.

The captain pulled the bloodied sword out of the man's body and quickly looked around. Andrea's barrier was up and no one had managed to penetrate it so far – in fact, none of the Legion's soldiers were even approaching it. His confidence grew, but he knew better than to start celebrating early. He looked around to see if Alexander was in sight, but there was no sign of his mentor anywhere on the chaotic field.

Hoping Alexander and Diana were both all right, Jacob continued to push through the swarms of fighters as he made his way to the front of the Legion, where he knew Erik Cadar would most likely be.

* * *

Cassie felt the walls of the small room shake again from the thunder. She had been sitting on the bed for the last hour or so, trying to process what had happened and what *was* happening. Magic, Meredith, Azgadar, the civil war, the forest…everything that had happened seemed like a blur to her now. *This* was real; the battle raging outside the city gates was real. The soldiers that fought outside the gates, no doubt giving their very lives for the city to stay free, were real. It was *all* real.

And now Andrea, the only person in this strange place that Cassie actually gave a damn about was out there risking her life. And there was nothing Cassie could do to help her friend.

Friend. Cassie shook her head. She never thought she would make one here. Damea was so hostile and dangerous, with most of the people she had met trying to either take advantage of her or destroy her. Sure, Elisa, Kye, and even Diana had been trustworthy so far, perhaps even Jacob and Alexander, but Andrea had really been the only one who had made the effort to be anything more than someone who did not want to harm her. Cassie felt a pang of regret as she knew Andrea, while an enchanter, did not deserve all of the scorn that Cassie had thrown at her. Now she might never get the chance to change that. *So much for making friends here.*

Or whatever she and the enchanter were.

She had not forgotten about how strange Andrea had acted, how she had struggled to stay calm and collected about going into battle, how she had kissed Cassie and left without a word of explanation. Cassie was not really sure what kind of explanation she was expecting, but *anything* had to be better than just saying *nothing* and leaving. *Nothing I can do about it now*. She would have to think of something to say when Andrea returned…if she did.

Kye's lute sounded from outside the room. He was playing a song she had heard a few times during her stay in Damea. The song, slow and beautifully mournful, carried well thanks to the acoustics of the building and the strength of Kye's voice. No doubt he was in the main hall of the inn, distracting frightened citizens from the battle happening far too close to them for comfort. Cassie decided to go out to the tavern and sit with the others. She was up for just about anything as long as it would take her mind off of what was happening.

* * *

Andrea continued to focus all of her willpower on keeping the barrier up. So far it was impossible to tell which side was winning from where she stood, but based on the reactions she was seeing from the soldiers that guarded her and the gates, Gurdinfield was not lost yet.

"What's going on? Can you see anything?" she shouted at the guards over the deafening roar of the battle.

Roe, who was standing not too far in front of her yelled back. "We appear to be pushing forward, but not by much! Keep that barrier up!"

"I will…try!" Andrea knew she could not keep this up forever, but she had to last long enough for the offensive to be effective to the point that the Legion's strategy to take over the city would be ruined.

* * *

"Fire!" Elisa shouted and another onslaught of arrows was launched from the battlements. She looked down at the sight below where she and her men stood. The bodies of dead soldiers from both sides littered the now bloody field. Piles of corpses were quickly forming. With a deep breath, Elisa realized that while their initial attack had been effective, the Azgadaran Legion's soldiers were too numerous and well-trained – the Gurdinfield army would be outmatched soon.

She scanned the field, wondering if she should call for Jacob and Alexander to retreat. It was only a few seconds before she saw *him*.

It was difficult to be certain due to the storm and the growing darkness, but her gut told her that she had spotted General Cadar. The general, flanked by his personal guard, appeared to be calmly walking toward something, a…structure of some kind? A sinking feeling gripped Elisa as she began to panic. Why had she not seen the trebuchets before?! She knew several of the Legion's tactics, which at times included firing rocks and such from trebuchets at the walls of a city or fortress, but she did not foresee such a small fraction of the Legion's force hauling trebuchets across Damea. The Legion's trebuchets were designed in such a way that they could be disassembled and hidden by surrounding soldiers until they were ready to be deployed for combat.

She shook her head and quickly spun around to face her men. "Aim for the trebuchets!" she shouted and pointed at Erik and his men, who were now operating the ranged weapons and preparing to fire. On the closest one they had loaded what appeared to be a massive crate that was…*on fire*? She quickly realized they were going to use the trebuchet to launch it at the city wall!

"Ready!" she yelled, giving her men very little time to prepare. They needed to hurry or the trebuchet's ammunition would be launched directly at the city's wall where Andrea had her barrier. While she had confidence in the enchanter's abilities, Elisa was uncertain if the barrier could withstand such a force. She watched as the archers scrambled to reposition themselves to hit the men operating the ranged weapon. *Faster.* She wiped away the rainwater that had mixed with the sweat on her face. *We have to be faster.*

She screamed for the archers to fire and watched in horror as the trebuchet was released – its target: the barrier.

* * *

"Get back! They are launching!"

"Move! Get to the city!"

Andrea watched in confusion as some of the soldiers around her began shouting in panic and fear for their comrades to move back and even into the city. A few of the guards ran up to the edge of the barrier but could not break through. They frantically pointed upward and Andrea's focus followed where they were pointing.

The chaotic blasts of noise from the battle went quiet. She

heard the shouting, but their shouts were muffled and she could not comprehend what they were saying as she stared up at the sky, frozen in fear and indecision as the massive ball of flames hurtled through the sky toward her.

Her last thoughts were jumbled, flashes of memory and concern for the people in the city that would be vulnerable once the gates were breached. She knew she would not have lasted much longer on her own anyway.

"Go!" she screamed at the fighters around her.

With the last of her strength, she gathered the barrier magic that had been flowing around her over the duration of the battle and threw it at the rapidly approaching projectile as hard as she could. The collision of magic against magic exploded into a scorching ball of fire and light, sending out an earth-shaking shockwave in all directions.

Andrea heard the deafening screams of everyone around her before she saw nothing.

✷ ✷ ✷

The ground shifted violently beneath Cassie, nearly knocking her to the floor. Several patrons screamed in fear and held on to whatever they could – tables, chairs, each other. Kye dropped his lute, and several glass bottles behind the innkeeper's bar crashed to the floor, shattering on impact. Within seconds, the shaking stopped.

"W-what the hell was that?!" Cassie stammered. The other patrons looked at her with wide, fearful eyes.

"The gates..." Kye realized aloud. His voice was strained and raspy and Cassie felt dizzy as she quickly understood what Kye was saying.

"They've gotten through. That means..." Cassie didn't finish her sentence. She grabbed Kye by his shirtsleeve. "Let's go. We need to get to the gates." To her surprise, he did not argue. Instead, he turned to the frightened patrons. "Everyone stay here. We'll be back." The crowd appeared shaken but most nodded.

Cassie flew out the door of the inn and began racing down the slick city streets as fast as her legs would carry her. Kye was not far behind and quickly caught up. "The gates! Look!" he shouted and nodded in front of him.

Cassie stopped running and rested her hands just above her knees, with Kye stopping behind her. Panting and drenched, she looked at the terrible sight before her. The heavy gate that had once shielded the city was no longer intact. Something very large and heavy had ripped a massive hole through the metal grates. The edges of the impact had left the metal melted and twisted. Swarms of the city's soldiers surrounded what was left of the gate, trying to make sense of what happened and position themselves to barricade the open space.

"The device..." she breathed.

"We...we have to find Diana!"

Cassie spun around. "She won't be able to help. You see those men?" She pointed as she spoke. "If the Legion can blast a giant freaking hole through a metal gate, who's to say they won't do it to those soldiers?" She strained her eyes to try to see further, but the rain made it difficult.

"I need to find Andrea. She was supposed to be holding up that barrier. If they got through...oh, *no*..."

"Don't think that way–,"

"I should have *been there*. I *told* her it was too dangerous to do on her own! Damn it, Andrea! Sh–,"

"She might have gotten out of the way in time," Kye said quickly. He looked up at the towers. "There has to be *some* way we can help."

"Can't...I don't know...can't you put up a barrier? Just a small one to give me time to find her?" Cassie pleaded.

Kye looked at the ground guiltily. "I...I can't. I don't have that kind of control, Cassie. I'm sorry. My powers don't work that way."

"*Damn it!* Then what *are* you good for? Setting random crap on fire?!" Cassie shouted angrily at him as she grabbed his shoulders. She knew this was far from Kye's fault, but between Andrea missing, the giant hole in the gate, and the massive army that would soon be in the city, she was slowly losing her grip on the situation.

"Cassie, I–," he tried to reason with her but she was past listening. Her gaze shifted from his face to the gate, then to the towers above. Her eyes lit up.

Kye was still apologizing when she interrupted him. "Let's go!" she exclaimed and grabbed his arm. She began dragging him toward the closest tower.

"What? Where are we going?" he demanded but followed her anyway.

"I've got an idea," Cassie said hurriedly as she led him by the wrist through the streets. "It's probably going to kill us both but you're going to have to trust me, okay?"

"You know, you're not exactly inspiring much trust when you say things like 'it's probably going to kill us,'" Kye muttered.

"Shut up. We have to get to the top of that tower." Cassie pointed to the Sky Tower.

"Why?"

"Stop asking questions and just follow me. Please." The last word sounded softer to Kye. He knew Cassie was worried and that she had less battle experience than he did, which was practically none, save for their skirmish with the Moores. But she had given him no reason to distrust her.

"All right," he exhaled and gestured forward with his hand. "Lead the way."

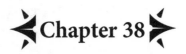

Chapter 38

Burning

When Elisa opened her eyes, she shuddered as pain shot up her back and to her head. The explosion had knocked her unconscious along with several of the archers on the battlement with her. She gritted her teeth as she climbed to her feet and began helping some of the archers around her stand up as well.

"What happened?" Victor grumbled, wincing as the ex-Legionnaire helped him stand.

Elisa rubbed the back of her head and looked down at the field below to assess the damage that had been done. Her chest tightened when she saw the charcoal-covered rubble that littered the ground where the gate and parts of the city's entrance once stood. The tightness spread to her throat when she realized that some of what looked like chunks of debris were actually the bodies of soldiers that had fallen when the blast went off.

Andrea. The realization hit her that the odds of the enchanter surviving the explosion were extremely low. She remembered seeing the enchanter use the barrier to counter the explosive before she was thrown back against the stone wall of the battlement. *Perhaps the barrier had been enough to protect Andrea.*

Looking out at the battlefield, Elisa could see that the fight had gone from strategic to chaotic. Soldiers clashed mercilessly into each other. She scanned the field to see if the Legion was loading more of the trebuchets. To her great relief, they were not. However, a small group of Legionnaires were preparing to make a run for the gate. Jacob and Alexander were not in sight, and Elisa knew she had to get down there and prevent the Azgadaran soldiers from storming the city.

"Watch the field. Hit them with everything we've got," she ordered Victor.

"Aye, will do!" he barked.

With all the speed she could muster, Elisa sprinted across the battlements toward the city's entrance, where a long flight of stone stairs, slick from the rain, had managed to hold up in the explosion. The air was thick with smoke and the strange, burned scent of magic stung her nostrils.

The area near and around the city gates was in disarray. Most of the soldiers were scrambling to form a barricade while others were combing through the rubble in a desperate attempt to find survivors.

"Elisa!" she heard someone shout. She turned and saw Diana running toward her. The queen was covered in the same charcoal residue that covered most of the city entrance but otherwise appeared uninjured.

"Are you hurt?" Diana panted as she approached.

Elisa shook her head. "I'm fine. Are you all right? What about the people in the city?"

"We're all fine. The explosion…was that–,"

"Yes. They used a trebuchet. It hit…it hit the barrier," Elisa said, her voice lowering almost to a whisper.

The queen's eyes widened. "Where is Andrea?"

"I don't know. I–,"

"We need to find her!" the queen exclaimed. She turned to the fighters that had lined up behind her. "You three!" she barked at a few of them. "Find Andrea! The rest of you, follow me!" She met Elisa's gaze again, and the ex-Legionnaire could see the stress and tiredness in the queen's eyes. "Jacob?"

"It's too chaotic on the field." Elisa tried to keep her voice steady and even as she spoke. "We need to get a barricade up. There are Legionnaires preparing to charge the city gates." She looked up at the ruined distortion of metal and stone. "Or what's left of it, anyway."

Diana nodded. "Understood. I'll prepare my men in case they get through. Can you hold this position?"

Elisa nodded. "We'll try to for as long as we can. If the Legion launches another explosive, though, we're done for."

"I…I understand." Elisa could tell that the queen was trying to remain calm but the growing panic in her voice said otherwise.

"We can't help them now. We need to focus on what's happening here," she said, knowing that Diana was still thinking of their comrades.

Diana bit her lip. "Right. Stay safe," she said and began to back away.

"You, too," Elisa replied with a nod and watched the queen turn and run back into the city with her remaining guards.

* * *

"Almost...there," Cassie panted as she and Kye neared the top of the long spiraling staircase of the Sky Tower.

"So at what point are you going to tell me about this plan of yours?" Kye demanded. His legs ached from climbing so many steps and his lungs burned from breathing in the quickly cooling air.

"There's no way they'll be able to hold the city against the Legion," Cassie explained as they finally reached the top of the tower. She pushed the heavy wooden door open and led Kye out onto the deck. "What I'm about to ask you to do is really dangerous and might kill us all, but I think it's our only chance."

"There's that word again!" Kye whined, shaking his head in dismay. "'Kill'. Don't we have some kind of explosive we can drop on *them* so that we don't have to die?"

Cassie grinned despite their surroundings. Were she with Andrea right now instead of Kye, the enchanter would probably be going on and on about saving the world and refuse to make light of the situation. She regretted the thought immediately, however, when she thought of the very real possibility that her friend might be dead.

"Okay," she said, looking out at the battlefield. "Look, what I'm about to tell you is going to sound really insane but you have to trust me, all right?"

"Just tell me what the plan is," Kye insisted. "We can deal with the insanity of it later."

Cassie held out her arm. "I'm going to feed magic into you and you're going to hit the Legion with your powers. It'll be ten times more powerful than if you tried it by yourself."

Kye raised an eyebrow. "What? How is that even possi–,"

"What did I say about trusting me?!" Cassie shouted. "Just do it. Look at that." She pointed to the battle below. "We're losing. I'm no war expert and even I can see it. Now, are we doing this or not?"

Kye looked at the battlefield, then at Cassie, and then at Cassie's outstretched arm. "I-I don't know if I'll be able control it," he admitted.

"You can and you will!" Cassie insisted, raising her voice over another clap of thunder. "Just…please, Kye." The fire that had burned in her eyes since they left the inn had given way to sadness and worry. "I can't…I don't know if she's alive, but if she is, she needs our help."

Kye breathed deeply and nodded. "All right. Let's do it."

Cassie smiled faintly. "Good. Now," she said with a grimace, "whenever I've done this with anyone else it's hurt me…a lot. Whatever happens," her voice was edged with dread, "don't let go. Promise me."

Kye nodded solemnly. "I promise."

"Good. Ready?" Cassie held her arm out. She was visibly shaking as she remembered her experience with Meredith in the Black Forest. *At least this time I'll be doing this for a good reason.*

Kye wiped the water and sweat from his brow as he mentally prepared himself before conjuring a small ball of energy in his right hand. "Ready." He watched as Cassie closed her eyes tightly and clamped her hand around his left wrist.

There was nothing Kye could have done to prepare himself for the overwhelming surge of power that shot through him. He staggered and fought to maintain his balance as Cassie let loose a shrill cry of pain.

"Cassie!" he shouted. The brightness of the energy in his hand was so intense he had to look away before it blinded him.

"I'm...fine!" Cassie groaned through clenched teeth.

Kye turned to face the battlefield again and lifted his free hand, aiming for an area directly in front of a large cluster of Legionnaires. Drawing on Cassie's power, he launched a series of shockwaves that rippled through the air and smashed into the ground, surprisingly not far from where he had attempted to aim. The sheer force of the spell sent soldiers flying through the air. The soldiers behind them quickly scrambled backwards. Some frantically tried to regroup while others panicked and looked up, wondering where the attack had originated.

"I did it," Kye whispered in awe. "Cassie, I did it!"

Cassie did not respond. Her grip on his wrist, while still tight, was already beginning to loosen. There was no doubt about it – Kye required a staggering amount of magic for his spells. The connection with Andrea during spells, while tiring, was methodical and steady, but having Kye draw on her power made Cassie feel like her very life essence was being ripped from her.

"I'm going to hit them again!" he announced. Reaching inward and grasping the newfound energy that flowed from

Cassie and through him, Kye conjured another powerful shockwave, wincing as Cassie's screams of pain filled the air, and hurled it at the panicking soldiers below. The impact was even more violent than the first spell, killing some of the soldiers instantly and tossing others about like ragdolls.

A spark ignited on the field followed by a loud bang. Within seconds, the radius where the shockwaves had hit exploded into flames. Soldiers cried out as they were quickly immolated by the rapidly spreading fire. Legion commanders frantically barked orders at their subordinates in a vain attempt to get them to regroup and attack again.

"Oh, no," Kye muttered. He looked up at the sky, which was still delivering punishing amounts of rain to the battlefield. He hoped the rain would be able to control the spread of the fire before it reached the city.

* * *

Once the ground had stopped shaking beneath her, Elisa looked around frantically trying to figure out what had just struck the Legion, taken out several of its soldiers, and caused a massive fire on the field, worried that perhaps they had other explosives and one had detonated accidentally. If they had one more, then there was a good chance that they brought several of the devices. She noticed that many of the Legionnaires were looking up and toward the Sky Tower, however. Following their gaze, she tried to focus on what appeared to be a figure, maybe two, standing on the top deck of the tower. It took her a moment to realize that something or *someone* up there had used magic. But who? Andrea had still not been found, and Elisa doubted that the enchanter had survived the earlier blast.

Kye. The name quickly surfaced in her mind, giving rise to frustration and worry. If he was up there then there was no doubt in her mind that Cassie had not stayed in the inn either as they were both ordered to. *I'm going to kill them once I get them off that tower.*

"That was impressive, Elisa. I'm not surprised to find you here, though. Had I known you had enchanters under your command, perhaps I would have brought my own. It's always interesting watching their kind fight each other." That voice. Elisa knew it – she both admired and loathed its owner.

Slowly turning, she found herself a few steps away from none other than Erik Cadar. He was, of course, clad in his custom-made general's armor – a full suit of leather and metal emblazoned with the crest of the Azgadaran Empire on the front of the metal chest piece. A gold-hilted sword hung from his belt.

"Erik," she growled and drew one of her long daggers.

Cadar narrowed his dark green eyes at her. "That's General Cadar to you," he said icily. "Of course, a deserter and traitor such as yourself would not care for manners or respect. It seems I expect too much from you yet again."

"Leave, before I have my enchanter turn you and your men to ash," Elisa threatened.

The general gestured toward the field where the battle was still being fought fiercely. "You should tell your forces to surrender while you still can, Elisa. I'm sure you saw the successful deployment of our new weapon. Having your enchanter throw the barrier at it was clever, but your walls are still exposed, and I have no doubt we will take the city by nightfall."

Elisa tightened her grip on the dagger. She could strike now but Erik was fast, probably too fast, and there would be Legionnaires on her within seconds if she tried. Most of Gurdinfield's forces were further out in the field or guarding the entrance to the city, too far to help her.

"I wouldn't try that if I were you," the general said, as though he had read her mind.

"You deserve to die for your crimes."

"*My* crimes?" He laughed. "I'm not the one who harbored a criminal for years and lied to her commanding officer, her empress, *and* her closest friend about it."

"You will *not* speak of my father!" Elisa spat, her anger quickly reaching a boiling point.

"And why shouldn't I? Hoarding magical artifacts is one of the worst crimes you can commit, Elisa. Or did you forget that part of your Legionnaire training as well?"

"I suppose then that I shouldn't bother asking what you told your sister," she snapped.

Cadar grinned. "I told her the truth, of course."

Elisa shook her head. "You're a liar. Ithmeera knew how upset my father was after Philip's death. She would have understood–,"

"All that the *empress* needed to know was that there was a dangerous criminal in Azgadar who had locked himself up with who knows how many magical artifacts. With that much power, he could have posed a threat to Her Majesty's safety," Erik declared angrily. "The fact that I was able to remove *you* – a thorn in my side – was merely a byproduct of the transaction."

"Calling my father's murder a 'transaction' shows just how far you've fallen, Erik," Elisa growled. "You've been nothing but envious of Ithmeera for as long as I've known you."

"You know nothing of our lives!" he retorted.

"I saw it! Philip saw it! You'd skulk the halls and question Ithmeera about everything! You were worse than Alden!" she continued.

"Silence!" Cadar yelled and drew his sword.

"You were always the jealous one. You hated that Ithmeera spent more time with her *husband* and I than you," Elisa taunted, the hints of victory beginning to show on her face.

"And you were an unnecessary burden from day one!" he shot back. "That is why I will *never* stop being Ithmeera's family and you...you will be forgotten as nothing more than a pathetic excuse for a soldier who, along with her sick, addict father, plotted her *dearest* friend's assassination as a sick sort of revenge for her brother's death!"

Elisa stared back at the general in shock. "You...that's what you told her? That I was...plotting her death? Are you mad?!"

"My sister knows what she needs to know," Cadar answered with a sinister smile.

Elisa drew her other dagger. "You're going to pay for what you've done, Erik."

"Not likely," the general said calmly as he held up his sword. "I am sorry it's come to this, Elisa. You had such potential and yet you threw it all away for an old man. A pity, really. I will give you one last chance to offer your surrender."

She raised her blades. "Let's get this over with then," she said. "I challenge you."

Erik looked at her in surprise but quickly composed himself and gave a curt nod. "A duel? With you? How can I refuse?" He took a few steps back to create space between them. "I'm sure I don't need to explain to you how this goes. Or did you forget how to duel like a Legionnaire as well?" he taunted.

Elisa did not answer. Instead she charged, daggers out and aimed for the sides of the general's torso, where his armor seemed the weakest. Erik, while surprised, quickly recovered and lifted his sword up to block her attack before the daggers could pierce the leather. He pushed back against Elisa, throwing her backwards. Glaring at him, Elisa attacked again, swinging her daggers downward in a spiral of blades. One of the knives caught on Erik's arm and sliced through. The cut was superficial, but angered Erik nonetheless. He used his sword to block the brunt of the attack again and charged into Elisa with his armor-plated shoulder. The impact left her gasping and knocked her to the ground.

Before she could get up, Erik strode over and pressed his heavy boot against her throat. She coughed and wrapped her hands around his leg, trying to push him away.

"Attacking before your opponent is ready? You truly *are* a coward and a traitor," he sneered and applied pressure to Elisa's throat. She gasped and choked, clawing at his boot in a vain effort to breathe.

Erik glared down at her mercilessly. "I sentence you to death,

Elisa of Sadford, for treason, espionage, and deserting your active post in the Azgadaran Legion." Keeping the pressure steady on her throat, he raised his sword and prepared to drive it through her chest.

Chapter 39

Pummeled

"Hold on, Cassie!" Kye yelled as he felt Cassie's hold on him weakening. He looked back at her quickly and was horrified to see that she was on her knees, blood dripping from her nose. There were tears streaming down her face and Kye could see the beginnings of bruising already starting to show under her eyes and on her cheeks. Her eyes were bleary with pain and she had been alternating between hyperventilating and crying out since they had begun contact.

"I…can't, Kye," she wheezed as her hand slipped from his wrist. "I can't–,"

"Yes, you can!" he cried. He grabbed her arm tightly and met her eyes. "Come on. Look, we've got them running scared!" He pointed to the field, where Legionnaires were being yelled at by their commanders to regroup, though by this point most were panicking and trying to avoid the fire that raged through the grass.

Cassie coughed, her throat sore from screaming. "Kye, *no*…"

He squeezed her arm. "Please, Cassie. You said it yourself – this is the only way we can win."

Cassie squeezed her eyes shut and then opened them again.

They were bloodshot, making the blue in them look unnaturally bright. "I can't, Kye. I just…it hurts too much. I can't."

Kye felt a confidence he did not know he had rise up within him. "You *can*. And if you won't do it for them, then do it for *her*. She wouldn't want you to give up," he said, his voice strong and unwavering much to his own surprise.

Even through her pain, Cassie rolled her eyes. "You…you people and your…stupid speeches," she grumbled and gripped his arm again. "I-I can't last much longer. Make it quick."

A smile broke out on Kye's face as he nodded and turned back to the battlefield. "Here we go," he declared and reached for the power for one final spell. When he found the magic he was looking for, he inhaled deeply and fired one final powerful spell, a massive shockwave wrapped in purple flames, at the field below.

The pain that the exchange wreaked on Cassie shot through every part of her body and blurred her vision to the point where she was blinded. She thought she heard a scream, perhaps her own, before she collapsed.

* * *

A mighty force barreled into the general, knocking him to the ground and sending a splatter of mud everywhere. Erik found himself on his back as flames slowly surrounded him and Elisa. Before he could react, the cold metal of his own sword pressed against his throat.

Elisa stood over him, soaking wet and covered in mud and

ash as she held the general's sword, prepared to drive it through him if necessary. "You will take your Legion and go back to Azgadar," she said, her tone low and dangerous.

"I'd sooner die!" he growled.

"You will if you do not," she stated plainly and put slight pressure on his throat to prove her point. "When you return to Azgadar, you will tell Ithmeera the *truth* about everything. Do we understand each other?"

Erik looked puzzled. "You're...not going to kill me?"

The ex-Legionnaire shook her head and stepped back. "As despicable as you are, you're family. As much as I'd like to run you through with your own sword, I am not you." After picking up her daggers and sheathing them, she extended her hand to him.

Surprised, the general took it and allowed her to help him up. "I...thank you," he spoke hesitantly. "Perhaps you are right. This...grudge has gone on for far too long. I will talk to my sister."

Elisa tilted her head. "Truly?"

"Yes," he replied with a nod. Looking around at the flames that were closing in, he said, "We had best get moving before this fire gets any closer. Your enchanters are ruthless."

Tossing the general's sword on the ground, Elisa sighed and closely followed Cadar away from the fire. She had relaxed for only a moment when she saw the flash of steel that appeared at the general's side as he quickly drew his dagger and spun around with the intent to drive the knife into her chest. Her thoughts a blur, Elisa drew her own blade in a race to block his attack. Realizing she was faster than him, she flipped the dagger and easily dodged his weapon before driving her own into the side of his neck.

The general did not cry out, but instead stared at Elisa with wide, disbelieving eyes as he fell to his knees. He grunted and struggled to crawl toward her for a few seconds until he collapsed on his side. He made a quiet gurgling sound before he lay still.

The battlefield, once roaring and chaotic, now seemed quiet to Elisa. Scanning her surroundings, she saw the once formidable Legion forces were beginning to pull back to escape the fire, the unending arrows that rained from her archers above, and the steadfast Gurdinfield soldiers that still fought fiercely on the field. The magical attacks from the Sky Tower had ceased, and she could no longer see the figures at the top of it. The rest of the Gurdinfield army that was not on the field was successfully holding the barricade in front of the city.

Panting, Elisa stared down at the dead general. Her throat tightened as tears pricked at her eyes, and she could not tell if it was from the fires that were slowly being extinguished either by the rain or on their own, or because she had just slain a man that she had once considered family. She shakily walked past Erik's body, where a small pool of blood had formed under his head and neck. Grabbing his sword from the dirt and drawing her battle horn, she took a deep breath before lifting the sword high in the air and blowing the horn, signaling to the armies of Gurdinfield and the Guardians that the Legion's general was dead.

* * *

Darkness wrapped around Andrea, cradling her. She could still feel the magic coursing through her, though most of it had gone to counter the massive force of magic that had been thrown at her. The rain seemed louder than usual but the sound of it was comforting, almost soothing.

She felt pain, but it was distant. There were shouts, but she was not sure how they related to her, if they did at all. A familiar smell permeated the air. Bill's trademark stew, perhaps? The shouts became louder and clearer and she realized her mother was calling for her. Probably needs me to deliver another batch of vegetables. *She wanted to tell her mother about Meredith and her offer but it seemed too soon. There was a buzzing in the back of her mind that grew louder the more she thought about her mentor.*

She would just have to tell her when she got home. No doubt her mother would want to meet Cassie as well.

Cassie? She was still at the inn, though. Andrea would just have to get her after the battle was over and they could celebrate.

But when had they won? Where were Jacob, Diana, and the others? The barrier had been lost but the Legion had not managed to get through…had they?

The buzzing had evolved into a roar that pounded in her head. The rain seemed…wetter, louder. Something dripped around her shoulder. There was a rush of air and a man calling out to her, though she did not recognize his voice. Where was–

"YOUR MAJESTY! Your Majesty, we've found her!"

Pain slammed into Andrea, knocking the wind out of her and leaving her gasping for air. Her ribs ached, making every breath nearly unbearable, and her shoulder throbbed, alternating between excruciating pain and exquisite numbness. The first thing she saw was the dark, clouded sky and the side of Roe's weary, dirt-covered face, which meant she was being carried.

She tried to speak, but every movement made her dizzy. There was a roar followed by loud cheering. Had they won? What was going on?

Before she could think on it anymore, her vision blurred and darkness took her again.

* * *

The fog that kept Cassie anchored in unconsciousness finally lifted. Her eyes were still closed, but she knew that she was awake again. More importantly, that she was alive. She wanted to laugh or even cry at the ridiculousness of it all – she had somehow survived the horrible ordeal of battle, a battle in some foreign land, on top of it all – but both her body and mind felt beaten and fatigued beyond measure.

There was noise, but it was distant and muffled. As she became more acclimated to her surroundings, Cassie realized that the noise was actually someone speaking, though she could not tell whose voice it was. After a few moments, however, it was clear that the speaker belonged to a male, and that there was more than one person in the room.

"...than we could have hoped. It'll take months to repair but it...done if we keep to the schedule...discussed earlier." The words came in bits and pieces to Cassie, but the voice was at least mostly recognizable now. She slowly opened her eyes and saw Alexander, no longer in battle attire but instead dressed in a simple grey tunic and dark pants, standing with his back turned to her a few feet from the bed she was lying on. He was speaking to a younger man Cassie did not recognize, though she was still learning the names and faces of the higher-ranking Gurdinfield officers.

"I will inform the others. That will definitely help morale, sir," the other man replied. He looked past Alexander and noticed that Cassie was awake. Nodding in her direction, he spoke once more. "I'll go see to the arrangements, sir."

Alexander turned and upon seeing that Cassie was awake, gave her a brief smile before facing the officer again. "Thank you. Oh, and please tell the queen that I'll be there shortly."

The man gave a slight bow. "Of course, sir." Once he had left, Alexander turned again to face Cassie. "You're awake, I see," he observed. "You are back at the inn you so hastily ran away from, against my orders to make things more interesting." He smiled again. "How are you feeling?"

Like crap. "I'm okay, I guess," she shrugged. She tried to push herself so that she was sitting up but as soon as she made the attempt, a sharp pain tore through her arms and ribs. She let out a small gasp that she tried to muffle, but not before Alexander noticed.

"You should try not to move around too quickly. Your injuries are still healing, it seems," he suggested as he took a few steps toward her and began assisting her in sitting upright. "There." He took a step back and looked at her with concern.

"That was a very interesting display of skill you and the boy showed on that tower. My people have their own theories, but I'm more interested in what *you* have to say, if you would not mind explaining – later of course. For now, just know that your actions saved a lot of people and enabled us to win that battle."

Cassie was unsure how to respond. Andrea had made it very clear early on that she was not to tell anyone about her abilities and...Andrea. Kye. They had won the battle? What had happened?

The sudden panicked look was not missed by Alexander, who placed a hand gently on her shoulder. "Your companions are all right," he said calmly. "Kye carried you down from the tower and is doing just fine, if shaken up a bit. I imagine that was his first time doing anything of the sort."

Cassie gave a short laugh. "Yeah...that wasn't exactly something on my 'to-do' list, either." She finally comprehended that he had mentioned her "companions" – more than just Kye. "Um...what about the others?" she asked hesitantly.

The Guardian leader grabbed the wooden chair that sat in one corner of the room and sat down next to the bed. "Di-Lydia was able to keep the city safe from the Legionnaires, no doubt the result of your friend's efforts with the barrier. Lord Harrington is fine as well. Jacob has a few minor injuries, but nothing that will not heal with time. Elisa, well, she actually fought General Cadar on the field."

Cassie's eyes widened. "S-she did? What ha–,"

"Cadar is dead," Alexander interjected, and Cassie thought she saw a hint of remorse cross his face. "We took the field shortly after."

Finally, Cassie fearfully asked the question that she had been holding in since their conversation began. "Andrea? She's... she's okay?"

Alexander gave a slight nod. "When the explosive was launched, your friend used her barrier to counteract it. She is injured, but she will live. Were it not for her quick actions, that explosive would have done far more damage than it did and many innocent civilians would have perished."

Cassie felt a massive weight lifted from her as she heard the news. Andrea wasn't dead – no, in fact the enchanter was nothing less than a hero to these people now. *I'm going to kill her.*

"I'm going to go see her. Where is she?"

Alexander raised an eyebrow. "You really should rest until your injuries have had more time to heal."

But Cassie had made up her mind. "I'm fine. I feel like I've been in this bed forever anyway." She looked down and noticed she was wearing new clothes – a black long-sleeved shirt and dark pants.

Alexander chuckled before standing. "It's been about two days since the Legion retreated back to Azgadar. Many of the fighters are still recovering and probably will continue to for some time. Come, I'll take you to her." He extended his hand and Cassie took it, using his arm as support to climb out of the bed. She gingerly tested her balance for a moment before letting go of his arm. The aching and wooziness were still there, but she could stand and walk at the very least.

"Will they come back?" she wondered aloud as he guided

her out of the room and down the main corridor of the inn's second floor. The Lion's Den was mostly quiet, though Cassie could hear the murmurings of patrons downstairs and the clinks of glasses and dishes from the dining area.

"I doubt it – at least not without some kind of courier to threaten us ahead of time," Alexander explained with a crooked smile. "The empress will be devastated at the loss of her brother, but she is a smart woman. She knows the cost of waging a war with a united nation like Gurdinfield will be higher than she is willing to pay."

He stopped outside a closed door, the second from the last at the end of the corridor. "She is in there. I am unsure of her current state, but if you require assistance please call on anyone here. Your other companions are most likely around here somewhere. We've run of the city until the repairs to the palace and gates are complete, though I suspect many of the soldiers will want to go home soon." He started to walk away but stopped. "Also, there will be a celebration of sorts soon. Lydia would no doubt appreciate your company there." He walked away, his footsteps heavy on the wood floor, leaving Cassie standing outside Andrea's room.

She hesitated a moment and inhaled deeply. The last time she had spoken to Andrea, the enchanter had been defensive and stubborn before suddenly kissing Cassie and running out of the room. She sighed. *This is going to be weird.* She grasped the door handle and slowly turned it before entering the room.

The room was small – barely large enough for the bed and side table that sat across from where Cassie stood. She moved into the room, her limp obvious as she struggled to keep her balance and close the door behind her. She turned back to face the bed that Andrea lay on. The enchanter's eyes were closed and she appeared peaceful, an expression Cassie rarely saw on her companion. Andrea's dark hair was spread across the pillow, and her face sported several fresh scratches and bruises. Under the new, white blouse the enchanter wore, Cassie could see thick layers of bandages wrapped around the girl's left shoulder.

She approached the bed cautiously. With no chairs in the room and her body still aching, Cassie decided to sit on the end of the bed. She waited quietly, taking note of the various patterns in the grain on the floorboards.

To cope with the silence, she began to think back on the battle. Being on the top of the Sky Tower and watching Kye defeat an army with magic – *her magic* – only made her realize that whoever she was back home was nothing compared to who, no…*what* she was in Damea. If entire armies fell because of her magic, if crazed enchanters chased her and her new friends across *countries* for the very same power…Cassie did not finish the thought. She knew the conclusion. She had become dangerous, a threat. And now the entire Gurdinfield army knew about her abilities. It was probably only a matter of time before her very *presence* put her friends in constant grave danger. They *had* to get to Rhyad and she *had* to get home before word of her power spread. If not–

"And you say *I* talk to myself too much." Cassie jumped when she felt a hand on her arm. She looked up and saw that Andrea had woken up and that the enchanter was now sitting up and staring at her, a faint smile on her face.

"Uh…you're awake." Cassie blurted.

Andrea nodded weakly and pulled her arm back. "Yes."

"Uh…how are you feeling?" Cassie met the enchanter's hazel eyes quickly before staring down at the bed's comforter.

"Tired. My shoulder hurts." Andrea gestured to her bandaged injury. She gave a quiet laugh. "Everything hurts, actually."

The two were silent for a moment before the enchanter spoke again. "How long?" she wondered.

Cassie shrugged. "Couple of days, I guess. Long story short, we won." She thought for a moment, then added, "You saved a lot of people with that barrier, you know."

Andrea bit her lip and shifted slightly. "I…you know what happened then?" she asked, her voice quiet and frail.

"I was still here when they threw that explosive at you guys and when *your* dumb ass decided it was a good idea to be a hero and go at it with your magic," Cassie retorted.

"I wasn't trying to be a hero–," Andrea began to protest. But Cassie put her hand up to stop the enchanter from continuing.

"I know," she said firmly, struggling to keep her voice from shaking. "I know. I was just…" she looked down again. *When the hell did talking get so hard?* "I'm glad you're okay is all."

"Oh," Andrea said, though she seemed confused. She noticed the bruising on Cassie's face for the first time since she had woken up and looked at her friend worriedly. "Your face."

Cassie involuntarily reached up and gingerly touched her cheekbone. "Oh, well…yeah."

Through her tiredness, the enchanter managed to narrow her eyes at Cassie. "'Oh well'? That's all you have to say?"

"It's just a bruise. It'll go away," Cassie said with a shrug.

"You...you used your power! How–,"

"I helped Kye, all right?" Cassie cut in defensively. "We heard the explosion and went to find you and when we saw what was happening...look I wasn't just going to sit on my ass while you and everyone else was out there! I told you that."

"And I told *you* to stay here where it was safe. You..." The enchanter clenched her fists. She spoke slowly, but her voice was shaking with anger. "You mixed your powers and...and *Kye's*? Do you realize how unstable that magic could have been? How *stupid* it was to even *attempt* something like that?!" She buried her face in her hands for a moment before glaring at Cassie again. "You could have been killed. *Kye* could have been killed! Everyone could have been killed!"

Cassie's eyes widened in surprise and she stood up and held her hands up. "Whoa, hang on! We were just doing what we thought would *help*. Your barrier was gone, we couldn't find you, and there was a giant hole in the city gate so no, I was not going to just *sit here* while everyone else was risking their life out there!" She waited for Andrea to yell back or get even angrier. But the enchanter just closed her eyes for a moment, opened them, and stared straight ahead.

"I-I need to sleep. I'm tired," she said monotonously.

Cassie rolled her eyes. "Fine. Whatever." She began to leave the room, shuffling slowly due to her still-aching body. With her hand on the doorknob she turned to face Andrea.

"See you around, I guess," she said. "Let me know when you're ready to leave. The sooner we get this magic crap over with the sooner I can go home." With that she left, leaving the enchanter alone in the room.

Once Cassie had gone, Andrea sighed and the emotion and tears she had been holding back for days rushed back as she put her head down on the pillow once more and tried to fall asleep.

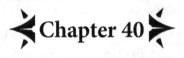

Chapter 40

Aftermath

Fimen's Hope, Gurdinfield

"Where *are* they?" Meredith muttered as she rummaged through her things for the gloves she could have sworn she had packed when she left her mansion in the Black Forest. With winter nearly upon Damea, the enchanter had made sure to pack warm clothing as she was unsure how long it would actually take her to find Andrea and bring both her apprentice and Cassie back home. She had spent the last few weeks traveling toward Gurdinfield, stopping at many of the small fishing and farming villages along the river. When her new constructs had been destroyed, she had been able to use the projection created from their destruction to track Andrea and Cassie to somewhere along the Rhyad River. Now she was packing, preparing to depart Fimen's Hope and make her way to the next town while discreetly asking the locals if they had seen any sign of the girls.

She considered returning to the bar to see if perhaps she had left the gloves there. Before she could make a move to do anything, however, a familiar dull hum rang in her ears. *Magic. A projection.* She slowly sat down on the bed in the room she had rented at the inn and closed her eyes. Concentrating, she pushed through the buzzing and other external distractions until she saw it – a clear path of blue light leading to a much brighter center. It was fading, Meredith could tell for certain, but she figured based on its brightness and how quickly it pulsated that it was very recent. *Andrea?* No, this projection was not the steady, predictable stream of energy that her apprentice often left behind. This magic was raw, untrained, and far more powerful. The sheer amount of energy told her that Cassie had played a role in this, along with possibly…another enchanter?

She opened her eyes and grabbed her bag again. She reached in and felt around for the object she was looking for – her map. After unfolding it and placing it on the bed, she tried to pinpoint exactly where the projection had come from. Allowing her memory and years of experience to guide her, she let her hand drift across the parchment until she stopped, placing her fingers on the location of the projection's origin.

The City of Towers. A least a week's journey from Fimen's Hope, probably more. It had been years since she had visited the capital city, and if the rumors she had heard bits of around town held any truth, then Gurdinfield truly was at peace again. The youngest Taylor had survived the assassination and had taken her place as queen. Meredith wondered what that would mean for her, her research, and the future of enchanters in Gurdinfield. Would the academy reopen?

She'd have time to ponder these questions, no doubt, while traveling to the City of Towers. She glanced out the small window in her room. It was nearing midnight, and she needed to finish packing. But first, she needed to find her gloves.

* * *

City of Towers, Gurdinfield

"...and once that is finished, we can make the final arrangements to start moving our operation to the palace."

Diana brushed her dark hair out of her face and pointed to one of the many papers stacked on the desk she and Alexander sat at. The owner of The Lion's Den had graciously offered them his largest room as a base of operations while Alexander assisted Diana in planning the next steps toward getting the monarchy running again. "*Another* tax?" she asked incredulously. "Alexander, we've only just reunited Gurdinfield. The last thing its citizens are going to want is a tax to pay for the crown's curtains."

The Guardian leader glanced at the paper the queen was pointing to. After reading it, he shook his head and turned to Diana. "This is for the restoration of the palace. We've put forward the funds we can spare from our forces toward the royal treasury, but Diana – we must be careful here. It's been over twenty years since the region has paid anything to the crown. Gurdinfield's citizens will understand that in order to maintain this kingdom and its army, changes will have to be made."

Diana ran her hand through her hair anxiously. "As much as I want to do this the right way, part of me wishes we could just skip this and discuss tomorrow night's celebration."

Alexander smiled and placed his hand on her shoulder. "We will in good time, don't worry. For now, let's finish what we can and then have some dinner."

A knock on the open door startled them both. They looked up and saw Jacob casually leaning on the doorframe. The Guardian captain had a few minor scratches on his face and a superficial head wound that had scabbed over, but otherwise he had come out of the battle unscathed. "Apologies for the interruption," he spoke. "I only wish to speak with Diana."

Diana thought she saw Alexander flash the captain a knowing look before standing up. "Of course." He turned to Diana. "We can pick this up after dinner or tomorrow morning."

"I...if you say so, Alexander," she answered blankly and watched her adoptive father give a polite nod to Jacob before leaving the room.

Jacob turned to face the queen and grinned. "See? All better!" he declared and held his arms out.

Diana was unamused, but stood up and walked to him anyway. "I thought I told you to rest." She wrapped her arms around him and he immediately embraced her. They stood in silence while holding each other for a moment.

"I did rest. Now I'm up and ready for my next assignment," he explained as they released each other and walked to the center of the room. Aside from the large desk, a small bed was situated in the corner along with a few chairs and an old nightstand.

Diana looked at him, puzzled, as she sat down again. "You were given another assignment? By Alexander?"

Jacob shook his head. "The assignment was one of my choosing, but I did run it by him first." He pulled up a chair and sat facing the queen.

Diana could not help but feel disappointed. Another

assignment? How would this affect them? They were finally together and he wanted to take an assignment somewhere else. She felt her frustration growing. "H-how long?"

He shrugged. "Hopefully indefinitely. My partner would be the one to ask about that, honestly."

She raised an eyebrow. "Your *partner*? Who? Victor?"

He laughed loudly. "Ah! No…Victor's a good lad but I'm afraid we're just not compatible that way."

"Why not? You've been on many missions together before. What's changed? And where is this assignment, anyway?" Diana knew she was firing off questions at him faster than he could answer, but she could not help it. This was infuriating. *After everything he said, he would rather abandon all that we've worked toward for some…assignment?!*

"Nothing has changed, love–,"

"Don't *call* me that," she said bitterly. Her anger only grew when he simply smiled at her.

"Is that not what you are?"

She glared at him. "I am your queen. And nothing more, apparently."

He reached over and took her hands. She tried to pull away but he held them firmly. "As I've said before, you are indeed my queen. Everyone is looking to you right now to rebuild Gurdinfield and their lives. I can't say I envy you."

"Did you come here to say 'goodbye', Jacob, or to tell me how to do my job?" she snapped.

"The capital city," he said simply.

"What?"

"My assignment, assuming I am cleared for it. It's here in the capital city."

She frowned. "Are you...you're not joining the city guard, are you? Those positions were not intended for Guardian officers and–,"

"No, love. Not the guard. The assignment is quite large in scope, you see, and requires me to perform a variety of duties, most of them having to do with your well-being," he said tentatively. To Diana he seemed almost...nervous?

Her eyes widened. "You are becoming a Guardian. A-a true Guardian?"

He winked. "You were never very good at guessing games, Diana. No, I was thinking perhaps I would rather have command of the Guardians. It's a role I believe I am well-suited for, assuming you agree to it of course."

The queen shook her head. "But...that role is reserved for..." She trailed off and went silent, her eyes still wide in shock as she sat there gaping at the man across from her.

"Alexander told me your mother was the finest woman he'd had the privilege of serving. She led the Guardians well and chose only the best to protect her family," Jacob stated calmly as he squeezed her hands gently.

Diana was still speechless as Jacob released her hands and reached into his shirt pocket. He pulled out a small brown pouch. "Do you realize how difficult it is to find a weaver in this city that would do this on short notice?" He emptied the pouch into his hand, revealing a bracelet made from a variety of threads and colors. Blue and gold overlapped and intertwined with a deep red. "I thought it might be appropriate to stick with the familiar." He held it out to the queen, who stared at it in disbelief for a few seconds before shakily reaching out and taking it.

"It's…beautiful, Jacob," she breathed.

He grinned. "I'm glad you agree. So…" He paused, nervousness creeping into his voice again. "It would be ah… proper if the queen herself would approve this new assignment request. That is my hope, anyway."

Diana looked up at the captain and shook her head in faux dismay. "You're impossible," she said and slipped the bracelet onto her right wrist. It fit perfectly, evidence that it was indeed made specially for her. A warmth immediately shot through her arm and spread throughout her being, no doubt a sign that the magic the bracelet had been enchanted with was working as intended. The sensation left her somewhat breathless.

"That…was incredible," she whispered and met his gaze again. Her eyes were glossed over with tears of joy. "Yes, of course, Jacob. I…I don't think I've ever wanted anything more."

Beaming at her, Jacob stood up, nearly knocking his chair over, and pulled Diana to her feet as well. "It appears we are in agreement then!" he boomed.

She narrowed her eyes at him. "Alexander knew about this, didn't he?"

"I told him after the battle. He had some concern over the fact that you are royalty and well…I am not, but after everything we have been through together, the last thing he wanted to do was let politics and formalities get in the way of your happiness," he explained and wrapped his arms around her waist.

She leaned in toward him. "*You* are my happiness, Jacob," she declared and held up her bracelet. "We shall have to get you one."

He smiled. "It is already done. I will wear mine at the ceremony."

Diana laughed. "A ceremony? You've already planned this?"

Jacob shook his head. "Of course not, love. I would prefer we do that together if it's all right with you. It is not my intention to impose or interfere with your rule, however."

She placed a kiss on his cheek. "I would never think that. And yes, a ceremony would be nice. The kingdom should know what its queen is up to. But first, we need to put the kingdom back together."

"Agreed. After, then?" he asked hopefully.

She nodded before leaning in once more and kissing him deeply. "Yes, my love. After."

* * *

A soft knocking on the door woke Andrea. As the groggy enchanter opened her eyes, the door slowly opened. She noticed a flash of copper hair first as Elisa walked in with a bottle and a small, white cloth in one hand and Kye's lute in the other.

"Sorry to wake you," the ex-Legionnaire said while using her boot to close the door. She set the lute down, propping it up against the wall, and approached the bed.

Andrea tried to sit up and answer, but instead she let out a sharp cry as her pain arced through her shoulder. Grabbing her injury, she lay back down, breathing shallowly as she waited for the pain to subside.

Elisa sat down on the bed next to the enchanter and opened the bottle before setting it on the nightstand next to the bed. "Don't move so much," she ordered and began undoing the buttons on Andrea's shirt to allow better access to the enchanter's injury. "This will numb it, but only for a short while. It needs to be reapplied three times a day until your injury heals more."

Andrea said nothing but nodded and watched the older woman pour a few drops of liquid from the bottle onto the cloth before applying it to the enchanter's shoulder. The pressure of Elisa's hand caused Andrea to hiss in pain, but she soon felt an odd, numbing sensation in her shoulder and relaxed.

"There," Elisa said and withdrew her hand. "I'm glad you are not dead," she concluded as she closed the bottle and set the cloth on the nightstand next to it. "To be honest, I am still not entirely sure how you survived that blast."

I don't really know, either. "I am…trying not to think about it too much," Andrea admitted.

Elisa nodded. "I can understand that." She looked around the room before catching the enchanter's gaze again. "I am sure the others will want to know that you're awake so that they can attack you with questions."

Andrea could not help but sigh. She really did not want visitors right now. Especially visitors who were going to ask her a lot of questions.

Elisa easily read the younger woman's expression. "I can just as easily not say anything…for now. Cassie would probably want to know you're awake, however. I can go and get her if you like." She began to stand up but not before Andrea grabbed her arm.

"No!" she exclaimed. "I mean…that is, I saw her already. I'm…not sure when, but she came to visit me."

The ex-Legionnaire sat down again. "You should have told us about her abilities. But I understand why you didn't."

Andrea shrugged and began buttoning her shirt. "We agreed not to say anything. We argued about it when she came to visit me earlier. I…made her leave."

Elisa nodded. "Were it not for her and the boy, we would have lost."

"I know," the enchanter whispered.

Elisa stood up completely this time. "You also played no small part in our victory. The queen is very grateful for what you did." She picked up the bottle and cloth. "Unfortunately, she pressed me for information on the two of you. I had to tell her what I knew about Rhyad. I am sorry," she said guiltily.

Andrea's throat tightened. If Diana knew why she and Cassie needed to get to Rhyad, what would that mean for them? Would she try to interfere? Forbid them from going? "But…I–,"

"Calm down," Elisa said. "She is in talks with that Harrington to get the Northland Bridge opened for you two. Once you and Cassie have ceased your latest pointless squabble, I'm certain you will be free to go about your business in Rhyad."

Andrea blinked in disbelief. "Really?"

Elisa rolled her eyes. "Yes. Now, I need to return that lute to

Kye and then get some sleep myself. Foolish boy left it on the floor behind the bar." She walked over to the lute and picked it up. "I will return tomorrow morning. Good night."

"Good...good night," Andrea repeated blankly as she watched the older woman leave.

* * *

Kye wandered about the tavern of the inn, peering underneath tables and behind chairs for the lute he had left behind during the battle. He thought perhaps the innkeeper had taken it back to his room and was about to head there when the instrument was suddenly hovering inches from his face.

"I believe this is yours," Elisa stated as she held the lute out to the enchanter. Kye hesitated before taking it. "T-thank you," he said, flustered. "I...I was looking for that."

"I noticed. Try to be more careful with your gifts," she scolded before turning abruptly and starting to walk away.

"Wait!" Kye rushed and quickly caught up to her. "You-are you all right? I heard you fought Cadar and–,"

"I am definitely *not* in the mood to chat about that right now," the ex-Legionnaire retorted. "You should go practice. I am certain they'll ask you to play at the celebration."

But Kye stood his ground. "Why won't you tell me what happened?"

"I killed my brother-in-law, boy. What more do you want to know?" she snapped. "I am not proud of it." She continued to walk to her room, the young man following close behind.

"But why? Why would you fight your own family, Elisa?" he pressed.

She opened the door to her room and entered. He followed her inside, continuing to ask more questions. "Why did you leave the Legion, Elisa? What is it that you haven't told us yet? What–?"

The ex-Legionnaire spun around, her face contorted in anger. "Fine! Look, you want the truth? I joined the Legion because my family needed the money and to be honest, my life up to that point was *boring* and I had some natural talent. My brother's company was still new and the Legion offered steady pay and good training. I was not *planning* to become Ithmeera's personal guard and I certainly did not plan to betray the empire."

"Betray the–," Kye breathed in disbelief before lowering his voice at Elisa's harsh glare. "Betray the empire?"

"Yes, boy," she spat and stepped forward threateningly. "That's right. I *betrayed* Ithmeera. Your empress. Your country. Is that what you wanted to hear?"

Kye blinked a few times before cringing as guilt set in. "N-no, of course not, Elisa. I...I'm sure you had g-good reason for doing whatever it is that you did."

The ex-Legionnaire sighed sadly as she sat down on the bed in her room. "I was a fool," she admitted and ran her hands through her hair. "I did the stupidest thing you can do while in the Legion. I...entered into a relationship with another Legionnaire."

Kye's eyebrows raised. "You did?"

"Yes. Ben, he...he and I were assigned to the same group during training. We became friends as we rose through the ranks and then later we became...closer." She closed her eyes briefly, as though reliving a memory, before opening them again. "He always was the better soldier. Became Erik...General Cadar's right-hand officer, in fact."

"Is that why it did not work out between you two?" Kye asked.

Elisa shook her head. "No. When Philip died, my father fell into a deep depression. It was just him – my mother had died many years earlier. I'm not sure how much of this you know, but it's not a well-kept secret that magic can be...addictive." She pinched the bridge of her nose. "Enchanters can safely extract magic from objects. With the right equipment, non-enchanters can...well, they can get a high from it. My father began spending all of our money, including the money I sent back to him from working for the Legion, on whatever magical artifacts he could get." A blend of guilt and shame crossed her features. "In Azgadar, that means utilizing the black market."

Kye swallowed nervously before taking a seat on the bed next to Elisa. "What happened next?"

But Elisa waved her hand dismissively. "I've talked too much. You should go rest. You need it."

Kye would not be so easily defeated. "I really want to know, Elisa. Will you at least tell me why you left the Legion?"

"You are incredibly obnoxious!" the ex-Legionnaire declared and threw her hands up. "Fine. Things between Ben and I became serious and so I decided to invite him over to our home for dinner. He unintentionally discovered my father's...habit."

She bit her lip. "I asked him, no, *begged* him not to tell anyone, but he wanted to do his 'duty to the empire,'" she said bitterly. "And he was right, of course – I would have done the same thing, honestly. The next day, General Cadar was at our home and ordered me to arrest my father. I couldn't do it."

"Of course not. He's your father," Kye said simply.

She shook her head. "You don't understand. When you take the oath of the Legion you swear to uphold certain tenets. Protecting the empire from magic abuse is one of them – probably the most important of them all. I failed to keep that oath."

"If I recall, the Legion's job is also to protect the citizens of the empire. Your father was a citizen. Take his magic but don't arrest him!" Kye exclaimed.

"Mm, that's a nice thought but a naïve one, boy," Elisa replied. "I did refuse, though. Cadar declared me a traitor to the empire and ordered my execution. My father…he tried to step in, but the general ran him through with his sword before he could do anything to help."

Kye's dark eyes widened in shock before giving way to sadness. He hesitated before touching her arm. "Elisa, that's terrible."

Her green eyes flashed with anger as she pulled away quickly. "I don't need your pity."

"You have it regardless," he stated. "No one should have to witness that. But couldn't you have told Ithmeera? You were friends. Surely she could have helped you."

"No. I…I ran after my father was slain. Didn't even get to

bury him. I barely escaped the city with my life. My mother's family lives in Gurdinfield, so I made my way there and ran into Alexander in one of the villages in the Southlands. After talking for some time, similar to how we are now, he convinced me to help the Guardians."

"He told you who Diana was?"

She nodded. "Yes. And I knew that running from Azgadar was…cowardly. It still is. If I had any honor I would return to Azgadar to be judged by the empress. But I don't…and so I am here."

Kye could not tell if Elisa was angry or guilty over her actions. He had one final question. "You were the empress's bodyguard and her sister-in-law. Why would her brother be so eager to brand you a traitor?"

"Oh, Erik couldn't stand me," Elisa explained with a proud smile. "He'd always been jealous of my and Ithmeera's friendship. For a long time, she would tell him everything. I suppose you could say that I took that from him."

"Seems like a silly thing to be jealous over."

Elisa shrugged. "It was. Erik Cadar is an arrogant man who has always been in second place." She sighed. "It doesn't matter now. But there, you have my story." She met his gaze. "And don't think for one minute that I've forgotten about how you disobeyed a direct order to stay here."

Kye stood up immediately. "I was trying to help!" he protested.

The ex-Legionnaire stood up as well. "Yes, despite my best efforts, you don't seem to *want* to stay alive. Rather, you throw yourself into danger every opportunity you get."

"Best efforts?" he asked.

She glared at him. "*Yes.* Jacob wanted to allow you to fight, but I asked him to keep you here. Apparently, his orders mean nothing if you don't actually *follow* them, though."

Kye frowned. "But...but you saw me fight, Elisa! You *know* what I am capable of! You–,"

He was silenced when the ex-Legionnaire placed a hand on his shoulder. "I am aware of your abilities," she said calmly. "I also know that you barely escaped with your life from Azgadar and I had no desire to watch you throw it away in a fight that the three of you shouldn't have been involved with in the first place!" She sighed and withdrew her hand. "But...you did what you did and...you saved my life and turned the tide of that battle. I owe you a debt, it seems."

He shook his head. "No. You risked a lot getting me out of Azgadar. We are even."

After studying the young enchanter for a moment, Elisa smirked. "If you say so, boy. Now, if you'll excuse me, it is late and if there is to be a celebration tomorrow night I'd like to be somewhat awake for it. You should rest, too."

A thought crossed his mind. "I will," he promised. "I need to find Andrea and speak with her first, though."

Elisa seemed amused as she nodded. "You'll want to check down the hall near Jacob's room. As odd as this may sound, Andrea and Cassie are not on speaking terms...again."

"Again? Why not?" Kye wondered, though he had a good idea of what the reason might be.

The older woman shrugged. "I suspect it has something to

do with the fact that Cassie revealed her abilities to everyone on that battlefield. Hard to believe something like that is even possible. *You* would know more about that than I, though."

Kye rubbed the back of his neck. "Yes, well," he replied nervously, "I did not believe her when she told me, either. After seeing…well, you saw what happened. I can understand why Andrea wanted to keep that a secret from us."

"She's an idiot," Elisa grumbled while practically pushing the young man out of the room. "A hero, but an idiot just the same. Both of them are. In any case, I need to get some sleep. Good night."

Kye was about to answer 'good night' when the door shut in his face. He stood at the door awkwardly for a few seconds before finally adjusting his grip on the lute and walking down the corridor to find Andrea.

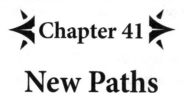

Chapter 41

New Paths

"Tonight, we toast to our victory. We have done the impossible and have reunited our people and defended our land from those who sought to shatter us." Diana spoke loudly and steadily while maintaining the solemn and respectful atmosphere in the inn. Many soldiers from the Gurdinfield forces now stood around the great central table where the queen sat along with Alexander, Jacob, Lord Harrington, Elisa, Kye, Andrea, Cassie, and the Guardian officers, holding their cups as they prepared to celebrate their victory as well as honor the fighters who had died during the battle against the Legion.

"Let us first take a moment of silence to honor those who made the ultimate sacrifice to defend our great land," she continued before all went quiet as everyone in the room bowed their heads in respect for the fallen. "This victory could not have been achieved without the aid of our allies," she said after a pause, smiling at Lord Harrington and then at Andrea, Cassie, and Kye. "This took all of us, and we should be proud. And as your queen, I hope to guide this great nation to a new era of prosperity and more importantly – peace." She lifted her cup. "To Gurdinfield!"

"To Gurdinfield!" the room echoed as all raised their cups in victory.

Even Cassie responded to Diana's toast before taking a sip of her wine – which was not terrible – and setting the cup down on the table. The inn broke into discord as the feasting eagerly began, and after grabbing food of her own she began to observe what her companions were doing. Across the table, Kye had pulled out his new lute and had begun playing requests, with many of the Gurdinfield fighters including Victor and Roe cheering him on. Cassie had never heard any of the songs before but some of them were quite good, and she took note to ask Kye to play them again for her later.

Diana and Jacob sat at the end of the table as several guests approached them to offer their congratulations on the couple's engagement. Cassie did not know much about their relationship other than the fact that Jacob had been hesitant to make any commitment until recently due to Diana's heritage. But now that all of that was dealt with, Cassie found herself feeling happy for them. There was very little happiness to be found in Damea, or so she had thought so far, but seeing them together gave her hope.

Across the room, she saw Elisa speaking with Alexander. He seemed frustrated, but understanding at the same time as the ex-Legionnaire shook her head at him. Cassie could not hear what they were talking about, but seeing as how news traveled rather quickly in this circle she suspected she'd find out sooner or later.

She realized she had not seen Andrea since the celebration had begun. She had sat across from the enchanter during the queen's speech, and Andrea, who was still not speaking to her, had avoided eye contact at all costs. As she looked around,

Cassie's gaze caught the door of the inn closing but not before she saw the back of Andrea's dark head as the enchanter walked out. Making sure no one would miss her, Cassie stood up and left the inn as discreetly as she could.

* * *

Andrea stood on the front patio of the inn, leaning forward on the wood railing. The inn's location on the hill gave it an impressive vantage point over the great city sprawled out below. The enchanted torches that lit the cobblestone roads in the trade district flickered brightly as a light, chilly breeze blew through the capital. The City of Towers was quiet now, and it was difficult for the enchanter to believe that the city had nearly fallen only days earlier.

She winced as her injured shoulder suddenly throbbed with pain. According to Diana, the explosion had left her partially pinned under debris. Her entire body was sore, but her shoulder had taken the brunt of her fall. It was not until just this morning that she had felt strong enough to try to use magic to slowly heal her injury. She had considered asking Cassie for help, but after their last fight she was afraid to approach her friend about, well, anything really.

The high-pitched creak of the inn's oil-starved front door closing pulled Andrea from her meditation. She sighed. Someone had followed her outside. Taking a deep breath, she turned her head and was genuinely surprised to see that it was Cassie. She turned back to face the city and heard the other girl slowly approach on her right.

"Mind if I join you?".

Andrea turned her head again and looked momentarily surprised before stepping aside to make room near the railing for Cassie. The two stood in silence for a few minutes before Cassie finally spoke up again.

"Not in the mood to celebrate?" she asked, gesturing toward the door.

The enchanter smiled faintly. "I suppose not. To be honest, I had considered going to my room early, but I figured I wouldn't be able to sleep anyway."

Silence again.

"Uh…so," Cassie mumbled as she absentmindedly picked at the railing. "How's your shoulder?"

Andrea shrugged. "It's fine. Better than before." She was not really sure what else to say.

"Yeah? You do that healing magic thing on it?"

What does she want? Is this her way of apologizing? "A bit. It takes a lot more energy to heal something like this so I have to do it a bit at a time."

"Oh." Cassie paused. She turned to the enchanter. "I could uh…help you. You know, if you want, that is."

Puzzled by Cassie's awkwardness and the entire conversation in general, Andrea faced her companion. "Oh! That's…that's all right. I don't mind doing it myself."

"All right. If you say so."

"Yes. Thank you, though. For offering, I mean."

"Sure."

They both faced the city again, neither saying a word as they took in the view and the quiet. After a bit, however, the silence began to annoy Andrea. Why was Cassie acting so strangely? The other girl had outright broken her word to keep her abilities a secret and had been nothing but rude when the enchanter had tried to explain to her how dangerous using Kye to tap into those abilities was.

She could have been killed. She nearly was, from what Kye told me. The young man had found her the night before and had explained in detail everything that had happened during the battle with Cassie on the Sky Tower. *She's so reckless – always wandering off, diving in head first without thinking, and then getting angry whenever things don't go her way. Then she has the audacity to yell at me. And now she wants to talk as though nothing happened. Probably going to tease me about Meredith again. Typical.*

And yet, as she watched Cassie stare out at the buildings below, the enchanter felt a strange, calming presence around her companion. She would not admit it to Cassie, but not sharing a room with the other girl for the past few nights had been oddly lonely for the enchanter. She scolded herself for being so dependent on someone who had done nothing but frustrate her lately.

Cassie's voice finally broke the silence. "I'm sorry, you know, for earlier," she said quietly.

Andrea glanced at her friend and then back at the city. She relaxed and shook her head. "No, don't apologize. I shouldn't have gotten angry like that."

Cassie shrugged. "Eh, I kind of deserved it to be honest.

You're right – it could have been way worse and people could have been hurt. I wasn't-we weren't really thinking, I guess."

"You were trying to help. I probably would have done the same thing," Andrea pointed out. "If it weren't for you and Kye, we probably would have lost."

Cassie shifted uncomfortably. "I know but...I'm also sorry for what I said to you. That wasn't right and you didn't deserve that." She sighed. "I was upset and...and worried and I let my emotions get the best of me, I guess." She turned to Andrea. "What you did for these people was really brave. I don't know them, but...I think your parents would be proud of you, enchanter or not." Then more quietly. "I know I am."

The enchanter smiled warmly at her friend. "T-thank you. It...means a lot to hear you say that. I wouldn't have gotten this far without you, though. I think..." A breeze blew some of her hair in front of her eyes and she pushed the strands to the side. "I think having you at my side has pushed me to do things I would have never thought I could do."

Cassie moved closer to Andrea and leaned on the railing again. She shrugged. "You're just saying that because you want to keep your little 'map' around a bit longer," she joked.

Andrea rolled her eyes. "Don't flatter yourself. You know you're as invested in this now as I am. Otherwise, you wouldn't have dragged poor Kye into the battle like you did." When she saw Cassie's surprised expression, she elaborated. "I spoke with him. He told me you were very concerned when the explosion happened, and you convinced him to help the rest of us by using your abilities."

"Yeah, well, Kye's a liar," Cassie grumbled, making the enchanter laugh quietly. She continued, "I didn't give a damn about the rest of them. But…" she hung her head, her tone shifting to guilt. "I knew that…that if anything had happened to you that…I could never forgive myself for letting you go out there."

Andrea thought she had been around Cassie long enough that she had seen every side of her friend. This side, however, was new, and the enchanter was at a loss for words. She exhaled nervously and returned to staring out at the city, focusing intensely on the countless flickering torches that lined the winding streets below. "You…you really mean that?"

Cassie snorted. "Yeah, Kye's a total liar. Have you heard him play? I don't believe for one second that he hasn't had *any* musical training."

"That's not what I mean–,"

Cassie cut her off with a frustrated huff. "I *know* what you meant and…yeah, I mean it." She hesitated before slowly placing her hand over Andrea's on the railing, giving the enchanter more than enough time to pull away. But Andrea did not move her hand.

"You kissed me," Cassie said simply, as though she were commenting on the weather.

The enchanter inhaled sharply. *Here we go.* "I-yes. Yes, I did. I'm sorry if–,"

"Why?"

'*Why*', *indeed?* But Andrea quickly realized that she did not need to think hard for this answer, as she had known it for quite some time. "I…I didn't know if I would see you again," she whispered fearfully.

Cassie gave a soft laugh as she turned to face Andrea. "Well, it looks like you're stuck with me for a while longer." She gave the enchanter's hand a gentle squeeze and moved even closer to her. At this distance, Andrea could see the reflection of the sconces outside the inn flickering in Cassie's blue eyes as well as the dark, purple swirls of bruising on the girl's cheekbones that were far more visible now than they had been when the girls had last spoken.

"Your face," she said, "it's still all bruised."

Cassie smiled wryly. "Yeah, that tends to happen for some reason when I do the whole magic thing without you. It'll go away, though." She shrugged. "Just a bruise, right?"

Andrea swallowed. "You shouldn't have to deal with that. Do you mind if I...?" She tentatively lifted her free hand to explain her intention.

Raising her eyebrows in surprise, Cassie nodded slowly. "Yeah, I guess it's okay."

The enchanter moved her hand away from Cassie's and faced the other girl. Using her left hand, she slowly reached up and hesitantly touched the side of Cassie's face, her fingers coming into contact with one of the darker bruises. Andrea was surprised by how soft Cassie's skin actually was, and for a moment, she forgot to actually transfer energy toward healing the bruise and simply held her hand there.

"You all right?" Cassie asked, startling her.

"Hmm? Oh! Yes, sorry. Just...trying to concentrate," the enchanter said lamely. "This should just take a moment." The bruises were far less complex than her shoulder injury, and within a few moments, she was able to channel enough magic toward them so that they became nothing more than faded marks.

"All…all done," she announced, though she had not moved her hand away. "The rest should go away soon, as you said. O-or we could try again later? I'm sorry – healing isn't really my specialty."

Cassie gave her a teasing smile. "Now you're just *looking* for an excuse to do magic on me." But she did not pull away, either. Instead, she reached out and placed her hands on the enchanter's waist.

Andrea felt her face heat up as an overwhelming number of thoughts and questions ran through her mind, not to mention she was not entirely sure how to process what Cassie was doing. "I-I would never!" she protested. As Cassie held her gaze, however, the enchanter found herself unable and unwilling to move her hand away from her friend's face, and unconsciously brushed Cassie's skin with her thumb. She froze up immediately, certain that she had crossed a line that could not be undone. But when she saw Cassie actually close her eyes briefly and lean into her touch, Andrea repeated the gesture, terrified and at the same time, curious as to what would happen next. "Cassie, I–,"

Cassie stopped her abruptly by closing the distance between the two of them and kissing Andrea softly. The enchanter tensed up at the sudden contact and involuntarily began drawing power from Cassie. The flow of energy was gentle and the warmth it generated gave Andrea courage she did not know she had. Tentatively, she kissed Cassie back and moved even closer to her, the nerves and worries beginning to fall away.

She withdrew her hand from Cassie's face, cutting off the flow of magic, and wrapped her arms around the other girl's neck. Cassie responded by pulling the enchanter into a tight embrace, deepening the kiss for only a moment before suddenly pulling away. Terrified that she had done something wrong, Andrea stared at Cassie, who was biting her lip as a brief flicker of fear crossed her features.

"I'm-I'm sorry," she breathed and turned away, her voice rougher than usual.

"I...that..." Andrea stammered. She touched her own lips gingerly with her hand. "You...why?"

Cassie took a deep breath. "I thought...were you not okay with that?" she asked in an uncharacteristically small voice.

Before Andrea could answer, she heard the front door of the inn slam shut and the sound of someone clearing their throat. Diana stood next to the door with Jacob directly behind her.

"Sorry to interrupt," the queen spoke.

Andrea shook her head vigorously, remembering etiquette. Wondering if the couple had seen what had just transpired, her voice came out in what sounded more like a squeak than the appropriate way to speak to royalty. "Not at all, Your Majesty. How can we help?"

Diana waved her away. "Please, Andrea, it's just 'Diana'. I can't even get used to 'Lydia'."

Andrea nodded. "Of course."

Diana continued. "We just came by to tell you that the Harrington forces will be clearing from the Northland Bridge. Rhyad should be open to you now."

The enchanter grinned. Finally, the way to Rhyad was open! Now she and Cassie could travel to the northern region and find out where the magic was being kept so that she could try to release it. And then…

She looked at Cassie. Her companion still had no idea that Andrea did not possess the power or the knowledge to send her home. What should she say? *There* must *be a way to send her back and you just need to figure it out. Perhaps with research? But…why?* What had just happened between them – she did not want to destroy it before she found out what it meant for them, if anything. It was selfish, the enchanter admitted, but she did not want to give it up just yet.

Her thoughts were racing and she did not hear Diana's question.

"I-I'm sorry?" the enchanter asked blankly.

Diana smiled faintly. "Jacob and I are offering to join you if you would have us. The path to Rhyad is a treacherous one that you two should not embark on alone."

Cassie raised an eyebrow at the couple. "We don't even know if we're going to find anything. Plus, who's going to watch things here while you're gone?"

"Alexander is more than capable of handling the day-to-day affairs while we're gone," Diana explained.

"I wouldn't want you to risk your own lives for this, Your Majesty–," Andrea started.

"Your actions in the battle had significant impact on us," Jacob cut in. "It's obvious what you plan to do in Rhyad will as well. We cannot just stand by and not help, especially after all that you've done for us."

The enchanter was not quite sure how to respond and exchanged glances with Cassie to see if the other girl had an opinion on the matter. But Cassie simply shrugged, letting Andrea know that she did not mind either way.

"If you're sure," the enchanter said slowly, turning back to Diana and Jacob, "then we would welcome your assistance. I've never been to Rhyad before. We can't be sure what we will encounter."

Jacob held up his hand. "I know men who have. It is a cold and dangerous place with very little in the way of roads or trails. You'll need proper gear to make it through there without freezing to death."

"I can arrange that," Diana offered. She turned to her betrothed. "It's settled, then." Turning back to Andrea and Cassie she said, "I'll make the necessary preparations and let you know when everything's ready."

Andrea nodded. "Yes, Your Majesty."

The queen of Gurdinfield glared at her. "Seriously, Andrea, for the last time–,"

"Why don't we get back to the celebration, dear?" Jacob interrupted. He flashed a grin at Andrea and put his arm around a still-protesting Diana while leading her back inside the inn. "We shall speak more later, my friends!" he called back as the front door shut behind them, leaving Andrea and Cassie alone once more.

Avoiding eye contact with Cassie, the enchanter absentmindedly kicked at the dusty wooden planks that formed the floor of the patio. Her chest and throat felt tight and Andrea knew she needed to get back to her room before she said something foolish to Cassie. *Perhaps she didn't think anything of it; maybe we can just forget about it and get on with the mission–* "Okay, then," Cassie sighed heavily. "So…"

"I should get back," Andrea blurted, cursing herself inwardly at her awkwardness. "I…need to get some sleep. It's been a long day and…and well, good night." With that, the enchanter turned on her heel and began to head back inside.

Before Andrea had taken more than two steps, Cassie reached out and grabbed her arm. "Andrea, wait," she said, the urgency in her voice making the enchanter cringe as she turned around slowly to face Cassie.

"I…" To Andrea's surprise, Cassie actually seemed quite nervous. "I'm not blind, Andrea. And…I don't believe what just happened was some fluke. Or maybe," she shifted her weight from one foot to the other, "maybe I don't want to believe that it was a fluke. But…look, I'm not just going to act like nothing happened…unless that's what *you* want. So," she met Andrea's gaze, "if you want to pretend that kiss didn't happen, that you don't feel that way and it was all just a big misunderstanding, then just say the word and we can move on. We can go to Rhyad and I…I can go home. But," she hesitantly took the stunned enchanter's hands, "if there's some part of you, *any* part, that wants to stop denying this, well…I guess tell me, because to be honest I don't really understand all this but I know that…that what I feel is real, Andrea." She let go of Andrea's hands and stepped back. "So uh…yeah," she finished awkwardly. "That all sounded a lot better in my head."

Andrea had only silence to offer in return. Stunned by

Cassie's admission, she tried to speak but failed to find the words she needed. Instead, she simply stared at the other girl.

Cassie took Andrea's silence to be her answer. "Yeah," she breathed and forced a faint smile. "I get it." She paced back and forth for a moment before turning back to Andrea. "I uh…I think I should head in, too. I want to get an early start to pack and everything so that we're ready when Diana is." She gave a final nod to Andrea and started to walk away.

The tightness in Andrea's chest and throat that had been building up finally released as the enchanter called out to the other girl, her voice shaky and broken. "I don't!"

Cassie froze and turned slightly. "What?"

Andrea pushed forward and positioned herself so that she blocked Cassie's path to the inn. "I don't want to pretend it didn't happen…because it did. And…" She swallowed as she pieced the jumble of words in her mind together as carefully as possible, though it all came out in a rush despite her efforts. "I don't understand it all either, and maybe I never will because I have absolutely *no* idea what I'm doing but I *do* know that what…what I feel is also real." She cringed, waiting for Cassie to get annoyed at her babbling or just walk past her. But the other girl simply smiled.

"You rehearse that?" she teased and tucked a loose strand of the enchanter's dark hair behind her ear, causing Andrea to involuntarily lean into her touch. "Because I think that was the best rambling from you I've heard in a while."

Andrea rolled her eyes. "No, and you're not funny."

Cassie grinned. "Yeah, I am." She took Andrea's hands in hers once more and leaned in so that their foreheads were touching. "You know, you could have just told me earlier and saved me from having to make that big awkward speech just now."

The enchanter laughed quietly, the warmth she felt earlier spreading throughout her again. "I think it's about time that *you* were the one doing the nonsensical rambling for once." Still feeding on her gathered courage from earlier, she moved forward and shakily wrapped her arms around Cassie, who returned the embrace.

"You were right," she continued softly as she leaned into Cassie's hold. "I need to learn to relax for once but..." She looked up at her companion. "I wasn't lying, Cassie – I really have no idea what I'm doing."

Cassie shrugged. "Well, I'm not exactly an expert, either. So, why don't we make it easy and just take it one day at a time, hmm?"

Andrea nodded slowly. "O-okay. I would like that." She looked up at the other girl. "I...ah, I think I would like to try again. If that's all right with you of course!" The nerves that had released earlier began to rapidly tangle up inside her once more.

Cassie looked puzzled for a moment. "Try again with-oh," she realized. "Oh, yeah, I mean...you don't have to ask, Andrea."

The enchanter smiled shyly and nodded before leaning forward and pressing her lips against Cassie's once more. The kiss quickly deepened as time seemed to stop around them and even the shouts and laughter from inside the inn could no longer be heard. Cassie wrapped her arms around Andrea's waist and the enchanter felt a deluge of emotions rise up within her. She wanted to analyze them, to ponder what they meant and how they would affect everything but...she did not. The stress and heaviness of the mission dissipated and for what seemed like an eternity, it was only her and Cassie, and that was all that mattered.

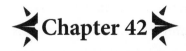

Chapter 42

Losses and Gains

Azgadar, Azgadaran Empire

A strong, cool gust blew through Azgadar, a telltale sign that the warm mornings of autumn in Azgadar would soon give way to winter rains. The early morning bustle of merchants making their way to their carts in the marketplace carried on as it did every day, seemingly oblivious to the events that had recently transpired in Damea.

Another breeze swept through the window of Ithmeera Cadar's bedroom and rustled the papers on her desk. The crumpled parchment at the end of her bed, where the empress now sat, stayed put. She hesitantly picked it up, as though seeing it for the first time, and made a half-hearted attempt to smooth out the edges of the paper. She knew reading it again would do nothing – that the news of the Legion's loss and of her brother's death would not have changed.

A single tear ran down her cheek from her already bloodshot eyes and fell onto the parchment. This was her fault – Erik's death was her fault. The death of those Legionnaires was her fault. She refused to deny it, but that did not lessen the pain that had overwhelmed her since receiving news from the courier of the battle at the City of Towers.

Upon reading it the first time, the letter had ignited nothing but anger and a desire for vengeance against the new queen of Gurdinfield. But Ithmeera was never one to make rash decisions, and after calming down she realized that more war would bring nothing but ruin to both nations. The harsh reality was simple – Gurdinfield had truly reunited and was once again strong, perhaps stronger than the empire. What this meant for Azgadar, the empress was unsure of.

"My lady, your uncle requests an audience with you," Petra's voice sounded from outside Ithmeera's bedroom after a sharp knock on the door sounded.

Ithmeera sighed and folded the courier's letter carefully before walking over to her desk and placing it in the top drawer. "Please let him in," she called back.

Moments later, Alden Cadar entered the room as Ithmeera's lady-in-waiting bowed quickly and left them alone. The empress sat on her bed once more and gestured for Alden to take the desk chair.

He folded his hands and cleared his throat after sitting down. "I...trust you've told Marco?" he said tiredly.

Ithmeera nodded. "I have. I am not quite sure he understands completely, but he will in time." She met his gaze. "Uncle...how could I have been so short-sighted? What did we do wrong?"

But the aged man waved his hand at the empress. "You did nothing wrong, dear. You were doing what you felt was best for the empire, as your father and I have taught you."

"They won't send back his *sword*, Uncle!" she said angrily, clenching her fists. "His sword!"

"His body is on his way here as we speak," Alden said calmly. "I admit, I was surprised when Queen Lydia offered."

"His body...it is no longer Erik, Uncle," Ithmeera explained. "I'll have...nothing of his to remember him by." She wiped away the new tears that streamed down her face.

"The queen seemed adamant in her letter to hold onto his sword, unfortunately," Alden admitted with a nod. "All I can say is that this is one of the consequences of–,"

Ithmeera stood up, enraged at her uncle. "Do not speak to me about *consequences*, Uncle!" she spat, pointing an accusing finger at him. "All of this...our losses, Erik...this *never* would have happened had we just continued what my father started!"

"Your father would have *handed* the empire over to Gurdinfield had he been around!" Alden yelled and stood up as well.

"You will *not* speak of him like that!" Ithmeera shouted back.

"We're low on magic, Ithmeera. The empire will not last another year with the way we've been carrying on," Alden warned. "Gurdinfield is still weak. The only reason they won is because of their enchanters! We can use this to our advantage and–,"

"*No.* I will not have it!" the empress cut in. "This war-mongering of yours has gone far enough, Alden! The empire survived The Starving, and it will survive this, too!" She sat down again, visibly exhausted despite the day having just begun.

"That Sadford girl *murdered* your brother, Ithmeera. The courier confirmed that. Will you truly do nothing?" Alden demanded.

Ithmeera sighed heavily. "I...Erik knew the risks, Uncle. As did I. And...we've paid the price. Perhaps..." she said with a small laugh, "perhaps we're still paying it." Her expression hardened as she looked at her uncle again. "We are done here. I will meet with the royal enchanters and we will start trying to find a way to conserve the magic we have left. Then, we will reach out to Queen Lydia and establish an alliance."

"Those backwater ruffians will never agree to an alliance with the empire, Ithmeera," Alden declared. "The council–,"

"Will help me decide on the best course of action to establish such an alliance," Ithmeera finished for him. "And...you will not be part of that decision, Uncle."

The older Cadar blinked in surprise. "Ithmeera, I know you are upset over the loss of your brother, but–,"

"I've made my decision," she said firmly. "The council will convene later today to discuss your...resignation." She stood up and turned her back to him, facing the open window instead. "Please leave me in peace, Uncle."

Alden bit his lip in frustration and restrained himself from pressing the matter further. "As...as you wish, Your Highness," he grumbled before briskly leaving the bedroom.

✳ ✳ ✳

City of Towers, Gurdinfield

The scent of food drifted from the dining hall of The Lion's Den and slowly wafted throughout the rooms. Cassie began to stir when she smelled the various dishes that were being prepared for that morning's breakfast. She slowly opened her eyes and rubbed the sleep away from them before realizing that she had fallen asleep on a stack of pillows propped up against the headboard of her bed.

Wait. She blinked a few times and scanned her surroundings. She was not in her room and this was not her bed. She glanced down and grinned. Her arm was wrapped around Andrea, who was still fast asleep on Cassie's chest. The sound of the enchanter's steady breathing relaxed Cassie to the point where she thought she might fall back asleep herself. Both still wore their clothes from the festivities the night before, and had stayed up late into the night before finally falling asleep just before sunrise.

The grin remained on Cassie's face as the memory of what had transpired only hours earlier surfaced. They had retreated to Andrea's room so as to not risk being interrupted again, which Cassie was perfectly fine with. But upon arriving at the enchanter's room, Andrea had insisted on staying up and talking for *hours.* To Cassie's surprise, Andrea did not bombard *her* with questions this time. Rather, the enchanter had divulged nearly everything about her life in the village she was from – Ata, growing up on a farm, her parents, how she discovered her abilities, her training with Master Jheran – all the way up to how she met Meredith and the work they did in the Black Forest together. While Cassie had patiently listened, and was more than happy to learn more about Andrea's past, she found it increasingly difficult not to nod off as dawn approached.

She sighed happily and gently kissed the top of Andrea's head, making sure not to wake the enchanter. Her focus was suddenly directed toward the door as it slowly opened, revealing none other than Elisa. They stared silently at each other for a few seconds before the ex-Legionnaire's expression transitioned from indifference to amusement.

"Still asleep? You two have gotten lazy since winning that battle." In her hands were the bottle and cloth she had been using on Andrea's injury over the last few days.

Cassie was about to offer a sarcastic reply when she felt Andrea stirring. She froze as the enchanter mumbled something unintelligible before wrapping her arms around Cassie's midsection and falling silent once more.

Breathing a sigh of relief, she looked back at Elisa, who had been watching the scene before her with mild curiosity. "Need something?" she demanded quietly.

"This needs to go on her shoulder three times a day," Elisa said and set the bottle and cloth down on the nightstand next to the bed. She took a few steps back. "News of your upcoming journey to Rhyad has spread quickly."

Cassie sighed. *Great, now everyone knows. Perfect.* "Really?" she asked worriedly, thinking back to her worst fears about what could happen now that so many people knew about her abilities.

"No." Elisa shook her head, receiving a glare from Cassie. "Diana told me last night and I offered to accompany you. I refuse to sit around here while the queen unnecessarily risks her life again."

"None of you have to go, you know," Cassie said.

"That decision isn't in your hands anymore," the older

woman replied. She pointed at the bottle. "Do not forget to put that on her," she instructed and began to walk away.

Cassie did a double take. "That's it? You're not going to say anything? No comments about how stupid we are or what a terrible mistake we're making?"

Elisa folded her arms across her chest. "If you're referring to *this*," she said, motioning to both Cassie and Andrea, "then all I can say is that I would advise you not to let your feelings get in the way of your mission." She gave a crooked smile. "But you've never listened to me on that topic before. No doubt you'll be back to bickering soon enough. Now, I have important matters I need to see to that are far more pressing than chatting with you about what color threads you're going to pick for the bracelet."

"The what?" Cassie asked blankly.

"Never mind," Elisa sighed. "Three times a day. Do not forget." With that she left, quietly closing the door behind her.

Rolling her eyes, Cassie looked over at the nightstand where the bottle and cloth sat. *Guess it's time to get up.* Typically, Andrea was awake long before she was, so having to wake up the enchanter was rather new to her. She looked down and shifted slightly before gently shaking Andrea awake.

"Hey, you uh…have to get up now," she blurted awkwardly.

Andrea stirred again before opening her eyes. She shook her head and blinked as she looked up and tried to focus. "Cassie?" she asked.

Cassie laughed quietly. "Hi."

"Hello." Andrea smiled sleepily before suddenly grimacing and looked at her shoulder. "This…is a little uncomfortable."

With a groan, she removed her arms from around Cassie and pushed herself up. "I need...has Elisa come by already?"

"Yeah, she uh...left this stuff for you," Cassie said before reaching over and grabbing the bottle and cloth. "You have to put it on three times a day."

The enchanter sighed with relief. "Ah, good. Thank you–," she stopped and her eyes widened. "Oh...so, you spoke with her?"

Cassie raised an eyebrow. "Um...yeah? What did you think I meant?"

Andrea slowly took the bottle and cloth from Cassie. The enchanter was clearly nervous. "Well, I mean...we were–," she stammered.

Cassie grinned. "Relax. She just made some comment about how we're just going to start fighting again and something about a bracelet – whatever the hell that means – and then left. She's also going with us to Rhyad, so we'll probably have to put up with her saying dumb crap about us."

She stopped herself, unsure if she had said too much or what Andrea's feelings were about how public their...whatever it was...was going to be, especially in front of their friends. "Er...we're not, I mean, this isn't something you wanted to keep a secret...right?" she asked, slightly fearful of what the enchanter's answer would be.

Seemingly satisfied to have placed Cassie in an awkward position for once, Andrea smiled again and shook her head as she carefully poured some of the bottle's contents onto the cloth before reaching under her shirt to apply it to her shoulder. "Of course not. I was just-wait, *bracelet*?" she exclaimed and froze up.

"Yeah, I don't know. What do bracelets have to do with anything?" Cassie asked with a shrug.

"Ah…it's nothing we need to worry about," Andrea answered quickly, her cheeks turning pink. She finished tending to her injury and handed the bottle and cloth back to Cassie, who set them on the nightstand. "Now, I'm actually quite hungry. How does breakfast sound?"

Cassie nodded vigorously and stood up to stretch. "Have you ever known me to say 'no' to food?"

"Right," Andrea confirmed. "Stupid question. Shall we?"

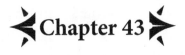

Chapter 43

Practice

Kye breathed deeply before conjuring yet another fireball in his hand. After a few seconds of concentration, he launched it at the combat training dummy he had set up in the stables just down the hill from the inn. As the dummy became engulfed in flames, the young man quickly switched to an ice-based attack and threw it at the dummy as well.

"*Yes*," he hissed in victory as the ball of ice rapidly extinguished the fire, letting off scalding clouds of steam. But before his celebration was long-lasted, the dummy ignited once more, this time dissolving into a pile of black ash in mere seconds. A few small flames burned on the dirt, which was sparsely covered with straw. Alarmed, Kye spun around to grab the bucket of water he had brought with him just in case, but was surprised when Jacob walked up behind him and grabbed the bucket, tossing the water on the flames before the young enchanter could do anything else.

"Nice one. How many was that?" Jacob asked with a grin as he set the bucket down.

Kye shrugged after regaining his composure. "I don't know. Six? Seven, perhaps?" he sighed, pointing at the nearly identical piles of black ash that were lined up next to his magic's latest victim. "Every time I think I'm getting closer to controlling my abilities, something happens to prove that I'm not any closer to controlling them than I was months ago."

"Nonsense. Your actions on the Sky Tower proved otherwise," the captain said.

"No. Had it not been for the rain, the city could have been set on fire," the enchanter pointed out.

"You changed the course of that battle, and I refuse to accept any other answer," Jacob said with a smile.

Slightly flustered, Kye bowed his head slightly. "T-thank you, sir. It was the least I c-could do." A thought crossed his mind. "Actually, I was ah…wondering. Do you think…do you think Her Majesty is going to consider reopening the academy?" he asked hopefully. "Elisa said-well, I think if I had some proper training that maybe…maybe I could learn to control my powers better. Not set everything on fire, for instance."

The captain sat down on a bale of hay and motioned for the young man to sit next to him. "To be honest, boy, I don't know," he admitted as Kye complied. "There are a lot of things that Diana needs to sort through before things can get back to… well, whatever you call 'normal' around here. First, though, we must take care of this magic nonsense in Rhyad. Then perhaps you can speak to her about your academy."

Kye looked up curiously at the mention of Rhyad. "Hold on a moment – you are going to Rhyad as well?"

Jacob nodded slowly. "Yes, to assist Andrea and Cassie with their mission. Elisa will also be accompanying us."

The enchanter frowned. "I had thought…they told me that Cassie needed to get to a village near Rhyad."

Jacob chuckled. "Ah, yes. Well, my friend, it appears that your fellow enchanter kept a few secrets from us up until recently. No, Andrea and Cassie think they know the location of our missing magic." He shrugged. "I don't know much more than that, but as it could affect the entire land it's imperative that Diana and I are involved."

Kye bit his lip. "And…Elisa is going with you?"

"She offered. Thinks Diana is going to wind up in some sort of danger that *I* apparently cannot protect her from." He shook his head. "I've fought beside Diana for many years. She can take care of herself, trust me. But…Elisa would have none of it. Not from me anyway," he finished with a short laugh.

"I should go too, then."

Jacob tilted his head. "What?"

Kye stood up quickly. "If you all are going then I should, too!" he said determinedly. "I-I refuse to stay behind while you all go to Rhyad."

Jacob raised an eyebrow. "From what I understand, boy, you're a wanted man in Azgadar. You survived the battle and now you are willing to venture to the most dangerous place in Damea? I cannot be responsible for you, and Elisa would not be pleased if you threw away the chance she has been trying to give you to start anew. Think carefully before you decide this as you may not come back."

But Kye had made up his mind. "So…you would allow me to go with you?" he asked excitedly.

"As I said, Elisa would not–,"

"Elisa does not get to make decisions for me," the young man protested. "I-I can hold my own and…and I could help Andrea!"

Jacob sighed. "That is something you would need to speak to *her* about. But…" He studied the enchanter for a moment. "You've done nothing but perform admirably in the time I've known you. Despite your…interesting and unpredictable abilities, I do believe you are an asset."

Kye practically leapt in the air with excitement. "So…you are letting me go with you?"

Jacob stood up. "I will…talk to the queen. But I make no promises!" he warned sharply. "And I cannot be your personal bodyguard should you get attacked by bandit or beast."

Kye nodded eagerly. "Understood…sir!"

The captain shook his head in dismay. "I need to get back to the inn. Try not to set the stables on fire," he said with a wink before leaving Kye alone with the combat dummies.

The enchanter turned toward his next target. If he was going to go to Rhyad, he could not be uncontrollably setting everything on fire. He needed to practice. "All right. Let's see if we can't freeze you this time," he muttered and prepared his next spell.

After finally finishing the last bit of paperwork for the evening, Diana was more than relieved to head to the dining hall for dinner. The last few days had been nothing but bureaucratic tasks as she and Alexander attempted to piece the kingdom back together. There was so much to go through, and the list seemed to be never-ending. Between the palace restoration, the reinstatement of royal taxes, rebuilding the city guard, and repairing the city gates, the new queen was overwhelmed and admittedly somewhat excited to be journeying to Rhyad, despite its dangers, if it meant she would not have to hold a quill again for at least a few weeks. Less time signing documents also meant more time with Jacob.

She could not hold back a grin as she felt the new bracelet around her wrist. The last few days since the Guardian captain had proposed to her, while busy, had been some of the best in recent memory. They were finally together, and the prospect of recovering Damea's missing magic in Rhyad, however unbelievable it seemed, was exciting as well. She and Jacob had decided to plan their wedding after returning home from Rhyad, and if Andrea and Cassie could truly find and restore the magic, then Gurdinfield's recovery as a nation would no doubt accelerate, or so Diana hoped.

By the time she arrived for dinner, the dining hall was mostly empty save a few Gurdinfield soldiers finishing their last drinks before retiring for the evening. In the corner of the dining hall, the fireplace still burned, which Diana was thankful for as the evenings had gotten quite a bit colder recently. Looking around, the queen saw several of the soldiers taking notice of her and bowing their heads in reverence. The concept of others bowing to her was still quite odd for Diana, but per Alexander's suggestion she smiled politely as she approached the corner of the room.

A large, worn couch and a few chairs were situated in front of the fireplace. Before she got too close, however, she noticed that the couch was occupied by none other than Andrea and Cassie, who were sitting quite close to each other. Letting her curiosity get the better of her, as Diana had known that the two were not on speaking terms due to Cassie divulging the secret of her abilities to the group during the battle without Andrea's permission, the queen took a seat at one of the large community tables in the hall and discreetly observed the pair as she waited for the innkeeper to bring out food for her. When her food arrived, though, she quickly realized she could hear bits and pieces of their conversation. She had not *meant* to eavesdrop, but she *had* just finished with a long day of work and she was not going to change seats *now*.

"…saying that you shouldn't rule it out just because of something he said that hurt your feelings." Cassie's voice was rarely this quiet, so it was difficult for Diana to hear what she was saying.

"You make it sound so trivial," Andrea replied, though it was obvious by the uncertainty in her voice that the topic being discussed made her uncomfortable.

Cassie laughed. "It's not. I know…not what you wanted…"

The queen was genuinely surprised when she saw the enchanter lay her head down on Cassie's shoulder. *Looks like they've sorted out their disagreement…for now?* "I will…think about it," Andrea considered. "No promises, though."

The other girl shifted slightly and wrapped her arm around Andrea, pulling the enchanter closer to her. "…could always get Elisa…yell at them a bit."

"Erm…no, I don't think…good idea."

Not wanting to intrude on her companions' privacy, Diana quickly finished her meal and got up to take a walk before retiring to her room for the night. Tomorrow she would start laying out the plans for their upcoming trip to Rhyad. She could not predict what they would encounter, but she was hopeful that with Andrea and Cassie no longer fighting the mission would have a greater chance of being successful.

Chapter 44

Road to Rhyad

City of Towers, Gurdinfield

One week later

The early morning chill greeted Diana as she stepped out of the inn. Her breath visible in the cool air, she could sense the beginnings of winter approaching. Grateful that Jacob had insisted she wear an extra layer of clothing today, she wrapped her cloak tightly around herself and began to walk to the stables just down the hill, where the others would no doubt be finishing up the packing for the journey to Rhyad. In the distance, she could hear a commotion, no doubt from her friends who had most likely headed down the hill before her while she finished sorting out the last of the administrative affairs with Alexander before leaving.

As the queen approached the stables, she could hear the commotion more clearly. Jacob was issuing orders to some of the Gurdinfield soldiers that were still on duty to fetch some of the various items – namely blankets, food, and other supplies – that they would need for the trip. Roe was assisting in loading the backpacks the group would be taking with them with the new supplies. Out of the corner of her eye, Diana saw a flash of bright copper hair. She turned and smiled when she noticed Elisa was in the stables with Kye. The ex-Legionnaire was teaching the young enchanter how to prepare the horses for travel. Diana marveled at her perseverance, and noticed that Elisa had grown rather protective of Kye over the past few weeks. Although the boy was a hero in his own right and had risked his life for a nation that was not even his own, Elisa had protested vehemently against allowing him to accompany them to Rhyad. She had finally given in after a few days of arguing, but only if the boy promised to learn some non-magical ways of combat to protect himself, at least until his unpredictable abilities could be studied and guided by a more experienced enchanter.

Diana heard faint laughter and turned her attention toward the far side of the stables. Andrea and Cassie were packing some of the saddlebags that the group would be carrying to Rhyad with them. More specifically, they were folding up a large camping blanket quite unsuccessfully, no thanks to their "teamwork". Diana raised an eyebrow as she watched the enchanter attempt to instruct Cassie on how to properly fold the blanket…with Cassie failing to do so on every attempt. At first, the queen wondered if Cassie truly did not understand Andrea's instructions, but quickly dismissed the thought when she noticed the girl grinning mischievously. Andrea exclaimed loudly in frustration before throwing the blanket at her companion, who simply laughed in return. Diana watched as the enchanter struggled to keep a straight face before finally smiling and shaking her head.

"Looks like they're having fun."

The queen turned and greeted her friend with a nod. "Good morning, Elisa. And yes, it appears that our friends are on good terms again. How's Kye doing?"

"Well enough. The horses should be ready to go at your command." A crooked smile appeared on her face. She nodded toward Andrea and Cassie, who had begun yet another attempt to fold the blanket. "Ah…that what they call it now? 'Good terms'?"

The queen nodded, looking out at the girls again. "Yes, I believe Andrea was quite displeased that Cassie let her abilities be known to us. They seem to be fine now. Almost as though…" She turned back to Elisa. "Tell me, my friend, have you noticed anything different about their behavior? Around each other, I mean."

Elisa smirked. "Which part? Where they stare longingly into each other's eyes like idiots or where they take forever to complete a simple task such as folding a blanket?" she finished with a shrug. She framed her mouth with her hands and shouted down at the pair. "Hey! You two were far more efficient when you hated one another. Stop gawking at each other and fold the bloody blanket already!"

The queen watched in amusement as both Andrea and Cassie froze while the others howled with laughter. The enchanter looked horrified and put her hand up to hide the deep shade of red that spread to her face and Cassie rolled her eyes obviously enough for Elisa to see. Diana covered her mouth with her hand and laughed quietly. "Oh!" she exclaimed. "I didn't realize…well, actually that's not true. They *have* been acting different lately. Nonetheless, I'm happy for them. It's nice to see something good come out of all the loss this land has suffered."

"Yes, well, I'd prefer that we *not* freeze to death in Rhyad," Elisa grumbled. "Blankets are a tad crucial to not freezing."

"Of course," Diana replied, still smiling. She gave a short nod. "I should probably go help them."

"As should I, or we'll be here all day," Elisa agreed. The two walked over to Jacob and Roe, joining them in preparing the backpacks.

At the other end of the stables, Andrea and Cassie had finally finished folding the last of the blankets.

"That should be all of them," Andrea announced and knelt to secure the final blanket to one of the backpacks.

"That probably took longer than it should have," Cassie teased.

The enchanter gave Cassie a knowing glance and stood up. "Yes, well…" She dusted her pants off. "When Elisa yells at us again, I'm not going to take *all* the blame."

Cassie was about to retort with a sarcastic remark of her own when Andrea's hazel eyes met hers. The enchanter simply shrugged and smiled shyly. Her eyes were relaxed, hopeful, something that Cassie had not seen from the enchanter since their time in the Gurdin Woods together. The remark she had been ready to fire back suddenly vanished and she scolded herself mentally for being utterly speechless whenever the enchanter simply looked at her lately.

"Uh…" she tried after clearing her throat. "Yeah, well, I'm sure Elisa's got better things to do than yell at us."

"You would think so," Andrea answered. She took the other girl's hand. "Come on. Let's go see if the others need any more help."

Cassie squeezed the enchanter's hand briefly before nodding. "Right behind you."

* * *

"You are certain you don't want me to accompany you?"

"We'll be fine, Alexander. Think of it as any other mission," Diana insisted. "Also, I don't really trust anyone but you to handle things here while I'm gone. We all know what happened *last* time I left the city."

"Come now, it was just a twenty-year civil war and nearly the end of Gurdinfield as we knew it," Jacob laughed.

The Guardian leader frowned and crossed his arms over his chest. "I would hardly call venturing into Rhyad 'any other mission', Diana."

Six of them – Diana, Jacob, Elisa, Kye, Andrea, and Cassie – all on horseback waited outside the city gates late in the afternoon as Diana handled the final preparations with Alexander before they were to embark on the long journey to the northernmost region of Damea. They each had their own mounts with the exception of Cassie, who had eagerly opted to ride on the back of Andrea's horse due to her dislike of riding at all. Work had already begun to repair the city gates, which had been severely damaged by the Legion's explosive launched during the battle nearly two weeks earlier. The palace restoration was underway and the capital city was slowly acclimating to having a new queen, a new government, and for the first time in decades, a hopeful future.

"I'll be fine. *We'll* be fine," Diana said confidently.

"And if not, then you'll never have to deal with us again," Elisa deadpanned, earning eye rolls from all around and a worried glance from Alexander.

"Please keep her safe," he pressed.

The ex-Legionnaire nodded solemnly, her demeanor shifting immediately. "Of course. Let's hope we're not about to be off on a wild chase for nothing then. Right, Andrea?"

Andrea grew nervous as she felt several pairs of eyes staring at her, waiting for some declaration of confidence that they would indeed find the magic in the Rhyad mountains and restore it to the rest of Damea. "I…yes, let's go." She glanced back at Cassie, whose arms were wrapped around the enchanter's waist. They had finally done it. They would be going to Rhyad – with help on top of it all – where Cassie's map would hopefully lead them to the lost magic the land had been missing for so long. The entire situation seemed surreal – they were *actually doing this.* She could not help but briefly reminisce on everything she and Cassie had been through to get this far. All the obstacles they had overcome. The friends and enemies they had made along the way.

The secrets she had kept.

Andrea still had no idea what she was going to do about the lie she had told Cassie in the Black Forest. She did not know how she would be able to send her home after they had restored the magic, if they even found it. Not to mention that things had changed – *they* had changed.

It was all still very new for the enchanter, having never

been...involved with another person before. A month ago, merely being around the other girl had been stressful and tried her patience very quickly. Now, it seemed she had to practically fight for time alone with Cassie. With their friends all aware of her and Cassie's new...whatever they were...it was as though the others tried to keep the girls apart on purpose, though of course the enchanter knew that was not true. Victor, Roe, and Jacob often invited Cassie to their evening dice games to teach her how to play. Diana had been stopping by Andrea's room nearly every afternoon to ask her questions about her training with Meredith, Cassie's abilities, and just exactly how Andrea knew the location of the magic. Thankfully, Elisa had mostly kept to herself about it, save the occasional joke at their expense, and Kye simply observed with a knowing smile most of the time, seemingly happy that his companions were finally getting along with each other.

On one hand, Andrea was happy that Cassie finally appeared to be acclimating to Damea. On the other hand, she was terrified of what Cassie's reaction would be when she found out that the enchanter did not know how to send her home. *What if there is a way to send her back, though?* Andrea had pondered that possibility several times and it was equally frightening. After all that they had been through, would Cassie still want to go home? Since the night of the celebration, when they had kissed in front of the inn and confessed their feelings for each other, they had not really discussed what that meant for them...not really.

What if she had misread Cassie's actions? Even if Cassie *wanted* to stay, where would they go after Rhyad, assuming they even made it back? Fleeting images crossed her mind – a small house in one of the coastal villages, Fimen's Hope, even back to the Western Hills – it did not matter where they were so long as she was with Cassie. She scolded herself for making so many assumptions, throwing her back to the reality that she would just need to talk to Cassie when the moment was right. *Whenever* that *will be.*

She sighed. She could do this. *They* could do this. And she would tell Cassie the truth…somehow. "Ready, then?" she asked.

Cassie nodded as a slight grin crossed her features – completely oblivious to the enchanter's internal conflict. "Yeah. Let's do this."

"I will have Harrington's soldiers send word once we've passed the Northland Bridge, sir," Jacob informed the Guardian leader. "We'll need to be leaving the horses there before we attempt to cross into the mountain range."

Alexander nodded. "Understood." He reached out and placed his hand on Diana's wrist. "Good luck," he said quietly. "Return safely."

"We will," the queen replied with a smile. She turned to Jacob. "Lead on, Captain."

Jacob bowed his head and gently spurred his horse to head north on the main road leaving the city, the others following closely behind him as they rode toward the first of many hills that would take them to the Northlands and the bridge that led into Rhyad. Looking back every few minutes, Andrea watched as Alexander and the City of Towers faded into the distance. There would be no turning back now. The six of them were going where very few Dameans had journeyed before. Wild animals, bandits staking a claim in the mountains, and harsh, snowy weather all awaited them in Rhyad. Despite the dangers, the enchanter could not help but be excited and scared at the same time. If this worked – if they really found the magic and released it – what would that mean for Damea? For enchanters everywhere? *Would Meredith know? And Richard...*

Andrea knew the more probable answer was that Richard's body would not be able to adjust to the new balance of energy were magic to be restored to the land. She shook her head. It was a cold reality that she had known might happen and could not afford to dwell on now.

"Ugh...I will never get used to this," she heard Cassie moan behind her only a few minutes after they had departed. "My stomach's already not agreeing with what we're doing."

"Perhaps you shouldn't have had that third pastry at lunch," Kye offered helpfully, his voice slightly raised so he could be heard over the sounds of the horses' hooves against the dirt road.

"Quiet, you!" Cassie retorted. She let out another groan and leaned against Andrea's back. "I...probably shouldn't have had that third pastry," she mumbled in the enchanter's ear.

Andrea's eyes widened. "Please don't throw up on me," she pleaded nervously.

"N-no...promises."

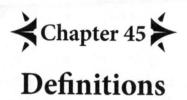

Chapter 45

Definitions

Rhyad

Three weeks later

The cold had rarely been a reason for Andrea to wake up. Winters in the Western Hills could get cool, especially at higher altitudes in the hills themselves, but the frigid, snowy weather of Rhyad was unlike anything she had ever experienced before, even in her years traveling with Meredith.

The enchanter groggily grabbed the heavy blanket that had bunched up at her waist during the night and pulled it over herself. Getting comfortable again, she was nearly asleep when a loud cry sounded from outside the tent that she and Cassie shared.

Startled, she bolted upright and looked to her right. Cassie was gone and the enchanter had no memory of her leaving during the night. Panic began to creep in as memories of their time in Azgadar surfaced.

Another cry sounded, followed by...laughter? Andrea listened closely. *Make that hysterical laughter.* She heard several voices talking at once and sighed with relief as she realized it was only her companions and that they were not under attack.

She frowned, almost sulking a little. *Time to get up.* She would not have declined more sleep honestly, but she could tell from the light that creeped into the tent that it was well into the morning and that they would most likely have to move out soon. It had been nearly three weeks since the six of them had departed the City of Towers. Jacob had kept true to his word and sent Alexander a message letting the Guardian leader know that they had reached the Northland Bridge, where Lord Harrington's soldiers had allowed them to pass without trouble.

They had crossed into the formidable Rhyad mountains a few days earlier and had so far been fortunate with the weather and terrain. Still, Andrea stayed alert as she utilized Cassie's map at least once a day to make sure they were on the right path. If the map was correct, the magic was trapped inside one of the larger mountains. The others theorized that there was a cave system there and that perhaps the magic was in one or more of those caves. The enchanter hoped they were right, for she could already feel the magic in the air destabilizing. It was subtle, but Andrea dared not try any strong spells and had advised Kye to do the same.

She poked her head out of the tent and gasped when she saw Cassie's head hit the hard-packed snow on the ground. The enchanter was about to rush out to help the other girl when Cassie's eyes snapped open and she started rolling on the ground with laughter. Looking up, Andrea saw Diana standing over Cassie and watched in confusion as the queen extended her hand toward her younger companion.

"Ah, you've decided to join us, finally," the enchanter heard Elisa's snarky tone before she even caught the gaze of the ex-

Legionnaire. Once Diana had pulled Cassie to her feet, Andrea left the tent and straightened out her heavy winter clothing as she stood up.

"Er...yes," she said in a voice that came out closer to a grumble. "G-good morning." Looking around, she saw Elisa sitting next to Kye on a fallen log across from the campfire. Both were eating what Andrea assumed to be today's breakfast. Jacob was nowhere to be seen and Diana and Cassie were standing slightly to the enchanter's right. Both were panting slightly and had knowing grins on their faces.

Elisa looked up at the sun peeking through the tall, snow-covered evergreens as she chewed her food. "Hmm. More like 'good nearly-midday,'" she commented, her mouth full.

Andrea could not stop herself from rolling her eyes. "Well, you could have woken me."

"It's fine. You seemed pretty tired last night, so I wanted to let you sleep. Besides, Diana wanted to practice some more!" Cassie said brightly and touched the enchanter's shoulder.

"It's true," Diana said with a nod. "I did promise her some hand-to-hand combat training back in Fimen's Hope."

"It's very fun to watch!" Kye chimed in before tearing into a piece of hard bread.

Andrea glanced down at Cassie's hand for a moment before smiling faintly. "I-thank you." She shivered. "I think it's colder today than it was yesterday."

"Stop complaining and eat," Elisa called out and pointed to the pan of prepared meat next to the campfire. "Jacob caught this earlier."

"Yeah, you can watch me practice," Cassie said. "I'm getting *really* good at this!" she added proudly.

"At what exactly? Being thrown on the ground again and again? If so, then absolutely," the ex-Legionnaire said smugly.

"*'Thrown on the ground'?*" Andrea asked incredulously and turned to Diana, who gave a sheepish laugh as she shrugged.

"It's perfectly safe, Andrea," the queen explained calmly. "And she *is* making progress."

"Yeah, I'm making progress!" Cassie declared in a huff.

"Well, I for one am enjoying watching Her Majes-er… Diana," Kye exclaimed before immediately correcting himself after Diana side-eyed him, "throw Cassie on the ground."

Cassie glared at the two of them. "You two are the worst support system ever."

"*I'll* watch you practice, Cassie," Andrea cut in quickly before an argument could start. She took a seat next to Elisa, who handed the enchanter a plate with the morning's meal.

"Where is Jacob?" Andrea asked.

"Out scouting so that we're not completely lost once we get going again," Elisa answered and glanced up at the sun again. "Which should be rather soon, actually."

Meanwhile, Diana was struggling to get Cassie to properly defend herself without going too easy on her. "Use your strength here…and here," she advised as she stood behind Cassie and positioned the younger woman's arms so that she was in the correct stance for when the queen attacked again.

"I did that before and you *still* kicked my ass," Cassie whined.

"No. You were lazy, let your shoulder drop, and I took advantage of it," Diana pointed out. "I'm not going to go easy on you, Cassie."

"Er…please don't get hurt," Andrea said nervously.

"Don't worry, I won't injure the queen," Cassie promised and grinned at the enchanter. She turned back to Diana, who had stepped back and was preparing to attack again. "Andrea could tell you how great my fighting skills are. Just ask her how we met."

The enchanter's cheeks grew hot immediately. "I-I don't think Her Majesty is interested in that, Cassie. Try to concentrate on what she is teaching you? At least a little?"

Diana chuckled at Andrea's reaction before focusing on Cassie again. "I'm sure that it is a riveting tale, Cassie, and I would love to hear about it later, but let's focus for now. Ready?"

Cassie nodded and tried to maintain the stance Diana had shown her as she raised her hands. Diana swiftly lunged forward, but Cassie was able to anticipate the queen's move fast enough to deftly move to the side. She retaliated by trying to grab Diana's arm, but the queen blocked her attack and grabbed Cassie by the wrist before reaching around just above the younger woman's chest and flipping her to the ground.

"Brilliant!" Kye clapped his hands in approval as Cassie lay on the snow, coughing. Meanwhile, Andrea had covered her mouth with her hands in concern and Elisa simply looked amused.

Diana reached down to help a spluttering Cassie up again. "That was much better!" she praised.

Cassie winced and rubbed her lower back after she was pulled to her feet. "Yeah?" she panted. Despite the obvious pain she was in, a proud smile crept onto her face.

"Yes," Diana confirmed. She caught a glimpse of Andrea's reaction and laughed again. "I think that is enough for today. You did well. We can continue tomorrow if you like."

"Great. Yeah," Cassie breathed.

"I wanted to see more," Kye grumbled.

"You'll be working on your swordplay with Jacob later," the queen told him. "Speaking of, we should start packing up so that we are ready to leave when he returns." She nodded to Elisa, who stood up. Minutes later, the five of them began breaking down the campsite to prepare for another day of traveling through Rhyad.

Andrea found Cassie outside their tent, stuffing cookware, rations, small blankets, and other camping accoutrements into her backpack. Since leaving Gurdinfield, there had not been an opportune moment – at least in the enchanter's mind – to speak to Cassie about all the things that were weighing on her mind. While traveling during the day, they were in the immediate presence of their friends, and at night they were usually too exhausted to talk much. She decided to speak up now. Perhaps not about everything, but Andrea needed to know the answers to at least *some* of the things she had been warring with herself on over the last few weeks.

"Erm…Cassie?" she tried.

The other girl immediately looked up and back at the enchanter. She grinned. "Oh, hey. Did you see that? I totally almost didn't get my ass kicked that last time."

Andrea smiled faintly. "Y-yes! It was very impressive, though I wish you would be careful. I…I don't want you getting hurt."

But Cassie waved her away and returned to packing. "Ah, it's fine. It was just for practice." She stopped as though she realized what Andrea meant and stood up to face the enchanter.

"Don't worry," she said more softly and lightly touched the enchanter's arm. "I'm not going to screw up so royally that I get myself killed or something and you lose your map." She snorted at her own words. "Heh. *Royally.* Get it? Because of Diana and…yeah."

Andrea looked confused for a moment before immediately shaking her head. "Oh, no! That's not-I didn't mean it like that. I just don't want you to get…hurt." She scratched her head and sighed. "I'm not very good at saying things sometimes."

Cassie raised an eyebrow. "Only sometimes?" she teased.

The enchanter pushed her slightly. "Quiet." The lightness in her mood and voice shifted to nervousness again as she quickly remembered what she had wanted to ask Cassie about. "I need to talk to you."

"You're talking to me right now."

"I know-I just…" Andrea sighed before everything she wanted to say all came out in a rush. "What I wanted to ask was…about us and-well, we really haven't discussed it since the night of the celebration and I didn't want to say anything because I didn't want to overstep since you had said to take it one day at a time, but I don't really know what that means sometimes as I've never done this and you–,"

She had nearly run out of breath when Cassie cut her off by kissing her. The enchanter relaxed, closed her eyes, and put her arms around the other girl, sighing into the kiss and nearly forgetting about what she had wanted to talk about in the first place. They held each other for a while before Cassie slowly pulled away.

"Did that answer your question?" Cassie asked wryly.

"I-I..." Andrea stuttered, her face turning a bright shade of pink as she struggled to regain her composure.

Cassie laughed quietly and leaned in again, but as the enchanter recovered, she suddenly remembered why she had even approached Cassie to begin with, and pushed the other girl away. "No!" she protested. "It-it does *not* answer my question!"

Still laughing, Cassie stepped back and put her hands up. "Okay, okay. So, look," she began hesitantly, as though she were choosing her words carefully. "The whole 'taking it one day at a time' thing – I said that because I didn't want you to feel...I don't know...*pressured* into anything you didn't think you were ready for."

Andrea nodded slowly, trying to understand. "I...suppose that makes sense. But...us-I...what is *this*?" She gestured at the space between her and Cassie as she began to grow frustrated again. "What are–,"

Cassie reached out and rested her hands on the sides of Andrea's arms. "Easy, there. Remember what I said about relaxing?"

The enchanter said nothing but nodded.

"Okay, good," Cassie continued. "To be honest, I've been trying my best not to overcomplicate this. I'm with you and... well, I guess you're with me. We're still *us*. If..." She hesitated, and for a moment Andrea saw her eyes flash with worry. "If that's what you still want, I mean."

Andrea felt herself finally relax and let out a sigh of relief as she stepped forward to embrace the other girl. "Of course it is."

"Good." Cassie grinned as she held the enchanter. "So...was that it?"

Andrea debated asking Cassie about the other things on her mind, including telling her the truth about sending her home and whether or not she would consider staying even if the enchanter *could* fulfill her promise. But they had already discussed one topic. Surely the rest could wait for now. *And Cassie actually seems... happy for once.* The enchanter sighed again as she sunk into the embrace. *One thing at a time.*

"Were you two going to join us or were you planning on freezing to death in that pose?"

The enchanter reluctantly untangled herself from Cassie's hold and tried her best not to glare at the ex-Legionnaire, who stood a few steps away from them holding a backpack and looking very impatient.

"Jacob has returned and he is ready to go when we are," Elisa said. "If you two are done, then we should depart."

Andrea glanced at the older woman before turning back to Cassie, who gave her an encouraging nod. "We'll...be ready to leave shortly," the enchanter answered.

"There are a few...complications in the trail ahead. Jacob can explain more on the way. Finish packing so we can go!" Elisa ordered before stomping off in the snow.

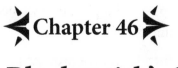

Chapter 46

The Blacksmith's Son

"That can't possibly be safe."

Jacob smiled faintly at Cassie, who like the others stared worriedly at the rickety wooden bridge before them. "It's not," he admitted.

"I-isn't there another w-way around?" Kye asked, his teeth chattering in the cold. They had spent much of the day trekking through the snow-covered hills of the lower mountains of Rhyad. Jacob had scouted ahead earlier that morning and had seen the bridge from his vantage point. The temperature had dropped steadily throughout the day and upon reaching the bridge, harsh winds began kicking up. The bridge itself was a haphazardly thrown together construction laid out between two sheer cliff faces. Old, rotting wooden planks scattered across the bridge served as a walkway, and torn-up rope lining the sides of it offered a precarious-looking rail. A long drop and sharp, jagged rocks awaited anyone unfortunate enough to fall through.

The Guardian captain shook his head as he adjusted his fur hood. "Not that I could see," he replied, raising his voice slightly as the wind grew louder.

"I agree with the boy. We should find another way," Elisa suggested.

"No," Jacob said. "That would cost us at least another day or more worth of supplies. Supplies that we need for the return trip if we cannot find food."

"We're nearly there!" Andrea protested. She pointed at the taller mountains in the distance that had grown quite a bit closer over the last few days. "We could go across and–,"

"If we *fall to our deaths,* then it won't matter how long it takes us to get there," Elisa snapped.

"Jacob has a point, Elisa," Diana spoke up, shivering. She looked up at her betrothed. "There must be *some* way to make it across."

"Across without dying, preferably," Cassie deadpanned.

Jacob knelt near the cliff's edge and inspected the bridge closely. "Hmm. It may be stable enough for one person." He touched one of the wooden posts that the ropes were tied to. Perhaps..." He stood up and faced the group again. "Perhaps someone could make it across with a rope, tie it to the post over there, and then the rest of us can use that as a...safety precaution. Of sorts," he finished with a shrug.

"That all sounds fine except for the part where we'd all fall through that sorry excuse for a bridge before we made it halfway across!" Elisa answered bitterly.

"Yeah, and with all this equipment...I don't think that's going to work," Cassie added. "It's just too heavy."

"Then we think of another way!" Andrea declared.

"What do you think we are trying to do right now?" Elisa retorted. "Plan a party?"

"I can do it," Kye spoke up quietly. But no one heard him.

"That's *not* a mature response to the situation at all!" Andrea argued with Elisa.

"I think it's a valid idea!" Jacob defended.

Kye tried again, raising his voice this time so that he could be heard above his friends' bickering. "*I can do it!*"

The other five fell silent as they stared at the young man, some in shock, others in confusion.

Kye swallowed nervously and pushed himself to continue. "I'm the lightest and fastest one here. I can make it across with the rope before the bridge breaks. Once I've done that, you can follow me."

While the others exchanged thoughtful glances, Elisa stepped forward and angrily shook her head. "Absolutely not and you're an idiot for even suggesting it."

"Elisa, he wants to help!" Diana said sharply.

The ex-Legionnaire looked back at the queen quickly. "Your Majesty, he's done nothing but undermine every attempt I've made to keep him *alive*."

"I can do it!" Kye repeated.

"If the boy wants to do this, I say we let him!" Jacob agreed.

Elisa glared at the captain. "With all due respect, Jacob, he is *not* your responsibility."

"I'm not *your* responsibility, either!" Kye shouted. He threw up his hands. "Why are you like this? Always telling me what to do! When will you learn that I'm not a *child* and–?"

"When *you* get it through your thick skull that *throwing your life away* will *not* bring them back!" Elisa yelled.

A stony silence fell upon them. All was quiet save the harsh sound of the wind blowing.

"I-I…I want to do this, Elisa. Please, trust me?" Kye pleaded, his voice breaking. "I know that…I know I cannot bring them back. Nothing will."

The others remained silent and looked to Elisa as they waited for her to answer. Biting her lip, the ex-Legionnaire glanced at her companions before focusing on Kye. "I do trust you," she finally exhaled. "I would rather not see you die pointlessly because you felt the need to prove yourself to us somehow."

Kye frowned. "I want to help. That's why I came along." He crossed his arms over his chest. "This is for *me* more than anyone."

"We are out of time," Jacob pressed, looking up worriedly at the slightly darkening sky. "Shall we do this?"

Elisa did not take her eyes off Kye, instead holding his gaze steadily as she considered what he said. "All right." She pointed at the younger enchanter. "He takes the rope, runs across, and ties it to the end. We'll follow one by one."

Kye sighed with relief and grinned. "Thank you," he said gratefully.

Elisa shot him a final, concerned glance but said nothing as Jacob grabbed the rope from his backpack and proceeded to tie it to the wooden post closest to them.

"You'll take this," he said to Kye before handing the young man the remainder of the rope. "The faster you are, the better. Try not to settle your weight in any one area too much. I don't know how much that bridge can actually take."

Trying to appear confident, Kye took the rope from the captain and nodded. "Understood."

"Good. Tie the rope around yourself so that if you fall, we can pull you up. Got it?"

"Yes," Kye answered. After securing the rope around his waist he turned to face the bridge, his expression slightly shifting from confidence to nervousness.

"Go, then. Good luck."

Kye took a moment to look back at his friends. Jacob had his arm around Diana's shoulders and nodded at the young man encouragingly. Cassie looked solemn and Andrea appeared quite nervous and was fidgeting with the loose threads of her heavy cloak. Elisa simply stared back at him, her expression void of emotion, and the young enchanter wished he knew what was going through her mind.

He could figure that out once they got across safely. Right now, he had a job to do.

Facing the bridge, he took a tentative step forward, his boot crunching down on the snow, then another. The first step onto the bridge resulted in a protesting groan from the old wooden plank. Kye involuntarily froze with fear as the ropes holding up the bridge creaked loudly.

"Easy, now!" Jacob called.

Kye gulped and nodded as he continued to step as lightly as he could across the bridge. From here, the distance to the other side seemed *much* farther than he had previously thought, and it took all his willpower not to look down. He tried to keep his breathing steady and focused on every step while gripping the rope around his waist. The wind howled all around him, swaying the bridge slightly, which made him freeze up again.

"You're almost there, boy!" the captain yelled out, his voice nearly drowned out by Kye's focus and the winds.

Kye looked up and realized that Jacob was right – there were only a few more steps between him and the other side. He closed his eyes and breathed deeply before launching into a sprint to the end. The boards under his feet threatened to snap as his boots pounded them.

He thought he heard someone scream his name, and that perhaps it was Elisa, but he could not be sure as he made a running leap and flew through the air for a moment before landing and tumbling onto the snow. He had done it. He was alive, and the bridge was still intact.

He tied Jacob's rope to the post while the others cheered loudly. "All right. It's ready!" he yelled.

On the other side, Jacob immediately turned to Diana. "You're up next, Your Majesty," he prompted.

"But I–," Diana began to argue.

"*Go*," Elisa said forcefully and led the queen to the edge. "Hold on to the rope and *do not* let go. Quickly, now!"

With a nervous pause, Diana glanced back at Jacob worriedly before stepping onto the bridge. Ignoring the wobbling as best as she could, she steadied herself on the new rope and moved across the bridge quickly. It was not long before she was on the other side with Kye.

"Who is next?" Jacob asked.

Cassie pushed Andrea forward. "Go on," she said.

"No! You should go first," Andrea replied stubbornly. "That bridge could break at any moment and if you fall–,"

"Don't be stupid. You're the only one who can actually *do* something with the magic once you get there," Cassie pointed out. "Look at those mountains. You *know* it's there. Plus, I'll be fine."

"She's got us here!" Jacob grinned while Elisa sighed.

Andrea hesitated. "I…"

Cassie rolled her eyes and pushed the enchanter toward the bridge again. "We can fight about this later. Go!"

Andrea took a tentative step onto the bridge and shakily held onto the rope as she began slowly crossing it. About halfway across, the board under her right boot snapped, the pieces falling into the gorge below. The enchanter cried out and clutched at the rope, causing the bridge to sway dangerously. The ropes on both sides of the bridge began fraying and unraveling.

"Andrea, *go! Go!*" Elisa yelled, her voice almost lost in the cacophony of shouts from the others.

Terrified, the enchanter raced across the remainder of the bridge toward Kye and Diana. Upon making it to the other side, she collapsed onto the snow, panting heavily.

"That nearly ended horribly," Elisa said dryly. "Who is next? I doubt the bridge will be able to withstand all of us."

"You or Jacob should go," Cassie decided.

"Andrea cannot find the magic without you, though," Elisa said skeptically.

Cassie shook her head and pointed at the mountains. "It's in there. She...she knows that. She needs you two to help get her there."

The ex-Legionnaire appeared conflicted, as though she knew Cassie had a point but did not want to endure Andrea's wrath if Cassie was somehow left behind.

"Elisa, perhaps you should go next and I'll stay with Cassie. If the bridge holds, I will take her across," Jacob offered. He looked back at the bridge. "It might work if she and I go together."

"No," Elisa said firmly. "You go. I will take Cassie across."

"But–,"

"We'd be lighter and have a better chance, anyway. Diana needs you there, Jacob," the ex-Legionnaire insisted.

Jacob looked at the two women and sighed. "Fine. I'll try to be quick so that the bridge might still hold." He turned and grabbed the rope to begin easing his way across. The bridge groaned but the side ropes surprisingly held and none of the planks broke. Once he had reached the other side – and after the queen briefly embraced him – he called back to the remaining two. "Quickly, now!"

Elisa nodded and directed her attention to Cassie. "Are you ready? We must be swift if we're to make it across before it breaks."

Cassie adjusted the straps on her backpack. "Yeah, let's do this."

"Then go first," Elisa instructed her. "I will be right behind you." She held her breath as Cassie took the first step onto the bridge. When it held, the younger woman began moving across at a steady pace, with Elisa following closely behind her.

"Come on! Hurry!" Andrea cried, with the others echoing her plea.

As they passed the halfway point, Cassie spoke up, her voice audibly shaky. "You all right, Elisa?"

"I'm fine – concentrate on what's in front of you," Elisa ordered.

They were only a few steps from the end when the ex-Legionnaire heard the terrifying snap of one of the ropes behind them. Fear spiked in her as the bridge began to buckle under their combined weight. She looked up and grabbed a frozen Cassie by the back of the girl's cloak before pushing her roughly toward the other side. The younger woman, propelled by the push, took the boost and jumped to close the distance between her and Jacob's outstretched arm.

The bridge jerked to the side as the other rope broke before the entire structure began to fall. Cassie tumbled toward Jacob as Elisa fell down with the bridge, which was anchored only by the quickly fraying ropes on the side of their destination. The ex-Legionnaire desperately grabbed one of the planks to keep herself from falling into the chasm. The others screamed in horror as the Guardian captain reached out.

"I've got you!" he gasped, barely catching Cassie by her arm as the rest of her body was suspended over the edge of the cliff.

"*Elisa!*" Kye yelled while Andrea rushed forward to help Jacob pull Cassie up.

Meanwhile, Elisa struggled to hang onto the board and pull

herself up. The weight of her backpack made it more difficult, but she managed to climb up a few planks before the bridge groaned and one of the two remaining ropes snapped, sending her back down a few feet.

"Diana! Give me another rope!" Kye cried, an idea forming in his mind.

The queen swiftly grabbed a rope from her backpack and held it out to Kye, who handed her one end of it and tied the other to his belt. "I'm going to go down there and get her," he explained hurriedly. "You pull us up!"

"Hand it here!" Jacob commanded. "Diana, stand behind me – this might take all of us."

Double-checking that the rope was secure, Kye began to climb down the side of the cliff, holding on to whatever rocks were sticking out far enough for him to grab. He stayed along the side of the bridge and let himself down until he was close enough to reach Elisa.

"Take my hand!" he called out and extended his hand toward her. The winds were louder than ever as the frigid air rushed through the gorge.

Stunned for a moment, Elisa shook her head before reaching her hand out. The shifting of weight caused the plank she was hanging onto to snap.

"*No!*" Kye shouted, swinging forward and grabbing her wrist just as the bridge fell – crashing down onto the sharp rocks below.

The combined weight of Elisa and her gear worked against Kye as he struggled to maintain his grip on her. "*Pull us up!*" he screamed. "*Now! Now!*"

"You heard him! Pull!" Jacob ordered as the four of them put all their strength into pulling Kye and Elisa up the side of the cliff.

Holding onto his arm, Elisa looked up at Kye, her green eyes bleary from the wind and her arm and shoulder burning with pain from the fall. "I can't...I'm losing hold of you!" she gasped.

"No! Don't let go!" Kye cried and wrapped both arms around her, hooking them underneath hers so that she could hold onto him. With Jacob's continued encouragement and the others pulling them up, the enchanter and Elisa eventually made it back on solid ground. After separating from the ex-Legionnaire, he rolled onto his back in the snow, breathing heavily while recovering. The others took a moment to catch their breaths as well.

Elisa, still on her hands and knees, pushed her disheveled hair out of her face and crawled over to where Kye was. "You," she panted.

He sat up immediately and prepared to be scolded for endangering himself once again. Instead, he was stunned when he felt the ex-Legionnaire throw her arms around him.

"You're a bloody idiot. Thank you," she whispered, her face buried in the crook of his neck.

Seeing that all eyes were now on him, Kye cleared his throat and awkwardly patted Elisa on her back. "Erm...you are welcome," he replied slowly before she pulled away.

"Damn, it's cold!" Cassie observed after a long silence among the six of them. She shivered and drew her cloak tighter around herself.

Elisa sighed as she stood up, still clutching her arm. "Your... skill at pointing out the obvious is remarkable, Cassie. I can see why Andrea would want to court you." She laughed. "Though I wouldn't be surprised if she prefers your other ability that delays us from packing up camp."

"Oh, that's rich. You nearly die, and you *still* just can't keep your commentary to yourself," Cassie scoffed as Andrea looked at her feet, struggling to appear unaffected by Elisa's words.

Elisa gave a short laugh. "Where is the fun in that?"

"Perhaps we should continue," Diana interjected quickly, though her tone gave away her amusement. She looked up. "It's going to get dark soon."

"Agreed," Jacob said. "We can stop once the sun sets." He secured his backpack before swinging it over his shoulder again.

"We'll need to find another way back, I suppose," Kye pointed out as he climbed to his feet.

"We will figure that out when the time comes," the Guardian captain answered with a brief smile. "Let's move, shall we?"

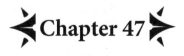

Chapter 47

Reflections

"Ugh, it's cold and I'm hungry." Cassie practically threw herself onto the ground near the campsite Jacob had chosen.

"Impressive. You've only said that three times today instead of the usual six," Elisa said dryly as she set her gear down on the snow, the others following suit. She removed her hood and glanced up at the darkening sky. The tallest mountains of the Rhyadan range peeked just over the top of the tree line. "If that map of yours is correct, Andrea, we should reach those mountains sometime tomorrow afternoon," she stated while Jacob and Diana began to build a fire.

"'*That map*'? I have a name, you know," Cassie protested while fumbling through her backpack for dinner rations.

Elisa feigned shock. "My apologies, Cassie. I simply didn't know what Andrea's new pet name for you was so I figured 'that map' was the safer option." Jacob and Kye laughed loudly. Cassie grumbled some profanity as a response and Andrea said nothing, but instead bit her lip while trying to appear intensely focused as she frantically searched her pack for her own food rations.

"All right, leave them be. All of you," Diana finally broke in, shooting her betrothed and the youngest enchanter a warning glare. The two men were immediately silenced, though Kye had to stifle his laughter with one hand. Andrea looked at the queen gratefully and Elisa chuckled lightly before sitting down on one of the blankets in front of the fire.

An hour later, all six of them were sitting around the campsite, most bundled in heavy blankets for warmth. Their meal rations for the night had been eaten, and their supplies as well as a few lit lanterns were scattered about the campsite. The night was clear, cold, and quiet save the crackling of the campfire and Kye's gentle strumming on the lute.

Jacob and Diana sat outside their tent in silence, listening to the young man playing and drinking the hot herbal tea Diana had made for them.

"The boy's quite good. We should have him play at our wedding," Jacob suggested, breaking the silence.

Diana took a cautious sip of her tea and looked over at the young enchanter, who seemed lost in his own world as he strummed the instrument. "He is talented. But I wouldn't want to impose–,"

"Nonsense, he's a nice lad," Jacob said eagerly. "Besides, I could probably make a deal to continue giving him swordplay lessons if he agrees to play."

Diana raised an eyebrow at the man. "Self-defense is one thing to make Elisa happy but…Kye set an entire battlefield on fire with his magic – do you really want him wielding a sword, too? Although, perhaps that might be safer…"

Jacob laughed deeply and put his arm around his future wife, who leaned in closer to him. "I'm sure it will be fine, love. He probably wouldn't mind having an outlet for that sort of thing." He clarified. "His music, I meant, not the sword fighting."

"Of *course*," Diana replied and gave him a knowing look.

They were interrupted when Elisa stepped in front of them. "I'll be in my tent getting some sleep, Your Majesty. Let me know if I can be of any assistance." The ex-Legionnaire gave a short bow.

"How is your arm? And really, Elisa, it's just 'Diana,'" the queen insisted.

"Of course, Your Majesty. And it's fine. Just a slight pull, but I'll be fine in a day or so, I'm sure," Elisa answered and winked at Jacob, who grinned in return.

Once the ex-Legionnaire had left, Diana turned to Jacob and gave a longsuffering sigh. "Honestly, I don't know how many times I have to tell her."

"Hah. It's protocol, love – I'm sure she's only trying to be respectful." He pondered his words for a moment. "Erm...in her own way I suppose. This *is* Elisa we're speaking of."

Diana slapped him playfully. "Oh, stop it. Though you're probably right," she admitted.

"You could lock everyone up who calls you 'Your Majesty,'" he suggested.

The queen laughed. "I think that might be frowned upon, Jacob. *Thank you* for the suggestion, though."

Jacob shrugged. "What? It's a sound strategy!"

Diana sighed. "I do wish she had accepted my offer. Perhaps

I can convince her when we get back to Gurdinfield."

The captain shook his head. "The woman swore an oath, Diana. You cannot ask her to go back on that oath, no matter how good a friend and ally she is."

"The empress does not deserve Elisa's loyalty," Diana said bitterly.

Jacob chuckled and lightly kissed the queen's forehead. "No doubt Ithmeera would say the same about you."

On the other side of the camp, Andrea and Cassie could hear only a muffled version of Diana and Jacob's conversation. When Cassie saw Diana playfully slap Jacob, she laughed quietly, getting Andrea's attention.

"What is it?" the enchanter wondered.

"Those two," Cassie replied, nodding toward the couple. "It's nice that they let their guard down around each other like that. I used to think Diana took herself too seriously. I guess I was wrong."

"She's been through a lot. We all have," Andrea mused, the airy music from Kye's lute relaxing her. She was suddenly reminded of how tired she really was.

"Yeah, I can't say I'll be making a return trip to Rhyad anytime soon once this is over," Cassie declared. She shivered. "It's freaking freezing up here."

Andrea took a deep breath as the tightness in her chest returned, as it did every time the subject of Cassie going home was brought up. *I cannot dance around it any longer. I should tell her. I'm sure she'll understand – we're toge-well, we're us now. That has to mean something to her.*

"Cassie?" she asked slowly. When she was sure she had Cassie's attention, she continued nervously. "Have you...well, you know...given any thought about wh-what, I mean, yes." She exhaled heavily. *Just say it.*

"Yes? 'Yes', what? I don't get it." Cassie looked puzzled but seemed to be trying hard to understand what the enchanter was asking.

Andrea rubbed the back of her neck anxiously. "What I mean is, what are you going to do if we-no, *when* we find the magic and release it?"

Cassie's eyebrows raised in surprise at Andrea's question. "Oh," she said steadily. "Um...that's a good question. I mean, I guess I had thought you'd be sending me home like you said, assuming we don't die in some horrible way." She let out a nervous laugh but quickly went quiet when she saw the enchanter looked sullen and was staring at the ground.

Cassie cleared her throat. "But um," she continued, "I think that things have...changed." She gently placed her hand on Andrea's shoulder, causing the enchanter to meet her gaze. "Right?"

Andrea said nothing but nodded.

"So...I think maybe it wouldn't be a crazy idea to stick around for a while," Cassie suggested with a small shrug. "You know, to make sure you and the others get back safe and uh... well, I didn't know if you had anyone to go with to Diana and Jacob's wedding and who knows when that will be, assuming we don't all, again, die horribly up here of course."

Andrea couldn't help but smile at Cassie's rambling and

felt a weight lifted from her shoulders at her companion's suggestion. "Of-of course," she stammered. *She doesn't want to leave.* Everything was going to be fine. They would find the magic, release it, and then the two of them would be free to go wherever they wanted in Damea.

She should have been ecstatic. But the lie she had told Cassie that fateful night in the Black Forest still ate away at her like a parasite.

"Hey." The enchanter felt Cassie's arm wrap around her and pull her in close. "You all right? I mean, I can leave if you really want me to," Cassie joked.

Andrea exhaled quickly and could not hold back a laugh. "Yes, yes I'm fine. And no," she said, looking at Cassie, "I don't want you to leave."

Cassie gave a short nod. "Good." She removed her arm from around Andrea and started to push herself up. "I'm going to go get some more wood for the fire and stretch my legs for a few minutes. I'll be back in a bit, okay?"

"Do you want me to go with you?"

Cassie shook her head. "No, no, I got it. I'll be back soon, promise." She grabbed one of the lanterns and a rope from her backpack.

"All right," the enchanter replied, wrapping her cloak tightly around herself. She was caught off guard when she felt Cassie give her a quick kiss on her cheek before leaving. As she watched the other girl walk away, the giddiness Cassie had left her with slowly began to dissipate. She knew she would have to tell Cassie the truth eventually. Andrea could not live the rest of her life with that lie on her conscience, especially if Cassie was going to be around.

Stop. The thoughts racing through the enchanter's mind came to a halt. She knew she was thinking too far ahead, making too many assumptions. This…whatever it was between her and Cassie was new. *One day at a time, right?* She sighed and reached toward the pile of blankets behind her to grab another one. Hopefully Cassie would be back soon and Andrea could stop worrying about this…for now.

* * *

Walking slowly around the nearby woods with the snow crunching underneath her boots was surprisingly relaxing to Cassie. She had stayed close enough to the campsite that she could still hear the faint melodies of Kye's lute but far enough away that she could get some quiet time away from everything to just reflect.

She had expected Andrea's question to come up eventually ever since the night of the celebration in Gurdinfield. What she had not expected was that she would actually *want* to stay in Damea. *Things are different now, I guess. I could go home but… Andrea isn't there.* Cassie had even considered asking Andrea to go with her, but she knew the enchanter would not want to leave the place she had fought so hard to save. *Even if mostly everyone here is a little crazy.*

She placed the lantern on the snow and began gathering pieces of firewood from the area. Jacob had done well in picking a campsite, and there was plenty of dead wood and branches to be found. Once she had gathered enough, she used the rope she had brought to tie most of it together so that she could drag it back to camp. She grabbed her lantern and was about to head back when a quiet, eerily recognizable voice pierced the stillness of the woods.

"Lovely evening for a stroll, no?"

Cassie gasped and dropped the rope and lantern. The light source fell on its side and rolled a bit before coming to a stop, casting an ominous glow on the figure in front of her.

"Don't be afraid, dear. I'm not going to hurt you." Meredith's form stepped into the light, covered mostly by her heavy cloak and hood, which she removed.

Cassie wanted to scream or yell out for help but was too stunned and paralyzed to do anything.

Meredith took another step forward. "You can yell for help but by the time your friends get here I will be gone. I am merely asking that you hear me out, Cassie."

Cassie found her voice. It was raspy and unfamiliar. "The… the hell? How did you find us?!"

The older woman shrugged. "You didn't *really* think that you could hide from me, did you? I've been tracking you since you and Andrea left, Cassie. A shame, really – Andrea should know better. She's more familiar with my tracking abilities than anyone." She took another step. "Once I reached the City of Towers, it was quite easy to figure out where you were headed next. Just about all the soldiers at the inns knew of your journey to Rhyad."

Without thinking, Cassie drew the dagger Elisa had given her and pointed it at Meredith. "D-don't come any closer, you crazy bitch!" she breathed. "I don't-I don't care what you want. J-just…just turn around and go back the way you came."

The enchanter gave a harsh laugh. "Dear, put the knife away and just listen to me. Or go fetch your friends – I don't care either way. Although, I think you're going to want to hear what I have to say."

Cassie held the dagger steady and shook her head. "No. I'm serious. Get the hell away from us or I'll make you wish–,"

"I know you've found the magic," Meredith said plainly, "and I can tell you that releasing it is the *worst* thing you could possibly do."

Cassie shook her head vehemently. "Look lady, you're crazy and there's no reason I would believe anything you have to say, so you might as well just go. You tried to kill us!"

Meredith laughed. "That's a tad dramatic, no? I sent simple constructs after you. I knew Andrea could easily dispatch them with your help, of course, and that the energy from that would allow me to find you. I would never try to kill my own apprentice!"

"You need to leave. Now."

Meredith held out her hands. "Will you at least hear me out? Releasing the magic here could have catastrophic consequences for Damea. It could kill both you and Andrea…and possibly all of us!"

But Cassie did not lower her weapon. She felt a shiver run down her spine as standing in the cold began to affect her body and the hand holding the knife began to shake. "Yeah, right. Andrea told me everything. You're just afraid that if we release the magic then all that work to wake your husband up will have been for nothing. He's *dead* – you have to move on!"

She expected the enchanter to lash out or yell, but to her surprise, Meredith simply nodded. "You're right, Cassie. Releasing magic that has been contained here for so long will no doubt affect my work on Richard. What *I'm* more interested in is the fact that you continue to blindly accept the word of a failed apprentice that has been lying to you this entire time."

Rather than take what seemed very much like bait, Cassie stood her ground and gestured at Meredith with the knife. "Right, and I'm just supposed to believe you after you kidnapped and tortured me?" she panted, her breath visible in the frigid air. "Nice try, lady, but it's going to take a lot more than you calling Andrea a liar to get me to listen to you. You have the next five seconds to get out of my face or I'll yell for the others."

The enchanter chuckled. "Mm, yes, and what exactly could they do against one of the most powerful enchanters in Damea, hmm?"

"Well, they ended a decades-long civil war and kicked the Legion's sorry ass back to Azgadar. I'd say they'd have no problem taking you on," Cassie challenged.

Meredith smiled faintly. "When Andrea left-no," she corrected herself, "when she *abandoned* her duties, she could barely conjure the simplest fireball. I believe she needed *your* help for that. I find it rather odd that you accuse me of torturing you, Cassie, yet you willingly provide Andrea with whatever power she needs."

"Maybe because it doesn't feel like she's trying to kill me when she does it," Cassie countered.

Meredith studied the younger woman for a moment before finally nodding her head in understanding. "Ah...of course! It was probably *her* magic that pulled you here from...wherever it is you are from." She nodded again, as though she were working out her theory in her head in front of Cassie. "Yes...I must have simply helped *complete* the transfer. Impressive, even for Andrea. Still, there's much she needs to improve on."

"Yeah, well, you must have been a crappy teacher," Cassie retorted. "Andrea's done more for this land than you ever will."

If Meredith was offended, she did not show it. If anything, Cassie thought she seemed amused. "I understand she was helpful in defending the capital city from the Legion, though of course the truth is that we both know that barrier didn't last very long. Perhaps...an assessment from her teacher might be in order? It would certainly be entertain–,"

Anger spiked in Cassie as she quickly moved forward. "You stay the hell away from her!"

Meredith narrowed her eyes at Cassie for a moment, as though she were studying her. "Interesting," she mused. "You seem to trust her completely when she's done far worse to you than I. Clearly, your little dalliance with her has clouded your judgement and yes, I know about that." She flashed another smile. "I saw you two earlier. I'm surprised – truly I am. You and Andrea...well, it just seems like a tragedy waiting to happen."

"You don't know crap about her or me. This is your last chance, psycho. Leave."

"Did she tell you she could send you home if you helped her?" Meredith sneered. "You *do* know that's impossible, right?"

"Shut up. And why am I still talking to you?" Cassie fired back.

"My dear, it took a *massive* amount of energy to bring you here, and that was an accident. Do you really think a mere apprentice who, by the way, has not completed her training, would have the ability or the raw power to just...send you back?" The enchanter paused for a moment. "As for this magic you're so graciously releasing back into the land, have you stopped and considered if perhaps releasing what is probably the most unstable energy *in the world* on an unsuspecting and unprepared population is the brightest idea?"

"Okay, I'm through with you, now," Cassie growled. She sheathed her dagger and picked up the rope and the lantern. "Are you actually going to do anything or was this just a long, boring lecture to make you feel like you are still somehow relevant?"

Meredith sighed and for a moment, Cassie saw what appeared to be *remorse* cross the enchanter's face before she returned once more to her confident self. "You have nothing to fear from me, Cassie. I merely came to warn you and Andrea. She's still my apprentice, and despite what you may believe, I still care about her. If you two would just come back to the Black Forest, we can try to make this right."

"I suppose you're going to tell me that only *you* can send me home somehow?" Cassie snapped.

The enchanter shook her head slowly. "I'm afraid not, dear. If you truly are from...somewhere else, I could try to recreate the environment in which we brought you here. But without doing more research, I could do more harm than good."

"You've done plenty of harm to me already," Cassie said bluntly. "Why do you care now?"

"Perhaps my initial methods for you were...rash. I should have asked for Andrea's help in channeling your power far sooner. Magic in this land has been waning for far too long and it is rapidly becoming more unstable." She looked around. "Especially here. You wonder why I haven't attacked you, Cassie? I dare not risk casting magic in this region. Can't you feel it? How unbalanced and unstable the energy here is?"

Cassie glared at the enchanter. "Yeah," she growled. "I'm leaving now. Don't try to follow us or talk to us, or get in our way. You got that?"

Meredith stood still, expressionless, and said nothing for a few seconds. Finally, she waved Cassie away. "Go on, then."

Cassie scoffed. "Yeah, great talk." She turned to start walking back to the campsite but after a few steps, an odd feeling nagged at her. She spun around and saw that Meredith had vanished.

"Psycho," she muttered and headed toward the camp again. Her heart rate had mostly returned to normal and the adrenaline rush she had while she had been holding the dagger had faded. While Cassie did not trust Meredith, not by a long shot, a few things irked her. *Why would Andrea want us to release the magic if it was so dangerous? She wants enchanters to be able to use magic freely again; she wouldn't try to hurt anyone on purpose. Maybe she really doesn't know what could happen.*

This brought Cassie to the ultimate question. Why had

Andrea told her she could send her home if she did not actually have the power to do so? *She wouldn't lie to me about something like that.* She thought back to when Andrea had asked what Cassie's plans were after they found and released the magic. *She asked you because she wanted you to stay so you could be together, dumbass.* Guilt set in, and Cassie scolded herself for being ungrateful toward Andrea. *She gave up a lot to get you away from that crazy bitch and here you are accusing her of being dishonest and…evil. All because her crazy torturer teacher is a creepy stalker that said some spooky things to you. Idiot.*

She pushed the doubts away. Meredith could go jump off the Sky Tower for all she cared. She considered alerting her friends of Meredith's presence, but when she arrived back at the campsite she saw that they were all already in their tents. *Probably sleeping.*

After tending to the fire, she crawled into the tent she shared with Andrea. The enchanter was wrapped up in blankets and fast asleep, no doubt exhausted after the day's long trek and the incident with the bridge. Cassie did not want to wake Andrea up just to alarm her, especially since Meredith had readily admitted that she would not attack them. *I'll tell her tomorrow and we can worry about it then.*

She grabbed her own blankets and gently placed a kiss on the enchanter's cheek before lying down herself. Sleep claimed her soon after.

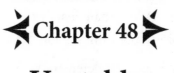

Chapter 48

Unstable

"Almost there! It's just up this hill."

"This 'hill' is ridiculously steep," Cassie grumbled. "Whose stupid idea was it to put this hill here, anyway? My legs hurt."

Kye snorted with laughter and brushed some snow off his pants. "Mine as well. I think I've got snow in my boots."

The formidable peaks of the Rhyad mountains finally stood before them. The only thing separating the mountains from the group was a series of rolling hills that led out of the forest. They were fortunate enough to have the weather on their side today – the air was clear and the sun shone down brightly on them, reflecting glimmers of light on the snow.

Jacob chuckled and continued. "I believe I saw the entrance to those caves we suspected when I scouted this morning."

"The magic is in there," Andrea announced, breathing heavily as she trudged through the deep snow with the rest of her friends.

"How can you be so sure?" Diana asked.

The enchanter gestured around her. "The air – the energy here is unstable. The way it flows here is unlike any magic I've felt before. Something is affecting it and I'm betting it's inside those caves," she explained and pointed ahead.

"I trust you have an actual plan for when we find it, yes?" Elisa questioned. "Other than just 'we'll figure it out,'" she finished while doing a poor impression of Cassie's voice.

Cassie put her hands up defensively. "What? We probably *will* figure it out! And I don't sound like that."

Andrea smiled at their exchange. "Well, I'm not exactly sure. We don't know what caused the magic to become trapped here in the first place. Once we find that out, making a plan to release it will be easier."

"See?" Cassie exclaimed at Elisa while pointing at the enchanter. "She's got it all taken care of."

Andrea turned to Kye. "Remember what I said about doing magic here. Even the smallest amount of energy drawn could harm us."

The young man nodded. "Of course." He appeared in thought for a moment before speaking again. "Actually, I was wondering if you had put much thought into what you were going to do after this. If it's not too much trouble, I would be very grateful if you could teach me some of what you know, Andrea."

Cassie grinned as the enchanter looked back at Kye in surprise before looking quite flattered. "Oh!" Andrea exclaimed. "Well, I-I suppose. I'm not really an expert by any means." She glanced back at Cassie, who offered an encouraging smile. "Maybe... maybe we could talk more after we're done here?"

Diana spoke up. "There is still much to be done to rebuild

Gurdinfield, but I will investigate what this will mean for the Enchanters Academy," she said to Andrea and Kye.

"Thank you!" Kye beamed at both of them while Elisa looked on in approval.

"Yes, that's very generous of you, Your Majesty," Andrea agreed gratefully.

The queen sighed. "Again, it's just 'Diana'. And it's no trouble, really."

As Diana and Andrea continued to discuss the academy and what reopening it would mean for Gurdinfield, Cassie eventually ignored them and focused instead on trudging through the snow, which was proving rather difficult as the snow was deep and she was growing tired. Hopefully, they would stop and rest soon before heading into the caves.

She worried about what they would find in those caves. What if the magic was dangerous and killed them all instantly? What if Meredith had been right, and releasing the energy would cause more harm than good? She sighed. *Stupid Meredith.* She had all but forgotten about her encounter with the enchanter the night before. She knew she needed to tell Andrea what had happened, but she did not want to alarm her, either – not when they were so close to finishing this.

"You all right?" Andrea's voice broke through her thoughts.

Cassie looked down and realized the enchanter had taken her arm. "Hm? Oh, yeah." *No, you need to say something* now. "Actually…I have a question for you. It's probably really stupid."

Andrea smiled brightly at her and squeezed her arm. "What is it?"

"Well, um…" Cassie began. Surprisingly, she was a little nervous, but she knew she needed to be able to be honest with Andrea about things, especially now that they were together. "Have you, you know, given any thought to the possibility that releasing all of this magic could just make things worse?"

Andrea tilted her head. "What do you mean?"

"Uh…well," Cassie pushed herself to continue, "what if releasing it causes more instability? Damea hasn't had a lot of magic for a long time and you're going to be releasing a ton of it at once."

The enchanter nodded slowly, as though she were still unsure of why Cassie would be asking such a question but tried to explain anyway. "That's…a good point. I suppose you *could* be right – this isn't exactly a tested solution we are attempting here," she said with a light laugh. "Any result would have to be better than it is now…Azgadar can barely power their farms since they have so little magic. Plus," she added, "any magic we release could take quite a while to distribute completely."

Several questions suddenly surfaced in Cassie's mind. "Well, how do you know it won't just destroy us all?"

"I've been studying magic for quite a while, Cassie. Trust me, I want to be careful about this." Andrea appeared slightly offended.

"I mean," Cassie continued, "if it takes a while to distribute, I'm guessing you wouldn't have been able to send me home right away."

Andrea frowned. "I thought-I thought you wanted to stay?" she asked quietly.

Meredith's harsh words about Andrea echoed in Cassie's head as she noticed the enchanter appeared to be suddenly uncomfortable with the conversation. Her emotions got the best of her and she began to grow suspicious. At the same time, a strange feeling of dread began creeping in on her thoughts.

"That's not the point," Cassie told her and stopped walking to face the enchanter. "I was just asking."

Andrea grew slightly pale as she released Cassie's arm. "I… well, I don't know then, Cassie."

No. The feeling of dread grew, and Cassie knew exactly why. Perhaps she had always known and had not wanted to admit it to herself because then she would have to deal with the horrible reality of it all. "Did you ever?" she demanded, her voice nearly a whisper.

"What? Where is this coming from?" Andrea asked.

The dread that gnawed away at Cassie slammed into her as her expression quickly shifted into a glare. *She lied to me. She's been lying to me from the very beginning. Everything…* "Oh, wow…I can't-I can't believe she was right. That bitch was right!"

"*Who?*"

"Meredith."

Andrea's eyes widened. "*Meredith?* She-she was here?!" she said fearfully.

Cassie nodded, her expression unchanging. "She's been following us since we left. I saw her last night."

The enchanter narrowed her eyes at Cassie. "You saw her last night and you didn't *tell* me?"

"Again, you're missing the point, Andrea. You...you don't know if you can send me home. You...you lied!"

Andrea bit her lip. Her hands were shaking. "Cassie I–,"

"Admit it! Just admit it. Did you lie?"

Andrea tried again. "What did Meredith say to you?"

Furious, Cassie stepped forward so that she was face to face with the enchanter, looking down slightly at her. "Shut up about Meredith for one freaking second! Did. You. Lie?"

"What are you two bickering about, *now*?" Elisa demanded.

Andrea reached out and touched Cassie's arm. "Cassie, please–,"

But Cassie pushed the enchanter away and staggered backwards. "*Seriously*?! You...everything?" she yelled. "Was this all just a way for you to get your stupid magic quest done? All of this...*us*...was it all a lie?" Her knees felt weak along with the rest of her tired body from traveling, and for a moment she thought she might collapse.

"No! Of course not!" Andrea cried.

"Cassie, Andrea – please, let's not do this now," Diana pleaded.

Cassie ignored the queen. "Was this all just a game to you?" she growled at Andrea. "Using me?"

The enchanter shook her head frantically. "No! I would never. Cassie, I *care* about you!"

"Hah!" Cassie laughed harshly. "Somehow, I doubt that."

"Stop it! Both of you!" Kye exclaimed, but like the others he was ignored.

"I do!" Andrea insisted, her eyes filling with tears. "More than I've ever-,"

"Liar. If that was true you would have told me the truth from day one!" Cassie cut her off.

Andrea reached up and touched the side of Cassie's face. "Please," she begged, tears streaming down her face.

But Cassie pulled away quickly. "No. I'm done. I'm done with all of this – magic, Damea…" She took one last, disappointed look at the crestfallen enchanter. "And especially *you.*" With a heavy sigh, she dropped her backpack on the ground and stormed off, heading toward the caves, leaving a shaking Andrea alone with their bewildered companions.

"Cassie," she tried feebly and took a step forward. But Elisa, who had observed the entire fight, intervened and pulled Andrea back.

"No," she said, almost gently. "Let her go." When she finally got the enchanter to face her, she asked. "What is going on, Andrea?" The others leaned in with concerned interest.

Andrea sniffed. "I…Cassie is not from Damea, Elisa. M-my mentor and I…we brought her here from…from somewhere else." She used her sleeve to wipe away her tears. "When I met Cassie, I…told her I could send her home." She sighed. "But I can't. I can't."

Jacob was the only one who could collect his thoughts quickly enough to reply. He looked out at the distance, where Cassie had disappeared over the hill and was no doubt closing in on the mountains. "She won't survive long on her own," he said worriedly. "We need to follow her."

ENCHANTERS

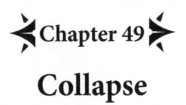

Chapter 49

Collapse

Perfect. Just freaking perfect. Finally reaching the top of the hill, Cassie stepped out of the snow and onto the hard, rocky ground of the cave's entrance. She paused and sat on a nearby boulder, her legs burning from the steep hike.

As she faced the sprawling hills and forest below, she still could not completely process what had happened. But there was no doubt about it now. Andrea had lied to her. She had been lying to her since that day in the Black Forest when they had first met.

Cassie sighed. She knew Andrea had lied to her in order to use the map to find the magic. The enchanter would never intentionally hurt Cassie – she was no Meredith. *That doesn't make it okay for her to lie to me. I would have understood.* But, the more she thought about it, the more unsure she was. Their first meeting had been…less than pleasant, and looking back, Cassie was not sure if she would have agreed to help Andrea if the enchanter had been honest from the start. *Guess I'll never know.* Now she was stuck in a rather awkward position – she could not go back to Andrea and she could not go home. She considered trying to find Meredith again. The older enchanter had made it very clear that there was no way to send her home, at least not without a great deal of experimentation. Maybe they could at least try. *As long as that crazy bitch doesn't try to torture me again.* Then she might be able to just go back to her normal – if boring – life.

If that was even what Cassie wanted now. She had admittedly grown accustomed to being in Damea, despite its strangeness and its dangers. It had become another home for her, or at least Andrea had. Her throat tightened as the shock began to wear off and the sting of betrayal began to set in. She could not deny she deeply cared for the enchanter, but even thinking about Andrea simply hurt too much right now. *Maybe that's what makes this such a crappy situation.*

Her thoughts were interrupted when the ground shook slightly. Startled, she jumped off the boulder. Small rocks crumbled from the ceiling of the cave's entrance and tumbled onto the ground. A low, pulsing hum filled the air, something Cassie had not realized was present before. Andrea had been right. The magic was close.

"Finally. I've been waiting all afternoon. Could you have walked any slower?"

Cassie spun around, facing the mouth of the cave, and froze when she saw Meredith standing a few steps away from her. "You again?! Get the hell away from me," she snarled.

Meredith put her hands up. "You mustn't do this, Cassie. It will only end badly," she pleaded.

But Cassie waved the older woman away. "I'm so freaking tired of all of you stupid enchanters. I just want to go home."

Meredith frowned as she looked past Cassie. "Where is Andrea? Where is the queen and the rest of your companions?"

Cassie turned away from the enchanter. *I don't need this right now.* "She's not here."

"Ah," Meredith said, understanding. "I take it something happened between the two of you then? I doubt she'd venture far from you if you held the key to finding this place."

"It's none of your business. Now leave me alone. You know where your stupid magic is. Go do whatever you want with it," Cassie retorted.

But Meredith did not leave, much to Cassie's annoyance. "You confronted her then? I am sorry, Cassie – truly, I am."

"Oh, shut up!" Cassie exclaimed angrily as she turned to face the enchanter again. "You wasted my time last night rambling on forever about how we were a 'tragedy waiting to happen', so don't act like you care now."

Meredith smiled sadly. "I admit, I said that to try to sway your opinion of her so that you would not release the magic. As I've said, Andrea is still my apprentice and I do care for her." She took a step toward Cassie. "I've seen you with her and I can tell that you do, too."

"Go away. You don't know anything about me."

"Come back to the Black Forest with me. We can sort this out."

Cassie's eyes widened in anger. "No way. You just want me to do that so that you can experiment on me again for magic. No, I'm done with all of you."

Meredith laughed softly. "I promise I will not attempt that again. I know it was…unorthodox of me–,"

"That's an interesting way to describe torture," Cassie snapped.

The ground shook again.

"Do you feel that, Cassie?" Meredith gestured at their surroundings. "The magic is dangerously unstable here. We need to leave, *now*."

"Cassie, get away from her!"

Both Cassie and Meredith turned and saw Andrea standing at the cave's entrance. She was flanked by Elisa and Jacob on her left and Diana and Kye on her right.

"Andrea!" Meredith said with genuine surprise.

Andrea stepped forward and pointed an accusing finger at her mentor. "What are you *doing* here? You tried to kill us!" she exclaimed. "You...you took energy from another *person*! This isn't what you taught me, Meredith!"

Not appearing even remotely threatened by her apprentice, Meredith simply shook her head. "I don't need to explain myself to you, Andrea," she stated calmly. "Leave this place and go back to Ata while you still can."

"I'm not going anywhere!" Andrea declared.

Suddenly, the ground rumbled more violently than before, shaking the foundation of the cave's entrance.

"Move back!" Jacob yelled and grabbed Diana before pulling her backwards. The stone ceiling quickly broke apart into large chunks of rock that came hailing down on them, the largest of the rocks directly above Cassie. Kye moved forward to help her, but was quickly yanked back by Elisa before one of the rocks could fall on him.

"Cassie!" Andrea yelled and lifted her hands up.

Meredith backed away, but when she saw what her apprentice was doing, she immediately lunged forward. "Andrea, *no!*"

Cassie barely had enough time to look up in horror as Andrea's barrier formed around her, stopping the jagged boulder just before it came crashing down on her. She met Andrea's terrified gaze for a moment before the shield flickered and disappeared. Meredith grabbed them both and pulled them back into the cave as the remaining rocks crumbled down and the entrance collapsed in a roar, kicking up thick clouds of dust all around them.

∗ ∗ ∗

"Cassie! Andrea! Argh, it won't budge!" Kye yelled his frustration as he put all his strength into trying to move the heavy boulders away from the entrance.

Jacob shook his head as he helped Diana stand up. "No," he panted. "Those rocks are far too heavy."

Elisa inspected the collapsed entrance. "Surely this cannot be the only way into these caves."

"Andrea used magic," Kye realized. He looked back at his friends worriedly. "What if something happened to them? What if we don't find them before her mentor does something terrible to them?"

"We have to try!" Diana pressed. She pointed to the right of the cave, where the hill sloped up against the mountain. A possible path up was visible in the distance. "Over there. Perhaps these caves lead up to the top. That may be our way in."

Jacob nodded grimly. "Let's go."

✳ ✳ ✳

Cassie opened her eyes and was greeted with nearly total darkness. She immediately coughed as the thick dust settled around her. Her eyes were watery and her arm stung badly where it had scraped against the ground. Light peeked into the cave through the cracks between the massive boulders that blocked the collapsed entrance. Upon inspecting her arm, she could see that she had bled through her shirtsleeve.

"Damn it," she muttered, hissing in pain.

"…Cassie?" Andrea's voice was faint and somewhat muffled.

"Yeah," Cassie breathed. In the dim light, she could see the enchanter lying face up on the ground. The other girl's breathing seemed shallow, but Cassie could not tell for certain. "You hurt?" she asked as she crawled over to the enchanter.

"Are you two all right?" Meredith called out.

Cassie ignored her as she reached Andrea. The enchanter still had not moved, and Cassie was not sure why. "Hey. Let's get out of here. I think the others are outside." The unsettling dread she had felt earlier returned.

"I…yes," Andrea answered quietly. But she did not move.

Cassie took a deep breath and reached under the enchanter's back, trying to lift her up. "Come on, let's go," she pushed. Her voice sounded shaky and she was not entirely sure why.

But as soon as she let go of Andrea, the enchanter fell back down. Cassie caught her before her head could hit the ground. "Whoa," she gasped. "You okay, there?" What was going on?

The gnawing dread that now wrapped around her made her chest and throat tighten, almost painfully. *You know.*

"I'm fine. I…" Andrea's voice grew fainter and trailed off.

"Andrea?" Cassie pressed, her voice sounding more ragged now. The enchanter's eyes were closed and she was not responding.

She heard Meredith approach slowly from behind. "Andrea…" she whispered.

"What's wrong with her?" Cassie demanded, looking up at the older enchanter.

"I told you – the magic is extremely unstable here. Stopping-stopping those rocks…was a mistake. She's…" Meredith covered her mouth in horror.

"What?" Cassie snapped. "What the hell–?"

"She has the sickness that plagues all enchanters when they use too much energy or…" Her voice lowered to a faint whisper. "Or when it is too unstable. Like here."

"Wait," Cassie said slowly as she tried to process what Meredith was saying. "Like your husband?" The dread had transformed into nauseating fear and threatened to overwhelm her. "Can't you stop it?"

Meredith shook her head. "No. I gave Richard a very specific drink to keep him alive. That drink no longer exists."

"Okay, fine," Cassie said while trying to control the panic in her voice. "So, what do we do?"

"I…nothing," Meredith answered sadly as she looked down at her apprentice. "There's nothing we can do. The illness…it is fatal. No doubt it's accelerated as well, given where we are."

"No…*no!*" Cassie said angrily. "That's not the answer – *do* something!"

"I can't!" Meredith cried.

"You're an enchanter. Figure it out!"

"I...there's not enough magic and–," Meredith tried to explain.

Cassie stood up and grabbed the older woman by the collar of her shirt. "You and I both know that the magic is at the center of these stupid caves," she said fiercely and pointed toward the dark corridor nearby. "If you release it, will she be okay?"

"I don't know!" Meredith pushed Cassie away and glared at her. "I cannot predict what will happen, Cassie."

"We have to try!"

"...Cassie?" Andrea whispered.

Meredith paused and looked at Andrea again before returning her focus to Cassie. "I make no promises," she said harshly. "Get her and follow me."

Cassie did not need to be told twice as she knelt next to Andrea. "Hey," she said softly. "We're going to head into the cave, but I'm going to carry you, all right?"

Andrea barely opened her eyes and gave a weak nod.

"Okay. Think you can hold onto me?" Cassie asked. When Andrea nodded again, she allowed the other girl to wrap her arms around her neck and lifted her up so that the enchanter was on her back.

"You're going to carry her the entire way?" Meredith asked doubtfully.

"Just go. I'll follow you," Cassie said, her expression hard with determination as Meredith began to lead them into the caves.

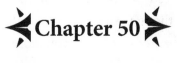

The Conduit

"Stay close. I can see light coming from the center of the caves, which means we are not far," Meredith said as she walked slowly through the long corridor.

With Andrea on her back, Cassie followed closely behind the older enchanter and noticed that there was indeed a faint blue glow that reflected off the walls, pulsing in time with the ever-present hum of magic. The ground still rumbled occasionally, but it was nothing like the earthquake they had experienced earlier.

"Cassie?" Andrea mumbled.

"We're almost there," Cassie answered as she struggled not to to let her tone betray how scared she actually was.

"I know. I'm…sorry."

Cassie sighed. "Don't worry about that right now. We can… we can talk about it when we get home."

She heard Andrea's ragged breathing pause. "Home?"

"Yeah. We need to take care of this nonsense first, though," Cassie explained while trying to keep the mood light. "Your mentor really is a nutjob, by the way."

"I heard that," Meredith grumbled from up ahead.

Andrea gave a weak laugh. "Still…funny. Cassie?"

"Hm?" Cassie did not mind talking to Andrea if it would keep her awake, though part of her was afraid that the extra strain on the enchanter would be even more detrimental to her already deteriorating condition.

"Where is home?"

"I…" Cassie didn't actually know how to answer. She did not know where 'home' was anymore or even why she had said that. *Yes, you do.* She just wanted Andrea to be okay and for all of this…Meredith, the magic, Rhyad – everything, to be done with. "It's wherever you want it to be, I guess," she finally answered.

"Oh," Andrea said. Then, in a frailer voice, "I don't feel so good, Cassie."

Tears pricked at Cassie's eyes and she swallowed hard as she tried to push them back. "What was the name of your village again?"

"A-Ata."

"Alright," Cassie said. "Well, we can go there if you want. What's it like?"

"Boring."

"I found it quite charming, actually," Meredith spoke up.

"Just keep walking," Cassie snapped at the older enchanter. Then, more quietly to Andrea, "I think 'boring' sounds good after all this, don't you?"

"My…my parents," Andrea mumbled. "They won't–,"

"I'll be right there with you to let them know how you saved the world. It'll be fine. I...promise," Cassie said as they rounded a corner.

"H-hopefully you are better at...keeping your promises... than I am," Andrea responded weakly.

"Oh stop. Now you're just being dramatic," Cassie teased half-heartedly. The humming grew noticeably louder and the corridor brighter as the three of them approached the center of the cave.

"I am never...dramatic," Andrea answered. There was a long pause as they neared the end of the corridor before the enchanter spoke again, this time in such a faint whisper that Cassie could barely hear her. "Cassie?" she repeated.

"What?"

"I...I think I love you. I just...you...should know that."

Cassie could not fight back the tears that came this time as a few made it through the emotional barrier she had struggled to keep up and rolled down the sides of her face. She sniffed and adjusted her hold on Andrea, who suddenly felt much heavier than she had moments earlier. "I–," She stopped when she heard how faint Andrea's breathing was. "Andrea?" No answer.

"What is it?" Meredith asked as they left the corridor and passed into the center of the cave.

Both were left speechless as they took in the sight in front of them. The cavern was huge – its ceiling higher than anything Cassie had imagined possible in a place like this. The walls of the cavern were lined with pale crystals that emitted a faint blue light. But it was what was in the center of the cavern that made her gasp.

A massive sphere lay before them, its bright, pulsing blue light nearly blinding them as energy visibly rippled all around it and the surrounding air. Up close, the faint hum from earlier was now a dull roar.

"This...this is incredible!" Meredith said breathlessly, her voice reverberating off the cavern walls.

"Is that...the magic?" Cassie asked as she gazed at the sphere in wonder.

Meredith nodded slowly. "It appears to be." She put her hand to her mouth. "I can't believe it," she said shakily. "It was...it was here all this time!"

Cassie did not want to waste any more time. "Let's do this, then. Andrea, you ready?"

The enchanter did not respond. In fact, Cassie could not hear the familiar sound of Andrea breathing at all.

"Hey, come on. Let's get this done so we can go," Cassie tried again. She knelt on the ground and laid the enchanter down carefully. Her heart sank when she saw the paleness of Andrea's skin, and the sweat that drenched her brow and the roots of her dark hair.

"Andrea?" she whispered.

"Allow me," Meredith offered, kneeling next to Andrea as well. She leaned in close to her apprentice and bit her lip when she drew away. "She...is still breathing," she said sadly. "But she is at the end of the sickness. My theory was correct – it has... accelerated." She looked up at Cassie. "She will not wake up, Cassie."

The tears came rushing forth again – only this time, Cassie

did not bother to fight them. "No!" she protested. "That's not acceptable. The magic is right there! Use it and *fix this!*"

"You think it is that simple, girl?" Meredith shot back. She stood up. "I've been working for over *twenty years* to bring back my husband and I've failed. I've failed!"

"You didn't have *that!*" Cassie cried and pointed at the sphere of magic. "Can't you do anything with it?"

Meredith inhaled sharply as she slowly approached the sphere. Her hair stood on end as she grew closer to the magic, the air crackling all around her. As she studied it, she began to understand how it worked, though not why or where it had come from. It was cyclical, she knew that for sure. Gathering the magic from Damea was something it did slowly and methodically, which would explain why it had taken years, hundreds of years even, for Damea to get into the state it was in. But it *was* magic, and like all other magic in Damea, it could be harnessed. The energy was tightly coiled, and it was almost as though whatever had constructed this had intended for the magic to be contained in the sphere. *Like a conduit.*

Conduits could be overloaded.

"I have an idea," she said as she turned to face Cassie. "You recall those devices I have in my lab? The ones I used to transfer the magic I acquired from you into those containers?"

Cassie glared at her. "You mean when you tortured me?"

Meredith ignored her comment. "This sphere is a version of that, but on a larger scale. If we overload it with energy, we may be able to release the magic."

"Releasing the-but you said that could be dangerous," Cassie pointed out.

"It very well could be," Meredith explained, "but it's our only option. Damea is slowly dying as the magic continues to be drained from it. Restoring the magic could rebalance the energy throughout the land and perhaps stop or even reverse the symptoms of the illness."

"And...she would be okay? She'd get better?" Cassie asked hopefully.

Meredith shook her head. "I don't know. That is my best theory and it's all we have right now."

Cassie thought of something else. "But what about Richard?"

For once, Meredith did not appear to be the calm, arrogant enchanter that Cassie had grown used to. Instead, she was but a broken, tragic shade of who she once was. She turned her gaze to Andrea. "There comes a point in every endeavor when it is time to let go." She sighed. "I did not find this magic. Andrea did. She does not deserve to die for...for my failure."

Cassie nodded. "All right," she said. "How do we do this, then?"

"We will need more energy poured into that sphere," Meredith explained. "You will need to provide that." She looked back at the sphere. "It will try to take your power from you on its own, but to overload it we must transfer the energy quicker than what it can handle."

Cassie's hopeful expression fell as she realized what Meredith was saying. "*You're* going to transfer the energy, aren't you?"

"It is the best option, Cassie. I know what this means, but it must be done if you want for this to have even a small chance of succeeding," Meredith stated plainly.

Cassie shook her head. "I don't know...what's to stop you from just stealing my power and going back home to your husband?" she asked suspiciously.

"Nothing," Meredith said simply. "You will need to trust me, Cassie. Also," she added, her tone of voice growing more solemn, "we don't know what kind of result this will give us. This...thing is designed to absorb magic. Transferring your power to it...well, it may kill you. There is a good chance that it will."

Cassie hesitated as she heard Meredith's cold words. She glanced at Andrea and then back at the older enchanter. "If I do this," she said slowly, "then you need to promise me a couple things."

"You've stated multiple times that you do not trust me, but go ahead and ask," Meredith replied.

"If I...if I don't make it," Cassie began, "then you get her out of here and take her back to her parents. You explain everything to them."

Meredith looked surprised but nodded. "I can do that. What else?"

Cassie took a deep breath. "*If* we pull this off, you leave us alone. You don't follow us, track us down, or do any of that other stuff. Got it?"

"I don't see how this helps me," Meredith answered coldly.

"Because I can still say 'no' right now. Andrea will die and it will be your fault. And I *know* she wouldn't have wanted me to do something like this if it meant you were just going to make us miserable afterwards," Cassie countered.

"Oh, enough! Fine," Meredith snapped. She waved Cassie over. "Hurry up, then."

Cassie took one more moment to look down at Andrea. She took the enchanter's hand in hers. There were words she wanted to say, words she had held back from saying, but she did not want to say them while the enchanter was unconscious or while Meredith was staring at her. *She deserves better than that.*

"Be right back," she muttered and released the other girl's hand. She stood up and walked over to Meredith. The hum of magic was starting to give her a headache. "Let's do this," she said finally.

"Are you ready? After we begin, there is no going back," Meredith warned.

"Yeah. Do it," Cassie ordered. Her hands were shaking as she hoped with every inch of her being that this would work.

The first contact made her gasp in pain as Meredith grabbed her wrist with one hand and reached into the sphere with the other. There was an intense pressure in her head as she gritted her teeth and tried to concentrate on anything other than what was happening right at that moment. The hum evolved into a high-pitched scream as the sphere pulsed brighter and everything around her began to shake.

Cassie yelled out as the pressure turned to white-hot pain that coursed throughout her body. But Meredith's grip on her wrist only tightened as the sphere shook dangerously and the scream of the immense amount of energy building up escalated into a deafening roar.

She heard a snap, then another, and another as white light

engulfed the cavern – so bright that she was blinded, though the pain only continued. Then, as she was on the precipice of fainting, Cassie felt a small shift within her chest. It grew slightly, until it became a tug, and then spiraled into a force so strong it threatened to tear her apart. As she howled in pain, she was surprised to hear another voice crying out. Meredith's grip had loosened slightly, but not enough to cancel the transfer as the pressure in the sphere reached critical mass, giving off an explosive force that tore Cassie and Meredith away from each other, throwing them to the ground.

Cassie grunted in pain as she rolled before coming to a stop. Looking up weakly with blood gushing from her nose, she saw Andrea was only a few feet in front of her and that the sphere was about to explode. It took every bit of strength she had remaining to crawl over and shield the enchanter with her own body just as the sphere exploded in a blur of white light. Cassie clung to Andrea as tightly as she could while countless particles of magic and rock rained down on them for what seemed like forever until the sphere was finally depleted and the cavern fell silent.

Chapter 51

Magic

Higher up the mountain, Diana struggled to keep from falling as the earth shook below them. She looked over at Jacob, whose gaze was focused on the snow-covered rocks that trembled on the cliff side above them before breaking away from the mountain face and plummeting to the ground.

"Move!" the queen yelled. The four of them scrambled to escape the oncoming avalanche as the rock and snow collided with the surface of the mountain. Spotting a crevice in the side of the mountain where they might be shielded from the incoming avalanche, Diana pulled Jacob into it and waved for Elisa and Kye to follow.

"In here! Hurry!" was the last thing she yelled before a brilliant, blinding white light lit up the sky. All four crouched down, shielding each other from the light and the snow that charged toward them.

But the light soon as quickly as it had appeared, and the rocks and snow stopped short of hitting them. Still cringing, Diana tentatively opened her eyes and removed herself from Jacob's hold.

"W-what happened?" Kye asked shakily while brushing snow off his clothing. "What was that light?"

"I don't know," Diana answered slowly as she emerged from their shelter.

"I do," Elisa whispered and removed her hood. "Your hands." She pointed at Kye. The young man gasped as he saw the glowing rings of blue around his hands and arms.

"What-what is this?" he demanded, clearly frightened at what was happening.

Diana had been looking at Kye along with the others when something else caught her attention. "The sky," she gasped. As the others looked up, they saw the sky, once a greyish blue, was now much brighter and clearer. As the queen looked around, she realized that it was not only the sky that had been affected, but all of their surroundings. Everything around them, from the forest to the very air they breathed, felt more alive than ever.

"They did it," Kye gasped. A few moments later, the blue glow around his hands faded, though he still felt slightly dizzy from the new flow of energy that coursed around him, something that he had never experienced before. It was not an overwhelming surge as it was when he had used Cassie's abilities. The new energy felt natural, as though his body had been starved of it his entire life. "They found the magic."

✶ ✶ ✶

Azgadar, Azgadaran Empire

"Mother! Mother!"

Ithmeera Cadar was alarmed by the sudden bang of the doors to her study swinging open as six-year-old Marco Cadar burst into the room. The heir to the Azgdaran throne had the same olive skin and curly hair as his mother and the light-brown eyes of his father.

Ithmeera stood up, breathing a small sigh of relief as her son did not appear injured or upset. In fact, he seemed quite excited. "What is it? Where is Petra?" she wondered, growing slightly annoyed.

As though on cue, her lady-in-waiting came running in as well. "Your Grace!" she exclaimed breathlessly. "I am deeply sorry to disturb you, but you should come outside."

The empress was confused. "Why? What's wrong?"

"I-I'm not certain. The city-well, you should see for yourself, Your Highness."

Glancing at a bewildered Petra and a practically jumping Marco, Ithmeera shook her head and sighed. "Very well, show me," she said as the young boy took her hand and practically dragged her out of the palace – where there was a discord of shouts from the servants and guards alike – and onto the steps leading down from the entrance.

The citizens of Azgadar had gathered outside and most were pointing at the sky, which the empress immediately noticed was a more vibrant blue than she had ever seen before.

Cries sounded from all around the palace gates as well, and as Ithmeera turned around, she could certainly see why. The streetlamps were flickering erratically. The great spire of the palace was...*shimmering*? As though by...

"Magic," she gasped. "But...how?"

"Mother!" Marco cried happily. "Look!" He held up his hands.

The empress did a double take as she took in the sight before her. A bright, blue glow emanated from her son's hands.

"Your Highness!" she heard the cries of her royal enchanters as they ran up behind her, reporting in a rush the latest events that had occurred, including machines powering back on, buildings lighting themselves, and potential enchanters manifesting their powers much sooner than thought possible. But she did not need for them to explain. She knew.

Magic had returned to Damea.

* * *

Ata, The Western Hills

"Garrett? Where are you going?"

Garrett grabbed the walking stick he had propped up against the house on his way inside earlier. "Be back in a bit," he called back to his wife as he held the front door open. "Just need to grab those other sacks I left this morning in the outer field."

"Oh, all right, then," Isabel answered from inside the house. "Dinner will be ready when you get back!"

Garrett smiled. "Thank you, dear!" He jumped off the porch, skipping the two wooden steps that led down from the front door. As he made his way through the fields, he could not help but admire the late-afternoon sky. Its purple, blue, and orange hues seemed noticeably brighter today than they had in days past, and with the temperature settling at a comfortably cool level, Garrett did not mind going back for a second trip to the outer field at all.

As he approached the sacks of the remaining harvest, he heard an odd grinding noise. Curious, he ignored the sacks and began walking in the direction of the noise. There was nothing out here that he knew of that would make such a strange noise. Other than crops, the only thing he remembered leaving out here were just those old, useless machines that –

Machines?

He broke into a run. It was impossible – the old farming contraptions had not functioned in generations and there was no way they would be able to function now, at least not without a great deal of magic. As the sun began to set, he sped through the bare fields, kicking up dirt and dust as his boots hit the ground. The sound grew noticeably louder as he approached, and he realized that the grinding now resembled more of a whirring. A mechanical whirring.

He stopped, panting and resting his hands on his knees. He tried to call for his wife, but could not find the words. Before him lay the two metal machines – one for planting, the other for harvesting.

Both were running, their engines working loudly as though they had never died.

"*Isabel!*" Garrett yelled before racing back to the house.

* * *

Rhyad

Her mind was heavy, clouded – such that it was almost impossible to focus. She thought she heard her name, but it could have been what she wanted to hear. Was she even there anymore?

She saw it in front of it – the tightly wound energy that had been just out of reach for what seemed like forever. They had come so far to find it. It seemed like years, eras even, when she knew it had only been a few months. Cassie had been the key, she knew that. The key to affecting so many. All those lives lost – the soldiers of nations fighting for the last scrap of energy, the countless enchanters that had perished over an era, and soon... her. She could have stopped all of that. "Saved the world" as Cassie would have put it.

Why?

She couldn't let those rocks go down. Couldn't let them destroy the key to the most important question in Damea. It wasn't Cassie's fault she was here. Key or not, she would not let Cassie pay the price for Damea's misfortune. She had been too selfish already.

There was a final, all-encompassing surge of energy that dissipated almost immediately. Then there was nothing. No light, no beacon, not even the steady, safe pulse of Cassie's energy well that she had grown so accustomed to. She felt lost and empty.

Her body went numb before the tingling sensation took over. Soon after, there was pain but only briefly. There was something else, something that she could not understand but at the same time somehow knew would change everything...

As soon as her eyes fluttered open, Andrea gasped as air rushed back into her lungs. As she winced from the burning of learning to breathe again, she realized she was pinned down. *Oh...this again.* The top half of Cassie's unconscious body was draped over her, and the enchanter was too weak to do anything about it. A flash of red caught her eye. The side of Cassie's shirt and her sleeve had splotches of dried blood on them. The other girl also had the remnants of a nosebleed and her face was slightly swollen underneath her eyes.

"Cassie?" she whispered fearfully. She tried to look around her. They were in a cavern, or so it appeared. The room would have been darker if it were not for the pale blue glow on the walls. Crumbled rocks were scattered across the ground, but other than that, the cavern was empty.

She tried to push the other girl off of her. "Cassie, please get up," she tried again, surprised at the roughness of her own voice. *What happened?* She tried to mentally retrace her steps as she remembered reaching the caves in the mountains, her fight with Cassie when the other girl had found out about her lie and…Meredith. *She was there!* Her mentor had been talking to Cassie about…something. She did not know what, but then there was that earthquake and she had put up a quick barrier so that the rocks would not hit Cassie and…

She closed her eyes as the memories of what had transpired surfaced in a dizzying rush that left her light-headed. She was sick…no, *had* been sick. She tried to pick apart the blur of events, but her thoughts were still a jumble. *I was talking to Cassie…she was carrying me? Meredith was there and…did I die?* She could not help but smile despite herself, figuring that dying was a rather stupid conclusion as she would not be awake otherwise.

"Hm?" She heard Cassie finally stir above her. The other girl's face immediately contorted in pain, no doubt from any injuries she had suffered doing…whatever it was that had happened.

"Cassie?"

"Ouch."

"Are you all right?" Something didn't feel right. Almost as though she was missing something.

Cassie shifted slightly, letting out another groan of pain. "Yeah, I think so. Think I landed on a rock or something and–," She paused when she opened her eyes and realized she was looking down at the enchanter. Her eyes widened. "You're not dead."

Andrea raised an eyebrow. "Not that I'm aware of, no."

"Okay," Cassie replied, breathing slowly. "I'm not dead, either."

"I can see that." Andrea paused as she realized what was missing. "Cassie…your power," she breathed. "It's…it's gone!"

"What?" Cassie asked, confused. She winced. "Ow. Okay, I need to get up." With great effort, she moved off the enchanter and stumbled to her feet before extending her hand to Andrea.

"It's gone. I-I don't feel any energy from you at all," Andrea continued as she allowed Cassie to help her up.

Cassie blinked a few times before scanning their surroundings. "It worked," she finally whispered.

"What worked?"

Cassie turned to face Andrea again. "The magic – it was here. Meredith and I…we tried to overload it or something. I guess it worked." She looked down at herself and laughed. "Either that or this is a really weird dream."

But as she assessed the situation before her, Andrea realized that Cassie was right. Her companion's ability was indeed gone, but the air around her felt alive and full of energy. It was a strange, foreign sensation that somewhat resembled what she had experienced in the Gurdin Woods, only far more balanced. Finally understanding what had happened, Andrea broke into a fit of laughter.

"What? What is it?" Cassie demanded.

"You...you did it!" the enchanter exclaimed, struggling to speak between bouts of laughter. She threw her arms around Cassie's neck, not noticing the other girl grit her teeth in pain. "You saved us! Saved...saved me," she added softly. For a brief moment, the enchanter almost leaned in closer, forgetting about their fight, forgetting about how angry Cassie had been at her, and the limbo in which their relationship currently lived.

Cassie smiled wryly. "Yeah, well, it was your crazy mentor's idea. Also...ow!"

Finally noticing the pain her companion was in, Andrea pulled away gingerly. "Sorry," she said sheepishly. She looked around. "Where is Meredith?"

Cassie echoed the enchanter's action and looked around as well. "I guess-I guess she's gone. She must have left...after." She sighed, as though with relief. "She won't be following us anymore."

Andrea tilted her head. "She helped you? Even though Richard–?"

"Yeah," Cassie answered with a shrug. "Turns out she still kind of cares about you." She shook her head in dismay. "I still think she's crazy, though."

"I...I see," Andrea replied with a slow nod. *Richard...gone?* The fact that Meredith had chosen her over Richard...she would not have believed it any other day. Realizing something, she looked up at Cassie again. "Wait, 'overload'? *You* and Meredith? As in you..." She did not finish, and instead only stared at Cassie in shock.

Cassie snorted. "Yeah." She pointed to her partially swollen face. "I guess it's bruise time again."

The enchanter's expression went from shock to anger quickly as she punched Cassie in the shoulder. "You *idiot!*" she snapped. "You could have been killed! How many times do I have to explain this to you?!"

Cassie threw her hands up. "I don't get you! First, you spend months lecturing me about how we need to save the world. Then we *do* save it and you *still* lecture me?" she exclaimed, cradling her shoulder where the enchanter had hit her. "I can't win!" She gave a long-suffering sigh. "I'm tired and my face hurts. Can we go now?"

Andrea was not sure whether to laugh or cry. It was all so ridiculous, but they had done it. They had found the magic, restored it to Damea, and had managed to both come out of it all alive. She nodded, suddenly feeling much more tired and weak than she had originally thought. "Y-yes," she said. "Let's go."

Cassie must have noticed the enchanter's drop in energy because she quickly leaned in and allowed Andrea to lean on her as they walked through the corridor opposite of where they had entered the cavern, making their way through and eventually exiting the back entrance of the cave, which overlooked a familiar sight.

"Hey, they made it," Cassie observed and pointed to where Elisa, Kye, Diana, and Jacob stood on the mountain slopes below.

"Yes," Andrea agreed. Her attention was directed toward the sky, where the sun had begun to set. "I've never seen the sky so *bright* before," she said in awe.

Cassie laughed. "We weren't in the cave for *that* long," she joked.

"No!" Andrea said excitedly. "It's the magic. It's…it's changed things. Fixed them."

Cassie shrugged. "Well, if that's taken care of, we should probably meet up with them and head back to…wherever we're going. Have I mentioned how freaking cold it is here?"

Andrea looked up at her companion guiltily. "Cassie, I'm sorry for…well, for everything. I shouldn't have lied to you. I promise as soon as we get back to Gurdinfield that I will do everything I can to research and find a way to send…why are you laughing?" she demanded.

Cassie placed her hands on Andrea's shoulders and met the enchanter's gaze. "Because you were about to do your nonsensical rambling thing again," she explained.

Andrea rolled her eyes. "It's not nonsensical. I was *trying* to apologize."

"I know," Cassie replied. "But," she removed her hands, "look – if we're going to be together, we can't be keeping things from each other like that. All right?"

Andrea closed her eyes briefly and nodded. "I know, I know," she agreed. "I truly am sorry and I *promise* – wait," she paused. "You…ah…still want to be…together?" she asked nervously, wringing her hands.

Grinning mischievously, Cassie took one of the enchanter's hands. "I did say you were stuck with me, didn't I?"

"But that was before–," Andrea started but stopped herself. She took a deep breath. "All right. If-if that's what you really want."

"It is," Cassie replied sincerely. She looked down. "But uh… can we skip the life-threatening magic plague this time?" She gave a nervous laugh. "Not that I don't appreciate the help back there with the falling rocks and all, but um…maybe you could not ever do that again? You kind of scared me for a moment there."

Andrea tilted her head as she noticed that while Cassie still had a slight smile on her face, she seemed…sad? She reached up and tentatively touched her companion's face, forcing Cassie to look at her. "No promises," she whispered, meeting Cassie's blue eyes. "I'm sorry if I scared you, though."

Cassie's grin returned quickly as she pulled the enchanter close. "'Scared' is a bit of an understatement, but sure – we'll go with that."

Andrea could not hide her happiness as she leaned into Cassie's hold. If Cassie was right and this *was* a dream, the enchanter hoped she would never wake up. "Ready? They're probably worried."

"Yeah," Cassie sighed. "Let's go."

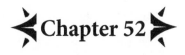

Chapter 52

Restored

City of Towers, Gurdinfield

Two months later

After rolling and hiding just outside her opponent's line of sight, Cassie took a moment to recover and quickly scanned her surroundings so that she could weigh her options. She attempted to control her breathing as each exhale drifted visibly in the cold around her.

Arming herself once more, she quietly peeked over the top of her cover, trying to see if she could spot her opponent. But her concentration was quickly broken when a small, frozen projectile collided with her shoulder, instantly breaking apart on impact and sending snow onto her face and clothing.

"Ack! Damn it, Kye!" she shouted as she stood up from behind the snow-covered hedge in the palace courtyard and wiped the freezing water off her face.

The young enchanter stepped out of the shadows of the nearby staircase that led up to the double glass doors to the palace, a grin plastered on his face. "That's three out of five! I win for real this time, Cassie," he announced.

Cassie shook her head stubbornly. "Best out of seven!"

But Kye just laughed. "Not a chance. It's starting to get really cold and we've already extended the game twice."

"You're being boring right now. Best out of seven or I'll tell Elisa the *real* reason you skipped lessons with Andrea yesterday," Cassie threatened, a smug smile forming on her face.

Her victory was short-lived when she saw the usually nervous boy just smile. "Go ahead. I'll tell her who *really* spilled beer all over her new cloak last week."

Cassie shook her head defiantly. "No way. That was all Victor!"

But Kye's daring grin remained. "Elisa doesn't know that."

"You're terrible," Cassie retorted. She gathered up more snow in her hands and flung it at the enchanter. The snowball missed its target, instead hurtling through the air past Kye and toward Diana, Jacob, and Andrea, who were talking amongst themselves as they walked down the stairs to the courtyard, completely unaware of what was going on.

Kye warned them first. "Look out!"

Fortunately, Andrea saw the snowball before the queen or Jacob did and quickly deflected it by summoning a small, contained barrier. The snowball harmlessly disintegrated upon colliding with the shield, catching the attention of the other two.

"Impressive reflexes, Andrea," Jacob praised. Diana nodded in agreement next to him as Cassie and Kye approached them.

"Sorry," Cassie panted. "I meant to hit Kye," she explained after Andrea gave her a puzzled look.

"Yes, she meant to hit me," Kye supported.

"Well, at least you know you made the right choice when choosing your royal enchanter, love," Jacob chuckled as he gave the queen a joking nudge with his elbow before absentmindedly adjusting the woven bracelet around his wrist. It had been over a month since the wedding – he and Diana had married at the top of the stone steps leading up to the palace at the peak of the capital. The entire city had attended, and the celebrations had lasted for nearly a week after. After the ceremony, when each of the city's residents lined up to wish the new royal couple their congratulations, Diana had offered Andrea the position of royal enchanter, the first of its kind for Gurdinfield. The enchanter had been very hesitant to accept at first, but after a few days of consideration she eventually agreed.

Diana gave her husband an amused glance before smiling at Andrea. "Indeed. I think that's the fastest I've seen you cast that shield of yours, Andrea."

Cassie laughed quietly as she watched the enchanter turn slightly pink at Diana's compliment. She could easily see that for all of Andrea's shyness about the new position, the enchanter was very proud of her new role. Diana had even offered Cassie a job as well – training with the Guardians as an apprentice. She had never considered going into military service, but the brief lessons she had taken from the queen during their journey had piqued her interest in learning more about combat. It also helped that she enjoyed Jacob, Victor, and Roe's company and was not against learning new things if she was going to remain in Damea. Andrea had stated her concerns with the arrangement early on, but Jacob had assured the enchanter that he would personally oversee Cassie's training and that it would be completely safe.

"I-thank you, Your Majesty. And ah…thank you again for the generous research space you've given me," Andrea answered gratefully, though her expression still showed signs of embarrassment.

The queen sighed. "Dare I even bother to tell you to call me by my name?" she asked, making the enchanter stumble over her words even more.

Deciding she'd try to rescue Andrea from herself, Cassie jumped in. "So, she makes shields. Big deal! *I* kicked Kye's ass in our snowball war," she bragged.

Kye narrowed his eyes at Cassie while Andrea stifled a laugh. "You did not," he insisted. "You lost. Many times, in fact. Your aim is actually quite terrible."

But Cassie held up her hand to silence the young man. "Denial won't get you anywhere, Kye. Also – and Jacob can attest to this – I have become an *expert* at dice."

Diana raised an eyebrow as Jacob beamed at his newest comrade. Andrea spoke first. "You *do* realize that game is entirely up to chance and you cannot be 'an expert' at it, don't you?" she pointed out.

"Oh, I don't know – I think she's done well. And I am not such a bad player if I do say so myself," Jacob countered.

"See?" Cassie exclaimed at Andrea while pointing at the captain as though he were living proof of her claim. "You're just jealous."

"And you're delusional," the enchanter countered while shaking her head.

"*Anyhow*, it is nearly dinnertime. We actually came out

here to see if you two were hungry," Diana finally cut in before another argument began.

"Oh," Cassie said, somewhat disappointed at the debate ending but excited over the prospect of food. "Yeah, I could eat."

"Where is Elisa?" Kye wondered. "I haven't seen her all day."

Jacob and Diana exchanged apprehensive glances. "She is in the stables packing, I believe," the queen replied.

Kye's eyes widened. "Packing? Why?"

"She is leaving tonight," Jacob explained with a nod. "She asked us to keep the news somewhat quiet, but she let us know some time ago that she would eventually need to return to Azgadar."

Kye bit his lip as an awkward silence descended upon them. "I…see. If you'll excuse me, I-I think I should at least go say goodbye."

"Of course," Diana said kindly. She turned to Andrea and Cassie. "She will not leave until later if you wish to eat now before saying your goodbyes."

The others agreed and followed the queen and Jacob back inside the palace. Kye, on the other hand, sped down the hill and toward the stables, where, sure enough, he found the ex-Legionnaire, fully outfitted in her armor and traveling gear, preparing one of the horses for travel.

"They said you were leaving!" he panted as he came to a stop and rested his hands on his knees. "Why?"

Elisa looked up from her task for a moment, amused, before returning to what she was doing. "I have some things I have to take care of," she stated calmly. She grabbed a sword from a nearby bale of hay and sheathed it before strapping it to the rest of her supplies.

Kye noticed the gold hilt of the sword immediately. The blade had belonged to General Cadar. He knew the empress had asked for it back more than once and that Diana had refused every time. "You cannot go back to Azgadar!" he protested. "I know Diana offered you a Guardian position and that you turned it down because of the empress. You cannot trust Ithmeera – she'll kill you!" He stepped toward the older woman. "I'm going with you."

He expected Elisa to snap at him or even scold him. But she simply chuckled without facing him as she continued packing. "If I recall, you have your training under Andrea that you should continue," she reminded him. "You also promised the innkeeper at The Lion's Den that you'd perform every few nights for him. *And* I believe Jacob has set aside time twice a week for you to improve your swordplay."

Kye shook his head. "But I want to go with you!"

The ex-Legionnaire stopped and sighed. "As annoying as it would be to have to carry you across Damea *again*, your duties are here."

"But the empress–,"

"I'm *not* going to Azgadar," she said, exasperated. "I'm going home. To Sadford. I have some affairs I need to settle there."

"Oh," Kye blurted, feeling a little foolish. "But…aren't there Legionnaires there, too?"

Elisa shrugged. "Perhaps. Nothing I can't handle."

"I should still go with you," the young man declared stubbornly. "I could…help protect you from Legionnaires."

The older woman gave a rare, genuine smile as she walked over to him and placed her hand on his shoulder. "Stay here and protect our friends. You've done a fine job of that so far. They need you more than I," she explained.

Kye sighed sadly and looked down. "Will you come back?"

"I cannot and will not make a promise like that."

"Will you try?" he pleaded, looking back at her.

Elisa's smile quickly faded. "Fine," she grumbled. They stood there silently for several seconds.

"I don't hug," she finally told him.

"You did in Rhyad," he reminded her.

The ex-Legionnaire rolled her eyes. "That was a moment of weakness after nearly falling to my death and most certainly does not count."

But her protests were ignored as the young enchanter stepped forward and pulled her into a tight embrace. Helpless to do much else, Elisa awkwardly patted the boy on the back before he finally released her.

"Go," she ordered. "You've a show at The Lion's Den tonight, if I'm not mistaken."

"I do," he confirmed with a nod. "You should come watch."

"I'll be long gone by then," she admitted. "But…good luck. Now, I should get back to packing. You've distracted me long enough with your ceaseless whining." She shook her head as he laughed. "At this rate, I won't be able to leave until next week."

Kye grinned back at his friend before finally turning around to head back up the hill to the inn, where he knew he would soon have an audience waiting to hear him play.

* * *

"I don't think I've heard this song before," Victor claimed before taking a long sip of his ale.

"Sure you have – you just don't remember because you were too busy yapping about your stupid new post on the Sky Tower." Roe shook his head before chuckling quietly as he noticed most of their friends sitting around them were laughing at his and Victor's exchange.

It was late in the evening, and The Lion's Den was a fair bit more crowded than usual. Since returning from Rhyad a hero, Kye – along with his music – had grown quite popular amongst the citizens of the capital city. Many came to the inn to watch him perform, meet the other "heroes of Rhyad", or simply just to pay their respects to the queen who, unlike her predecessors, could often be seen walking around the city during the day and frequenting evening events such as this one as a way to get to know her people better. It was a strategy that seemed to be working as Diana had easily become more popular amongst the people of Gurdinfield than her father had been decades earlier.

"It's a good post! I'm tired of wandering about the woods all day and night!" Victor argued. He nodded toward Jacob, who sat at the table behind him and Roe next to Diana, with Andrea and Cassie sitting to her left.

Roe snorted. "Figures you'd want to get out of doing actual work," he quipped. He turned to Jacob. "Though…perhaps I should apply for a post on the tower as well." He and Victor exchanged glances and broke into laughter.

The Guardian captain grinned. "Laugh it up, boys. We'll see how smug you are when you're running the hill all day tomorrow." He turned to Cassie. "Not you of course, Cassie. We'll continue training as usual."

"You shouldn't go easy on her, Jacob," Andrea spoke up. "That snowball earlier could easily be interpreted as an act of war." She flashed Cassie a knowing glance while attempting to remain serious.

Cassie raised an eyebrow at the enchanter. "You and your 'humor' again. You really should give up on it while you still can. It's not working and you know it."

Andrea laughed quietly as Kye's song ended and the inn broke out in uproarious applause. Out of the corner of her eye, the enchanter noticed a flash of copper hair before it quickly disappeared. Moments later, the front door of the inn slammed shut. Making sure Cassie could hear her over the sound of the crowd's cheering, Andrea leaned in close to the other girl. "I'll be right back," she murmured before giving Cassie's arm a gentle squeeze.

Cassie nodded. "All right," she answered as she watched the enchanter leave the table and head toward the front door.

✶ ✶ ✶

"I thought you would have left by now." Andrea took a few steps out into the cloudy winter evening as the door closed behind her. The frigid air sent a shiver down her spine and she wrapped her cloak tighter around herself for warmth.

Elisa turned slowly and offered a small shrug. "Thought I'd watch the show before heading out." She nodded toward her horse, which had been tied to a nearby post. "Which I'll be doing now."

The enchanter bit her lip. "You're actually leaving us, then?" she asked, not bothering to hide her disappointment.

The ex-Legionnaire sighed heavily. "This again? I don't need another guilt trip, girl."

But Andrea put her hands up. "No guilt trips. But I won't lie." She smiled faintly. "I'll miss you. And I think you'll miss us, too."

Elisa folded her arms across her chest. "You presume much. I doubt you'll have time to think about rogue Legionnaires when you've an academy to reopen."

They walked to the edge of the patio by the railing, which was covered with a light dusting of snow. "Nonsense," Andrea declared. "Also, I'm still uncertain about what will happen with the Enchanters Academy. I told Diana that I'd like to study the effects that the magic restoration has had on the land before doing something like reopening the academy."

Elisa nodded deeply. "Smart move. But then again, I'm no enchanter so I wouldn't know. Have you heard from your former mentor at all? Meredith, was it?"

The enchanter shook her head. "Ah, no. No, I don't believe I'll see her again. Cassie told me she made it quite clear that

Meredith was not to come near us anymore."

Elisa did not seem surprised. "No doubt some threat of violence was made in that exchange."

"Most likely, though Meredith is not one to give up easily."

"A trait that she did not fail to pass down to her apprentice, I see," Elisa stated. Andrea was not positive, but the older woman's tone came off almost *admirable* toward the enchanter.

"I…there's no way Cassie and I would have reached Rhyad without you, Elisa," she said quietly. "Thank you."

Elisa simply looked amused. "You're welcome." She began to walk to her horse. "I'll expect you to write if you two end up making it longer than a month without bickering with each other."

Andrea laughed as she watched the ex-Legionnaire climb onto her horse after untying it from the post. "I don't know if I can promise anything like that."

Elisa grinned. "It's hard to be surprised by anything these days. Good luck, and try not to do anything rash or stupid, as you are prone to do." She gave a final nod before spurring her horse into a light gallop that took the ex-Legionnaire down the hill, through the capital, and toward the city gates.

The enchanter did not hear the door open and shut behind her as she watched Elisa ride out of the city and across the snow-covered fields surrounding the capital.

"She's gone then?" Cassie asked as she stepped out into the cold night and stood next to Andrea.

"Yes," Andrea said regretfully. "I don't believe she wanted a lot of commotion around her departure."

"That's an interesting way of putting it. Before we left the palace earlier, she took one look at me, said, 'Don't get yourself killed', and left," Cassie summarized. She looked up as a light snow began to fall. "Hey, it's snowing again."

Andrea sighed. "Words cannot describe how utterly sick I am of winter," she grumbled.

Cassie wrapped her arms around the enchanter's waist from behind. "Reminds you too much of our favorite vacation spot?"

Andrea snorted. "I'd hardly call Rhyad a 'vacation spot.'"

"True. More like a death wish," Cassie muttered. An uneasy silence settled around them. The muffled melody of Kye's next song sounded from inside the inn.

"I'm all right, Cassie," Andrea finally said, leaning back against her companion.

"You almost weren't," Cassie mumbled.

The enchanter turned around before grasping Cassie's arms and looking up at the other girl. "If I had another chance, I would do it again," she vowed.

"I know, and I'm grateful that you did, but…" Cassie shifted uncomfortably. "I just don't really like you putting yourself at risk all the time like that." She looked down, avoiding the enchanter's gaze. "Between Azgadar and the wagon and… and the battle and then you were…that was just *really* close, Andrea."

Andrea nodded. "I know it was. But Cassie, I can't promise you that–,"

But Cassie cut her off. "You don't have to. I know that you're just going to keep doing what you do because that's who you are. That's why I accepted that offer to train and start learning some new stuff so that I'm not *completely* useless."

Andrea laughed softly. "You brought magic back to Damea. I'd hardly call that 'useless.'" She suddenly understood what Cassie meant as she realized for what must have been the hundredth time since they had left the cave in Rhyad what was missing. "You don't need your power to be useful."

"Well, that's a relief," Cassie said. She lowered her voice to a whisper. "To be honest, I was getting a bit tired of the whole bruise thing."

Andrea rolled her eyes. "Had you listened to me, you wouldn't have had to deal with those two out of the three times," she scolded.

"Again with the lecturing? When's it going to be *your* turn?" Cassie exclaimed as she released the enchanter.

"When I've done something worth lecturing me over."

Cassie narrowed her eyes at Andrea as a roguish smile spread across her face.

"What?" Andrea demanded.

"*Somebody* still needs to write to her parents to let them know we are coming as soon as this snow melts," Cassie reminded her.

Andrea frowned. "I said I would *think* about it!"

"Nope. You said you would, so that's what you're going to do."

"It's been over three years, Cassie – I wouldn't know the first thing to write," Andrea argued.

Cassie took the enchanter's hands. "Tell you what. You have two options. You can write them a letter telling them we're coming, *or* you can try my favorite drink. But…you have to drink the entire thing," she challenged.

It didn't take Andrea long to decide. "Fine," she conceded. "I'll write the bloody letter. Can we go inside before we freeze to death?"

"You know what really warms you up on a cold night?" Cassie teased as they headed back inside.

"I'm *not* having any of your foul drink, Cassie."

✶ ✶ ✶

Gurith, Gurith Coast

The tavern by the docks was remarkably quiet. The establishment was typically frequented by the sailors and merchants that came through in the later hours. Some arrived looking for a bed, dinner, and perhaps a drink or two while others stumbled in having already had a few drinks but more than willing to pick a fight with anyone who seemed like a worthy challenge.

But the quiet hooded woman in the back of the tavern just wanted to be left alone with her meal before retiring for the evening. Broken and guilt-ridden, Meredith had not returned to the Black Forest after the incident in Rhyad. She did not regret her decision to help save her apprentice, but that did not make the dark pit of anguish in her any less devastating. Twenty years of research, twenty years of her life – gone.

She had traveled to Gurith, the largest city on the Gurith Coast to meditate on her decisions and her life as of late. The owner of the tavern had been kind enough to allow her to rent out one of the rooms for as long as she liked, and the enchanter admitted that being so close to the sea brought to her a kind of peace that she had not felt for decades.

In the weeks that followed, rumors had reached the port city that the magic that had been lost to Damea for so long had been miraculously restored. Farmers could now work in their fields more easily with the assistance of magically powered machinery. Enchanters in the royal court in Azgadar could practice their craft without fear of succumbing to the illness that nearly took the life of Meredith's apprentice not so long ago. There were even whispers that the new queen of Gurdinfield was considering reopening the academy in the City of Towers.

She sighed as she held her hand out closely in front of her and struggled with all her willpower to create the very same simple orb of blue light that had drawn her apprentice to her cause in a tavern not so different from this one only a few years earlier. But there was nothing.

Her magic was gone. After transferring Cassie's energy to overload the strange phenomenon in Rhyad, Meredith had been left without the ability to cast so much as a small light. There was no lingering energy or trace in her that served as a relic that she had even *been* an enchanter. She struggled to push back the tears that sprang into her eyes as the depression that had pulled her down over the last few months threatened to overwhelm her again.

She finally gave up and shakily lowered her hand, opting to

pick up her spoon instead so she could finish her stew. It was going to be another long night.

* * *

The Black Forest

Three months later

High-pitched squeaks echoed throughout the laboratory as a small grey mouse scurried across the cold stone floor. It made its way past several large pieces of broken equipment, long since covered in dust and cobwebs, before reaching cover in a dark hole in the wall on the other side of the room.

A low hum sounded continuously from the broken conduits scattered across the floor as a single magical construct stood motionlessly in the center of the room next to the metal table where Richard lay. A dirty white sheet covered the enchanter up to his shoulders. On the floor, one of the cracked containers for storing magic began to flicker with a faint white light as the broken conduits began to hum louder.

With the hum growing to a reverberating roar, the construct shifted slightly. The table began to vibrate, and the room shook slightly as Richard's hand began to twitch ever so subtly. Then again. And again.

His eyes flew open.